A Tear To Remember

© by Michael John Murray, M.A.

Media Arts Productions.

Media Arts Productions
P.O. Box 48
New York, N.Y. 10475

Manufactured in the United States of America

To Khemali, Mikael, Georgette and
the family of Lillian and Ruppert
Stanley Murray, Sr.

Chapter One

Autumn is the beginning of the traditional hurricane season in the caribbean, which more than often diminishes the tourist trade, and always wrecks havoc upon the already strained fishing industry of the islands. Maritime warnings were posted at the dock, alerting the fishermen of the first fall storm, earlier in the day, and at noon, the changing weather began showing initial signs of the impending deluge. By afternoon, the torrential rains fell from the darkened gray sky and stirred the sea to dangerous undulations. Crests of whitecaps rushed, barely visible, across the ocean, spurred on by turbulent winds, to make a final awesome roar, as the waves pounded against the shoreline. In the distance, a small sea-worn fishing boat could be seen, hovering along the horizon, as the few remaining domestics idly viewed the weather from the safe vantage of the hotel bar, at the edge of the beach.

Life had become more routine in Martique, now that the furor of Independence had settled during the early years of the 1960's. The change had, of course, brought a great deal of speculation among the islanders that the country could now embark upon new economic programs and encourage foreign investment to stimulate private sector growth. Small light industries were promised by the governor. Mainly plastics and textiles. But, it was hoped that Martique would profit, in its quest to modernize, through the introduction of various ventures in electronics and high tech periphery which was just beginning to have an impact on international commerce. These were the plans that the people waited for patiently.

The domestics became bored of watching the fishing boat and returned to busy work around the empty hotel. Meanwhile, the small trawler struggled in the gale with the full weight of its catch. Although the fishing nets and riggings were firmly secured, the vessel's bindings strained with the tension of the boat's progress, as the craft made its way through the rough sea.

The crew of weathered seamen were gathered inside the ship's galley, engrossed with a card game. They appeared to be oblivious of the raging sea and placed their wages, experiencing gain or loss, matter-of-factly. The sailors' casual attitude contributed to a languid atmosphere in the hole, which made the extreme rhythmic pitch of bow and stern seem incidental, as the storm rolled the small vessel about in the ocean. A glimpse of each member of the crew through facial expressions and hand movements, as an occasional card passed onto the table, revealed their common bond of African ancestry.

At the controls, above the crew, was the skipper. His attention was riveted to the horizon, eyes focusing through the torrent, as the age-old saga of man and the sea was reinacted. There was a special powerfulness to his bewhiskered visiage, half hidden in his blue skully. His dark eyes sparkled against the hues of black skin, giving his countenance a look of sagacious concern, as he attempted to pierce the downpour while agilely guiding the craft through the rough waters with his huge but nimble hands. Intermittently, storm warnings blurted out from the marine band, through the otherwise static din of the radio.

Down below, the ship's steward emerged from the kitchen, bringing coffee to the card players. He was a well-built, rusty brown man of thirty-five. His light brown, oval eyes and full moustache contrasted in a pleasant way, lending intrigue to his already handsome appearance. Obviously a neophyte to the way of life of fishing men, his presence tokened a pause in their activity which turned to hearty exchange, as he poured the steaming liquid into the sailors' cups. Everett, a large bellicose seasman, began the spar, as he grinningly leaned back in his chair.

"Ah, yes, my good man, Fred. What does your culinary artistry bring to our palates, this evening?"

He purposely exaggerated, an already heavy West Indian accent, then glanced around the galley to gain support for the trist. Fred sensed the direction of the come-on and curtly replied.

"Gumbo."

Everett now sensed his bait had been swallowed.

"How can this foreigner, who should be thrown out of the islands with a name, such as Murphy, come up with all these delectible and choice items?"

Amused by the pun, he led the crew in boistrous laughter while Fred continued pouring coffee, waiting for the joke to run its course. Everett, not satisfied yet, pursued the spar.

"Well, feathertail, what have you got to say for yourself?"

Fred continued pouring coffee, seemingly unaffected, but quipped pointedly to the West Indian. "My father told me many of the kitchen secrets of your lasses!"

"Now that's choice! I didn't know we let the feathertails past the living room sill," Everett retorts, then spits into a bucket.

"There was always an open door policy to the kitchen for my father, you know," says Fred, momentarily interrupting his activity.

The crew became silent, awaiting the climax of the exchange.

"Is that right, man," asks Everett.

Fred began to pour coffee again, and dryly remarks, "my presence is testimony to that fact, Mr. Carter!"

A sarcastic glare suddenly transformed his face, as the two men's eyes were locked together. The other crewmen began edging the humor which was finally interrupted by a call from the skipper, fetching Fred to the bridge. As Fred departed, Everett spat into the bucket, again. Meanwhile, the crew laughed heartily.

Fred ascended the narrow stairway to the bridge and entered the small pilot's station, struggling with his coffee pot to keep his balance in the rough sea. Hampton, the skipper, was shouting into the marine radio microphone, but was unable to get a clear channel for ship to shore directives through the storm's impedence. He replaced the microphone and turned to Fred.

"Now, here is where you get to test yourself. See if you can keep her to within two minutes, as we pass the lighthouse. That way, we can probably pick up a couple of leagues, rounding the tip, and outrun those furies that Zephyrus is sending after us,'' he directs Fred. Although an older man, the skipper was enlivened by the adventure of work at sea and his skills capable enough to meet the challange, even at his age.

Fred's attention was split between the threatening storm and Doc's activity at the helm. He sat the coffee pot down. ''Never mind all that Greek shit, I think I can manage it. I have a thorough understanding of witches, you know.''

He began unfastening the apron from his waist.

''Now, if I can just get out of this straight jacket . . . you want some coffee, Doc?''

Chapter Two

As the storm began to subside, the afternoon sunlight broke through the overcast sky, spreading its last rays at sunset. The small trawler finally reached its destination and entered the harbour. A rainbow cradled the horizon, as the crew emerged from below to secure the vessel. Fred and Hampton were busy shutting down the systems and gathering their gear. The two men paused a moment, before disembarking, and Doc struck up a conversation.

"You did very well indeed, man! You just have to get out here more often. Perhaps then, the authorities might sanction my request for a navigator. By that time, you should have that other letter and all your documents will be in order. Then, we'll see how you feel about ocean voyages and sea travel . . . I tell you, the timing is altogether different. Lets a man get some depth to his thoughts, you know . . . take Everett, for instance . . . "

Fred testily interrupted Doc. "You take him. I can't stomach his horrible tastes, nor his flat sense of humor."

Hampton changed the focus of the conversation, sensing he'd touched a sore spot. "Yeah, well like I was saying, he's already figured his class-A license and has sound plans for his retirement. You know, a fellow has that type of time."

"Shit! I can't imagine that hard nosed Rastafarian in broadcasting. That's definitely not a boon for the industry," Fred mocks, as he picks up his gear and moves toward the stairs. Hampton continued his fatherly advice, as he followed along behind the younger man.

"He'll do just as good a job as you're doing . . . trying to steer this boat like a sports car! Anyway, Helena has already forgotten you, I'm sure!"

Undaunted, Fred replies, "yeah, he does talk kind of funny, at that! Maybe, he'll be able to reach a lot of people with his jejune banality!"

Fred's sarcasm was disconcerting for Doc, who snapped back, curtly.

"So do a lot of Geiches, for that matter!"

"Look, Hamp, don't play the forgotten man with me," Fred laughingly intones. "I know you rather choose the type of life you lead. Your momma didn't make no 'pissy-ass' cry baby. You just never let the Georgia Sea islands circumscribe your life's experience . . . but, you could have been a stick in the mud too, you know."

Doc took the younger man's comment as a source of comic relief and smiled broadly at the humor.

"Go on and laugh at the old man . . . but play with her nose a little bit, every chance you get."

"You talking about Helena, Doc?"

"Shit no, man, I'm talking about my boat! And there better not be any equivocation about that. I've got too many things to look after, besides you confused children," gripes Hampton.

Chapter Three

Daybreak came pleasantly to the island, showing no trace of the inclement weather which proceeded the dawn. Two seagulls listlessly rode the calm trade winds through the lingering mist, high above the activity on the wharf. The cold light of diffused sunshine accentuated the ebony colors of the crew, who were busy unloading the month's catch. Garbed in raingear, the men completed their chores with the accompaniment of lively song exchanges. The work progressed in a highly orchestrated manner which was reminiscent of African tribal behavior at harvest time. Hampton viewed the activity from the deckrail while a motor-scooter approached in the distance. Doc interrupted his supervision when the messenger arrived. The young boy dismounted the scooter and ascended the gangplank to dispatch an envelope. The skipper received the letter and tipped the adolescent, then carefully scrutinized the envelope to discern its contents. He held it up to the sun, which now shined through the overcast, then seat about seeking Fred.

"What do you know, feathertail?"

"Ah, Doc. Just tyring to awaken these dorsel fins this morning. The old man will probably have to put some heat on my back, after this haul. What have you got cooking?"

"Here's something come in for you . . . "

Fred took the envelope and proceeded to open it. "Ah, ha, what have we here . . . folks just won't let me have any time for myself."

Everett passed by the two men and looked nosily over Fred's shoulder. He testily comments, "call from the White House, feathertail?"

"Business as usual, governor," quips Fred. His offhand reply was spontaneous, expressing disinterest with the morning spar. The marked change in attitude was apparent to the skipper, who watched, as Fred moved toward the hole while disrobing from his raingear.

"Got to pull anchor and head to the Regent Hotel, Doc! Take care of my gear until I get back," he shouted, as he disappeared below.

"Alright," says Hampton. "I suppose I won't be able to get you out for another haul, now that the 'pressures' have got a fix on you."

Fred entered the crew's quarters and continued to undress. He paused a moment, reflectively, then re-read the telegram.

TRANSCONTINENTAL MEDIA PROMOTIONS; New York, September 29, 1963. Murphy: Our sources disclose the conservative interests within the textile offering shall attempt expansion in Martique . . . elements connected with N.Y. & Mid-West financiers and bankers seek co-optive parasitism . . . see Haber at Regent Hotel to counter ameliorative tactic . . . exploitive stratergy to be neutralized in representing our client, The Federation of Martique . . . expecting your return Oct. 1, 1963.

The telegram was signed, Lloyd.

Fred dressed in moments and assumed the poise of a well tailored public relations specialist. He emerged from the hole and waved to Doc, then walked along the pier, amidst the souvenir and fruit vendors, to a waiting taxi in front of the Anchorage Hotel. The cab left the poor section of the island, with its crowds of local peasantry, peddlers and squalor, and turned onto the main road leading to the more affluent parcels of real estate. There, the hotels catered to the middle class white tourists, who played all day in the calm waters of protected beaches and danced all night to the sound of calypso and reggae, or perhaps, gambled at the casino.

Watching the picturesque array of floral variety through the open window, Fred's thoughts focused on the textile industry, as the cab ambled slowly along the bumpy road. He knew that textile businesses were among the first large scale operations in America, which developed in the new country, after industrialization broke up the cottage industries of the old world. Now, the traditional families who controlled these businesses were being replaced by the new generation of immigrants. He also knew of the fierce competition in the industry which stemmed from the Asian influx and the rise of synthetic products, after the war. But, the main problem for that kind of business still remained cheap labor, he thought. Since the unions remained the perrenial thorn in the side of textiles, and Martique presented a reasonably close third-world labor force, the probability of exploitation remained unequivocal. Fred thought over several strategies while the taxi approached the hotel. Finally he felt his job was clear: develop an agreement that would protect the workers and simultaneously contribute to Martique's economic development plans. The cab had reached the Regent, at last, and Fred gathered his portfolio, paid the fare and entered the hotel.

The Regent was a modern building, like most of the edifices in the area. Unlike the more traditional structures in the poorer sections, the decor was slick and camp. Fred thought the architecture was a poor attempt to emulate Miles Van de Rohe. Aesthetically, he preferred the influence of Frank Lloyd Wright and Corbuso who, he felt, integrated their structures with cultural and environmental factors in a more wholesome balance. Although he was accustomed to the 'grotesque distortion' of the island's natural beauty, to accomodate the 'petty bourgeois', he nevertheless felt resentful.

Fred entered the lobby and paged Haber from the main desk, then found a comfortable spot at one of the tables on the terrace, overlooking the seacoast. He sat there awhile watching the yachts in the bay, smoking contemplatively, and began constructing an imaginative conversation about the ensuing meeting. In his thoughts, Fred saw two Rastafarian labor leaders who were characteristically attired in dirty dashikiis with faded monograms of Haille Selasie. The men wore their hair in dreadlocks, down to the shoulders, and on their dirty feet were sandals made of old rubber tires. As Fred continued to muse with the scenario, he imagined the substance of the conversation.

"You speak of one hundred positions as if that's going to stimulate industrial growth, in and of itself. Don't you realize that we're not interested in passive exploitation of that type. Here you sit, Mr. Haber, representing joint financial holdings of approximately two hundred and fifty million dollars, which could be transferred into resources capable of wiping out a sizeable portion of the health and educational problems that presently plague Martique. Further, your international interests shall undoubtedly double those assets within the first five years operation on the island, purely from savings by using our human resources. No, Mr. Haber, we are talking about a joint proprietorship venture, managerial skills, and at least a minimal return to our waivering marginal economy . . . what the hell do you people think is going on in the world today, anyhow . . . it's not long ago that we put your 'constituents' out of here, you know!"

The labor leader spoke with a highly accented deep bass voice while his assistant nodded agreement. When the Rastafarian finished, his subordinate rose to speak, with an awkward modulation while he anxiously paced the floor.

"As I understand, Mr. Haber, the interests behind this venture do not at all reflect sympathetic views regarding our present economic situation. Those political lobbies, in the states and on the continent, continue to impede mature foreign policy and further the same colonial attitudes which you seem to be attempting, once again . . . "

The assistant sat, with an air of self-satisfaction, and crossed his legs. Haber had been sitting opposite the Rastafarians with a supercillious grin on his face throughout the diatribe, puffing at his havana cigar. He was a tall white man of forty five whose well-built frame accentuated the expensive tan summer suit. Wrinkles lined his weathered face, adding interest to a recently tanned visiage. Clearing his throat, momentarily, he began speaking with the drawl of a sophisticated southerner.

"Understand me, gentlemen. We cannot afford to overlook the lucrative potentials of this package. We are at the thresholds of a billion dollar operation which will inevitably spin off into Martique's economy. That should be obvious in such a long range undertaking. Now, I don't want to talk politics to you gentlemen. Presently we're not able to do anything in the social sector. But, this business deal which my colleagues and I offer is designed to stimulate economic growth. Once the success of our venture becomes known, there's no telling how much Martique's business community can expand . . . it just takes time and training. We're not out to rip you people off. We'd like everybody to get a little of the gravy, if you understand me!"

A big smile shined on his face, as he leaned back in his seat, satisfied, and puffed at the havana. Fred leaned forward, obviously interrupting the two anxious Rastafarians.

"Very succinctly, Mr. Haber, the commercial value of Universal Textiles does outweigh the type of project you're trying to implement in Martique. Besides my client's sensitivity to the political sentiments of the company's larger stockholders, there is the real issue of guaranteed cash flow in a world recession. Perhaps you can arrive at a more amenable economic exchange in your offering; stock options, residuals, profit sharing or what have you. It's a matter of control on the one hand, as I'm sure you readily agree. Then on the other hand, it's a concern of labor relations. With the competitive edge your company gains by operating here in Martique, you're just going to have to be more realistic in your offering."

Fred fixed his eyes upon Haber's, as he inhaled smoke from a cigarette. He weighed the imapct of his statement on the opposition, before making the next point.

"These people have their own prospectus for economic development. Although my client realizes your good perception of its labor potential, you have severely underestimated the government's foresight . . . they do have the option of opening up bids to tap their market potential . . . "

The smug grin turned sour on Haber's face and his voice lost its former paternalism.

"You must be the Murphy from New York!"

Fred smiled at his daydream which was suddenly interrupted by a suavely dressed white man.

"Murphy? . . . Jonas! We're waiting for you upstairs."

The two men left the terrace while, in the background, reggae sounds intoned social themes from the hotel bar jukebox. New arrivals cluttered the Regent's lobby, as the men entered the elevator, and in the distance a jet streaked across the horizon, setting its flight path to the states.

Chapter Four

Autumn came late to New York that year. By October the leaves on the trees in Central Park were just beginning to turn pastel. The city was undergoing transition at that time, reflecting changes in federal allocation policies which were making headlines in the news across the nation. Urban renewal of the 1950's had reached a hiatus, leading the feds to follow a course of review and accountability. Locally, politicians, eager in their opportunism to gain constituents, were quick to espouse the virtues of the new government programs of community renewal which were ushered in in 1960. It was now three years later, and competition between neighborhood hegemonies were the pervasive outcomes of local control. For Mayor Bailey, a new element had been introduced to the partisan politics of the city. The Blacks, who had carried the traditional democrat party line for decades, were no longer a passive block. Spurred on by the civil rights activity of the South, a new militant attitude characterized the neighborhoods of Harlem, Bedford Stuyversant and the South Bronx. Adding fuel to the fire, the Puerto Ricans, who had come in droves during the 1950's and were considered thirty years behind the Blacks, were forming coalitions with the activists. The mayor, facing a critical situation in housing, employment and education, steered a tenuous course between the second and third generation European immigrants and this new emerging force. The melting pot was about to explode, and people were choosing sides very early.

For the moment the political situation was veiled in the lower East-side. The real estate interests, eager to capitalize, welcomed the displacement of old world immigrants because of the increased rent charged for each new lease. A pattern of catering to the known transient populations of students, leftist radicals, Blacks, Puerto Ricians and artists emerged, which led to a curious anomoly in neighborhood organization. This disparate admixture of marginals occupied a territory between Fourth Avenue on the West, which ran North to Fourteenth Street, then East to Avenue D, and South to Houston Street.

In this area one could find expensive boutiques on Eighth Street, with their tiffany lamps and hand carved furniture, Andy Warhol and other pop art posters, head shops and their smoke paraphrenalia, as well as disco joints. A stroll along First Avenue introduced open vegetable stands, army and navy stores, coin operated laundries, and small food stores among the large variety of ethnic restaurants. On Fifth Street the motorcycle gangs hung out, and derelicts converged on Second

Street, around the Men's Shelter.

The multi-ethnic and generational community was promoted as New York's 'true' Left-Bank, in contrast with the more status conscious West Village. But, even in that quasi-integrated neighborhood, the spectre of political machinations were to be seen in the intermittent renovations which, overnight, hiked the real estate values out of the reach of the average denizen and simultaneously altered the demographic composition of whole streets.

Fred chose to live in that neighborhood at 88 East Third Street, between First and Second Avenues. The building was old, built around the First World War. Indoor toilets had just been installed. The landlord promised continued renovations, but meanwhile, the faded brown paint peeled from the gloomy narrow building which was squeezed among the other walk up tenements near the corner of First Avenue. The narrow stairway was like an obstacle course to navigate, but somehow Fred had moved his furniture in without damage. This was home for the last two years. Apartment six, on the third floor, which overlooked the graveyard that faced Second Street.

Inside his apartment again, Fred was busy making dinner. With his shirt collar open and sleeves rolled up, he moved about the small kitchen area with stylized precision, bringing together a meal in a matter of moments. The television and FM were both playing at low volumes, which contributed to his way of relaxing. Occasionally, fragments of colloquial Spanish could be heard over the din, as passerbys conversed while traversing the building's hallway. The news came on, and the commentator elucidated details of the Vietnam War.

"For the second day this week navy pilots bombed the Viet Cong supply routes along the Ho Chi Minh trail. All the aircraft returned safely to the carrier Nimitz . . ."

Fred took a seat in front of the television, engrossed in the news while the FM oozed with progressive jazz, making a strange contrapuntal to the ravages depicted on the screen. The telephone rang.

Fred reached over the side of his chair and picked up the receiver, abruptly intoning, "Fred Murphy . . . yeah, how you doing, man? What's up . . . uh, huh . . . right, I've got you!"

Just then there was a knock on the door.

"Hold on, man, there's someone at the door."

Fred's agile movements took him to the door in less than two seconds. He returned, followed by a casually dressed brother who exuded a smooth placidity in his demeanor, as he made himself comfortable. Returning to his seat, Fred picked up the receiver and continued the conversation.

"Okay, I'm back. Look, Jomo just walked in the door, so we can go over that right now. I'll work on it over some brew, tonight, and have it ready in the morning. Okay later."

Fred motioned Jomo toward the kitchen area of the small flat. "There's more of this in there, Jomo. Help yourself . . ."

Tall, lean Jomo stood to the side of the television set watching coverage of civil rights protests in Montgomery.

"The city of Montgomery exploded today, as civil rights protestors mounted their campaign for more jobs. . ."

Jomo shook his head and says, "no, that's alright. I stopped by the little kitchen on my way over here. Had a nice little bite to eat. What's happening, man . . . where've you been for quite awhile?''

"I've been playing ship's steward on a trawler, Jomo . . . down in the islands trying to take some kind of vacation."

Jomo hiked his jeans and took off his denim jacket.

"You mean on old Doc's fishing boat, huh?''

Fred moved toward the kitchen area to clean up.

"Yeah, I was down in Martique for about a good month, before the 'presssures' got a fix on me, as Doc says."

"Say, Fred, didn't I hear something about a big textile deal that you and Doc swung for them dudes?''

"Is that what you heard, or did you read that?''

"Come on now, Murphy, it was you who got that connection squared away. I do read the exchange sections in the newspapers, sometimes. I am also aware of what effect that venture could have on international trade. But, what intrigues me is, how in the man's name did you work that shit out through all them Rastafarians?''

"Doc gets a lot of respect from some important folks, down there, Jomo."

Jomo rubbed his bald head in amazement, and adds, "and I suppose you made out like a fat rat!''

"I imagine you had better straighten out your information on that point, my man!'' Fred's tone was markedly caustic, but Jomo played down his companion's peevishness with a broad knowing smile. "Somehow news articles can't help making provocative innuendos. Fortunately, I happen to know you people have scruples."

"That makes my job all the easier, I would imagine, Jomo."

"So, you don't plan to correct the public information?''

"No, not at this point. We've been impressive enough for the time being, and news comment doesn't adversely affect our public relations."

Fred lit a cigarette and took a drag, inhaling deeply, while Jomo made himself comfortable on the floor.

"Well, the textile industry is in for a revolution," says Jomo.

"You better believe it!''

They laughed awhile, then Jomo raised himself from the floor and walked to the refrigerator. During the interlude in their conversation, the television commentator presented news about the impending election.

"In the city, tongiht, the mayoral candidates are scrambling for last minute endorsements as the election date draws near. . .''

Jomo returned with a beer and squat in front of the set.

"How many people are you taking with you on this assignment, Jomo?''

"Two"

"Should I question their abilities?''

"No, man, it's just another dude besides myself. One other cat who's gotten good over the years."

"Oh, I see, you're cutting back to get the job done more economically, eh?''

"You know him, perhaps . . . John, the pretty boy from uptown."

Fred mused for a second, reflectively, then says, "no, I can't say that I do, offhand. But, anyway, I'm sure Ferguson is going to be facing a great deal of tension and I think we should do our best to give him the right type of treatment. No mess ups! It's got to be clean from start to finish . . . how many pieces are you bringing?''

"There'll probably be three cases. They're small and quick. Nothing should go wrong with the thing. I'm sure I can count on John . . . who are you bringing?"

Fred stretched a moment, while yawning.

"Oh, I'll probably go with Les. He's done this type of thing before."

"Oh yeah? Well, what time do we set up in the morning?"

Fred got up and walked to the small desk which sagged from the weight of his opened attache case and other work materials, spread on top.

"Take a look at this itinerary, Jomo. Then you can get a better idea of what you're doing."

Approaching each other in front of the table, the two men spread out the materials and began to chart details. Fred guided his hand over the paper to emphasize the itinerary while Jomo looked on, memorizing the information.

"This is where he'll come in from the East of Lenox Avenue."

"Alright, if it gets too congested, we'll pull back to the interior position."

"Try not to go inside unless it's absolutely necessary, Jomo. If you can keep all the activity on the streets, it would be fine."

"I got you. What about the timing . . . I'm going to have to move downtown pretty fast, after that!"

Fred looked at his watch. "At most it'll be five minutes. Come in about 11:35 and I should have set it up for you."

"Okay, Murphy . . . so I start my movement at 11:30. The rest will take care of itself."

The two men paused. Music from the FM became the focus of thier attention. Jomo turned up the volume and they were engrossed with the sounds of Charlie Parker.

"How's the governor looking these days, Fred?"

"Oh, Mr. Carter," Fred strains in a cajoling dialect. "He's linked up with some nice broadcast plans."

"I got that info myself, man . . . fill me in," Jomo prods.

"It's simply that we're going to need a lot of communications vehicles in the future. So Doc has already started talking to some people about it. So it goes, he seems to be gaining a lot of ground with Parliament. Since he did need an island boy up front, he opted for Everett. The cat's been Doc's right arm down there."

Jomo rubbed his bald head.

"Well Helena tells me he's doing quite well, too. Said he was licensed and all that shit . . . oh, by the way, that's how I found out you were on your way back to the 'big apple'."

Fred shook his head, obviously disgruntled. "Hmmm, it seems like folks think I need a constant wet nurse."

Jomo smiled. "No offense 'poppa', but I'm expecting to hear a little more than those sketchy details from you. What's he into, Fred?" After all, your time was spent getting up in the morning with the man.

"Broadcast is tricky, Jomo. Especially in mountainous terrain. I guess what I'm really waiting for is cable. Better quality control. Anyhow, Doc has got some gas and oil interests behind the broadcast idea for Martique and it looks like the deal will be completed within a few months. Everett will be on his way, after that."

"Well that's terrific . . . you and Doc should be sticking your chests out, then. What the heck are you so down for?"

"Man, look . . . I'll do the business with Everett . . . I'll do it all the time, for any brother who's got the sense and industry to move forward! What I don't like about Everett, is his sense . . . he doesn't have enough sense to stay out of my personal business."

Jomo used both hands to rub his slick head, as he felt Fred's temper rise. "Helena is his sister, man," he offered a note of balance. "We all know how you feel about it. But did you ever consider what other folks are going to feel about your situation? I'm not one to say that you made a mistake, or encourage you in any way . . . lord knows I don't see how you made all of them pressures, for as long as you did. I must really premium my freedom, because I'd never put up with what you've gone through. But I can still see the guy's point in doing what he feels is part of his responsibilities."

"I hear you, Jomo, but I guess I just haven't matured, as much as the thirty some odd years. . ."

"Dig you over there . . . peeping around the corner at forty, talking that nonsense about maturation. Why don't you just talk to the brother and smooth things out?"

"I'm not about to start sounding like a talking asshole. It's bad enough that I look that way, too often for my own comfort!"

They laughed heartily a moment, then Jomo finished his beer and went to dispose of the can.

"I understand she's going to move out to the West coast," he comments from the kitchen area. "She's constantly being a part of what's happening." He returned to the living room while continuing the conversation. "She got out of harlem, you know . . . down on Central Park West, somewhere. Ah, if you want me to find out about her next move. . ."

Fred was peeved by the gossip, and quips, "look, man, I'm not suffering from malnutrition. But, if she decides to let me see Amber Ujima, she knows where to reach me! I'm not going to get hung up on tracing her obvious whereabouts around town. I'm not interested!"

Jomo lowered his head, obsequiously, sensing he had overstepped the bounds of a confidant.

"Yeah, well, I guess it's time for me to ease . . . loosen some more of them buttons on your neck, son, so we know where you want us to put the noose."

Jomo exited the apartment, as placidly as he had entered, while Fred remained seated in the same position, losing himself in the commercial.

Chapter Five

The crowds on 125th Street were much larger than expected. There were perhaps fifteen hundred people gathered around the new State Office building. Expectancy pervaded the throng like a magnet, attracting curious passersby, and busy shoppers away from the overpriced stores. The excitement over recent changes in local politics was everywhere in Harlem. Even petty hustlers turned out. Scattered among the crowd, they added distinctive contrasts, decked in their leather and sharkskin outfits and maroon wing-tip shoes. They stood around with their velour hats cocked to the side, brims broken over their eyebrows, eager to see what kind of connection they could make. Calculation was their game, and they were quick to drop a fifty or hundred dollar bill into the campaign fund for future favors, in the event they ran afoul of the law. The cops were there in force. Both uniform and plainclothesmen moved through the crowd along with the local panhandlers and vendors. To the West, on Seventh Avenue, a campain van equipped with loudspeakers could be seen, parked at the corner. The message blurting out of the public address system reinforced the hype of the affair, which complimented placards posted on streetlamps, promoting Councilman Charles Ferguson for mayor.

Jomo and John were rushing now. Events had taken on a different character, and they were forced to move their operation indoors. Exiting the elevator inside the Theresa Hotel, they scrambled down the corridor, cases in hand, to room 5F, which Jomo had reserved for such an emergency.

The men sat their cases down on the carpeted floor, as Jomo fumbled for the key. Finding it, he unlocked the door, and the two entered with their load. The men sat the equipment aside and scrutinized the view from the window. They were facing East and could see the entire scene downstairs clearly from the vantage high atop the building. Satisfied, they returned from the window and opened the cases. Their precise activity worked like a military operation. Cameras emerged and were connected to the wireless transmitter in the nagra recorder. John fastened a 500 millimeter angeniux lens to the eclair, and Jomo made a few minor adjustments. John opened the window for Jomo, who braced the rig against the frame, to focus on the entrance of the State Office Building. The men worked very methodically and set up a shooting in minutes. Downstairs, a small coterie emerged from the towering edifice and lingered at the entrance. Jomo checked his timepiece. Eleven thirty four showed on the dial.

"Roll 'em."

John turned on the recorder and listened attentively through the earphones.

The campaign staff was busy exchanging small talk, awaiting their exclusive media coverage. Fred knew that Les was busy polling the electorate and gathering editorial and other research data for their work on TMP's campaign contract, elsewhere. They would meet later at the corner of Lennox Avenue. He checked his watch. It was eleven thirty five. He had been waiting for the right psychological moment to capture the candidate's interaction with the excited crowd. His eyes were fixed upon Ferguson, as he watched each subtle movement of the councilman while the tension mounted in the air. He took a drag on a cigarette and extinguished the butt, then snaked his way through the throng. As anticipated, Ferguson was clearly perturbed, but held his composure, as Fred approached.

"Well, I see you people can fall short on commitments, after all is said and done. What's the matter, didn't I contact you early enough?"

He was an imposing black man who's almond shaped eyes and thick moustache contributed interest to his arresting visiage. As he walked toward Fred, in his Hart Schaffner and Marx blue pin stripped suit, the crowd surged forward shouting his name. His athletic frame accentuated the meticulous tailoring of the expensive suit, and only graying temples gave any indication of his fifty-two years. His entourage became dismayed, meanwhile, and expressed chagrin among themselves about the seeming foul-up. Fred walked toward Ferguson with a provocative smile, but before he was able to interject one of his quips, a tall, conservatively dressed elderly woman stepped from the group and positioned herself between the two men.

"You know those boys from the newsrooms would belabor the point that we hadn't notified them of this event. And after all, an outfit of such prestigous esteem as Transcontinental Media Promotions . . ."

Rita Callandar was a suave old timer to the machine in New York. She had gotten over by paying her dues, several times over, and she carried a lot of clout. Fred respected her influence and wasn't about to ruin his relationship with her, or make the company look bad. He bit his tongue. After all, she was district leader and councilman from Brooklyn's Bedford Stuyvesant community.

"You're not implying that you wouldn't have time for conversations with your fellow citizens, anyway, now that you're out here, Ferguson? This commencement is for your public audience, isn't that right," plys Fred. "Well, how about speaking directly to your constituents."

There was a method to Fred's ploy. He wanted the candidate to appear unrehearsed and spontaneous, rather than over-conscious of his camera image. Ferguson began to size up the situation, recomposing his temperament.

"Don't tell me you spent all that dough just to bring the people out today, Murphy?"

"Just relax, councilman, and talk to the people about reclaiming some of this choice land from the downtown interests. Keep yourself faced in the general direction of the Theresa while you speak   . . .   here, let me prepare you, properly."

Fred took a wireless microphone from his pocket and pinned it to the councilman's collar.

"You never know what you'll gain from being honest and open-minded," Fred winked.

Ferguson's coterie had listened with guarded interest, but were befuddled by such capricious behavior. The candidate was also, more than wary. But, his shrewd political savvy and trust in Fred's boss, led him to follow the public relations directions, even though seemingly unconventional, to say the least. Ferguson sublimated his anger and approached the crowd, which was exactly what Fred had wanted.

"What are you going to do about that educational mess, councilman," shouts a fat lady who stood at the front of the crowd. She was dressed in African garb and, like many of her neighbors, was sensitive to the identity crisis of the times. Her comment brought forth new waves of outcry from the people.

"I'm hoping that we can work very closely with the Board of Education and the various neighborhoods throughout the city to develop the kinds of programs that are suitable to each respective community. I'm on my way now to district five in the Bronx, to look into a proposed plan to use para-professionals in the schools. Should that prove to be as dynamic as it appears on paper, perhaps we can look forward to setting up community boards throughout the city. Today is a very special one for me to examine educational concerns . . . ''

Chapter Six

Transcontinental Media Promotions occupied a renovated city firehouse on East Thirteenth Street in the lower East Side. The spacious layout housed a complete media operation within three floors, which was a vital part of the public relations business. The ground floor was divided between a reception area, offices for the economists and social scientists and libraries. Journalism activity took up the entire second floor, where the magazine and newspaper writers worked, while the constant din of wire services and typewriters pervaded the large open space. The top floor was being completed and would eventually house the commercial artists, public relations personnel and executive offices. Only the projection room was functional, at present, where Fred and Lloyd had just finished viewing a screening of the day's shooting. The film had been edited earlier, and now the two men consulted about the assignment, while the office buzzed with late afternoon activity.

"You shouldn't have shaken up Ferguson so much, there . . . it's okay, otherwise. It's got a clean natural look to it."

Lloyd carried his fifty-five years well. He had been around public relations when it wasn't fashionable for Blacks to be on staff. Benevolence of his many social contacts had gotten him into the field, and now the experience was paying dividends. He knew his work thoroughly and worked hard at it. Fred was looking at the wrinkles on Lloyd's forehead which appeared like finely etched carvings on granite, as his boss casually sat, with his tie unfastened, taking care of business. The short, clean cut, pipe smoking man carried a great deal of information upstairs under his fully grayed head of hair. Fred admired his superior's professional ability, but more importantly, he respected Lloyd's integrity and wisdom.

"I thought you'd like the first outtakes, most. You know, in the beginning was the word . . . candid situations usually provide a lot of choice ones," Fred glibly remarks, grinning sarcastically at his success. Lloyd ignored the bait.

"If we can get some more exclusives like that one on Ferguson, I think we can start to wrap up that phase of the project." He turned to talk to a waiting secretary. "Get me the news desk on that six o'clock special about our prospective mayor." Another worker peeked into the room and interrupted the conversation. Lloyd paused momentarily, in his busy schedule, to read an assignment. "That's some pretty nice copy . . . get it over to McNally and Rand right away. They have a hold on that layout, and it's four hours behind . . . now, what was it you were saying, Fred?"

"I was saying that Ferguson has a special facility with words."

Lloyd puffed on his pipe and curtly remarks, "Save your humor for young ladies and cocktail sips, my man. I need about three or four more profiles of Ferguson for this campaign, and you're not getting off the hook until the chores are completed!"

"Is there any way I can do it all in one day?" Fred quips, still grinning.

"I want some magazine spreads in the next two weeks. Try to focus on arts and cultural affairs . . . then you can hold off for a little while, until somthing big comes up."

"I'll be sure to set a little hay for the horses and some slop for the pigs, Lloyd."

"Yeah, well with the price of food the way it is, are you sure you're going to be able to eat, yourself?"

"Alright, already, I'm available," replies Fred. "Shit, I haven't hustled like this since I was twenty!"

Lloyd leaned back in the chair and puffed his pipe. "Well, keep the machine oiled, Baby!"

Fred got up and began to leave the projection room. When he reached the door, Lloyd asked, "How's Doc moving things along?"

"Doing swell. He sends the 'Rasta-pressure-house' his regards. Says he's going to make a navigator out of me, yet. He plans to hijack me from the city and thereby save my soul."

Lloyd gave a half smile, pipe in mouth, without saying a word. He emitted a blank stare. Fred got the message and abruptly exited.

Chapter Seven

About a month had elapsed now, and the company was having marked success. Pumping the hype of a political campaign came rather easy, as a result of Ferguson's polished charisma. Once the candidate adjusted to the Fred's unconventional style, working together became rather enjoyable. He had captured a sizable portion of the electorate and was shaking up the partisan loyalties, in an untraditional manner. But, although he was a household symbol, there was still the problem of gaining important endorsements.

Events had quieted down somewhat around the office, as Lloyd continued to work on new strategies. While he sat alone in his office, there was a soft knock on the door. He raised his head, as Fred cautiously opened the door and entered. Leaving the door ajar, he was followed by the lithe catlike movements of Jomo, who in turn, was followed by John. They entered, closing the door behind them, and spread was followed by John. They entered, closing the door behind them, and spread casually around the room. Lloyd hadn't changed his position at his desk. He sat there in an unpresuming manner, pipe still in hand, without emotional expression on his face. During the long interlude, Lloyd silently scrutinized the group, as if they were a bunch of street thugs.

"Okay, listen up! The City Council hearing should wind up the documentary portion of the campaign project with Ferguson. Now, thus far, we've had pretty good success with his image, and it looks as if things are going reasonably well with the man. He's more accustomed to the intrusions we make on his activities, so there shouldn't be any problem during this shooting, right? I just want to say two things . . . look out for Callander. She's probably withheld a lot of stuff, just for this part of the hearings. She'll undoubtedly have a great many goodies, so try to anticipate her for dramatic force. Then, I want you to play down the other council-members . . . slight distortion, rough edges, or whatever. The important thing here is to overemphasize the situation. Have you got that? Now, are there any questions?"

A long silent pause descended while Lloyd puffed profusely at his pipe. Finally, Fred moved toward the door, followed by the feline motions of Jomo, with John bringing up the rear. They exited, easing out as casually as they had entered, leaving Lloyd to his work.

Chapter Eight

A fine mist shrouded the city that morning, making a dismal atmosphere for the hordes of workers, trudging to their jobs. The army of civil servants mixed indistin-guishably with the cadres of private sector employees, as they exited the crowded subway tunnels and buses and entered the towering office buildings to punch their timecards before the clock struck 9:01. Downtown, in the Wall Street area, traffic was congested, as usual, and the light rain added to the delays. Along with the city's daily flow of its large work force, the weather contributed a peculiar kind of fore-boding to lower Manhattan where the awe-inspiring edifices loomed high above the drudgery at street level.

Ferguson's limousine snaked through the traffic on Lafayette Street and turned right at the Municipal Building, heading west toward Broadway. There, the car turned south and proceeded to the official driveway at the beginning of City Hall Park. The chauffer eased the limousine into a waiting parking space in front of City Hall which stood, insignificantly, at the base of the Brooklyn Bridge. Ferguson stretched his large frame as he got out of the car while the film crew emerged from the doorway, lending a documentary air to his entrance. He was accompanied by Rita Callander whose open raincoat revealed a stylish man-tailored suit that accen-tuated her, once slim and youthful figure. Although she remained small, age had come upon her. Now, the stockings were chosen to conceal the advancing varicose veins. Colors were more demure, as well as the styles she wore. But, even at this stage of the life cycle, she was still an attractive woman.

"This business gets more exciting as the time goes by. What are you dudes doing up so early in the morning, anyway? That's phenomenally uncharacteristic of black folks. You had better be careful, or you'll wind up changing our image," she joked.

Her demeanor always carried a combination of incisive analysis and shophisti-cated street-wise jibes which Fred found entertaining.

"My boss suggests that inflation is coming and advised me to beat the food costs by keeping prompt appointments," laughs Fred.

"He should've written me that advice, so I could present those kinds of solutions at this hearing," replies Callander. "You know, the city could use that type of fiscal policy for budgeting."

"Rita, do you think you can stretch the agenda and get into that concern, today?"

"Well, Fred, I'm sure we could introduce the issue for the council's consideration. The membership might assign a committee to study and evaluate the threat of inflation . . .''

Ferguson had been silent on the way up the stairs, but was seriously reflecting upon his companions' conversation. He saw another political advantage to upstage his opponents in the campaign.

"That should be the first recommendation you make, upon recognition by the chair, Rita."

"Then, you would have a logical prelude for presenting the educational plan for the council's approval, right?" asks Fred.

"Your insight is correct again, Murphy. Livingston Street is one hell of a complex to overhaul," Ferguson continues. "But, it's got to begin soon. Otherwise, the city is going to continually have economic crisis and social problems, draining the tax base."

"What kind of support can you caucus from the black teachers, Rita?"

"I've done a lot of preliminary work to insure it, Fred. Their dissatisfaction with the union is about to erupt into another municipal explosion."

The threesome had reached the second floor. The brief exchange had stimulated Fred and his mind percolated with ideas. He would have to sort them out and go over a strategy with Lloyd.

The group reached the City Council chambers where they were greeted by other councilmen and their aides, as the membership entered the large official quarters.

Ferguson spotted the council president approaching and beamed a warm smile. "Eugene! Well, I see the traffic didn't stop you from getting here on time."

The two men shook hands and shared small talk as the membership moved to their respective seats. Inside the chambers sat a small audience comprised mainly of public interest groups, waiting patiently, as the councilmen settled down to the business of the day.

Eugene Landers was a capable city council president and an astute politician. Although he represented the last vestige of White Anglo-Saxon Protestant influence, he had broad partisan support in the city and related to the various political factions in an uncharacteristically wholesome manner.

"By the powers vested in my office, I call this hearing of the City Council of New York to order. If there are no requests for reading the minutes of the preceeding session, the secretary will enter today's proceedings into the public record . . ." He turned to the other councilmen, inquiringly. "Very well, then, the agenda reads as follows . . . item one of today's business is the recommendation of the transit committee concerning operating revenues for mass transit. Under review is the committee's study of the Transit Authority's proposed rate increase and the related issue of wage demands of the Transportation Workers Union . . . item two deals with the education committee's study of the proposed neighborhood school boards." He turned to Ferguson and made a cursory aside. "I think your proposed ideas are scheduled for presentation, Charles. If I recall correctly, that whole item might require a separate hearing . . . next is the problem of rent control and the issue of fixing ceilings on rent increments. Lastly, we have the stalled construction projects in our capital improvement program, and the issue of discrimination in jobs and contracts, which will affect federal monies slated for the city by HUD . . . perhaps, by the end of the week we will be finished with two committee reports and testimony." He paused to sip some water. "I hope we can get out of chambers before vacations begin to roll around!"

Fred found a seat in a secluded corner of the room while the councilmen laughed at Landers' joke. He had just gotten comfortable when an aide excused herself and occupied the adjoining seat. She was an unimposing white girl who's youthful attire belied her twenty-nine years. Holding a bundle of files close to her chest, she obtrusively makes her presence felt.

"Ferguson looks a lot calmer now," she whispers.

"Oh, yes, I've noticed that, myself," Fred replies, half-interested in the small talk.

"You fellows have been doing quite a smart bit of public relations, I must say."

Fred sensed the curiosity which usually pervaded staff workers in all walks of life, who were always eager to get the latest inside dope to contribute to the grapevine. He decided to be polite. After all, he could use a connection in City Hall to help round out his work on the campaign. Then, you never knew when something important might arise in the future.

"Thanks, but I don't think we've met, have we?"

He beamed his million dollar smile.

"I was hoping that I could be casual . . . but, what the heck, sometimes a person is a little gawky . . . so you're the Murphy character behind all of the things coming out on Ferguson?" she flashed a broad smile and obsequiously adjusted her partially opened blouse.

"Fred Murphy, to be exact! And who do I have the pleasure of meeting . . . despite the gawkiness, of course?"

"I'm Christine Jordan . . . this is the first opportunity I've had to get into council chambers during these hearings," she confides to Fred" . . . How do you do?"

"Alright . . . and, ah, who are you with, Christine?"

"Councilman Landers. We're doing the opening on the transit situation."

Fred figured he had scored a good mark and reached for a cigarette, as he sized up the lady.

"Do you smoke?"

Christine smiled and adjusted the papers on her lap. She was more comfortable, now.

"Only occassionally when I'm relaxed," she replies.

"I imagine you've done a lot of homework on that material. Did you lose a lot of sleep?" Fred took his time purposely. He didn't want to be too obvious, nor did he intend to pull teeth to get information.

"Oh, yes indeed! I worked very hard on these reports. It appears that the grand dragon will have a long way to travel, yet, for more funding. It's a real political football, and I don't have too many job prospects," she comments.

"Uh huh."

Fred's relaxed demeanor captivated the talkative aide, who was too busy satisfying her own basic emotions to suspect his ulterior motives.

"You know, Fred, it's really unbelievable the way transit has gotten all those hikes. And, to boot, they're still tying up people's movements. It almost takes a half hour to get there from Brooklyn Heights. I shudder to think of what it's like for those unfortunate of the mass who come from further out in Queens, or up in the Bronx. How about yourself . . . do you find it difficult getting around?"

"I almost live in the neighborhood."

"Well, then, I guess it's a hell of a lot easier for you," she remarks. "Tell me, though, do you feel comfortable blowing the lid on the school situation?" Christine probes.

"Fortunately, I've been able to insulate myself from a lot of political liabilities. But, why don't we wait and see what Ferguson's committee will present, okay?" Fred replies, in a pensive manner. Christine was quite aggressive, he thought. "Anyhow, I really don't see any cause for alarm on your part."

Charles Ferguson stroked his finely trimmed moustache, waiting expectantly as the council listened to the committee's presentation of transit operating problems. Landers was questioning the officials on other fiscal matters, however. His aide had uncovered a pandora's box, and he was calling for a full investigation for possible wrong doing in the agency's management of its pension fund. Ferguson thought the situation might pay dividends. He had weighed the alternatives as the facts were disclosed and was convinced of his position. While there was a sizeable number of black transit workers, he didn't feel his platform could be completely pro-labor, in an indiscriminate appeal to the blue collar voter. He needed endorsements by labor, it was true, and he had addressed labor concerns to some extent. But, his main strategy was to direct a broad based appeal to the poor. He felt that he could swing enough of the working class votes, through his tactic of linking the problems of the poor with general consumer issues which cut across socio-economic status lines. Backed with his position on a tax reduction package and calling for more federal subsidies to stimulate business growth and employment, he felt his decision would work well. Ferguson felt he would support Landers' 'muckraking' of the transit bureaucracy, thus gaining positive campaign promotion by adding government accountability to his platform. The trade-off would be fruitful down the line, he thought, as Landers could bring in other traditional endorsements from the establishment, which he vitally needed.

Fred was busy playing up to Christine, like the farmer carefully feeds the cow to later draw upon its milk.

"Chris, I can almost feel those bloodshot eyes from months of tiring research and sleepless nights, as I listen to Landers' presentation. But, I wouldn't worry about somebody putting a price tag on your head, at this point."

"Shucks, I thought I could count on a position with your organization. When this little item hits the news, all my efforts won't amount to anything if I have to hit the streets. And, all that exhaustion ain't going to take care of me, then, you know what I mean?"

A demure smile played upon Fred's lips as he listened to the young aide's heavy come-on. "There haven't been too many layoffs around the city, lately. Look, it seems to me that you did a very impressive job. You won't go hungry, I'm sure. But I really wonder if you need much sleep . . . maybe something else is the matter, the way you're clutching those files," he teases her. Fred couldn't resist toying with Christine's inquisitiveness. And, after all, if push came to shove, he wasn't beyond a pretentious, screw-for-inducement. His ploy affected her, and she became self-conscious.

"Well, I'll keep that in mind when I consider your offer."

"You can use my name as a reference, Chris. I like having fat-legged young ladies around me," he remarks, as he raises himself from the chair. He glanced at his watch while walking to Ferguson's seat. It was already 11:30. The councilman leaned forward as Fred whispered in his ear. "I've got to phone the office, Charles. The crew know what to do should your proposal come to the floor."

Callander leaned over to participate in the conversation.

"Could you be a little quieter back there, Fred? You've got me cracking up, over here," she quips. "I don't want to be a spectacle up here, you know. This is my big film debut!"

"Rita, if those big ears of yours weren't so valuable, I'd stuff them full of cotton!"

Callander smiled, and retorts, "You're in for a rude awakening the moment I withdraw my affections and care for you, Baby!"

Fred returned the well-poised woman's smile, and says, "with that forwarning, Rita, I'll excuse myself."

Lloyd poured over a new contract draft which the company lawyer had presented to him earlier in the day. Returns from TMP's work on the mayoral campaign were already flowing into the office. Black entrepreneurship was a novelty during the early sixties, but Transcontinental Media Promotions' vanguard efforts were being received very well by major industries. Now AT&T had opened its doors in response to the unique proposal which the company presented to the utility, and Lloyd was pleased with the herculean effort Fred and the crew put into the package. The phone rang and Lloyd impatiently picked up the receiver.

"Hello . . . yes . . . what's going on over there now . . . right . . . well see if you can hang on there until they break up. Perhaps Ferguson's proposal will be presented this afternoon . . . dosen't look like it, huh . . . okay, make sure they're squared away, before you move out from there!"

After the conversation with Lloyd, Fred felt tired. It seemed like he had been working around the clock, since his return from the islands. He sat at the desk in the empty office and wondered if the view of the harbour would be pleasant from the World Trade Center which was currently under construction. He stood up, yawned and looked out of the window. Christine quietly entered the dark room where she found Fred standing alone at the window, shilouetted in the misty light.

"You do get lost rather quickly, don't you Fred?"

"I thought I might catch a breather in here, before the afternoon session."

She joined Fred at the window and stood awhile, casually brushing her long flacid hair to the side.

"They're serving club sandwiches and asparagus salad. . ."

Fred's mind was full of mental gymnastics as he calculated.

"Thanks, would you mind if we ate in here, away from all of that activity?"

"Oh, let me put down these papers. I'll get lunch," she says. Christine placed the bundle on the desk and moved obsequiously toward the door, obviously satisfied with the new found interest in her position.

"Your salary covers an awful lot of extrinsic activity, Chris," Fred says in a supportive way.

"Your sweet, dear, but I'm used to the chores, with or without women's liberation, you dig?"

"Yeah, I can understand that," he remarks, comfortingly.

She exited briskly, leaving his silhouetted figure staring out of the window. After viewing the lunchtime activity on the street outside, awhile, Fred turned to the documents which Christine had conveniently left on the table. He perused the material casually, thumbing through the files for a general impression. Finding nothing noteworthy, he carefully placed the research neatly back in order. Christine wasn't long in returning, and entered, carrying their lunch on a tray.

"Do you like ruhbarbs, Fred . . . I put some in your salad."

"Ah yes, just fine . . . say, have you any idea of the sum of unaccounted money missing from the transit pension fund?''

"Oh, my goodness, that's a sure enought scandal. Those poor-johns have a pretty tight little union operation, alright. But, their pension fund is a bureacratic mess. It's not managed like other city agencies," she says excitedly.

"I imagine not. The city usually invests in stable, slow turnover markets. But, apparently those jokers in transit could have the worker's dough tied up in any kind of national or international ventures. That could be political machination if it were managed by unscrupulus forces . . . but, you weren't able to get any assistance from their accounting office . . . I don't understand that. Isn't that information accessible to the City Council?''

Chris cleared her throat, and says, "it's all outlined in my research, since you took the liberty . . . there's some report I came across, a Neilson paper, or something like that. But, I don't know what it is, or how it figures in . . . maybe it might shed some light on the rumors that the city is investing in South Africa.''

"Oh, I guess I must not have gotten to that," Fred says, with a wry grin on his face. He took the tray from her and placed it upon the desk where they dined in the silhouetted light.

The afternoon session was about to begin, as the straggling politicians lingered in the hallway to finish their lunchtime conversations. Ferguson had been going over his strategies with Rita, about obtaining endorsements. He had been candid with her about the use Landers could play in making alignments for his campaign. Callander had agreed to help persuade the chairman to make some deals for the candidate in exchange for Ferguson's support on the transit investigation. Everything seemed to indicate a nice cozy arrangement which pleased Ferguson. Now it was back to work on the education committee's report.

"Well, Rita, I guess we'll have to go through another day before we can present this thing. . .''

"Yes, I'm tired too, Charles. I started to say where's our boy, but I see him coming now. . .''

Fred and Christine were finishing their conversation about the transit investigation, as they casually approached the council chambers. Meanwhile, Ferguson was eager to get the information about his impending deal conveyed to Lloyd, but he awaited a more appropriate moment. It wouldn't be opportune to divulge his intent, prematurely, in the presence of Landers' aide.

"How'd you enjoy your lunch, people," he says, to cover his excitement.

"I like my gumbo. I'll have to treat you to some, when you get the time. . .''

Fred also had a mind full of thoughts, but he kept them to himself. Callander was the only one among them without cogitations, at the moment, and lead the group into an afternoon spar.

"With all you men doing way out cooking, what are the sisters supposed to be doing in the kitchen, Fred?''

Fred eagerly took on the exchange to relieve his mind of pondering the, yet, elusive information.

"I have some ideas I'd like to let you in on, Rita!''

"That's alright, Baby. I don't think I'm ready for anything that you're going to tell me, right now. It might be a literal translation of 'Naked Lunch'!''

Christine sensed the direction of the jokes. She excused herself and went off to attend to Landers, not caring to be the brunt of the exchange. Ferguson, who was more stoic, anyhow, finally grounded the two songbirds.

"Looks like it'll be another day before we go on, Fred. What do you people think you're going to do about handling that?"

"You sit tight, and I'll pass on some instructions to the crew. I'm not going to be hanging around any longer, anyway. But just in case you do go on, they'll be able to handle it, until I arrive . . . they know where to reach me . . . just remember to watch the pace of your delivery."

"Oh, I see you're easing," says Callander, still keyed up for the perennial sport of the dozens.

"Just a little bit of business, uptown, baby," Fred quips.

Ferguson interrupted the digression. "Alright, I think I can make a solo on this one, if anything should come up."

"Later," says Fred, as he moves out of the conversation, as smoothly as he had entered.

After finishing his instructions to the crew, Fred started the journey uptown. He descended the short stairway and made for the doors, in a rush to grab a cab. His mind on other things now, he quickly approached the exit, unconsciously bumping into another man who was simultaneously hurrying into City Hall. Fred turned half interestedly to see with whom he had rubbed elbows, as a loud voice boomed out a greeting.

"Fred Baby!"

"Hey, man, how're you doing," Fred replies, as the huge light complexioned brother engulfed him in an affectionate 'bear-hug'.

"Fred Murphy! I'm doing alright!"

Wendell had the build which could have gotten him a spot as a guard on the New York Giants. Towering above Fred, he pulled Murphy to the side of the lobby. His eyes darted around the vestibule, exuding tense hyperactivity, as he talked to Fred in the syncopated rhythmn of a jazz tempo, while accentuating his points with bodily gestures.

"Tell me where you've been for a month of Sundays? Here I've been trying to get a hold of you, to do something for my outfit, you understand, and people are telling me you left the country! I know you're not messing around with no nefarious import-export thing, are you?"

"Nah, Wendell. That gangster shit is not my thing. I've just been learning how to sail, man. Navigation and shit like that!"

"You mean you got hooked up with old Doc and that crew of British niggers down there in the islands, huh," Wendell remarks, as he takes out a handkerchief and wipes perspiration from his forehead, then blows his nose.

"Just for a month or so. Where are you on your way to, in here of all places . . . you still operate out of the same palce, uptown?"

"Indeed! I'm not moving . . . I was just running over to the Planning Commission's office to check on some work I did for them . . . consulting architect and shit. But, I have to get some documents notarized, upstairs somewhere. Hey, I did get into a new domicile, though. Why don't you stop over and have a couple of brews or something? Got some nice lady friends, if you know what I mean?" He lifts his hand to his nose and sniffs the air loudly.

"I like the way that sounds. What are you doing around eight this evening," asks Fred.

"About that time I should be ready to sit down and do some serious playing."

"You still plucking at that bass, Wendell.?"

"Well, you know what I mean . . . now, I play some dynamite chords and shit . . . you heard me doing the back-up for Yusef's latest cut, didn't you?"

The two men shared a boistrous laugh for a moment, then Wendell straightened his garments.

"Well, I know you're still shooting their eyes out on the courts," Fred says, while mimicking a basketball dribble.

"Definitely! There was never any question about how bad I can shoot, now, was there? But as for the musical numbers, I'm 'fair-de-meddlin'."

"Okay, Wilbur Weir," Fred makes an 'in-joke', and pantomimes his friend, as he strums at an imaginary bass. "I might buzz by later on this evening to see what kind of duckets went into your new place."

"Right on, buddy . . . easy now!"

Fred departed, as Wendell walked agilely through the crowded corridor, despite his enormous size.

Chapter Nine

Fred entered the recording studio and was ushered past the reception desk where he was known as a familiar business contact. He walked past the expensive recording machinery and sound equipment, where engineers worked busily at the controls, toward the main control booth.. There he signaled a bald headed white man, who interrupted his activity and came to the door. Fred entered and, once inside, exchanged greetings over the crescendo of music.

"Yeah, Fred, he's around here somewhere . . . saw him a minute ago. Say, you still bringing those youngsters over to make tapes?"

"I'm trying to work out a date with their manager. It looks like later this week, if my schedule can handle it . . . oh, here he comes now. I'll be in touch, Leroy."

Sonny emerged, genie-like, seemingly out of nowhere. Very short and slim, he was dressed in way out pastel colored clothes. In fact, like a genie. His short steps and slow pace made it seem like forever, before he reached Fred. Purposefully disregarding greetings, he spoke with a high pitched voice, as if the conversation had been on-going. "I think I'd better let you know what I'm calling myself, these days . . . 'Olabisi', which is Yoruba for joy is multiplied. It's really feminine gender, but the content is just too much to be believed . . . what's to it, Baby?"

"She sounds like she's out of sight," Fred jokes. "How've you been, Sonny?"

"Fine. Just fine. I hear you got yourself out of the country . . . looking better, I might add . . . what's to this recording arrangement Leroy was telling me about . . ."

The din of music interrupted their conversation, so Sonny led Fred to a quiet room where the men resumed their talk.

" . . . says you're bringing some job corps kids here. There was a group of youngsters in the other day, you know. Some bad sounding individuals, I might add . . . if only I could keep better contact with you," he complains. "Some dynamite talent comes through the studio, occasionally."

Fred lit a cigarette and sat on the edge of the table. "You know how those youngsters make out. Or, don't make out, I should say. And it makes no difference if they enter jobs corps or other programs, these days," he criticizes.

"It is tragic."

"Well, they're going to make a statement on an interview show with the prospective mayor, who's campaigning about the quality of education. He's especially interested in promoting arts and culture to gain youngsters interest in the basic three R's. I want some good tapes of their sounds for the insert to the program . . . It's amazing to hear the story of how they got together. Let them run it down for you."

"Uh Huh, I'll do that, Fred."

"Good!"

"Well, how's that crazy lady doing? Casting spells on the government, or something?"

Fred smiled, and says, "Rita? Oh, she's there, taking care of business, with her crazy self . . . tell me about your new love."

Sonny beamed a self-conscious grin, and replies, "Ah, man, I tell you, it's so beautiful, I call myself 'Olabisi'," he repeated. "Being with this lady is so natural, it makes me feel like I've got all the keys to the mansion!"

They laughed heartily, as Fred paused to check the time. "There goes the mad-hatter, again," sulks Sonny. "Where are you off to now?"

"Got to check with the crew. The didn't call for me, did they?"

"No, I haven't heard from Jomo at all today. Neither John, for that matter. Are they going to bring in any tapes for transfer? Can't say I want to hear from John any too soon, anyhow. I'm into him for fifty dollars . . . so, say nothing about seeing me, brother!"

Fred was half listening to Sonny and turned to the phone.

"Can I use this?"

"Are you going to bring me any new business, Fred?"

Fred commenced to dial, as Sonny made idle activity.

"Is that you, Christine . . . well, it's been a matter of hours. Does it look like the hearing will continue awhile . . . okay, well, tell Jomo to stick with it, and I'll see the crew tomorrow at six. Later, sweetness."

Fred put the receiver back onto the phone while Sonny looked on with a super-cilious grin.

"Darn, Baby! No matter how much activity you get into, you always keep them ladies in order, don't you?"

"Privileged information, that's all . . . look, Sonny, we're trying to work something out with a broadcast operation in Martique. Do you think I can count on you for help?"

Sonny strained humorously at dialect, and comments, "sure thing, man!"

"Good, glad we can count on you. Now, before you ask, don't ask me anything about Helena, alright?"

Sonny smiled broadly, displaying the missing molars. "Everything is coposetic, amigo!"

Chapter Ten

The newly acquired poster of Krishna hung decoratively on the East wall of the apartment, adding picturesque contrast to the multi-colored hand woven Mexican sarape which hung on the opposite side of the room. Upon the hastily constructed book shelves stood two inexpensive machined wooden elephants, like sentries guarding the small treasure of esoteric literature. A brass Chinese incense burner rested on its three legs on the floor, waiting to fill the domicile with aromatic fragrances. The sagging table had since been replaced with the purchase of an antique bargain from the flea market. An opened book and several portfolios were on top of the newly scraped table, which carried the weight more securely, as it awaited a new finish. A once cold beer was growing warm on the floor in front of the television set which indiscriminately projected news to an empty room while the sounds of jazz from the FM filled the apartment with background music. The various curios and unhung paintings, piled neatly about the domicile, reflected a variety of motifs that would contribute an inexpensive cultural richness to the small railroad flat.

Fred emerged from the tub, which stood between the kitchen area and the living room. Although it provided no privacy, he had rigged up a showering mechanism to serve his needs. Wrapped in a towel, with a Christian cross dangling from his neck, he disrobed and dressed in comfortable corduroy slacks and an acrylic sweater shirt. The weather was changing now, and the old tenement wasn't the warmest place to be in the cold. Fred sat in front of the television set and sipped the warm beer. Relaxed, he focused attention to the last news item. As the day's tensions unraveled, Fred's visiage appeared somewhat older, more reflective of his age. The news ended. He got up and turned off the television, then went to the desk. He thumbed through the portfolios again, then closed the documents. Satisfied that he had a handle on the work, he picked up the telephone.

"Lloyd . . . yeah. I looked through the new campaign strategy and the press releases from Ferguson's staff . . . the news stuff reads like dead weight . . . I'll have to tune it up some. I don't know what it's going to look like, just yet, but I'll have their approval, before getting it to you tomorrow morning. Oh Lander's presentation was pretty impressive. I think I've got one of his aides in rapport, so maybe she'll work on things for me . . . there's bound to be a lot of trade-offs with that kind of shake-up, and Ferguson's campaign will definitely look all the better within the political controversy . . . by the way, what do you know about a Neilson paper, or something like that. You have heard of it. Can you get a copy for me? Okay, see you in the morning.''

Fred returned to the table and picked up the papers. He looked at his watch. It was six thirty. He pulled a chair to the desk and cleared the materials away from his typewriter, then settled down to work.

Chapter Eleven

The bright lights accentuated the expensive decor of Wendell's plush Sutton-Place apartment, located in East-midtown. Fred sat, dwarfed in the white huffman koos sectional couch which faced the large copy of Picasso's Guernica, hanging on the spacious North wall. He nursed the tall glass of brandy, carefully placing it on the coaster atop the glass covered mahogany coffee table. He didn't want to spill anything on the hand woven Persian rug, spread across the hardwood floors. He was impressed with the large varied selection of books in Wendell's library, enclosed in two large teakwood cabinets along with the latest in audio equipment. There was quite a compilation of world history, political science, anthropology and, of course, architecture. The full length drapery was opened, revealing a spectacular view of the East River and the Franklin Delano Roosevelt Drive. The large kitchen was located to the left of the oversized living room, again displaying the obvious affection for fine wood in the choice of dining facilities.

Wendell stood underneath the tiffany lamp at the bar, dressed in a flowing full length dashiki outfit. He was enjoying himself, being a host to an old buddy, and was piling on the gratuities of the house. There was no doubt in Fred's mind that 'Skinner' had invested a fortune decorating this place, in an unostentatious combination of modern and period design. It was a professional job, alright. But, Fred suspected a woman's touch.

"Man, this bitch is into some heavy cakes," he says, while carefully uncovering his stash of cocaine and arranging the drug paraphernalia. "I figured you'd get here by ten thirty . . . same ole 'ragged-de-ass' time when it comes to socializing." He walked across the living room to the couch and gave Fred the cocaine. "You'd think that a cat like you would be more attuned to decency . . ."

Fred took the drug and arranged it carefully on the coffee table.

"Had to work on some press releases and draft a speech for tomorrow, 'Skinner'."

"Sounds like a very diplomatic way of avoiding apologies," Wendell criticizes. "Go on and taste that lady. With all the work you say you took care of, Charles Ferguson must be looking pretty good, by now . . . I think you deserve some relaxation."

Fred sniffed some crystals, inhaling the bitter alkaloid into his sinus cavities. "This is a nice place. I like the arrangement. How did you run into her?"

"Through Elaine. She's an interior decorator. We teamed up on a couple of projects, you dig, and the whole thing went over very smoothly. She did this place, as you can imagine . . . her folks are into some heavy shit, you know what I mean?"

"It's not textiles, I hope," quips Fred.

"No, man, he comes from investment banking. That sort of old line stuff," Skinner replies, then pauses to do some of the cocaine . . . "Yeah, I dig the joint. It sure as hell beats trying to live out that uptown scene."

"Hmm, I know about the ghetto," comments Fred. "Everybody has long since split from the lower East-side too. I suppose folks are getting tired of policies based upon that melting-pot concept initiated by Moynihan. Now the situation is about changing our own lifestyles. There's just no future in reacting to the tease of miscegnation to pacify the labor party. That's genocide. Excuse the pun, Skinner, but we just don't melt in the politics of this society!"

Wendell cleared his throat, as the drug began its stimulating effect. "Hmm, but you know, I keep hearing shit about Chico taking over . . . so, I came down here and let the urban administrators worry about increasing law enforcement in the neighborhoods, you know what I mean?" He got up and adjusted the stereo.

"Uh huh," Fred replies. "But, fortunately, or however you look at the situation, my neighborhood is still pretty simpatico. A few freaks on bikes, now and then, but otherwise the usual. No real statistics to speak about. It's just that certain folks are skeptical about that violence shit, you know what I'm talking about, Skinner? Seems as if they want to stretch out and go places to gain perspective. So, it's pretty much a ghost town in my circuit."

Wendell stretched his big frame and arranged himself more comfortably on the sofa.

"Well, so much for the hot line about current events . . . so, you like the place?" He became enlivened by the drug and cleared his nose. "It's a pre-war building. Very warm and sturdy. I can't begin to think about living under the modern touch, since I know what type of materials they're using, you understand."

"Yeah, I just hope my next move takes me a foot away from the thing, instead of merely an inch." Fred remarks, glibly. "We can't all be as fortunate, as some, to run across such 'interesting houses' . . . " He snorts " . . . to live in."

Wendell took the joke personally, and retorts, "you want me to put my hands in shackles, or something . . . shiiit! But, I'll see what I can do for you, to help some promising architectural students."

"The idea is to let younger brothers get to Africa through the association. The effect will be two-fold; first, the exposure will add to their maturing perspectives, and then, by furthering good business relations, it will help get us into African development plans at the ground floor. Education is always an important rep! We're looking for students in city planning, economics, business administration and so forth, Skinner. Sort of beefing up the front line . . . you know where that's at," Fred remarks, convincingly. "I'm sure the State Department won't bother to scrutinize the project too closely. But, even if it does, we can go directly through the fed's support. I can do that too, through educational exchange, you dig!"

Fred had said more than he had intended, but he was sure Lloyd wouldn't mind, since he felt he had to play his cards openly to convince Skinner.

"I'll survey the prospects within a week or ten days. Let me have some more lady while I make a mental note of this thing," Wendell comments, and takes the cocaine from Fred.

"Don't hurt yourself, buddy!"

"No, no, I'm diversified, you understand. It won't take any effort whatsoever," Wendell says, pausing to snort the drug. "I'm interested in cats getting right into first hand experience. We all did our tenure in the school of 'hard-knocks'! But, I don't see why we can't turn around sometimes, like this . . . I'm only sorry I wasn't a couple of years younger, to do it myself, you dig."

As Wendell talked, his eyes began to dart around the room paranoically. He had become animated by the cocaine, and little beads of perspiration dripped from his forehead.

"Well, I'm sure you'll be getting a lot of calls for work, if it goes alright," encourages Fred.

"I can always use it!" Wendell snorted more cocaine greedily. "No matter how good all this seems, you understand, I've got to take care of my operation. And, most importantly, myself! You never know when some damn shit will hit the fan, and I have to guerrilla my way out of this situation, as pleasant as it may appear to the unwary."

"You tickle me, 'Skinner'," comments Fred. "You developed from 'basketball mentality' to become a prominent midtown architect and still talk about being afraid of your own shadow. Damn! I expect that from your white counterpart, or are you just that freaked out behind the young lady?"

"Are you talking about Yvonne," Wendell replies, smugly.

"That is, I assume, your lady friend?" Fred took a short snort of cocaine and cleared his nose.

"There is, of course, a certain complicity to this madness. But, I would say my nose is fairly dialated, sir!"

Fred smiled demonically, and quips, "you'd better take your head out of the shit-hole, before you lose it, 'Skinner'!"

The two men stretched out on the large white couch listening to the distinct arpeggios of Archie Shepp. The exhilarating effect of the cocaine lent to the keen attentiveness required to appreciate the music of this new wave artist. The talk in the avant garde circles compared Archie Shepp's subtleties to the progression of the old master, Miles Davis, and his excursions on the trumpet. It would take more time for the critics to agree conclusively whether the younger man would reach such artistic heights. The record ended, and the two men adjusted their attire during the interlude, regaining their composure while Wendell put on a disk of Rassan.

"Have you been to see the Knicks, lately, 'Skinner'?"

"They're nobody!"

The dozens were erupting again, and Fred was game for the exchange.

"You mean you're not going to play forward with Debucher and them other dudes?"

"They're nobody," repeated Wendell, emphatically. "Believe me when I tell you. Talk about guerrillas . . . here's a team that gets to the finals on a shoestring," Wendell picked up the spar with eagerness. "Now, how is it possible for them to out-shoot a team like the Celtics. You tell me, I want to know. Really! I can't make out how you figure the duckets, at all. You'll probably wind up a poor man!"

Fred smiled ingenuously, adding, "they looked pretty good Thursday night!"

"That's true, but watch what happens in this third game. Boston is going to be shooting their eyes out . . . can you imagine me snatching some rebounds off the boards, sucker?''

He got up and began to motion plays in the middle of the floor. His huge frame filled the large livingroom, but he moved with the smooth precision of a seasoned athlete.

"I'll shoot your face off, Murphy!''

Chuckling, Fred added fuel to the spar. "I'll lay out a light ten, if you want to do a little speculating on the outcome?''

"I don't know if I want to go along with that. Are you sure that's all you want to get into with me? You know you're going to be indebted for the ten, so why don't you stop pussy footing around with purse wagers and get down to some heavy betting?''

"Now, 'Skinner', I don't want you to hurt me, too bad! Let's just say I can't afford to live on your scale.''

"Bullshit, you black Jew! With all that dough you're carrying out of TMP, you could buy a basketball team . . . or take care of a struggling architect.'' Wendell laughed boistrously, pleased with his rouse.

"I couldn't imagine to whom I might offer such a professional subsidy,'' Fred laughs, taking the brunt of the joke.

Wendell had gotten his kick and didn't care to be anticlimatic. He continued in a more sober tone.

"You know, I can never get you really inebriated . . . you're too straight, nigger!''

"I got through the Indian trip very early, my man. I'm too aware of samsara. That's just to let you know I've got to keep this pace for the next five or so years. That way I can grow old gracefully . . . Lou Rawls style,'' Fred comments reflectively.

"Well, I can dig it. You cats have really stretched out in two years. Makes me feel like there are lessons to be learned. I guess that's why we haven't gotten together, before now . . . professional pride, you understand. But anyway, I wasn't ever ready to sacrifice those exhorbitant fees . . . heavy duckets, Baby!''

"There wasn't any other way around it, 'Skinner'! It had to be done, then! The timing was essential to coordinate the idea. You see, it's all about high level international communications. We've just been successful in utilizing the public relations gamut, that's all.''

Fred lit a cigarette and took a long drag, inhaling the smoke deep into his lungs, and continued.

"It was a very important step on an individual level, as well. Personally, I think it's important to expand in at least three areas, simultaneously, if you can. Otherwise, you'll grow tired in the mainstream of your progress, lose direction and be left with the drujas,'' he cautioned Wendell.

"So, you feel pretty optimistic about the future, huh, Murphy?''

"Relatively. Considering what's happening in education, these days, there's bound to be a shake-up in employment patterns . . . oh, I imagine there'll be political maneuvers, as usual, to thwart the increasing awareness, by control of the issues. That's traditional. I wonder how that's going to transpire . . . it seems clear that a purely business attitude is appropriate for this stage. Otherwise, folks are left with some kind of socialist philosophy. That's a vacuum, brother! Too many old timers got stung with that crap in the thirties,'' Fred remarks, critically.

"That's an awareness, too late in coming, and too costly for too many," Wendell says, reflectively.

"Let me put it to you this way. Self help is something real. Disregard the conservative ploy. Eventually, the system is going to respond to sustained economic effort. Historically, it's more strategic to operate from an economic perspective, due to the ripple effect in controlling the pawns. Elijah and his folks realize that, even down South."

Wendell weighed Fred's insight, pensively. There was a great deal he wanted to explore, but the effects of the drug had his mind reeling. He thought better of confusing the conversation with awkward extraneous probes.

"Most people don't get beyond flamboyant rhetoric, anyhow, buddy. But you're right! I can see it in terms of industrial relocation, myself. What are you folks doing in the South, Baby?"

"So far, only in Atlanta. Our interests are primarily tied to the two coasts, right now . . . it's obvious the large urban centers are important," Fred comments, becoming abrupt for the moment. He figured 'Skinner' had enough information. It would be up to him to act. He took another drag on the cigarette and put the butt out.

"Well, there's no doubt about a change in the man's attitude when you've got your own thing. Then you don't have to be fronting off, in no way," Wendell comments, behind a wry smile.

The two men glared at one another, silently, while reflecting on the statement.

A taxicab pulled up to the curb and parked, downstairs at the entrance to the midtown building, and a young lady alighted from the vehicle with the assistance of the doorman. She was a very 'chic' white lady whose short meticulously coiffured dirty blond hair gave her a boyish appearance. As she passed Fred, who rushed by, glad to have caught a taxi so quickly, she turned to get a second look. Their eyes met, as she paused to give the doorman a tip. She lingered a moment in her unbuttoned mink coat which revealed an expensively tailored blue sequined dress, matched with a string of white cultured pearls. Making a mental note, she entered the building. As the cab took off, Fred looked through the rear window at the elegantly dressed woman, as she disappeared into the expensive edifice.

Upstairs, Wendell stood next to the open drapery at the window, looking reflectively at the tugs in the scenic East River. The door opened, and the mysterious lady entered the apartment in a happy mood.

"Hey, Skinner." .

"What's up, 'Sugar'," Wendell grumbles, in a restrained tone of voice.

Yvonne paused while unwrapping herself out of the expensive mink. She sensed that something was bothering Wendell, so she took on a serious attitude.

"Was that your friend I saw leaving just now, comrade?"

"Good looking, brown-skinned dude? Must've been. We'd be the only two brothers coming in or out of this building."

Yvonne draped her coat over the sofa and fixed herself a drink. She returned to the couch and sat demurely, as the sounds of John Coltrane came to an end. There was a long uncomfortable silence which was finally broken by Yvonne's inquiry.

"Well, comrade, how did it go, tonight," she asks.

Wendell's mind had been going at fever's pitch, but he had long since become used to the side effect of the drug.

"Overall, the thing failed! I couldn't get what we wanted through the drug. That cat's got the stamina of a bull! I thought my tolerance was high, but he's got a tight lip about the operation," Wendell replies. "I did get some idea of what they plan in Africa, but I think I'll have to change my tactics, right away . . . and cut the comrade shit, okay! You know I'm not a kid, Yvonne. I'm aware of my responsibilities."

Yvonne listened patiently. She had been schooled to be patient, and knew how to deal with the erratic behavior that Skinner often went through when he used cocaine to induce information.

"Well, I didn't think the coke was going to work, myself. From what you tell me, he seems to be controlled more by the metaphysical," she interjected authoritatively. "Let's wait awhile, before we report back to the embassy. Perhaps the Neilson project will work out . . . if the association is as aggressive as you say, they'll inevitably come across our information. Then, we can relax and let Fred do our work as he designs packages for the organization," she concludes.

Wendell was not thoroughly convinced with Yvonne's strategy. He felt that she underestimated Fred. But, Yvonne had more time in the party. Indeed, she had recruited him, shortly after their romance began. She outranked him, and that precluded further argument on the matter. He also knew something about the force of her conviction. Yvonne had joined the left in the mid-fifties, following the major furor over McCarthyism. Her motives were purely emotional. Despite her parent's affluence, she had become disenchanted with the hypocritical social mores of the wealthy class, after being jilted by her fiance when she became pregnant. She had prepared to enter George Washington University Law School at that time, and her only recourse was Elaine, the sole black schoolmate, who arranged an abortion for her. Since then, she had risen in the ranks and had even received training by the East Germans, who had come to the U.S. through the Russian Embassy to beef up the party. Wendell knew this information well, because in his mind, it separated their motives. His involvement was purely pecuniary, while she suffered from deep rooted psychological needs. Neither of them would ever be more than mere flunkies in the organization, he thought. But he vowed never to burst her bubble.

"Well, we'll see . . . anyhow, I hope your evening went better than mine . . . I'm flying. Where's the tranquilizers?"

"In the kitchen," she replies. "Say, Skinner, don't you want to hear about the newest project we're working on in the women's cell?"

"What's up," Wendell remarks with a blase air while entering the kitchen.

"Women's rights! It's going to shake the hell out of this country in the coming years. The idea is to make women's concerns another big minority issue . . . it'll be another force to work pressure on the establishment. We plan to lobby, use boycotts, involve the church and media in a broad based attempt to spread the 'gospel' of women's liberation. What do you think?"

"All I can say is, don't count on me as one of your supporters . . . I'm a male chauvinist, you know!"

"Oh don't be such a pig, Skinner," she says, deflated, by Wendell's crass attitude. Yvonne felt that he would have been receptive, but apparently his failure tonight had made him moribund. She would have to help him realize success, so she could use his contacts in the black community to further her new assignment. She finished her drink. She had exercised enough mental gymnastics that night. Now it was time to change her tactic and work her womanly persuasion under the sheets of the bed.

Fred stood reading the opened telegram which had been left stuck in his doorway. His senses were keyed up, and he welcomed the assignment to work off the excess energy. It was the usual cryptic message that Lloyd dictated when in a hurry to get something important done, right away.

TRANSCONTINENTAL MEDIA PROMOTIONS
New York, November 15, 1963
"Fred: Contact Elaine in Washington, D.C . . . . Zambian bauxite interests are ready to review company prospectus . . . meet Mr. Abiola at the embassy tomorrow night . . . reception for several businesses . . . Les to pick up press releases at the airport."

Fred hustled, in a flurry of activity and pulled together a traveling wardrobe. Pausing just long enough to tune in some late night jazz, he moved to the bookshelf and pulled down a folder marked 'Swazi Bauxite'. Fred laid the material aside, while disrobing, and tested the temperature of the make-shift shower, leaving a trail of clothes strewn about the floor. His cleaning bill would be outrageous, but now he turned attention to the soothing refreshment of a hot shower, as he soaked his naked body in the water.

Chapter Twelve

The late fall sunrise was even more pleasant at the airport. Uncluttered by the towering architecture, the spacious vista presented a clear view of the horizon at dawn. Traffic was relatively light that Wednesday morning, and the taxicab driver made excellent time jockeying through the sparse traffic. Fred had enjoyed the ride to the Eastern shuttle at Laguardia and gave the driver a good tip, when they arrived. Once inside, he found Les waiting for him in the middle of the terminal. Fred spent a minute to tease Les about his anal compulsion, as he gave the press releases and speech re-write to his co-worker, but he was really glad there was no delay in his time schedule. They talked briefly, then the two men parted company. The boarding call for his flight was announced over the public address system, just as Fred joined the long line of passengers, moving to the waiting aircraft.

After unbuckling from the lift-off, Fred busied himself surveying the economic projections in the Swazi Bauxite prospectus which he spread on top of his portfolio, resting comfortably in his lap. He continued his review through the entire forty-five minute trip and was only interrupted, when the helpful stewardess offered to make a nearby passenger more comfortable. He looked down through the jet porthole, just as the Washington monument came into view. Fred put the material inside the attache case and paused to check the time. It was eight o'clock. He had made good time, he thought, as he leaned back and casually brushed his chin to smooth the morning shave.

The new subway system was not completed, yet, and construction continued to link Washington International Airport with the municipality. Meanwhile, the local politicians and city planners were heralding the capital improvement project in all the news media, as a boon for making the District of Columbia a cosmopolitan center. Inside the small terminal stood a lone black woman. Very smartly dressed in a brown suede suit and trenchcoat, she was an attractive cocoa colored lady in her mid-thirties. Her appearance and demeanor made stark contrast with the otherwise drabness of the airport. She checked her watch, just as Fred emerged from the crowd of baggage seekers. His wardrobe over one arm and attache case in the other hand, he deftly moved through the confusion.

"Hi, Baby!" Elaine extended her open arms in greeting. They embraced, kissing lightly at the lips.

"What kind of time are we making, loveliness?"

"The reception's not until eight tonight. But, I thought you should get here early enough for us to go over the details, before we get to the embassy, Fred."

"Here's the prospectus," he says, as they exited the terminal. She took the portfolio while they quickly walked the distance to the parking lot where the silver Mercedes Benz waited.

"You like my latest investment?"

"I was going to ask whose machine it was, Elaine. When did you start digging vintage automobiles . . . or have you recently caught a flare for the German?"

"I thought you'd have an interesting comment . . . you like? Thought about taking time to run it up to New York and open it up, but I just couldn't fit it in," she laughs.

"Has business got you that uptight, doll face?"

Fred lit a cigarette, as they entered the sedan, while casually eyeing Elaine's physique.

"It seems that I'm the only working lawyer around town, these days. People calling the office all the time. I can't even find time to keep up with the journals, mind you . . . and the little writing I do, doesn't leave me satisfied," she complained, as she started the powerful engine.

"So, what's new and exciting around town, besides jim crow," he says, then takes a long drag on the cigarette. He leaned back and stretched his legs comfortably, as Elaine drove out of the parking lot.

"Have you seen the morning papers? Home-Rule seems like it's about ready to get kicked around on the hill again, this session. I'm not too worried, actually. It should pass, after all the filibusters get their air time. There's really no point in forum any longer. Either it's enacted, or there's more fuel for the flames. That's the way I see it!" She shifted gears and capably guided the mercedes into the parkway traffic.

"That's good, because the possibilities of confrontation have me worried," Fred replies. "Subtle antagonistic provocation is strategically tactical, nowadays."

The mercedes moved at a rapid pace, bringing them to the Seventh Street Bridge in minutes. They passed the large government buildings and workers in transit to their jobs. Rush hour was less hectic in the District, but Elaine figured she'd gain time by taking a short cut around the federal enclave. Fred was delighted with the ease with which she handled the machine and took in the view, as the scene changed from office to residential buildings. What impressed him most was the air space afforded by the architectural style in the city. The buildings were built low, with very few high rise apartment complexes crowding the horizon. Elaine abruptly swung the mercedes onto Rock Creek Park and began weaving the auto along the winding paths.

" . . . Other than that, let me see. Melba Moore's in town, and Julian Bond is scheduled to speak . . . I think the Urban Coalition has set something up at the Shoreham . . . I really haven't been making the fund raising affairs, Fred. For that matter, I haven't found the time to keep up with myself, this last month or so," she exclaims, as she pulls the car in front of a comfortable home on a quiet residential street, just off the park.

Fred finished his cigarette and got out of the mercedes. He stretched and looked around at the scenery.

"You know, there's always a quiescence that captivates me when I come to D.C."

"Like the city that closes up its gates at sundown and pulls itself in to shelter it from the night," she teased him.

"Precisely, Elaine! There's always a feeling of enclosure in the offing."

They laughed at his perception and entered the small home. Fred was immediately relaxed in the smartly furnished living room, the moment the door closed behind him. The many fine pieces of art work decoratively arranged among the contemporary decor enlivened the house. He always found the baldwin piano fascinating, especially when she relaxed and made her special kind of music on the instrument. Then, of course, there was always the allurement of Elaine's fluid movement, as she made him comfortable.

"Oh, did I tell you I saw Anita?"

"No, you didn't. What is she doing these days, lady?"

"You know, the same old things . . . she went back to Ron."

"Is that right," Fred remarks, as he makes himself comfortable on the full length sofa.

"Yeah," Elaine laughs. "Her old man got her out of the way. Said he couldn't afford to take care of her, any longer. So, now she's back with Ron and the baby," she laughs boistrously. "Isn't that terrible?"

"You Washington ladies are really far flung . . . when did all this happen," he edged the idle gossip.

"What do you mean, you Washington ladies," Elaine snapped. "She's from Texas. Got old Ron in a spider's net . . . it's terrible the way these sisters are carrying their men through all those changes. I talked to her last week and she was telling me all about it. We've really got you men in our clutches. Baby!"

"More like mental straight jackets, by far. Only we're not supposed to know it. It's much heavier than two on one, I admit. However, I have faith in the male culture which makes all of your ladies' activities merely vestigal ritual," he grins at her.

"No more wet dreams for you, Fred?"

"I'm in good physical condition, Elaine, Just is case you're interested."

"Don't mind me, sport. I just have to laugh at all of the shananigintz you supposedly married people seem to get confused with," she mocks. "It behooves me to find an answer for all of that nonsense you folks go through, 'gettin' it t'getha'!"

"It's just that you're still into that Washington parochialism I've been telling you about, sister."

"Shit! Anita was doing that kind of crap, way back when. But then, it was a matter of getting through school. Coming home all tired and what have you, becuase nobody had any money . . . and then, she couldn't even eat any of the damned food all of her efforts earned. So don't talk to me about any male chauvanism crap, Baby!"

"Well, I'm sure as hell not going to talk to you about how big my heart is," quips Fred. "Sure, I'm on an ego trip. I found out how to take care of myself long time ago. Therefore, I just don't tolerate incidental shit like that!"

"You still don't realize that girl's got a death grip on your jones, Fred . . . or you won't admit it!"

"I'm not going to lie down and die about it, Elaine. Things have been quite good for me, these last couple of months, especially. What do I have to look backwards for, in order to see the future?"

"Why you dudes with these, 'oh, so heavy come-ons', are so damned shortsighted, escapes me," she criticizes caustically.

"Perhaps if you, for example, would cease challenging, that which amounts to a whole lot of banal insecurity, maybe some precedents could be made in establishing models for your sisters to relate to," he replies, incisively, as he lights a cigarette.

"I'm not sure I understand what you're implying, but it soulds like you feel that I should become a guinea pig to save the institution of marriage . . . now, that's a whole lot of banality!"

"Enough talk about idle inconsequentia," he responds, sensing an apparent dead end in their conversation. "Let's focus on something more blissful about life." Then, straining to be more charming, he affects a heavy accent. "What you got cooking for lunch, my dear?"

"The bar's over there," Elaine quips, somewhat deflated. She enjoyed being argumentive with Fred and hated to acquiesce to his chauvanism. Then, again, she found him cute when irritated. "You've been here before, so help yourself, sweetie!"

"In more ways than one," he grumbled.

"Excuse me, I didn't hear what you were saying. . ."

"I was a butler," Fred says offhandedly, to hide his ire. "A house boy in my former life . . . I haven't worked that out of my karma, but I think I can manage."

He raised himself to fix a drink. He poured the scotch over two ice cubes, gave the mixture a quick stir, and tasted it.

"Can I make you one?"

"If you like."

"Hennessy and coke?"

"Your're right on time."

Fred restrained his heavy hand and returned to the couch with her drink, in a more comfortable mood.

"So you haven't been in contact with Helena, then," Elaine inquired in a personal tone.

"No! Everybody seems to think that I'd do better by bending over backwards, but I can't see it."

"Fred, Amber Ujima is old enough to see you under a variety of situations," Elaine says, compassionately. "There doesn't have to be any more pain for her, now. Why don't you see her more often?"

"I don't appreciate the way her mother manipulates her like some kind of commodity. There are too many changes that I can bitch about, Elaine."

"If it hurts, Baby, we don't have to deal with it."

"Perhaps it's better that I talk with you about it. After all, I know you will be judicious where others have no discretion."

"Now you're talking my kind of language! Go on counselor. . ."

"Look, I really am worried about Amber. I had to get away for a month, just to survive, mentally," Fred exclaims. He leaned forward and extinguished the cigarette.

"I heard you went away. . ."

"I went to Martique and worked with Doc for a month . . . I don't think you know him. He's an old time musician out of New York, who went to the 'Gold Coast' in search of fortune and fame, but wound up down in the islands on a fishing boat."

"I guess that's what happens when you try to get at both hands at the same time,'' she philosophised to loosen him up.

"He was making out alright, out there . . . had a little houseboat and all . . . playing the clubs regularly. But the scene wasn't him. He had already become active from struggles back East. But, by the time he found out what kind of politics he was dealing with, out there, he had to split. They broke him financially and were moving to frame hime, as an example.''

"What's he doing down there in Martique?''

"Using what remained of his kitty to stimulate international economic liasons. A coterie sprung up around him, almost immediately, and he weilds a lot of influence . . . partially due to his connections with some powerful folks, back here. And then, he's trained a lot of good people for us.''

"That's fascinating,'' she said, and patiently listened while Fred talked. Eventually he would return to his primary marital problem, she thought. Meanwhile, Elaine enjoyed finding out his sensitive nature. It added to her appreciation of the man.

"Yeah, it was therapeutic, cooling out down there, rusticating in the sun and learning navigation . . . one of Doc's many skills.''

"I bet Amber would have enjoyed being there with you.''

"It would've been a great thing for her at this age,'' he comments, reflectively.

"Did you send her a card?''

"I can't do that! I'm not supposed to know where Helena is staying.''

"That's trite!'' She moved to the bar to refresh her drink. "I understand she's going out to the coast, too. Any idea where she'll be staying, Fred?''

"Los Angeles, perhaps. She's got some relatives there.''

"Well, what seems to be the difficulty?''

"She doesn't condone the way I'm going about getting things done. I haven't been able to explain to her that a cat like me just can't sit around and watch himself dissipate!''

"Don't you give her enough security, Fred?''

"It's not that . . . It's a question of time with substance. Look, you're probably the only one I can talk to easily about it. You realize that I'm not entirely happy about being out here, but that I have to be. After you pull that veil away, there's no other way. . .''

"Yes, I can understand what you're doing, I think. But, you're not expendible as far as Amber's relationship with her father. That's a very important bond.''

"You sure can make poignent remarks, Miss Lawyer. That is the significant point. But, I can only be responsible in that role in terms of what I'm doing in life. That's what is real to the relationship. There's no other philosophy than that behind my position. Helena seems to feel that I'm wrapped up in some sort of twentieth century masquarade,'' he complains.

"Come on, now, she's probably just as overbearing as a protective mother hen,'' Elaine interjects.

"I didn't know that nature exhibited such strikingly similar emotinal patterns,'' he replied with a broad quizzical grin.

"Sometimes you can be such a 'klutz',' she laughs.

"You know I'm right, Elaine! I've always taken care of the important things in our relationship. Now it's a question of time. I believe in what I'm doing! And that makes all the difference in our views about Amber.''

"Even though we all have the same basic pressure on us, maybe she just doesn't consider time as a possible benefactor. But it does seem that you would normally feel more inclined to provide more time to your family, is what I'm saying."

"Again, it's really how time is spent. Who I am and what I do, are integral. And that makes all the difference in the manner by which my family will grow. Therefore, I have to use time discriminatively for what I think is important about the future," Fred concludes, emphatically. He felt relieved to express himself succinctly, rather than ventillate extraneous emotions which had hitherto crowded his mind about the marriage.

"An entirely positive perception. It's a good thing you say, my friend, because it reflects a true understanding of your past, in viewing your daughter's future. It also makes me feel that you anticipate making your plans work for your family to reunite, eventually."

"I don't entertain for a moment any fantasies about us getting back together again . . . I'm no putting it out of the picture, is what I will say. Only that!"

"That's good, because I thought, for a moment, that you might evade making that kind of statement," she remarks, supportively.

"Not at all, Elaine. It doesn't frighten me, any longer. I just don't consider it, too often, nor any further than that. I think it would become dangerous to do so, at this time . . . whenever I get hung up with those kinds of considerations, I start making people irritated. I have to watch myself. . ."

"I can understand that. Lloyd and I were talking about it while you were away. Seems as if you got the image around the office of a callous sarcastic tongued son-of-a-bitch."

"Yeah," he laughs. "A veritable fire-breathing-dragon . . . the trip did me the world of good, though. I seem to be working out of the configuration of ken, now."

"Ah, yes," she mimicked Fred. "Let me see . . . that's the mountain . . . keeping still and stuff like that, right?"

"I see you've been doing some homework right along, haven't your?"

"I can't fool around with metaphysical systems, too much," sighs Elaine. "It always happens that I find myself in the midst of a configuration, before I'm aware of what's going on with the I Ching."

Fred laughed at her dilemma. "The Chinese is difficult, alright. I stay away from it, unless I have a problem to work out that really gives me a hard time."

"Oh, wait a minute," she exclaims, remembering her busy calander. "I've got to call the office."

As Elaine left the living room, Fred got up to look at the art objects which were placed at various complimenting locations around the house. Alone now, he assumed a contemplative poise, as he glanced out of the window at the Mercedes. The conversation had settled his mind a great deal, which allowed him to relax, for a change. He felt comfortable about the reception, as well, and began to daydream about the impending event. As he mused with the scenario, he envisioned Abiola as a short stocky Europeanized African. He imagined the tribal decoration scars would be less apparent on Abiola's deep black face. His native dialect would be tainted by an Oxford accent. Fred smiled at his own pun and thought of his conversation with the business contact.

"Since you like the prospectus, we can begin searching for investors to finance the project," Fred anticipated telling Abiola.

"Yes, I think it's very decent. There's already a certain 'hard line' in it that will ultimately give us the right kind of interest we are seeking," Mr. Murphy.

"Do you have any other ideas that you might want to express about your project?"

"No, not in the initial offering. That will come later. It's a good package. . ."

"Well, then, have you had an opportunity to see much of Washington, since you've been here?"

"No, and my itinerary is scheduled for New York and then to Western Europe. I will only have time to make a conference at the United Nations."

"Hopefully, you'll have time to share some entertainment while you're here. We've come up with something to show you part of the city life," Fred imagines the kind of public relations he will use to firm up the deal. He has orchestrated the meeting in his mind, so that Elaine would reach them at that very moment. "Miss Elaine Peterson, meet Mr. Ode Abiola. . . Mr. Ode Abiola, meet Miss Elaine Peterson"

Fred would have continued his daydream a littler longer, but Elaine had finished her telephone work and returned to the living room, interrupting his muse.

"Well, I've gotten a couple of things lined up for this evening. Abiola will have a nice selection," she comments, as she finds a comfortable spot on the sofa.

"Good girl! Now to look at the prospectus," he remarked, as he took the portfolio from his attache case and placed it on top of the coffee table. "I've researched the industrial market from stem to stern to put this package together. I even looked at fluctuations in non-related commodities for a thorough assessment of future industrial needs for bauxite . . . How'd you do with investors?"

"I'll have to admit, I'm still a little uneasy. I looked at institutional sources, mainly. A few insurance companies expressed interest, but I'll need prospectuses to follow up those leads," she replies. "I've got a feeler out on Capitol Hill, meanwhile, to find out about the political climate. I figure we should know the short run policy of government appropriations, too. Everything, from contributions to the International Monetary Fund to legislation governing industrial expansion, here at home. That way, we can plot several trends, and check prominent indicators in our estimates to develop a good projection for Abiola, if he okays this draft."

"Out of sight! Lloyd will be happy to hear that."

"Oh, by the way, remember the land leasing project that I spoke to you about. . ."

"Uh, huh. How did that turn out? What was it about, anyway?"

"Some young fellows passed though here a month or so ago, talking about leasing government land in the midwest. They claimed that financing for geological exploration was possible through natural gas companies who initially tap the soil. Apparently the venture will boom, as the gain is assured, even if oil isn't ultimately found."

"Oh, yeah? Who do they represent?"

"Investments Limited, up front . . . what's behind, I don't know. Their approach is similar to the Kiplinger Letter. My friend, Mr. Cook, the Grand Master of the local Masonic lodge, gave them a clean bill of health. He's an old family friend."

"Sounds decent, but I don't know about the conservationists. Anyhow, I wouldn't worry about it right now. We've got to get a reading from Abiola, before examining any ideas about expansion. Keep your eye on it for the time being," Fred advised.

Elaine appreciated the meticulous care which Fred brought to his work. It allowed her to contribute her keen professionalism to the job. As she skimmed the prospectus, she kept a mental note of possible legal ramifications to check, before their presentation.

"Oh, this is interesting, Fred. Where did you get this information?"

"I tell you, Elaine, I usually do my homework thoroughly to completion."

"Abiola's going to flip when he sees this. . ."

Fred had uncovered information within the transportation industry about future increases in the manufacture of airplanes, which used aluminum extensively. Elaine could always check the prospective move toward deregulation of airlines to verify the fact. Nevertheless, it was another potential need for the ore.

"What type of man is he, Elaine?"

"I'm told he's very astute, but unassuming. Now, that's good for me, as a girl, because you know how some of you vanguards can be at times. I rather think you two will hit it off, right away. From my impression, he's kind of bullish, too!"

Fred smiled, demonically. "Ah, then, he must dig your fat legs, almost as much as I do."

Chapter Thirteen

The embassy was located downtown in Northwest Washington, D.C., on the fringes of the small commercial district, near Thirty-Third Street. The low three story green and white building was inconspicuous in the transitional zone, only recognizable by the colorful emblem of the national flag which hung listlessly in the stagnant evening air. The formalities of the meeting took place, before the reception ceremony which was a pleasant gathering of international businessmen, government officials, influential socialites, fraternal groups, churchmen and aspiring politicians. Select invitations were drawn to assemble individuals who reflected conservative attitudes toward international affairs, business, civil rights and the arts and culture, to provide a lively exchange between the Blacks in the forefront of many countries. Although there was a sprinkling of Asians, Arabs and other ethnic groups mixed within the crowd, the embassy was filled with a preponderance of Africans. It was a beautiful spectacle of traditionally garbed women, in galees and flowing outfits, who contrasted with the more contemporarily dressed men.

Fred took it all in, letting the enchantment of the affair inspire his public relations work. He had made an aggressive effort and found Abiola a very receptive client. Elaine had helped immeasurably with her knowledge of international law. She was an excellent partner to have around. He couldn't help noticing her, now that it was over and the conversation more relaxed. She was an attractive woman, he thought. Both well formed and choicely dressed in an expensive low cut black cocktail dress with slits to the side, revealing her long legs, she presented an interesting compliment to Abiola, who was attired in a plain business suit. The music was turned on, and the light sounds of Miriam Makeeba filled the reception room.

"Excuse me for a moment," Fred said, politely, and left his companions to their conversation. The effect of the expensive champagne strained his bladder.

"Did you decide which of the affairs you would prefer to attend, Mr. Abiola," Elaine continued.

"Ode, please, Miss Peterson. I am not that familiar with your American performers, so I think I'd better leave that choice to your discretion . . ."

"Alright, that's just fine. I'm sure you'll enjoy yourself. Did our consultation prove fruitful, Ode?"

"Oh, quite, thank you. Mr. Murphy continues to be a challengingly interesting person. I might add, most direct and persuasive. I admire your selection, already, Miss Peterson."

"Well, thank you, Ode. I hope we can count on your recommendations back home."

"Thus far, they are first rate. Now, the problem ahead is growth. We have been able to circumvent many of the cultural difficulties in our developing country . . . traditional kinship patterns, urbanization, recurrent famine and so forth. But, the task of enlightened socialism is one which should not outstrip our very humanity," Abiola emphasized, while he stared at her with his cold piercing eyes.

"Are you still running into trouble with your railroads?"

"Just interim setbacks, Miss Peterson. We've received a great deal of support from the Chinese technicians. It looks as if our country will have adequate transportation within the next five or ten years," he replied.

"That's very exciting. Apparently war mongering from South Africa won't be an impedence to the impetus your country is demonstrating to the world."

"I have no doubts there will be continual attempts to thwart the goal of self-determination. However, at this time, there are too many concerted forces in the world to counter racism."

Fred was in a rush, but didn't stop to check when he found the bathroom door which he abruptly opened. To his utter surprise, the bathroom was occupied by a young lady, who in shock, hastily pulled down her garment. There was a momentary look of bewilderment on her awe struck face, then, she reached forward abruptly and slammed the door shut. Fred was startled by the bizarre incident and stood in front of the closed door for a moment. He finally gathered his composure together, stepped back, and adjusted his tie. After a few minutes the young lady finally emerged.

"Don't you know how to use your hands properly on the door, first, before entering, young man," she testily remarks.

"Excuse me, I was rather abrupt . . . kind of an emergency," Fred says, apologetically.

"There is no protocol for such decorum," she continues, curtly, while scrutinizing Fred with peculiar interest.

Fred listened to the diabtribe while he nervously massaged his fingertips. When she finished reprimanding him, a demonic grin spread across his face.

"I suppose you've never used a latrine in France," he quips. Fred watched the impact of his trist, as a whimsical smile began to float upon her lips. He felt his humor had worked, as their eyes met, but he could hold his water no longer.

"Pardon me," he mumbles, as he enters the bathroom.

Fred wasn't long in relieving himself. The record had scarcely been changed, by the time he returned to the reception room. Hugh Masakela's trumpet was sounding out the message. He liked the African artist's style. He also liked what he saw. As Elaine and Abiola came into view, there she was again, talking together with his companions. A fourth gentleman was there too, but Fred counted on his star that it was no more than a casual acquaintance. Because, if it was favorable, he wasn't going to waste any time. He maintained his pace; after all, he didn't want to let events escape him, as coincidentally as they had occured. He casually joined the group, maintaining a low profile while carefully controlling the rising animus.

"Oh, here you are, Fred. Let me introduce you to Vivian Delaney and Bob Johnson. Bob is a coordinator for the D.C. Youth Development Project and Vivian is a dancer."

Fred was careful. He exchanged handshakes with Bob, cordially, before directing his attention to Vivian. After all, he was a gentleman and respected propriety.

"I hope you found the lock on the door to be serviceable," Vivian responded to the introduction.

"It was really an emergency," Fred replies, smoothly, while beaming a million dollar smile. "I'm pleased to meet you, Vivian."

"My, that's a very surreptitious greeting," Elaine remarks. "Do you two know each other?"

"You might say, we ran into one another in passing," Vivian says, in a sparring tone.

"Well, it sounds exciting, anyway," comments Elaine, as she begins to size up the mystery. "Vivian is another school chum of mine, who looks like she has a very exciting career in the arts developing for herself."

"She's an extremely wonderful dancer," adds Bob.

"Is that right, Vivian," Fred casually inquires. He couldn't enter her game, just yet, as he didn't know if she was fair game.

"Well, I've been at it since I was a little girl," she answered, more civilly.

An embassy aide interrupted the conversation, summoning Abiola to the telephone.

"I would like to hear more about your youth program, Mr. Johnson, but you people will excuse me, for a moment." He left the group while Elaine took the opportunity to give Vivian the 'come-on-eye'. She had finally gotten wind of events and was now content to play matchmaker.

"Don't stop now, Bob," she says, drawing him aside to the chairs. "You can tell me all about your project while Ode takes care of his business."

Fred was still too busy thanking his star to notice Elaine's very overt cues. "A dancer," he mutters, to keep the conversation alive.

"In reality, a starving child of the world."

"Who do you dance with, Vivian?"

"Right now, The Repetoire Company. Have you heard of that group?"

"I'm not a native Washingtonian. I'm only vaguely familiar with the New York troupes, Martha Graham, Alvin Ailey . . . "

"Oh yes, they're very famous groups. Well, this troupe just started this year. Before that, there were a lot of tours."

"I guess the dance company is a plus for this area. But, my exposure to that art form is decidedly limited, I'm afraid."

Fred didn't know it, but Vivian had designs of her own. She wasn't a nymph, as Elaine liked to call her, but she did enjoy intriguing relationships, from time to time. Apparently, this was one of those times. She adjusted her posture to appear more alluring, shifting her small frame sensually, and remarks, "Really! I would imagine a cosmopolitan like yourself would be more abreast of the arts."

Fred smiled at her, as he eyed the fullness of her pert, but developed breasts which were partially exposed by the low cut of her blue evening gown.

"I really should be, of course . . . what's a dancer's life like, anyhow?"

"Long hours and hard work," she replies, with an air of vivacity.

"You must undoubtedly be endowed with the requisite stamina, since you've been dancing from the time of youth," Fred responds to her come-on.

"It's a special way of life now."

Fred wanted to pin down the vital question of her status, because he didn't want to be callous. Neither did he desire to be strung out, grasping at straws.

"It must keep you in broad touch with people, I imagine," he probes.

"I know only a few of the people here. Elaine invited me."

"Is that so? Strange people usually make for strange acquaintances," he jokes. "I've known her about seven years."

"And you, Fred? What are you doing with this life of yours?"

"Public relations, this time around . . . most people call me Baby."

"New to the field?"

"I'm constantly growing," he laughed at her quip. "You're a Scorpio, aren't you?"

"Second of November. My rising is in Gemini."

"An interesting season for birth," he comments, while conjuring a workable strategy to score with Vivian.

"Full of energy. I don't get the sleep we're supposed to require, though. Too busy trying to cram everything into my life, for that," she sighs, theatrically.

"Sounds very typical of Scorpio. And a dancer at that," he says, reflectively. "Would you like to dance with me, pretty lady? Perhaps you can help me learn something about the finer points of your art."

Chapter Fourteen

Fred had parked the Mercedes on Georgia Avenue, not too far away from the renovated movie theatre. As he walked along the deserted street, he again thanked his lucky star that events had turned out favorably. So it transpired, Vivian was indeed unattached, so he didn't have to step on anyone's toes. Since Bob was just a casual friend, merely escorting the pretty Vivian, Fred was able to arrange a date. He had sensed her adventurous personality and had been careful in presenting his proposition to play upon that aspect of her character. He was glad he didn't have to restrain his libido too much longer. It wasn't that he was a wantonly adventurous guy. His case was just the opposite. But, the long abstinence, since breaking with Helena, had made him quite 'horney,' Fred thought. He welcomed an affair to balance the rigorous austerities he practiced as part of his life styles. Putting aside the youthful excitement, momentarily, he reflected about the significance of the Repertoire Company.

Fred entered the lobby of the old building and browsed around, familiarizing himself with the range of activities offered by the company. From the directory he learned that the group had workshops in theatre, writing, photography and, of course, dance. The troupe was the professional pinnacle toward which the workshop students aspired. He perused the poster sized blow-ups of newspaper clippings, advertising critics reviews, and the slick high-gloss publicity photographs which decorated the walls, to get a closer look at the quality of activities. The organization probably got its funding from the newly established National Endowment for the Arts and other private foundations, he surmised. It was fashionable at that time to support black cultural endeavours in the neighborhoods. He knew the grants resulted from an ameliorative policy, used mainly to placate and counter the increasing militant movements which were springing up everywhere during that period. But, Fred thought, it served a purpose. Especially in the District of Columbia where the rising black community and, everything else for that matter, was overshadowed by the federal government presence. After all, he told himself, the entertainment industry made no bones of exploiting black artists. It was about time the system threw some crumbs at the struggling talent. He located the dance troupe on the directory and entered the theatre to watch the rehearsal on the main stage. The dancers were just completing their routine exercises which were executed with delicate precision. He watched Vivian, whose lithe body moved effortlessly with the other dancers through the intricate jazz routines, until the choreographer was satisfied and called for a break. From his seat in the front row of the small theatre, Fred took the opportunity to signal his new acquaintance. She left the group of exhausted dancers and approached him with a pleasant smile on her face.

"Hi," she sighed, and flopped into the adjoining chair to catch her breath.

"Hi," Fred returned the greeting. "How're you feeling today, Vivian?"

"Just great! We got through a whole movement this morning, and I feel like I'm floating now."

"You look very vibrant . . . shucks, it might be wise for me to change my lifestyle, if dancing makes you look that good!"

Vivian lowered her eyes demurely at the compliment.

"We'll be through in a minute. Sit tight," she said, and returned to join the dancers in their conversation.

Fred assumed an unimposing poise amidst the empty chairs and watched with interest, when the lively activity resumed. He didn't have to wait very long before the rehearsal was complete and was exuberant, as they left the theatre. It was easy to converse with Vivian. He casually directed the subject toward his plans for the evening, as they entered the waiting Mercedes. His agenda was clear: to spend the night with her.

"Where are we off to, skipper," she said, jokingly, and made herself comfortable in the expensive auto.

"Does it really matter," he replied, tactfully.

"I thought we'd stop by my parents place for dinner. I haven't been in touch for a while now."

"Oh, really," said Fred, disgruntled. He hadn't anticipated more socializing, but covered his anxiousness well. "I had in mind a stroll through the zoo, or something like laying out in the sun . . . "

"Say, that sounds great . . . now, I bet those ideas aren't a product of your New York culture. Let's do both! We can go over to the zoo now, and I can call my mother to have her set two extra places on our way over there. Okay?"

"Uh . . . alright, I guess," Fred mumbled, distraughtly. "That is, if you want to . . . "

"Great! I haven't been over to the zoo in years. It's terrible the way we overlook all the little goodies around here. I suppose artists aren't immune to neglecting many incidentals of life, in our mad quest for expression," she chatted on.

"I'll have to admit, you're quite right about that. It's usually too late for us, when we realize what we're doing. Then, all our efforts amount to a frustrated groping which makes events grotesque," Fred sermoned, as he geared the mercedes and headed for the zoo.

"Precisely," Vivian agreed. "In that way, we're no different from the millions of other people who spend their time trying to decondition themselves from the callousness they've built up over the years . . . it's very pathetic," she says, philosophically.

Fred enjoyed driving the mercedes while listening to the pleasant conversation. With the advanced suspension and steering systems, it handled like a sports car. He was a good driver and observed the local ordinances carefully, as he had long since outgrown the fascination with speed. As Vivian chatted, he headed across town along Columbia Road which led directly into the zoo, located in the middle of Rock Creek Park. When they passed the working class residences, his view of the pleasant homes gave him, yet another perspective of Washington's varied black communities. Unlike the poorer sections of the city on the South side of Florida Avenue, and elsewhere, the small sturdy structures were well maintained and the streets kept clean. Fred thought the residents were probably hard working upwardly aspiring citizens who, in many instances, had taken second mortgages to make requisite improvements that would stabilize their property value. He wondered if redlining was still a problem, which he had read about on previous visits to the District. As the light changed, he guided the auto across Sixteenth Street and shifted into low gear to descend the steep hill, before entering the zoo.

"The National Zoological Park," Vivian exclaimed, full of laughter. "What do you want to see first, the bears or the lions?"

"I kind of think the seals," Fred teased, captivated by her excitement.

Vivian sucked her teeth childlike, and says, "between the bears and the lions!"

"In that case, the bears," he replies. "Lions always seem out of place to me behind bars. I can even tolerate the statues in front of the library quicker than real live ones in cages."

"What statues are you talking about, Fred?"

"You mean you don't have lions outside your libraries, down here," he jokes, as they bundled up to face the chill.

"Washington's too provincial to have that type of pornography outside. They're a bunch of pompous victorian hypocrites!"

"You've got a point there," he adds, as they disembark from the vehicle.

Vivian took the lead, as they walked, and pulled him to the small pond which housed the seemingly endless variety of birds, with each species carefully guarding its own ecological niche.

"This is so exhilarating," she says. "I feel like a little girl, again."

"I'm sure that in your case, it doesn't take that much to keep the feeling alive, Vivian."

"You're so damned charmming!"

The trip to the zoo was an excellent idea. A reprieve among the hectic schedule of creative work, endless deadlines, research and the tensions of interpersonal interfaces, he thought. During the hour and a half of sight seeing, they relaxed and became more comfortable together. Fred enjoyed Vivian's kinetic energy and childlike enthusiasm, that lent a welcome excitement to their date, which he had not known since courting Helena. He bought her popcorn and a balloon, and buttoned her coat to protect her from the late afternoon chill. She clung to his arm, and kept up with his fast pace, as they made casual jokes about the different animals that they viewed. All in all, it was a pleasant way to break the ice and prepare him for the formalities of the family dinner engagement. Mrs. Delaney had already set the table, when they arrived, and it was not long before Fred could lose his lingering uptightness by stuffing his hungry stomach.

"This is really good, Mrs. Delaney. You'll have to excuse me if I make a glutton out of myself, but I haven't had the pleasure in such a long time, you know," Fred compliments with small talk to ease his tension. Somehow, he just couldn't stop feeling like a cad when he thought of his designs for Vivian.

"Darling, you just help yourself," Mrs. Delaney remarks in a motherly way. "There's nothing that pleases me more than to see a man enjoy my cooking."

Mr. Delaney was a quiet authoritative person who commented with patriarchical reserve. "Make yourself at home, son, we've got enough to go around. Vivian's always calling us up like a lost child. Since we never know when she's going to bring somebody over for dinner, mamma just naturally cooks for her, all the time.''

"It's not like she lives so far away from home, you know," Mrs. Delaney interjects, defensively.

"You prepare for her, all the time," Fred says, perplexed.

"It's nothing, I just make a little extra," she says, coyishly. "If Vivian doesn't come over, I usually eat her share for lunch the next day . . . maybe that's why I'm gaining all this weight, eating lunch everyday.''

Fred laughs. "I suppose we all would have to watch our weight if we had this type of food to eat, all the time." He winked at Vivian's younger sister, who smiled shyly and lowered her head.

"Well, thank you darling. You know that you'll always be welcome here with all the flattery you're giving me," says Mrs. Delaney, as she passes her husband a bowl of greens.

Mr. Delaney cleared his throat and changed the tone of the conversation to serious business.

"Well, how does it seem to be shaping up for that Councilman Ferguson in New York?''

"The prospects couldn't be better, at this point," Fred replies. "The news will be carrying a statement about his proposed plan to overhaul the Board of Education, sometime next week.''

"That's good," says the old man. "We need to have sound projects in mind, as we get acess to more spots in city governments. Down here, the educational mess will only be cleared up when we get our home-rule from the hill. It's going to be one hell of a big project for us when it finally takes place . . . sort of Reconstruction on a small scale, if you know what I mean.''

"I know, but I have faith that all of you are ready to handle the change when it passes, this session," Fred says, encouragingly.

"I wish I could share your enthusiasm, son. I've seen this thing battled around all my life. Although we're prohibited by the hatch act, the postal employees union is encouraging residents to work overtime on the issue. But, I still try to keep a sober mind of realism about it," comments Mr. Delaney, as he relaxed after a full meal.

Fred became interested with the old man's conversation. He thought about the point a moment, then expressed a thought to weigh his idea from Mr. Delaney's response.

"Like many other places, Washington has changed during this decade. Especially since the Civil Rights Movement began. When Whites fled to suburbia after the war, there was no other alternative but to revolutionize city politics. I think black representation is going to change in our favor primarily because of that. The cosmopolitan trend today is toward black leadership. There's no other way to go," he concludes.

"I understand you. I suppose they thought we were going to mess up the bureaucratic machine and get caught inside a fortified enclave," Mr. Delaney remarks. "All that talk about Whites reclaiming the city and urban violence makes me uneasy, though. It wouldn't take too much for this whole thing to backfire and set us back another hundred years, son.''

"The same attitude exists about private business, Mr. Delaney. You might say there was a failure to calculate our own innovative resource and persistent work,''

Fred replies. He felt assured that his role at TMP was worthwhile. Sober folks, like Mr. Delaney, undoubtably had clear insight into the message he strove to communicate.

'Well, how do you think New York will adjust to having a black mayor? We've had that experience, here in Washington, for quite awhile, now . . . even if it's only by appointment.''

''I think the election is just a ritual now, for something that's already understood to be the next fact.'' Fred glanced at Vivian, exuding another of his demonic grins. He couldn't avoid her stare any longer. Their eyes met, and the sensuality of her alluring smile captivated his imagination, again.

Chapter Fifteen

Vivian's apartment faced West, overlooking the small parking lot in the rear of the tenement. She had apologized for the untidiness and complained of the tiny rooms and exhorbitant rent which, to Fred, was an unbelievable bargain in relation to comparable quarters in New York. The sparsely furnished residence was tastefully arranged with inexpensive items, many of them 'hand-me-downs', which added a sense of homely comfort to the otherwise dormitory-like atmosphere. Fred felt at home immediately, upon entering the livingroom. He paused momentarily to view the vibrant image cast upon Vivian's face by the illumination of the full moon shining through the window. The colorful chiaroscuro lent dramatic impact to her free spirited personality. Fred sensed Vivian was 'good people'. Not a malevolent creature, like some of the obvious 'come-ons' that he knew. She ushered him to the worn sofa while she made herself comfortable.

"You can certainly show a girl a good time, Fred," she sighs, as she returned from the closet with a few marajuana cigarettes.

"I just get a glimpse of Washington each time I come here. You know, it's like fitting together a picture puzzle."

"It must be a fairly good composite to keep your interest. I mean, you do share a very precious sensitivity."

Fred lit the intoxicant and took a long drag from the joint.

"I'm married, Vivian. My wife and I are separated."

"That's a very apparent part of you . . . I guess I sensed it in your gestures. Do you think that it's always as perceivable, as you've made it with me, though?"

"I hadn't really thought about it. How does it affect you, Vivian?"

"Oh, very positively . . . unusually so, I suppose I'll have to admit . . nothing at all cumbersome with you, Fred."

"I've had thirty five years to learn to live outside the drudgery of life."

"You're just a young man," she says, pausing to inhale the marajuana. "There really isn't any need for despair, at your age."

"Perhaps. But, maybe judgement of this life will be diverted by a moratorium among the spiritual forces, and I'll have an opportunity to grow the next time around," he comments, pensively.

"I'm surprised at your melancholy, Fred. After such a beautiful day . . . how many flowers have you opened, my masterful friend,'' she inquires, probing his intrigue.

"Several,'' he replies, rousing himself from mixed emotions. "I see myself working with at least eight limbs.''

"It that right? I've just begun to open all of my chakras and I've been dancing for quite awhile. You must have some terrible resources, or a powerful kundalindi!''

Fred laughs and says;

"There once was a plump damsel of Martique,
Who wished dearly to be sleek.
She set about to practice austere,
Which continued approximately a year,
At the end of this time she became quite meek.''

"Very good,'' laughs Vivian. "But I'm really not quite that fragmented a Washingtonian you always seem to imply, Fred.''

"First of all, schizophrenia is idigeneous to New York. You see, your vivaciousness is just a bold relief within the overall picture that I get, whenever I come here. It's got to be a built-in mechanism of some sort that continually reminds me of where I am. Otherwise, I might get paranoic about Washington. I don't think I could handle two psychoses, you know.''

"Then, there's not even a question of you ever living here?''

"Obiviously, I wouldn't prefer it. But, as with everything, there's a way to circumvent those situations I don't like. That's not just here, though!''

"Washington is probably more like the rest of the country, if you think about it's size and parochialism. It's just that you've undoubtably gotten too used to your smug New York sensationalism! It's only false grandeur, that's all.''

"That could be so. But, talk is that everybody is leaving the city. New York experiences great exoduses periodically. Whatever cyclic pattern operates, it seems to be coming to fruition again. Old timers splitting to other parts of the world, new people coming in . . . I imagine it's healthy for continual changes like that to occur . . . in New York, as well. Oh the city can be a big enough place to absorb great transformations, and then, it too, can become stagnated like other localities,'' Fred says, analytically.

"I'm not sure that I'll leave this bizarre atmosphere. Despite all the accusations you've lain clear to me about Washington, this is my home. We've still got a degree of warm relations, so I won't be jealous of your New York,'' she responds while handing him the remainder of the joint.

"I wouldn't encourage you to get out of an obviously noncontending situation. If the skirt fits, wear it, Vivian!''

Fred acquiesced. He felt he didn't have to be cunning and played the gentleman.

"Of course, I don't rule out the possibility of tours and what have you, as taking me as far away as I might desire. But, I'll probably grow old and die here,'' she exclaims.

"Aie morto!''

Fred used a comic diversion to change the tone of the conversation.

" . . . I have this insatiable love of my life that tells me never to die in a place like Washington . . . Ah cabronia, no bet,'' he teased her.

"Gee, Fred, you haven't even given me an opportunity to talk about myself, with all this gabbing about New York and Washington," she laughs. "Have you got some kind of perverted fixation or something?"

"I know what you mean," he says, calming down a bit. "I haven't been a good guest, at all, I imagine. And you have such interesting attributes . . . I'm surprised you haven't thrown me out," Fred apologized.

"Tell me about it! You know how we ladies eat that shit up!"

Fred laughed and moved closer. "Are you prepared for all that comes along with my compliments?"

"We couldn't get too much more intimate than the way we met," she says, teasingly.

"That's not exactly what I had in mind," Fred responds

"I'm ready to throw you, you suave New York turkey!"

Vivian responded to the challenge of the overture in characteristic manner, Fred thought. The exchange animated him.

"Well, then, I become an old man and refuse your amazon from hurting my pride."

"I feign the alluring maiden, teasing the serpent of your most powerful drives," Vivian murmurs, while moving toward him and brushing her lips across his mouth.

"I know your sensuality, intimately, by the flower of my mind. Awaken pneuma naturalis. Open the senses of my body to the experience of senual bliss," Fred incants a psychic phrase. Although he didn't quite consider himself a magician, he had good command of many natural forces.

"I pull your old man with my harlot, teasing you to madness with the soft textures and womanly redolence of my mature responsive body", Vivian whispers enticingly.

The charm made Fred sanguine, and he responded to the natural urge with a playful attitude.

"Why, then, I metamorphose into a satyr and carry you off to the shadows of nightfall, all the while titillating your lower depths."

Vivian recoiled, feigning shock. "Shades of Diana, you move a sibyl to turn a trick! I was hoping to be your Nefertiti, my black lord."

Fred smiled. "You do have such wonderful legs, Vivian . . . "

"All the better to snake my body around you and squeeze the very fluids of life from your thighs. Tease me into bliss and die a thousand organisms, to awaken in heavenly repose . . . send the fire of your jissom into every abode of my shelter and fructify the life forces."

"I enter the innermost recesses of your maiden flower and transcend the throes of hell," he whispers, charmingly. "By twelve paths I travel through earth's womb and emerge from the misty caverns to discover the multitude of heavenly manna."

Vivian looked invitingly at Fred, as he handed her the dwindling joint. She puffed, letting the vapors through her nose. A pleasant smile of anticipation spread across Fred's mouth while he gazed knowingly at her bright twinkling eyes. She returned the marajuana. He took two quick puffs, then placed the thin cigarette to her lips. She drew upon it deeply, leaving moisture from her wet lips on his fingers.

"I am a honey bee seeking the nectar of your flower," Fred continues to ad-lib the drama of foreplay."

"I open the folds of my petals."

"My senses are kindled."

"I summon the wind to guide your wings to the pistils of my waiting violet,"

Vivian murmurs, sensually.

"I enter!"

"I shiver!"

Fred moved closer and held Vivian gently in his arms.

"We meet," he whispers, and kissed her lingeringly, as they began the evening's lovemaking.

The weather had turned colder during the night, and they had wrapped their nude bodies closer together for warmth. Their clothes were still strewn about the couch and floor, when morning arrived. Fred smiled at the scene, on his way to the bathroom. He had enjoyed the evening with Vivian and was glad he had allowed himself the indulgence. Although he guarded his life through rigorous metaphysical practice, he felt his purpose could be communicated to compatible mana. It wasn't often he found good spirited people. Vivian was such a person. Through her, Fred saw again, that work toward communion was well wothwhile. She had brough him closer to his human relations.

He had initiated her to the mystery of the journey. Casually introducing her responsive senses to the subtleties of nature, Fred had taken her spirit, gradually by degrees, to the bliss of celestial music with each successive orgasm. He used the lessons of the mantras well and, by the completion of their lovemaking had brought forth her astral body. Vivian had been captivated by the new experience. She brought a mature openess to the exchange which helped her comprehend the profound messages that accompanied her ecstasy. Cunalingus wasn't the only thing that Fred was good at, Vivian had thought. She slowly awoke in rapture from the deep reverie and, sensing Fred was not in bed, got up and entered the bathroom.

"Say, man, what are doing out of my bed so early in the morning," Vivian complains, while embracing his back. "You've got to be kidding. This is no breakfast scene!"

"If I say I'm going to return to that bedroom, I'd be realizing my demise," he quips, while holding onto his toweled waist. "You almost killed me with those powerful thighs, lady."

"Oh stop putting me on, tiger. You're not getting out of bed that easily, you know. Come on and let me rub you down."

"What are you commencing to do in this place, Vivian? First of all, I told you that I was an old man!"

Vivian's challenging character was emerging again and she just couldn't keep herself out of a spar.

"Well, then, it's classical! You know . . . front page mess with all of the sensation . . . old man dying at the thighs of young consort . . . further investigation discloses the fact that the grieving spouse is, in reality, the old man's concubine . . . pretty interesting, wouldn't you say?"

"I would never be allowed to be buried in New York," Fred replies, while trying to elude Vivian's aggressiveness.

"Oh, how terrible! I'm afraid we don't have anymore space in this area," she cajoles. "We'll simply have to unload the carcas into the sea . . . "

"Ah, then there's the possibility of washing ashore on Martique's beaches," he says, and pinches her nose affectionately. "I'd prefer to be ressurected there," Fred adds, while escaping her grip. "I have to get in an early morning call to the office," he apologizes, and blows her a kiss.

"New York wins, huh?"

"If it doesn't, I'll probably die of natural causes!"

Defeated for the moment, Vivian remained in the bathroom with her hands on her hips, complaining.

"Now I've got to barter all my goodies for a soft landing back into reality," Vivian comments, sassily. "I don't know about these sessions . . . I think I'll have to carry the austerities a little further, in the future," she says, sarcastically.

"It's all a matter of mind poise, Vivian," he replys, on his way to the living room.

"And that should keep you in my clutches a little longer, huh?"

"No, but it will keep you away from rigid thinking," Fred quips. He picked up the phone. "Collect to New York . . . 379-6475 . . ."

Vivian entered the kitchen, disgustedly, and put on a pot of water for coffee. The dawn light poured through the window, brightening her profile, as she moved about with unassuming womanly grace. She turned on the radio and began swaying rhythmically with the music. Opening the door to an almost bare refrigerator brought forth a laugh from Vivian, as she lazily searched for something with which to prepare breakfast. She finally found some sardines and mushrooms and quickly whipped together an omlette. The news came on the radio with a lead in story about a financial scandal in the New York City Transit Authority.

"In urban news around the nation today, New York's city council president disclosed a pattern of fiscal mismanagement in that municipality's transit authority pension fund. Commenting on the situation at a news conference, Eugene Landers called the problem a 'deplorable deception which shrouds the credibility of civil service accountability'. The councilman alleges that unaccountable sums have been diverted into speculative investments in several politically unstable and repressive nations throughout the world, including the apartheid government of South Africa. In a virulent attack, he placed responsibility with the incumbent Mayor Bailey and his political appointees, and is calling for an intervention by the governor's office. The councilman says that the State Commission of Investigation should examine the pension fund for possible fraud. The situation comes on the eve of the mayoral primary in New York City, and political analysts agree that Bailey's re-election is in jeapordy. The leading candidate in that contest, Councilman Charles Ferguson, is supporting the city council president's actions, and it is felt that Ferguson's minority status will gain most in the close election, as a result of this latest development in New York City politics."

Vivian reflected about the information, as she listened to the rest of the news. She wasn't exactly clear about how these events affected Fred's work, but she had a premonition of danger, which made her nervous for him. The music resumed, livening the atmosphere, and she cast the ill omen out of her mind and relaxed. Fred entered the kitchen in a happy mood which also helped displace her forebodence.

"Ah ha, there is some carryover to kitchen affairs this morning," he joked in a relaxed manner.

"Well, good morning to you, too," Vivian responded. "Did you accomodations serve to relax you, Mr. Murphy?"

"I'll be sure to make advance arrangements for my return visit!"

"You won't have to leave right away, will you?"

"No. The weekend is going to be slow, Vivian. I won't have to be at the office until Monday."

"Oh, that's great! Then I can turn off these eggs, and we can get back in bed!"

"No, baby doll . . . we're going to eat those eggs, and then, I'm going to help Elaine with some library work while I'm here in the capitol. I'll be moving between the F.C.C., the IRS and the Commerce Department, all day," he replies.

"Alright," she says, curtly. "I'm not going to fret about it today! But, you'd better not tie up my weekend running over to Elaine's. I can become more overt, you know!"

"Of course, I don't know that, right?" Fred grinned, and winked encouragingly at Vivian.

"My prowess have yet to be tapped, my dear," she smugly remarks, and casually slides the sardines and eggs across the table to him.

Fred cleared his throat in attempt to gather a glib reply, but says, "I don't think I'll be attempting that herculean feat, Vivian. I no longer have my aegis for protection."

"All that verbage means nothing to me, Baby! I've already begun spinning my web about you . . . now, go ahead and eat while I take a shower." She kissed him on the forehead and disappeared into the bathroom.

Fred was comfortable. He was also hungry after the evenings activities and quickly devoured the omlette. After completing his meal, he sat quietly listening to the radio. Fred became bored with soul music and switched to an FM jazz station. Now he was satisfied and went to make a telephone call.

"Hello, good morning . . . yes, I'm still on my feet. Thanks to you and Lloyd, I can be nowhere else, this morning . . . spoke to him earlier . . . yeah, I was expecting it to break. It puts our candidate in a fine position . . . right, I got you. See you at nine-forty-five . . . "

Fred returned and sat in front of the empty plate, just as Vivian entered the kitchen while unwrapping the towel from around her head.

"You might as well finish that omletee. I don't eat until eleven o'clock," she says, to make light conversation.

"Alright . . . you're sure, now? This stuff is pretty filling."

"You'll never fatten me, Baby!"

Fred almost choked while stuffing her portion into his mouth. He cleared his throat, laughing at the pun.

"I'm not going to bite that bait . . . anyhow, as I was saying, this stuff is body building protein. Nothing too fattening about this breakfast. Fish and eggs are definitely healthful!"

"It could become a habit," she says, curtly. "I'm only allowed two meals a day . . . ".

"Elaine wishes you a happy weekend," he interjects. "She says she's sorry about snatching your company away from you, but adds that she doesn't have any concept of leisure class lifestyles . . . so you'll have to excuse her early morning interruptions," Fred teases, humorously.

Vivian frowned in mock agitation. "I should curse both of you out! But, I'm still being charming, momentarily . . . "

Fred laughed at Vivian's flamboyant gestures. The two women shared an obvious good relationship, he thought. He decided to continue being a gentleman, especially to prevent them from double teaming him, later on.

"Can I drop you off at the studio?"

"No," she replies, somewhat deflated. "I think I'll tidy up around here, this morning, and go over later on in the afternoon . . . say, what would you like for dinner?"

"You don't have to cook, if you don't want to. I know how burdensome impromptu cooking can become, sugar. Perhaps we can run over to Billy Simpson's or something," Fred offers, to insure his welcome.

"Listen to me. I purely forgot who you're going to be with, today. Elaine will probably come up with some, or another affair to attend, anyhow! Call me later this afternoon when you find out what the devil she's got going on, first. Then, we'll see."

"Alright. But, I'm on you're side, remember," he remarks, supportively.

"Be careful of the sword over your head as you leave my front door, 'damocles'," Vivian responds, sarcastically.

Chapter Sixteen

The silver mercedes could be an exact duplicate of Elaine's, Fred thought, while watching the expensive vehicle pull to the stop light on Fourth Avenue. The white couple sat very stoically inside the car looking beyond Fred, as he paused for a closer look while crossing the intersection. Early morning traffic was just beginning to congest the streets of New York, along with the first wave of working class people who hurried by, as Fred continued his pace to the office. Something would have to be done for an outside sign, he mused, upon entering the building. The old firehouse was an easy enough site to locate, but there was no other identification other than the big white building number, for the one in a million client who happened to be passing by. He scaled the stairs to the second floor where he found Lloyd busy gathering news information from the wire services. With his shirtsleeves aready rolled up for work, the stocky officious businessman had stopped a moment, to read some of the material, when Fred approached.

"Buenos Dios, hombre. Como ca va," he casually greeted his boss, in a light mood.

"Bien! What brings you back to the city, my man . . . and at such an unbelievably early hour! You must've had a very inspiring little trip . . . how's Elaine?"

"She still manages to make Washington a lively place. She says she'd like to get up this way for a relief, some time soon, and asked me to relay her desires to you, directly!"

"That chic's dizzy! How's home-rule making out, down there on the hill?"

The two men walked toward Lloyd's office while talking and, when they entered the room, Lloyd made himself comfortable in his armchair.

"It seems the politico's are trying to cut through the filibuster, so there's a good chance it'll pass, this time. Although everybody's planning for a gala celebration, I hope their anticipations aren't let down."

"Hmm, all of that presumption would mean a terrible disappointment," Lloyd says, pensively. "But, after all, that stew has been in the pot for some time now . . . what else is occuring in the nation's capitol that makes you so exuberant this morning?"

"You know getting away always has a soothing effect on the beast within me, Lloyd. And then, you have to remember that I was in Elaine's company . . . she always has the therapeutic effect of bringing out the better side of me . . . ''

"I suppose I'm too old, or too ignorant to understand that, right?'' Lloyd picked up his pipe and began to smoke while relaxing in his armchair.

"She's pretty far along with her brief, I might add.''

"Yes, tell me about that, Fred. What did you get from it?''

"Well, although the station dumped the only black program, claiming government pressure about its editorial policy, she's not going to present the case simply from the free speech aspect. It's a very sophisticated labor management contest. I had no idea that she was planning that type of strategy,'' he reports.

"Yeah, man, that's important! See, this is going to be precedential in several ways. First of all, in confronting the communications industry through labor proceedings, there's greater impact forthcoming from the disposition. Therefore, it provides solid argument for the numerous civil suits that will follow . . . did she file for class action complaints, yet?''

"She's working on that now. I learned a lot that will help us in other areas. I'll write up a little outline for you, as soon as I can . . . what's been happening around here?''

"Well, our exclusives are giving the campaign a great deal of momentum. Once the primary's over, it'll be all down hill . . . oh, by the way, Jomo wants you to screen some rushes for this week's schedule.''

"Have you seen any of the footage,'' Fred asks, as he lights a cigarette.

"No. I haven't had the opportunity to scratch my back, since you've been away . . . So Elaine is going to shake up the communications industry and pull the carpet on the government, at the same time. Well, it's about time those jokers got caught in a trick!''

"From the looks of it, those people don't want any part of an assault like that. They've been busy enough trying to feel her out, but they're slick enough not to get caught in a minor conspiracy. All of their inquiries are unofficial probes,'' he remarks, and flicks an ash in the ashtray.

"It seems like a ripe situation for your talents, Murphy. I know you'd like to get a chance to even the score with some of the forces that broke you, but we can't spare you now. We'll just wait until they face our syndication,'' Lloyd comments, calmly.

"By the way, how is Ferguson . . . what's Callander talking about,'' Fred responds, changing the subject to more comfortable matters. Lloyd's perception was accurate, but Fred respected his boss's insight. It was better to be patient, he thought.

"They're both getting pretty excited, now that time is coming closer. You know, minor fears cropping up in a few of the districts. But, they're both holding their own.''

Lloyd paused to answer the telephone while Fred enjoyed his cigarette.

"Hello . . . how are you, Rita . . . yes, Fred's back. He tells me he couldn't find a job down there, so he came back to the dirty city . . . you are? Well, how does Ferguson feel about that . . . really? You might pick up tickets for me and mine, too. I'd very much like to do that . . . you didn't think I could afford the time, huh? Well, the head honcho around here could stand a breather, about now,'' Lloyd smiled, uncharacteristically at his humour. "For two weeks! A month would be more like it, at this rate . . . okay, I'll tell him . . . hang in there, Rita. Bye, now.''

"I always said she had big ears. What's she talking about, now?"

"Says she's getting ready to embark upon a caribbean cruise, to relax her nerves," Lloyd curtly replys.

"Shit, I'm interested in being her gigolo. When is she going?" Fred says, jokingly.

"I think you're going to have to take care of the store, this time. I told her to pick up passages for me, you know what I mean?"

"You know you wouldn't trust me running the whole show around here, Lloyd. You'd develop an ulcer wondering what the devil was going on in here!"

"Yeah, maybe so. But I could sure use a little vacation, after this election is over. It's running me into the ground."

"What else did Rita have to say?" Fred inquires, curiously.

"Oh, she's anxiously anticipating your return. Hasn't lost a wink of sleep, or some nonsense like that," Lloyd chuckles.

"I wonder where she picked that up from?"

"Anyhow, Fred, you, tell me, what Abiola was talking about," Lloyd cut the gossip short, with his usual officious attitude.

"Right! He told me that Martique could develop her commercial potential through trade agreements with international businesses in Zambia and other African countries. He figures such a coterie would only have to invest one hundred million dollars at the outset. So, he's awaiting our signal to arrange a meeting with his country's economic minister and the governor. Meanwhile, he's moving forward with the bauxite venture, if the insurance interests prove fruitful . . . he liked the prospectus very much. Especially the hard line we developed. Says it's just what he needs to convince his government, if the other project becomes a reality."

"He's scheduled to visit the United Nations soon, isn't that right?"

"Yes, from one arena to the next . . . that guy is going a long way in his country. Now, with our paws in industrial development, I'd say we made out like fat cats," Fred comments and grins at his boss.

"Well, that's good. Perhaps you can keep your belly full, for awhile. Since this liason is proving fruitful, the next step is to introduce our media expertise, when the time is right. I'd like you to go over there and check out the whole situation, the first opportunity that crops up, Fred."

"Man, am I ever ready for that!"

"You've got to move fast, now that opportunities are occuring for us. Because, by the time you blink an eyelash, other larger interests could swoop down on us and eat everything up like a cancer," Lloyd advises him. "That's why you're going to have to open up some other avenues for Lester to pursue on his own, after this campaign is over. It's true we need additional staff, but we're going to have to develop some heavies from within, right away!"

"What about using some of Abiola's people?" Fred suggests, and extinguishes the cigarette.

"That would be a wonderful idea, but then, they wouldn't be coming to us for assistance at all. They know their potential. That's why we have a serious task of insuring our survival while we grow with them. It doesn't take long for a developing country to capitalize on implicit communications!"

"Most assuredly! That's part of the design," Fred remarks.

"We're only a complimenting vehicle in this case, fitting into their long term plans. That's why we're in at the ground floor," Lloyd reminds him.

"Well, it's true that they're shrewd enough to know what to look for, but more importantly, they know which sources are helpful to reach their goals."

"Let's face it, Fred, without us getting direct investments like that, we'd be merely human resources, manpower, interpretively speaking," Lloyd continues to tutor Fred.

"Yeah, well I still think their attempt to modernize will be better off, if they open up the growth potential to the people of color, over here, who are developing their expertise the same way."

Lloyd paused a moment to weigh Fred's point while he puffed at his pipe. He knew the younger man's character was often hampered by fervent idealism. It had caused him problems in dealing with the viciousness of systems in the past. But, Lloyd felt that with proper schooling, Fred would develop the insight and wisdom which would allow his expertise to benefit, rather than to be destroyed.

"I guess I'm still a little conservative in my training and experience. More so than you. It shows. That's why I want you to be available to research this potential, thoroughly, very soon!"

"I certainly will be glad to do that!"

Lloyd felt he had said enough for the time being and became tactfully silent. He would file their conversation and work with Fred further.

"Meanwhile, I hope you're not letting any grass grow under your feet!"

"Hmm," Fred grumbled. "I didn't think you noticed. Do you want to keep Les on this campaign, now that he's with the candidate?"

"Baby, you sure as hell must think we're supporting you for nothing, around here. What do you think I'm paying you for, anyhow?"

"Sometimes, I get the impression that you dig my company," Fred replies, sarcastically.

"Until I start wearing skirts, or something, realize that your elocutions don't serve to palpitate my emotions, in the least . . . your glib just gives me gas pains, to say it in a gentlemanly fashion. You'll find your itinery on your desk!"

Fred raised himself from the chair to leave the office and made his last pun. "Take care of the old man for me, Lloyd."

Chapter Seventeen

Fred decided to take the subway downtown. He hadn't gotten last month's expense voucher in on time and wouldn't get the check for another week. Payday was four days away, and he was desparately short on cash. The short ride was quick enough, and he was glad the station was a few steps from City Hall. It was colder in New York now, so he quickened his pace. After presenting identification to the guard, he ascended the stairway and entered the council chambers. Fred noticed immediately that more people were present for the hearings, which was ostensibly a factor of the recent transit scandal. But, he was pleased to see additional black faces in the audience. Most of them were political activists and old line party hacks, he thought, and was satisfied with their turnout, as a reflection of his work on the exclusive media coverage of Ferguson. He found an empty seat next to Les and Christine and made himself comfortable.

"Hi people. How's it going . . . "

"We've been here, but nobody figured you'd be back."

"Don't tell me this is the place where that rumor about my job seeking originated, Chris."

"What's to it, Baby," Les says.

"I didn't find anything down there, except more work, Les. Behind that, you know I had to turn around and come back here."

"Everything here has been relatively stable," Les reports. "As you can see, Rita is giving her findings and suggestions."

"Yes, I'm watching the lady in the limelight. It's pretty devastating material, isn't it?"

"You can say that again," interjects Chris.

"And how've you been managing?"

"Still putting in those long hours, Fred. Besides that, alright I guess."

"Did Landers uncover any figures in the pension fund fiasco?" Fred inquires, as he lights a cigarette.

"Two hundred and forty million unaccounted for, to be exact. It was quite a disclosure for the public to stomach." she comments enthusiastically, in an eager attempt to be impressive.

"Hmm. Well, what about the the transit's demand for a pay hike?"

"The union is claiming that its demands are within fiscal capacity, but there's going to be a further investigation. The city can't cover a pay increase out of general revenue, at this time. According to the comptroller, there may have to be an across the board cut-back in operating costs, anyway, to keep the city from going in the red. Landers feels that a pay hike would just lead to other municipal drains, and New York is already straining," she concludes, in an officious manner.

"Doesn't look too good, huh? I guess the union raised hell."

"All over the weekend papers, Fred. They're threatening a strike again," adds Les.

"Landers is trying to make a case, and it looks like a good one, for a tight budget, until the city can be assured of federal aid from the Transportation Department. Now, if Callander makes a convincing presentation about the school issue, transit will probably be bumped, altogether," Christine critically analyzes probable events.

"Well that's interesting," Fred comments. "It seems like education is the hottest issue around the country. It's pre-empted all other concerns, thus far."

"It's the same in Washington, huh?" Les asks. "What does homerule look like, anyway?"

"I'm rather optimistic that D.C. will be successful . . . with minor reservation. But, there again, education is the first priority, Les."

The conversation was interrupted by Rita Callander's emotionally charged voice, which had become more dramatic as she emphasized each crisis while delivering her committee's findings.

"Last year alone, there was a twenty percent turnover within the teaching profession. The impact of this frightening trend presented critical staffing shortages in seven school districts which, coincidentally, are familiar to us as the precise locations of poorest grade score achievement within the city school system. The residents in those neighborhoods have sought a resolution of the dilemma, by presenting community guidelines in filling vacancies, and has met with repeated closure by the union structure. The Board of Education, in the interim, without clear policy guidelines, has raised the criteria for licensing para-professionals and removed the par-diem teaching category, altogether. This, of course, had led to a general staffing problem throughout the educational system and further exacerbated learning deficiencies, particularly within the problem school districts which serve a principally minority ethnic student population . . . "

"It's becoming more difficult within the civil service all the time," Fred remarks, philosophically.

"But, as with everyone else, there's no telling the teacher that she doesn't deserve every pay increase the union constantly demands," Christine cynically comments.

"How about you, Chris," asks Fred. "Haven't you gone that route?"

"The first four years out of college," she replies. "I can't say that I didn't enjoy the experience. I taught social studies at the high school level. Erasmus. I see it this way, after ten years, a person really has a very stable job. Then, should one enter administration, which is the usual route for the more aggressive, there are some comfortable monies involved in that profession."

"It really fits into that bureaucratic jungle over there on Livingston Street," Fred remarks, as he takes a long drag on the cigarette.

"That's why there's hardly any real innovation for forthcoming from the educational system, anyhow. It's another sector which functions, just to absorb a size-able portion of our educated population," comments Christine.

"I might add, toward perpetuating the drone sysndrome among our citizenry," quips Fred. "But, somehow I don't think I'd send my child to a private school. There are some virtues to public education, although I'm hard pressed to put my finger on them."

"It's only noticeable later in life, just what the public education system lacks," remarks Les. " . . . We are continually training as a response to the quantitative increases and suffering, because of qualitative deficiencies in both staffing and programming," he mimicks Callander.

"If that's not a direct quote, I'll treat you to lunch," Fred says, in a sparring mood.

They turned their attention to Rita Callander's delivery, which had climaxed and was in the midst of summation.

"We are continually training our young students in response to quantitative in-creases within our city population and subsequently suffering, because of oversights in meeting the diverse cultural and scholastic needs for both qualitative program-ming and staffing . . . "

"A roast beef and beer is good enough for me, Fred," laughs Les.

"You really know your work, don't you, Les," Christine remarks.

"She's really putting on a good show, don't you think," adds Fred.

"She's got a very professional delivery that seems so natural to her character," Christine observes. "I kind of like the way she comes on . . . "

"You mean, she's very easy to talk to," Fred interjects, sarcastically.

"Did I say something out of line?" she asks. He had caught her off guard, and she was lost for a moment, trying to decipher the innuendo. Christine didn't suspect that Rita poked fun of Fred, through the aide's very own conversations with her.

Fred smiled quizzically. "No, I suppose I did," he teased her.

"Listen," interrupts Les. "I'm going over to the office now. Put that lunch on your expense account, and I'll get to you later in the week."

"Alright, buddy. Take it easy now."

"It's been a pleasure working with you, Lester," Christine says, charmingly.

"Take it easy, you two." Les waved to the panel, as he left. Meanwhile the hearings had stopped for lunch break, and Callander strolled casually toward the two workers, leaving Ferguson talking busily with Landers.

"Well, how did you enjoy the sojourn to the Southern states, Fred?"

She was still keyed up from her presentation and displaced her excitement in a typical challange.

"You could be talking about South Africa, you know," he quips, with an eager response. "It's just that I don't taste the apartheid in your voice."

"Oh, did you go there too," Rita continues, provocatively.

"The trip was pleasant, Rita. A lot of work and what have you, but I just didn't seem to get enough sleep," Fred says, to edge the contest.

The trist worked on Callander, and she was momentarily lost for words in Chris-tine's presence. She changed the subject diplomatically.

"Uh, well, how are you Christine?"

"Watching my decorum, about now. You've made a very impressive presentation."

"Talking to a bunch of men is always exciting to me," she replies, regaining her composure. "I've sort of planned my career, so that I'll always have a male audience."

"And you have the audacity to speak to me of my pomposity, Rita," Fred exclaims through boistrous laughter.

"Well, Fred, you know how we women love to showboat. It's part of having a captured audience that brings out the best of us, wouldn't you agree, Chris?"

"I'm not sure if I do, or not, Rita. But, right now, I'm off to fetch some lunch. Do you care for any?"

Ferguson had finished his conversation and almost bumped into the young aide, as he approached the group.

"Where are you off to, in such a hurry, Christine?"

"Checking the daily menu . . . are you eating with the president, or with this group of prima-donnas?"

"With Eugene and the rest of that crew. Don't bring me a tray. I just came over to say a couple of words to Fred, since he found his way back to our illustrious city . . . so how's it going, fellah?"

"There must be something about going South that makes people associate unpleasant epithets with the person," Fred responds to Ferguson's uncharacteristic humor.

"It's alright, fellah, we all know that you're really an achiever, aspiring to break the yoke, as it were," he continued the tease.

"Let's just say, I'll never take you with me," Fred counters. "Obviously, things are going along alright in this part of the world, judging by your spirits."

"Quite," the councilman curtly replies. "But, tell me, what's going on in Washington?"

"You haven't mentioned a word about your visit, in the course of ten minutes," chimes Rita.

"It's too damned redundant now," Fred snaps, defensively. "You know, home-rule, education . . . what else is there to tell you two big city operators that you don't already know. Unless, of course, you want a rundown of the proceedings on the hill?"

"Now, isn't that being too damned smug!"

"I agree with you, Rita. This man goes to the District of Columbia and refuses to discuss current matters of importance. Next, he's going to tell us that he did a great deal of work, or something, and was too busy. What's on the agenda of the Urban League, the Urban Coalition and other organizations, down there," Ferguson plys the younger man like a drill sargeant.

"Wrapped up in plans and activities for home-rule," he retorts. "Everything is contingent upon gaining congressional mandate!"

"What are the people saying about the campaign?" Ferguson presses him.

"Everybody digs your image. I suppose, now that they're sure of your directions, the educational platform will augment your statue, moreso. They're anxious to see New York follow suit in this mayoralty election, since they've been accustomed to it for awhile, now," Fred concludes, briefly.

"Is that all, man? You've given a lousy report," Callander chastises him. "I expected you to have all kinds of useful informational tidbits, and here you go sounding like a buck-private, repeating general orders."

"What can I tell you. I don't run a Gallup poll," Fred quips. "My survey was extremely selective. What else do you want me to say . . . I went there on other business. I had very little time for city politics!"

"It isn't often that I walk away feeling a sense of incompletion, after having talked to you, but today is one of those days, I'm afraid . . . I'll speak with you after lunch," Ferguson criticizes him, then abruptly leaves the conversation.

"Uh oh, I feel I pulled a muscle, somewhere," Callander remarks, in an apologetic tone of voice.

"Yeah, right in the seat of my pants! What's to this concern with Washington, all of a sudden," Fred pleads. "Doesn't he know what office he's running for . . . after all, my work demands considerably larger fees for national campaigns."

"Let me smooth your feathers, darling," Rita consoles him. "Here comes our lunch."

Christine entered, carrying three trays, awkwardly piled on top of one another. Fred and Rita paused in their conversation and went to assist her. They arranged themselves in a comfortable corner of the empty chambers and continued their conversation.

"It's not as easy to stay on top of things, like Ferguson seems to thinks," Fred continues his gripe. "He gets me a little unnerved, the way he imagines our activities should coincide. He must realize the educational-industrial complex is one hell of a political bloc in this country."

"I'll have to admit, the manner he views the challenge to education is really on a national scale," Rita comments, maternally. She felt that her instigation had been too severe and became serious with the young man. The last thing she would ever contribute to, was unnecessary conflict between her black associates. That was professionally disdainful to her, not to mention culturally regressive.

"Well, that's good, overall. But I feel that his priority should be with the city, at this point," he remarks. "Those fellahs on the hill can reach pretty far. He has a long way to go, before he starts throwing around any weight."

"I missed that. But, perhaps he's thinking that he'll get a good head start," Christine idly remarks. She was being conversive, but unsuspectingly, out of place.

"At this point, it seems more than a little political naivity," Fred cautioned the young aide.

"He still views things hard. Part of his feelings about the impact the gray area project had upon educational policy," Callander comments, authoritatively. "It's a tough fight to come up with ideas that the administration will go along with, these days."

"We all know the effect of reports like that. Public interest groups have always looked for inroads into educational systems. It's easier to exploit young minds that way. Look, foundations like Ford, Carnegie and all the rest don't have problems entering the social sector, do they? Blatant conditions—grants and studies—all attempts to manipulate the situation. Once the money became visible, the focus of competition turned the educational system around, through policy battles, cooptation and what have you. Look what Moynihan is doing to get over," Fred remarks, bitterly.

"Gee, Ferguson must have really stirred the cock's nest, this morning," Christine interjects. She was eager to get all the dope with which to satisfy her curiosity and add to her self importance within the staff-workers' 'in-group' status clique.

"What Ferguson should include on his staff is a good sociologist," he asserts, dryly.

"My, the scope of that remark has national implications," Christine comments, encouraging Fred to ventilate.

"Undoubtedly! But, he can't stand that kind of opposition. Not until he's been in office awhile. That's what I think is politically naive, his timing," Fred replies. He was becoming tense from the conversation and lit a cigrette to counter the emotional upsurge. His analytical thinking was far superior when he remained calm, he thought, as he drew heavily upon the cigarette.

"You know that's not the case, Baby. He's been around the ball park long enough to draw some clout from past favors," Callander adds a note of reflection. "It's just a charged atmosphere of anticipation, and his anxiety about changing the cycle of despair is undoubtably normal."

"Perhaps, but his timing is important during this overall flux in administrating inner cities. People are demanding more sophisticated resolutions of municipal dilemmas. They don't want simplistic, callous policies that treat citizens like little children. Education is central to their priorities, true. But, quality of life changes threaten deceptive practices . . . "

"Well, how do you handle the situation, Fred?"

"Rita, you can deduce from ancient Chinese proverbs . . . constant issues and changing focii within successive decades," Fred ad libs.

"Then, we begin and end with a focus on civic affairs, am I right?" Callander inquires. She had a good command of logic and history, but found it wise to clarify Fred's esoteric philosophy.

"When the well becomes poison, the water is no longer a staff of life . . . "

"What does that imply, Fred?"

"It's clear that the city is the most realistic organizational unit. History confirms that view. I imagine many astute politicians have been mayors, first, then governors and so on," he says.

"Then, you're statement supports Ferguson's tactic, more so than your note of caution," she rebutes him.

"Not so," he says, patiently. "Right now I think we're playing an economic ball game within a context of international development, which introduces the problem of conflict. All of the present cultural events that are critical to emerging nations are occuring in principal cities, which are the gateways to the western world. A focus on civic affairs, as you say . . . But, when we turn to national politics here, this emphasis shifts drastically . . . where we should be speaking about urban administration, the focus is no longer clear. This country lacks a concise policy direction regarding the inner cities," Fred concludes.

"So, you imagine Ferguson should sit tight until he gets some indication of the contending interests he'll face in the coming year, before showing his hand," Callander infers from Fred's point.

"I couldn't have said it any more succinctly, Rita. When the educational focus returns to questions regarding quality of life issues, then he will be able to see clearly what forces are in control of civic affairs," Fred summarizes his point for her.

"Of course! But, as you said, there always has to be some campaign issues in the interim."

"Ostensibly," he comments. "But I'm afraid Ferguson is over-stepping the point. He mustn't jump from these findings to politicize the national educational dilemma. At least, not until he knows what the agenda is . . . those powerful boys on the hill will try to make any black mayor, of New York especially, look silly, if he rushes into the situation, prematurely!"

Fred looked up as the councilmen returned to the chambers. Rita left them and walked back to her seat on the panel while he made small talk with Christine, as they cleaned up their trays. The councilmen straggled into the room, continuing idle conversations, before the assembly finally resumed its parliamentary form.

"Well, let's see what the prestigous 'politicos' will resolve on matters germane to education," Christine sarcastically remarks. She wasn't sure if she had 'grapevine information', but it was interesting. "You know, the situation gets worse the further society progresses . . . "

Landers raised his voice over the din, as the hearing was marshalled to order for the afternoon session.

"By the powers vested in the office of president, I now call this council hearing to order."

Fred continued the conversation in a whisper. "Yes, I'm afraid you're right! By the time the industrial complex does it's number on 'higher' education, we're left with an insufferable population which, ironically, is similar to the impact of military training at lower levels."

"The chair recognizes councilwoman Callander's business," Landers commands in his officious tone. "Can we resume the findings of the education committee, without further delay . . . "

"You mean, by proselytizing academic pursuits for professionalism," she says. "There hasn't been a true academic community to speak about, for quite some time, because of that!"

"The problem may get worse in the future, if politics continue on the same course," Fred conjectures. "It's really a lack of a two way communications flow . . . either you learn scholarship and suffer financially, or you train for some type of a career, you know what I mean."

"Yes, I know what you mean. One hand finds it hard to recognize the importance of the other."

Callander had been impressed with Fred's point and drew upon her vast experience to round out a position she felt Ferguson might take within the party. The endorsements were still needed, and he was having some second thoughts about his platform, she would have to speak with him further, she thought. But, now her concentration was directed to the work of the committee.

"Outlined, in front of you, are detailed evaluations of Dr. Julian Frazier, noted child psychologist. He says, the level of achievement by the predominently minority students in the specified school districts has dropped steadily in the last three years. Statistics reflect the poor performance in math, science and english. Dr. Frazier finds inadequate motivation by teaching and counseling staff an important factor affecting this crisis . . . "

"The question of goals is usually circumvented. I'm really concerned about the kind of people we're putting out into the community," Fred remarks, and disgustedly extinguishes the cigarette.

Chapter Eighteen

Fred was busy reviewing the Neilson Report at his desk in the office. It was an impressive document, he thought, as he thumbed through the material. Although he didn't recognize any of the extensive list of contributing Phd's, their credentials seemed auspicious enough. The scholars were professionals within various disciplines in the behavioral sciences, such as economics, political science, sociology and anthropology. It was compiled by the International Society for Development and Training, which didn't ring a bell in Fred's mind. But, once again, the reference sources, which included The United Nations Research Institute for Social Development and The International Research Center, among others, were first rate.

Organized in three major parts; an historical overview, presenting the crisis of urbanization in less developed countries in their attempts to modernize; research findings, presenting principal statistical trends reflected within the cultural patterns; and a final section, offering a comprehensive plan for integrating developments in less developed countries with the modern world, it was a thorough package. Fred was concerned with the economic projections and checked the index on those statistics first. As he reviewed the complex charts, Lloyd emerged from his office and walked to the desk.

"I just got a call from Dan Coleman."

"What does 'Mr. campaign manager' have to say," replies Fred, momentarily interrupting his concentration.

"Chalk it off to overhead."

Fred lit a cigarette and marked the page with a piece of scrap-paper.

"Is he kidding? With all the duckets those folks are spreading around, he can't be complaining, as small as my stomach is, these days . . . where do those cats get all that dough, anyway?"

'You look better tailored in your clothing at that weight. We don't want you to get too fat, you know," Lloyd says, and shifts Fred's emphasis by perusing some material on his desk. "Says Ferguson should have more civic coverage. We want more radio. Have you got anything in mind?"

"Let me think . . . maybe something in Brooklyn. I was discussing the Restoration Project with Callander and him about two weeks ago. The theater presents some real good performances, and he hasn't been to a play in a while, he says . . . what do you think?''

"That's alright . . . That's good! Something like that, over there, could mean a great deal, right about now. What's playing,"Lloyd queried, to make conversation.

"Fortune in Men's Eyes. Have you seen it?''

"When it was playing uptown in Harlem. Out of sight . . . see if you can get somebody to write a few articles on that. The civic aspect . . . ''

"Let's see what Jimmy can do for us," he suggests, and inhales deeply on the cigarette.

"Okay. Remember, the weekend is an important spot for that.''

"Editorials?''

"The community approach," Lloyd says, curtly. "Perhaps something from a student, or somebody in the neighborhood.''

"Perhaps Lester could be helpful . . . ''

"Did I hear my name?'' Les approached the two men in a relaxed manner, carrying several portfolios under his arm. He rested the material on the desk and joined the conversation.

"We need some type of an article from the young folk for the weekend edition,'' Fred outlines the assignment. "Ferguson's planning to become more active in cultural affairs in Brooklyn, and we want to set a prelude with his visit to the Restoration Project. It would be good to get feed-back, you know. The college lowdown on his impact upon civic affairs in the neighborhood.''

"An article about Ferguson as a patron?''

"We want to keep the arts alive in people's minds, Les,'' Lloyd adds, patiently.

"Yeah, I know somebody that can do that.''

"Fred's going to work out compliance for the weekend edition,'' continues Lloyd.

"Just don't go and get some political science major.'' quips Fred.

"I know what you mean, brother,'' says Les, and winks knowingly.

"Avec une petite finesse,'' Fred cautions. "What else is new, Les?''

"My 'ole lady' hit the number!''

"I think this is where I came in,'' Lloyd sighs, as he leaves the two, grinning like chesire cats.

Les took the reprieve from work as an chance for relaxed conversation and sat on the desk. "The comptroller's office extends congratulations for our balanced coverage, thus far.''

"Everybody's expecting a tight budget, you know!''

"I guess Ferguson will be wrapped up in a financial snare drum for awhile, trying to iron out Bailey's incompetent administration,'' prophesizes Les.

"Changes in city administration tend to follow the national scene, in that respect,'' Fred observes. He stood up to stretch his body, as he smoked the cigarette. "That's why it's so important for him to get immediately at work on other priorities, and let the white collar boys downtown do their thing. There's a way to balance books.''

"Of course. But people are always forced into the trap of viewing administrative changes solely in terms of of their pocket books,'' Les counters.

"You'll have to include me amongst the proletariat!''

"Aw, come on now, Fred. That guise of a lower east-side hustler is like the little old rich lady who starved to death,'' Les comments, laughing at the joke.

''The family name just doesn't hit the register, but the form is quite similar . . . ''

''I'm not at all surprised at how easily you make that connection,'' Les criticizes. ''But, then, I suppose when I become rich and famous, like yourself, this will all become clear to me . . . ''

''Always make a point of developing your tastes, my friend,'' Fred glibly remarks.

''And when, or where do I find time to do that?''

''I started to tell you to work on Chris, to get more inside dope that we need so desperately. But, I imagine that would be too awkward,'' Fred teases him

''Shit, if you weren't behind the black belt, I'd be coming across the table at you!''

Fred laughed and crushed the cigarette in the ashtray. ''I beg your pardon, but I bet you'd be a bad number!''

''Hmm,'' Les grunts. ''Am I supposed to be flattered?''

''My friend, one day you'll wake up and see it's very hard out there . . . ''

The conversation was interruppted by the secretary, carrying work assignments to the staff. As the two men paused, she studiously thumbed through the portfolios on the desk, replacing completed materials with those in her arms.

''Hi, Wanda, how're you doing?''

''Okay, Les, what's to it?

''Nada!''

''These are due back in the library, Fred.''

''Ah me nana, me lito linda,'' he responds, in a flirtatious manner.

''Gracias,'' Wanda replies. ''Esta bien, hermano?'' She smiles, winks and turns excitedly, leaving in a tempetuous hip swirl.

''Is the governor likely to endorse the candidate,'' asks Les.

''Probably. Once Ferguson is past the primary and gets out there on the campaign bandwagon in full swing,'' remarks Fred. ''I expect that'll come late in the game . . . Executives have to reserve their commitments to insure favorable alignments, right?''

''Well, at least that will be an additional plus, whenever it comes. I wonder what kind of reservations he would have, if Ferguson were running as an independent?''

''You know, with a mind like yours, I can't see why you didn't go into law,'' badgers Fred. ''Come on now, this is New York . . . he's worked that democratic machine as the only way to amass a viable coterie. It's traditional. But, your question raises something else in my mind. I mean, even considering the times, where does a black man get all of that campaign backing?''

''Don't anticipate worms in the wood, my friend.''

''It's just an inquisitive imagination that I'm sharing with you, Les. Although Ferguson has tremendous popular credibility, it's really a monstrous proposition to run in this city,'' Fred exclaims. ''there must be some powerful sources behind his contributors. All of them are not progressive, I'm willing to gamble.''

''You're teasing my mind, Fred. What do you know about it?''

''It's a big question to me, too! Lloyd won't let me in on it either . . . I think we should know, though. Why don't you inquire and see what you come up with . . . off the record, of course.''

"If I find time to do that, I'll write a book," quips les.

"There's nothing wrong with that. Something like that would probably hit the best sellers list. I find it very fascinating, don't you?"

"Hmm. I'll look into it. Well, how're the hearings proceeding? Rita get finished, yet," he asks, to change the subject.

"Almost. She paved a way for Ferguson's proposed plan. Now we can sit back and laud her performance. She's another one who missed their calling," Fred comments. "I see theatre written all over her, and, apparently, she does also! Those chambers probably never housed such oration!"

"I did feel as if I were at an amphitheatre. The Acropolis, perhaps," Les jokes.

"Well, she doesn't spare any bones about being 'on stage'. And that's what makes her delivery hold so much impact. Has she commented on her screen image at all."

"Hasn't she told you she wants copies of all the footage sent to her agent," Les laughs. "I'm surprised she hasn't found her way over to the viewing room it sit in on the editing of the stuff for T.V."

"She makes an especially good public servant, though."

"My girl, Rita . . . you sure got that right! Another old timer who's finally got to see some light . . . I wonder wht she's going to do when she leaves the public eye." Les remarks in a serious tone of voice. "Women have a way of disappearing, once they terminate their political careers."

"To me, she's been one of the most powerful councilmembers to speak about. There's a subject for another biography, Les. What could be more appropriate for a black public relations man to write about, than the black women politicians? It has that special ring to it that would sell a million copies in the first year, man. I'm not joking, now," Fred coaxes. "We need that kind of documentation! The only reason I drop these ideas in your lap and don't do them, myself, is because of the types of approach a cat like you would give something of such importance, you dig?"

"One at a time, though. I don't know if I'd be so good at expose!"

"Well, see if you can find anything about the power behind his big backers for me, will you?" Fred left the probe at that point. He knew Les was a persistent 'go-getter' who would work arduously on the favor and, perhaps with luck, would solve the mystery, where for him, there was only closure.

"That sounds like a hard nut to crack, but I'll give it a try, sport."

"Lloyd probably wouldn't want me to have that kind of information anyway, because of the type of company I keep," Fred confides, surreptitiously.

"Well, is there anything else on the wire? If not, I'm going to try to keep some of these appointments on my schedule."

Les raised himself from the desktop and eased away, as Fred turned his focus back to the Neilson Report. Opening the document to his page marker, he resumed his perusal of interesting research information awhile, then stacked the material into his attache case. His immediate curiosity was satisfied. He straightened his desk, piling folders neatly together, and prepared to leave for the day. Fred checked his watch. The secretary passed in the distance, disseminating work to ther employees, as he hurriedly grabbed his attache case and scurried to intercept her. He was already behind schedule and was rushing, again.

"Wanda, I'm on my way downtown, should anybody call for me. There're some letters on my desk that have to be typed, when you get time . . . oh, I've taken the Neilson Report with me, in case you should be looking for it."

,"I've got you," she says, confidently. "Is that all, or is there anything else?"

"No, that's all. I still haven't gotten up enough courage to tell you what I want to say to you, doll baby," Fred responds, teasingly.

"Ah, shucks," Wanda exclaims. "I'll probably grow a moustache waiting for you to find the right pretext, old man!"

"I'll be you agent, if you do," Fred says, affectionately, as he smiles and blows her a kiss. "We're bound to make a million . . . "

"Kiss mine," she retorts, dejectedly, and rubs her rump.

Fred left Wanda to her chores of delivering work to the desk tops of the dozen, or so, busy employees. The wire service activated while he walked out of the exit, adding the distinct clicking of the machine to the din of office work, as the dispatch was automatically printed.

"MUTUAL BLACK NEWS, January 18, 1964
Caribbean Report: Offical sources in Martique disclosed an agreement today between Consolidated Broadcasting Company and the island's recently established government. George Hernandez, Director of the government's Information Agency said plans are in effect to begin limited operation in the Fall of the year. ed. ASP/FY exclusive.

Chapter Nineteen

It was cold again in Fred's apartment where he was busily reading the Neilson Report. Several reference books and esoteric literature were spread on top of the newly stained table, crowding the portable typewriter. Garbed in a comfortable sweater and slacks, Fred sat making notations for further investigation. He had been working all evening and was tired from the tedious mental activity of research. He took a break and went to the refrigerator to get a cold beer. He returned to the living room and flipped on the FM receiver and television for relaxation. As he made himself comfortable in front of the T.V. with the relaxing sounds of jazz filling the apartment, there was a knock on the door. The late night news show came on with a lead-in on the city council hearings. Fred hesitated until the commercial break, before answering the call. He found Jomo and Les at the doorway, bundled up for warmth during their nocturnal carousing in the winter weather. They entered and made themselves comfortable, unwrapping and settling down in front of the T.V..

"What's coming on the news, man?"

"An insert of Callander's final presentation, Les. What's up people?" Fred didn't mind the company. It broke the monotony of continuous reading.

"I'm tired of this thing now, man. I can't wait until it's over," Jomo comments. "Say, have you got another brew?"

"Check out the box . . . you want one, Les?"

"I don't mind if I do. Nothing like a cool brew for refreshment . . . "

"Wait a minute," interrupts Fred. "Let me see how this piece looks."

The commentator apeared on the screen as Jomo returned to the living room with two beers. He gave Les a can and, they watched, silently engrossed as the story was presented.

"Today Councilwoman Rita Callander concluded the educational committee's findings during city council hearings concerned with various problems in the municipality. She stated in her report that the Black Teacher's Caucus is calling for an immediate response to their grievances with the Board of Education's policies and is threatening a city-wide walkout, pending the outcome of the hearings. We switch now to an exclusive coverage of today's proceedings.

Rita's face filled the screen like a softly lit portrait.

"As a result of these findings, Mr. President, the educational committee rec-

ommends complete restructuring of the city's educational system. In view the gravity of social malaise forthcoming from an oversight in corrrecting present dilemmas
in this key institution, the committee advises the council not to weigh its action
solely upon the difficulty of such a comprehensive project . . . ''

The television screen switches back to the commentator.

''In further news on the crisis, Councilman Ferguson, candidate in the city's mayoralty race, disclosed he will present a proposed plan to resolve the educational
dilemma during the continuation of the City Council Hearings, tomorrow.''

Fred got up and turned the television off.

''That wasn't a bad piece,'' says Jomo, as he rubbed his bald head. ''It could've
been a little softer, though,'' he criticized his photography. He was a sensitive
craftsman. Sometimes even picky. ''I should have used the other lens . . . ''

''I thought it was alright,'' Les comments. ''You didn't want to get too theatrical
with her presentation. It would've taken away from the poigency of the message,
don't you think, Fred?''

''Yes, and no. We could begin to expose the television audience to artistic persuasion quite early, you know!''

''Cinematographically speaking, we would have stood a better chance of touch-
ing upon audience sensibilities the other way,'' adds Jomo. He understood their
public relations concerns purely in artistic terms. ''You know, personalizing and
such,'' he says. ''That's what you wanted, wasn't it?''

''The nail on the head! That's exactly what I mean, man. The people have got
to have a very direct involvement with this issue,'' Fred remarks, enthusiastically.
''Our chances of success increase, immeasureably, if we can attune the folks to our
work through the personal dimensions, more often. But, it can't be too
obvious . . . ''

''If we get too camp, the whole show is up in the air as blatant commercialism,''
interjects Jomo. ''And if we get too artistic, there are bound to be a lot of 'art-fart'
critics generating adverse propaganda to our progressive images.''

''Literally,'' Fred exclaims. ''You've got it one hundred percent right!''

''Shit! I'm really sorry I didn't go with that angeniux lens,'' he reflects,
disgustedly.

''Don't worry about it now, Jomo,'' Les consoles him. ''Just go with your intuition in the future. The likelihood is that you'll probably be reading into Fred,
anyhow. Do you agree?''

''Yes,'' Fred replies. ''Moreover, if there are any interpretive questions, don't
hesitate to let me fill you in.''

''You know I'll always check with you, if a situation comes up,'' he says. ''I
don't know why I didn't go with that angeniux in the first place.''

''Well, think about the things you can do with Ferguson,'' comforts Fred.

''There's a whole lot of innuendo you can explore with him. Everything could
be shot in extreme close up, letting us see that no sweat exudes from the pores of
our 'super savior','' laughs Les.

''Or cropping everything to frame just his mouth, so we can be constantly exposed to his compelling smile,'' jokes Fred, as he displays a set of perfectly formed
white teeth, in mock charature.

''Figure the candidate's pearly whites, huh,'' Jomo comments, catching onto
the humor.

"That's one way of approaching the personal side of the man," quips Fred.

"Could you imagine his whole delivery tomorrow, shot as a commercial," Les interjects. "That would be too much, wouldn't it?"

"It may have been better to introduce these promos much earlier in the campaign," Fred reflects, changing the tone of conversation to more serious matters. "Then, the commercial aspect wouldn't seem so bizarre in contrast with the documentary style . . . That's a good point, Les!"

"I don't think he's going to present too much trouble," Jomo remarks. "The only thing I'm worried about is his pacing. I suppose you'll remind him of his camera image, again?"

"I'll do all I can, man. But, you'll still be left with your own resources, I'm afraid."

While they discussed the technical and artistic considerations of the assignment, an exciting jazz recording was broadcasted by the FM station, filling the background with pleasant music. The conversation lulled while the co-workers listened attentively to the melodious sounds emitted by the radio. A relaxed mood captivated the atmosphere, changing the interest of their discussion.

"That was McCoy Tyner, wasn't it," Jomo asks, appreciatively.

"I think so," says Les. "The disc jockey isn't doing so much rapping, but I guess he'll come back later on, to fill us in on the jam . . . sounds pretty fly!"

"I think that was him," Jomo comments. "He's got a distinct sound, you know what I mean?"

"Yeah, unmistakeable," he reflects.

"Sounds like he should be getting onto some more wax, Fred."

"I don't even know him, Jomo," teases Fred.

"What about Doc? He ought to be able to work something out," Jomo persists with his interest.

"Probably," he says, somewhat disinterestedly. "But, I'm interested in new talent. He's undoubtably making out alright, anyway. What I'd really like, is to vamp on the young boys from D.C."

"Is that right?"

"Everytime I go there, Jomo, I hear some decent sounds."

"Say, excuse me for interrupting, Fred. But what does the National Association of Broadcasters have to say about the court situation in Washington?"

"Ah, man, they don't want no parts of us. It's like having the flu or something, when nobody wants you to come around, Les. They're pretty much out of the picture thus far, but Elaine figures they're behind the scene supporting WKBC-TV. You have to anticipate those organizations closing ranks at this point. In a situation like this, once you introduce a class action suit, the snowball effect threatens the entire industry . . . so, since they can't move the house, they'll erect a high fence, right quick."

"Any offers to settle the situation," queries Les.

"A few program changes, some additions to personnel . . . but, nothing as far as management or administrative policy. What can I tell you," Fred concludes, briefly.

"I can't understand it myself," interjects Jomo, half interested with their concerns.

"That's some pretty determined shit for a company to do in a city of seventy percent black population," observes Les.

"Means nothing," Fred reflects. "They've had a black mayor for awhile, too! But it's still the nation's capitol! Pressure from interests are on a larger scale. So the trade-offs are different. I'm really surprised at what does get done there, under the circumstances."

"You're talking about the local racism, huh?"

"Hey, Les, I've never seen anything like it. That city is tighter than a convent!"

"Well, I hope Elaine is successful in toppling the bastions of the communications industry, there. After all, the city does represent the seat of power in this country," Les remarks.

"All I can say is that I'm not interested in a studio gig when you people pry open some equal opportunities," Jomo comments, dryly, with a blase attitude.

Fred laughed at the dig. He recognized his companions aversion to large groups. It was a peculiar idiosyncrasy.

"What did you say, Jomo? No inside work for you, huh?"

"I thought you folks were ready to give up on the challenge," Les continues. "Is that accountant dude still running the show?"

"Yeah, he's still station manager," Fred answers, then changes the subject. "Ah, Jomo, how do you feel about going to Africa?"

"Are you kidding? I like that better than going to Hollywood, man! Have you got something lined up, my friend? Tell me quick, so I can brush up on the appropriate language . . ."

"I know you're not kidding," says Fred. "No, nothing concrete. But, there's a feeler circulating around, which might call for me to make the trip. I just thought you'd like to tag along."

"So pleased that you would think of me. Allah must be smiling upon my good works!"

"Well, if it comes through, it'll be a lot of hard work!"

"Ho hum," Jomo grunts, while casually examining his fingernails.

"I don't know about these 'cinematographer-types'," laughs Les. "There's always a subtle narcissistic air about them. Have you noticed that, Fred?"

"We each have to find the right lifestyle, my friend," comments Jomo, with his home-spun philosophy.

They paused again in their conversation, as the FM filled the room with the sounds of Alice Coltrane. The delicate music from her harp presented interesting variety to their jazz enjoyment, with the soft staccato of strings contrasting the timbre of the hard tonal music of the wind instruments, broadcasted earlier. They remained engrossed until the recording ended.

"I'd like to catch her in a set," says Jomo. "It's too bad she's not making live appearances anymore. Although, I can't blame her, too much."

"Hmm. I know what you mean," agrees Les. "She is beautiful, though!"

"Say, Jomo, could you shoot some stills of Ferguson attending a play with his family out in Brooklyn? We need a photo for a magazine layout."

"Don't catch me on one of my good nights, Fred. I don't have enough time for the ladies as it is, you know!"

"How does Wednesday sound to you," asks Fred, ignoring the humor.

"The sixth," Jomo comments, disdainfully. "Hmm, I'll have to make sure and be extra careful!"

The men shared a brief laugh at Jomo's superstitions, then Fred got up to refresh himself.

"Does anybody want more brew."

"I'll have another," says Les, while Fred disappears from the living room.

"I realize my limits, thank you," Jomo replies.

"That's good, Jomo. I don't want you to get stoned and hurt your eye," Fred jokes, as he returns to the living room with beer. "You'd be suing me down to my underwear, behind that!"

Jomo remained unpreturbed.

"An occassional brew, now and then, my man."

"I'm going to have to do something about this consumption, myself," Fred comments. "That brew is putting a hurting on my midsection . . . I'd better stop, before I get a mid-drift buldge!"

Les got up and disappeared, on route to the bathroom.

"Speaking about ladies, however," Jomo says, changing the subject to his kind of interests. "I'd like you to meet a friend of mine . . . some fat action, man!"

"Really? Where's she from?"

"Down from Boston . . . commercial artist, vegetarian and what not. I think you'd enjoy her company."

"Sounds interesting," Fred remarks, distractedly. "Maybe I'll do that some other time. I've been spreading myself too thin, lately. I'm going to catch up on my austerities."

"I really can't understand that, Baby," snaps Jomo, annoyed at the rejection. "You set a discipline on yourself about the ladies, but yet you sit around guzzling a whole lot of beer. That's really ass backwards to me!"

Jomo had meant to be sarcastic, and that peeved Fred.

"Well, maybe ass backward is a way of life for me, or something," he quips. "I don't know! I'm just feeling that I should abstain for awhile. You know how that is . . . you meet someone, she's nice, so you extend yourself a little. Then, before you know it, that hunger emerges and attempts to swallow you up whole . . . I have to take it easy now, anyway. The old man keeps rattling that forty linked chain in my ear."

"Hmmm," groans Jomo. "I guess I understand . . . just thought I might mention it."

"Are you really that concerned about somebody else's sex life, Jomo?"

"Take it easy, man! I'll find somebody else to turn her on. Shit, nobody meant to fuck with your austerities . . . it's a good thing I don't drink a whole lot of beer. It makes a person vile," Jomo counters, defensively.

"Forget it, Jomo. Maybe the next time I'll have some kind of heavy 'jones', or something. Right now, it's no show!"

"Now that's better, friend! Much more civil in your discourse," he remarks.

"You know what a klutz is," asks Fred, dismissing the friction with a note of levity.

"I wouldn't want to eat one!"

Les entered the living room just then, returning from the bathroom in a sparring mood.

"What's a klutz, Fred?"

"I don't know. I was called that too, recently . . . anyhow, from the context I understood it, Jomo, go eat a klutz!"

"Baby, you sure are vile," Jomo criticizes. "Maybe it's better that you practice some austerities, so you can clean up your house!"

"That's just what I'm going to do . . . talk to the old man tonight," he jokes.

"You rushing us out of here or something, Fred," Les badgers.

"What are you cats trying to put me through, tonight?"

"I think I might try one of them 'ole clutches' too, Jomo," Les teases him.

" 'Klutz, man, klutz,' " corrects Jomo, fueling the double team.

Fred held his head in mock dismay from the two comedians' onslaught.

"I think I was better off by keeping away from you two, altogether!"

"I'm not going to say any more about the matter, but you better not renege on your offer to take me to the homeland," Jomo says, to rub in the rouse. "Les sat right here and heard every word of the conversation."

"I'm here to testify."

"Look, you people can't stay around here giving me a headache," Fred pleads. "I don't have any aspirin . . . "

"You better start meditating, 'toute suite', my friend," Jomo remarks curtly.

"I think I'll have to take my activity up to the Cloister and spend a couple of nights a week in Fort Tyron Park," Fred complains.

"You getting tired of your neighborhood, Baby," Les quips.

"Just some neighbors."

"Look, we'll be running along in a little while. Just drink your brew and relax," Jomo continues the humor. "You can even change the subject, if you want. We're tolerant! Let's see, now . . . what did you make on the knicks? Thought Boston would tighten them up, did you?"

"Not me, but I have an architect friend who you could've put the squeeze on, after the playoffs . . . and he gambles with some heavy duckets. Probably lost a yard."

"Well, I couldn't stand to go speculating that heavily," Jomo sighs. "But I did make a little bit of change."

"On a shoe string, huh," goads Fred.

"It could've been a piece of thread, for that matter. They got over and brought me mine. That's all that matters in my case. I'm not interested in next season's starting five," he glibly remarks.

"Shit like that cheapens the sport," Les complains. "I bet you haven't been to a game in the last five, or maybe ten years."

"Crowds turn me off when I'm not working! Doesn't make too much sense, when I can sit in front of the 'boop-tube' for a re-run," counters Jomo.

"Speaking about the tube, though," Les says, changing the subject with the after-thought. "Isn't it interesting that so many local T.V. operations are beginning to proliferate. Look at the Star, in North Carolina and Miami. That's a pretty nice venture for a newspaper of its size . . . "

"Well, there's always an opportunity in the district. You know, there are some formidable businesses in Washington. The potential is there. All that's needed is the completion of the mass transit to alter the nature of the city, if anything is going to have a dramatic planning effect. The same thing is true of Los Angeles, although the iron horse is easier to construct in places like San Francisco. The point is, with more people moving around the inner city, the parochialism breads down. Aside from financial considerations of life-styles, the level of maturity helps diffuse a cosmopolitan attitude. Although, in D.C. I'm sure the extraneous influences don't want to deal with anything like a New York," Fred comments.

"It just goes to show you how things change, because the reverse is occuring here," Les remarks. "There's more activity, yes, but as I see it, the tendency is to use a lot of discrimination, nowadays."

"Does it seem that way to you? I can't imagine that kind of sophistication in New York among the 'flower' generation," criticizes Fred. "But, it's true, discernment is really a question of proper individuation in the growth process. That's the essential point of education which, unfortunately, the Board of Education has killed in this city."

"That's what I'd say," Jomo interjects, to continue participating in the conversation. He wasn't really interested in the subject, but figured he'd express a comment, even though offhanded. "There's really few things being done in the streets these days, except for the dudes hustling . . . things are pretty quiet in the big apple."

"Time for people to leave, I guess," reflects Fred. "A person can outgrow a situation."

"How about you, Fred? When are you going to make that move?"

"Whenever I do that, Les, it'll be to Martique."

"Hold on there, fellah! I'm not going to let you off the high horse so easily," says Jomo. He had found an opportunity to resume the tease which he found relaxing to his temperament. His mind-set didn't work overtime on intellectualism about the obvious constraints of the common man. "You said, in front of this man here, that you were sponsoring me on an extended tour of Africa. Now, what's to it?"

"We can sail there anytime the inclination hits us, Jomo! Doc is no 'tired old man', you know."

"The way you talk about them 'Rastafarian', 'Conkie Joe', 'Geiche', 'Creole' muthas, I don't want to be taking them to the homeland! They'd just be despoiling the place! We have to be careful of who enters our shores," he mumbles, with sarcastic humor.

"And, of course your geneology automatically entitles you to a visa," quips Les.

"Keep my passport in the bathroom, next to my shaving kit, so I can see it every morning when I start out, you understand!"

"I hear you, brother," Les laughs.

The FM emitted stimulating music again, prompting a pause in their friendly 'digs'. Fred picked up the Neilson report, distractingly, while the two co-workers listened to the jazz.

"Some heavy shit in here to put together some ideas about international trade . . . maybe some investment bankers might be interested."

Les read the message correctly and starts putting on his coat.

"Oh, really? Well, maybe some other time," he says. "I think we'd better split . . . do you want to share a cab with a Rastafarian, Jomo?"

"All I'm good for is the tip, anyway," he cajoles, as he gets up and straightens his attire. "So, it really doesn't matter who I ride with . . . easy, Baby. Don't work too hard:"

"I'll try a yoga posture for a half an hour," Fred replies. "If that doesn't work, I'll go buy some aspirin . . . ''

Chapter Twenty

The bright photographic strobe light froze the fleeting gestures of the frail chocolate colored lady, as she modeled a stunning silk evening gown, with a delicate flow of sensual poses before the camera. The high fashion layout was being assembled in a tiny boutique on Tenth Street, which was relatively new to the neighborhood. The innovative photographer had positioned himself on the floor to better compose with his 35 millimeter wide angle lens, alongside the confused arrangement of equipment and apparel in the cramped quarters of the dress shop. Fred entered the store during the awkward photographic session and accommodated the assistant's directives. He watched, interestedly until the activity was finished.

"Alright, I think that does it, wrap it up, Chico," the photographer says, as he raises himself from the floor.

The assistant sprang into action, pulling the lighting cables together and replacing the expensive cameras into their cases. Meanwhile, the photographer lit a cigarette for the thin young bald headed lady, and they exchanged small talk as she relaxed from the excitement. Fred approached, unnoticed, while the couple chatted with their backs turned toward the entrance.

"I didn't like that last one," he says, feigning ostentation.

"Make another take?"

The photographer turned and looked at Fred with an air of professional disdain.

"Fred," exclaims Pat. "What brings you to this part of the world!! You know you're only a few blocks away, but with you, it's like we're at two opposite poles of the universe!"

Fred kissed her affectionately on the cheek and looked around at the confusion.

"They let me out of the circus today, so I figured I'd buy a new costume. How's the best designer in town?"

"Just fine darling . . . Oh, this is Nat," Pat says, informally. "Nat meet Fred Murphy . . . Nat's doing a spread on me for Essence. It's a new magazine. Isn't it exciting?"

"What do you know, man?"

"Alright . . . I thought you were some kind of a comedian, for a moment, the way you came on."

"Oh, Fred's just an over critical old public relations man" she says.

"Really," Nat comments with interest. "Well, maybe you can get me some work. I can always use more of that!"

"I already have a cinematographer working with me. He usually doubles up on still work, but I'll take your card."

Nat reached into his jacket for his billfold, as Fred lit a cigarette.

"I've been working like crazy, getting these outfits together, this last month," sighs Pat. "It isn't easy doing a rush job in such a short space of time," she says. "But, tell me, what have you been doing, Baby?"

"About the same as yourself . . . where's Sherman?"

"In the back." She shouts, "Sherman!"

A cool effiminate light skinned Puerto Rican emerged from the back room with a tape measure thrown over his shoulder, holding sewing materials in his hands. Meanwhile, the photographer exited.

"What is it, Pat . . . oh, Fred, I didn't know you were here," he says, smiling charmingly. "When did you come in? You finally found time in your busy schedule to come visit us, huh?"

"What's to it, Sherman. Do you have a moment to fit me for some slacks?"

"There's a shortage of material around here right now. We've been using a lot of cloth to make samples for this shooting, but if you have time, I'll take your measurements . . . you'll trust me to select some out of sight fabrics, won't you?"

"Yeah, sure! You know what I like. Nothing too outrageous," Fred remarks, soberly.

"Ugh, I'm afraid I do! You really cramp my imagination with your terrible tastes," he criticizes. "Well, what have you been doing with your lecherous self, Mr. Fred?"

"This and that!"

"I can imagine, 'doll Baby'," Sherman responds, with a clandestine air of intrigue.

"Say, some buyers finally invited me to show my wares at the Hilton," interrupts Pat. "Do you think you'd like an invitation, Fred?"

"I'd hate to disappoint you. You know how my schedule is, these days."

"Make him promise, lady day." Sherman edges the situation.

"It would sure mean a lot for my status in New York! Plus, you stand a good chance of running into some nice little contacts," she pleads.

"Trying to suck me in on the same work pretext that I'm giving you, huh," he teases her.

"Well, how's a Detroit girl going to throw around any weight in this big New York City? Just tell me that you'll try and make it, because you want to help me out, and if you can't, I'll honor your good intentions, alright?"

"If you say no, I won't have your pants ready for a month," chimes Sherman. "And further, I'll put the word out to have all the girls close up on you!"

"Well, you two hardly give me any alternative!"

"Great," exclaims Pat, happily. "Then, I can count on you coming, if you can?"

"Sherman, I am not going to promise! And, all I'm going to say, is those slacks had better look and fit right," Fred cautions the whimsical young man.

Just then, a barking watchdog emerged from the back room and ran forward toward Fred.

"Down, Major," commands Pat, irritated by the animal's behavior.

Fred invoked Anubis so the animal would recognize his good spiritual forces. He rubbed the scruff of the dog's neck, and the beast responded to his karma and calmed down.

"What do you say, big fellah?"

"Do you see what happens when you threaten this delicate spirit," Sherman cajoles, in a vain display of feminity. "All the forces of retribution are unleashed upon you! . . . take heed, Mr. Fred," he badgers him, while removing the canine to the rear.

"I'm really glad to see you, Fred. As you can see, things have gotten on pretty well, since your last visit," Pat comments. "What about yourself?"

"Well, without going into it, if you don't mind, getting in and out of the city and working on the campaign. What can I tell you, I've been quite busy!"

"Then, relax a moment, while I fix some coffee." Pat walked sensually in the flowing gown toward the rear of the shop where she put on a pot of water. She returned, shortly, moving her delicate frame stately across the boutique with a self conscious display of allurement, in response to Fred's presence. "You know, hospitality demands that the guest reciprocate!"

Fred smiled, graciously. He enjoyed the casual affection that transpired between them. More importantly, he admired her industriousness.

"Where does he get of calling you, 'lady day'," with your beautiful bald head?"

"Oh, Sherman is so imaginative," Pat replies. "Tomorrow he might tell me I look like an African princess . . . you know how crazy he is, sometimes."

"Yes, but that's too fantastic . . . 'lady day'."

"Do you want to hear something really fantastic? I'm going to start school this summer. I've already registered," she says, excitedly.

"No kidding! Where will you study?"

"Fashion Institute of Technology. I'd really like to teach, someday . . . and it's only two nights a week," she rationalizes. "I think I can manage that! What do you think?"

"I think it's ridiculous," interrupts Sherman, returning from the back room. "She should be spending her money for a vacation, or something like that! Can you imagine her teaching a bunch of 'snotty nosed brats' the art of fashion designing?"

"Oh, you can return from the dead, huh," quips Fred.

"Sherman, you're just too damned supercilious," Pat castigates him. "I don't want to spend the rest of my life operating this shop."

"I get the impression that Sherman doesn't want to be left here, all alone," Fred says, to instigate him. "Well, there's always Major to look after and provide you company."

"You're a lot laughs, friend! But that girl has been working her fingers to the veritable bones. She needs to take a rest, not to go to school," he remarks, authoritatively.

"Well, maybe you're right at that. But, may I make a suggestion? Visit Martique, should you decide in favor of a vacation," says Fred.

"Oh no you don't, you two! I've already registered and I'm going to attend," Pat dramatically emphasizes her point, then abruptly leaves the conversation to fetch the coffee.

"What is this Martique you're pushing, Fred?"

"It's a small island in the Caribbean, Sherman."

"What's so exciting about Martique," he inquires, curiously. "I mean, island hopping is no new fad!''

"Well, just because it's no longer a popular tourist resort, a person can spend a very enjoyable vacation, without the normal ostentation from the travel agencies, you know what I mean!''

Pat returned with the coffee and rejoined the conversation.

"Sounds very rusticating," she says, as Fred helps with the chores.

"Oh, it's quite developed for its size," he comments. "It's just that the outside interests are minimal. Most of them were nationalized after independence. I think you'd like it, if you spent a month there, some time."

"I could never leave New York for a month, right now. With all of the orders I have to get out, I'd go broke," exclaims Pat. "Besides, when I do take a winter vacation, like I'm supposed to, I might want to go overseas!''

"I see you've caught onto the flair of success," Fred laughs.

"I still think you should consider this school thing more carefully," remarks Sherman, while punctiliously sipping the cup of hot coffee.

"I'll find time to handle it," she curtly replies, to dismiss controversy. "Perhaps you'd like to join me, Sherman?''

"Not on your life, 'dearie'! Those pedantic educators will never spoil my sensibilities! My mind is too precious!''

"Sherman, I think you'd probably make a very fine teacher," teases Fred.

"Undoubtedly! But, the world will never have that glorious experience!''

"Sherman's too damned selfish to teach," Pat criticizes him.

Fred winked at Sherman, as a prelude to his ploy. "There are a lot of fringe benefits in that profession, you know," he whispers, sarcastically.

"I left that petty hustling behind me when I turned twenty one, my dear!''

"No satire intended." Fred puns, while smiling demonically. "I was mentioning it, in terms of vacations . . . that is what we're talking about, isn't it?''

"Well, you two can argue," Pat concludes, "because I'm going to take myself right over to F.I.T., this summer, and start getting it together . . . ''

Sherman finished his refreshment and raised himself from the chair.

"Does anybody want more coffee," he says, disdainfully, while walking toward the rear of the store.

"Not me," replies Fred. "I've had enough caffeine for one day. That, and your conversation, will just give me indigestion!''

"The next time Major attempts to mess up one of your suits, I hope nobody's around," he retorts. "How about you, Pat . . . ''

"Alright, just half a cup, though!''

"Did you rearrange the walls in the back," asks Fred. "It seems a little congested, for some reason."

"Oh, heavens," Pat exclaims. "I forgot to have the assistant replace that rack of clothes."

"Maybe I can help you with that chore."

"Never mind, I'll get Sherman to do it."

"You're going to display enough designs in the show, I hope."

"I made seventeen. But, I think I'll only use eleven and keep the rest as back up . . . I want fresh designs available for anything else that should arise. It's a good practice, I think."

"It is a good practice to always be ahead," says Sherman. "Don't you think so, Fred?''

"You can't beat it," he replies. "Eleven pieces seems like a fair amount for a new comer to display, considering the interest of the designs, of course."

"Go browse through the rack and tell me what you think of your preview," she jokes.

"If what you're modeling reflects the quality of the others, I like your style, Pat. You'll probably knock them cold with that unique touch . . . young new talent hits the New York fashion scene, and stuff like that . . . "

Pat laughed at Fred's humor. "I'll be lucky if they mention my name in the news, at all!"

"I'm sure they will," Fred remarks, encouragingly. "On that scale, there are only a few opportunities for Blacks. It's almost imperative that they give you some decent coverage."

"We're counting on you to use your influence in the matter," Sherman interjects, dryly.

"Well, I don't know anyone in the fashion world, personally. But, I'll make a point of calling a couple of newspaper contacts, to set the stage for you," he says, supportively.

"You're such a darling!"

"I bet you tell that to all the guys."

"Only the very special ones," she says, coyly. "The rest are just 'sweeties'."

"Oh, this shit is so nauseating," exclaims Sherman. "Excuse me, please," he smugly remarks, then disappears into the back room.

"He's so bedeviled," sighs Pat, with frustrated concern. "I just don't know what I'm going to do with him."

"You might get him to work on some maternity clothes," Fred replies, with biting sarcasm.

"Can you imagine 'ole' Sherman working on some pregnant women's garments? That's a scream," she laughs.

"It might serve to strengthen his lip," he says. "It is a bit unrestrained, I'm afraid?"

"He just likes you, Fred. It's his way of showing affection."

"I like Sherman too. Qualified, like he relates to children," he snaps.

"You shouldn't be so sensitive. He's just confused, but you have no excuse. You know better!"

"Well, if I do, I'm not setting a good example for Sherman," Fred replies, "Perhaps, the best thing for him is a good reading of the book of Leviticus, chapter 18 in the scriptures!"

Just then, the door opened and a neatly dressed young Muslim courier entered, regimentedly carrying a bundle of newspapers.

"Your copy of Muhammad Speaks, Miss!" He handed Pat a paper, then turned his attention to Fred. "Do you care to purchase the latest copy of the Messenger's word, Sir?"

Fred reached into his pocket and produced some change, which he placed in the young man's hand.

"Thank you. The blessings of Allah be with you," he says, and turned very pompously and exited.

"Who was that," asks Sherman, poking his head out of the back room.

"I just purchased an exclusive copy of the message for you. Do you care to read it now, or will you wait until you have to use the john, Sir," Fred mocks, humorously.

"Oh, those folks can be so annoying, sometimes," Sherman says, as he returns to the front of the store, again. "I wonder if they intend to build a Mosque in this neighborhood?"

"Well, it would give the community additional variety," Pat comments, matter of factly

"I don't know, Sherman," Fred replies, while smothering his laughter. "But, it seems they're about to open a bank uptown in Harlem."

"Why? Aren't there enough black banks uptown, already," quips Sherman.

"It has to do with tactics," he says, authoritatively. "The few other establishments are traditional corporate attempts, whereas, the Muslims would be tying banking into economic programing. It's just a different kind of propaganda about life in the ghetto."

"When did you get your X, Fred," Sherman puns, caustically.

"I'm familiar with Semitic languages. I've been in contact with the Muslims, as they choose to call themselves, as well as with Rabbi Smalls and the Black Jews, uptown. If you've read the Bible, you would understand that their religous forms derive from the same cultural root in the old country. I don't need to carry a card, or profess their beliefs. I've made my choice. What about yourself?"

"I dropped my religious affiliations when I was in high school, my friend!"

"Are they really serious about a bank," Pat asks, gullibly, somewhat shocked by Fred's statement.

"Of course, that remains to be seen," he reflects, "but that's the rumor I picked up the last time I was uptown."

"Well, let's hope they don't abscond with all of the people's money, like other familiar traditions, Fred," quips Sherman.

"Will you ever grow up in this lifetime, Sherman?" Fred had to suppress his laughter, for Sherman had scored a good pun.

"It's just 'mother-wit' talking to you," he continues. "There's nothing like protective thinking!"

"Well, at least they won't be held up every week, like the Chase Manhattan," Pat sighs, reflectively.

"Another bank, such as that, would probably help redirect the 'robin hood' mentality of hoodlums toward other institutional pursuits," Fred philosophised.

"And, how do you propose to do that, Fred? Give jobs in the bank to all of the thugs," Sherman interjects, soberly.

"That might not be a bad idea," concludes Pat.

Twenty One

The day passed uneventfully in Martique, and now the sun poured forth its last rays of heat which made the already humid afternoon, even more unbearable. The tourists found the weather ideal for a variety of water sports, or perhaps took the occasion to tan their pale bodies, laying close to the shoreline. But, for Doc and the governor, the beach was a special reprieve from the cramped and stuffy quarters of the trawler, where they could hold a business conference. The two old men could be seen in the distance, walking at a stately pace toward the harbour. The chauffer followed the men at a respectable distance to allow them the privacy of conversation. The governor walked with a cane and occassionally gestured with the stick to emphasize his points. They had chosen to stroll along the lee-shore, in hopes of cooling off with an incidental seabreeze.

After a duration, the threesome finally left the idle tourists far behind them, and entered the more secluded sections near the harbour. They stopped to appreciate the various species of birds which mingled along the expanse according to their niche, as they scrambled for food. Doc was impressed by the governor's ornithological knowledge, as the statesman pointed out the snipes, sandpipers, plovers, and turnstones. The captain had explained that his familiarity with birds was limited to seagulls. They shared a laugh, as they continued their stroll, and were soon at the boat's moorings. After first ascending the gangplank, then climbing down into the hole, the two men were weary and exhausted. Doc took a moment to catch his breath, then began to make the governor comfortable.

"See if you can find a cozy spot in here, Adam. The galley is a little messy," Doc apologized. "But, it's the largest quarter on board . . . "

The governor eased his septuagenarial body, cautiously into a small chair and removed the sweat stained panama hat. "Whew! I don't know about those long walks, Hampton. I must be getting on in age, now."

"Can I get you some brandy, perhaps," offers Doc.

"Put it in some tea for me, huh."

"I figured you'd be moving fast, but I didn't expect you to be going that quickly," Doc continued the conversation, as he walked to a cabinet where the liquor was stored. "Developing minerals could really skyrocket your real estate over one hundred percent. But, what does the survey indicate about depletion of natural resources?"

"Ah, my friend, I'm not about to be entering long term leasing, just like that," Adam replies, defensively. "Through a solid program of agricultural rotation, separate parcels of land could be opened for ten year periods of extraction. I'm going to have another geological survey done by an international team, anyhow, just to legitimate our claims at the World Bank, before I open any doors."

"But, without speaking to the trade commission sort of precludes any speculative investors from making decent offerings, doesn't it? I mean, the whole package could conceivably be underscored in haste," cautions Doc.

"Not so, my friend," Adam replies, authoritatively. "I want an in-depth analysis of the island's total resources, double checked, and hear all bids on mineral developments. That way, I'm sure of talking to parliament with an air of assurance, because I'll have a total economic plan for development . . . what is it you say, youngblood, I don't want to go in there, 'half stepping'!'"

Doc laughed raucously at the governor's use of slang from Black American folklore.

"That's the only way to be, governor! Anything you do has to be done in depth. So, you want to have the whole package ready to present within a year, huh?''

"I think it should be timed to coincide with the next general election. I'm trying to leave office with a stable economic program before the electorate. That way, I can write my epitath into the progress of Martique, you understand."

"Definitely. I quite agree with you, governor."

"Where is that drink you're making for me, Hampton," says Adam, with mock irritation. "A man could die from want of refreshment, in the time it takes you to fix a tardy."

Doc had forgotten about the tea, but quickly moved to the boiling water and mixed up a special concoction. He poured the brew from the pot while continuing the conversation.

"This ought to take the tiredness out of your bones, governor," he says, as he handed him a mug of tardy.

Adam sipped the hot tea with satisfaction. It was part of a cultural vestige that that remained within his lifestyle habits.

"Ah! That's a good tea you brew, Hampton . . . now, something will have to be done with the minerals, once they're mined. I understand you have already looked into possibilities of tying in with Zambia . . . ''

"We did an investor's prospectus for a company in that country. The principal executive is trying to interest the minister of interior in an idea for an international business coterie. The mutual interest in mineral development could be decisive through that liason, so it seems. Fred worked on the package," he says.

"I see. And how is that young man about town?''

"I don't know, 'Governor'. I expected to hear from him, before now, but I suppose they have Fred running everywhere, covering the mayor's campaign."

"Well, when you get started, be sure to send for him. I like his style . . . he's married to Everett's sister, isn't he?''

"Yes. They're not together, though . . . that's why there are hard feelings between the two men. I try not to mention it, too much, even though I'd like to see them get back together."

"A man must make his way in the world," Adam says, reflectively.

"Yes, but 'Governor', it's a little different back in the states . . . a woman gets confused in terms of the space and all," Doc advises him with compassionate concern. "She's a good mother, but it looks as if she's a little on the pressing side, if you understand what I mean."

"Every woman can be pushy, you see. Even though that's not the way it was meant to be! But, it's up to the man to see the situation through to the end," he remarks, paternally.

"Well, maybe you should talk to Everett. He thinks that Fred is taking unnecessary advantage of his sister. They can't seem to bridge the gap and work together smoothly," Doc pleads.

"As long as his sensitivities do not impede upon the performance of the franchise he's got, I have no business in his sibling affairs," Adam curtly replies, maintaining an objective position of neutrality. "What is his sister's name?"

"Helena."

"Hmm. I must remember that one for future reference," the old statesman concluded the subject.

Doc saw it would be of no use to pursue his concern, so he focused the conversation on more germane issues.

"Say, 'Governor', what do you really think about a joint development with Zambia and other African countries?"

"If the man wants to come this way, we can arrange a suitable reception . . . I think I ran into a Mr. Abiola at one of the United Nations meetings of the economic and security council. Must have been several years ago, I think . . . I'll have one more tardy and then, I must run!"

"What did you think of Mr. Abiola at that time," queries Doc.

"We didn't chat too long, but he seemed to be an impressive sort of person. Why do you ask?"

"From all indications, it seems that his public career will net him a position as economic advisor to the government. So, if you know him, 'Governor', perhaps later plans could be facilitated much easier."

"Oh, Hampton, I must know a million faces through all my travels! It could be coincidental. I just happen to remember the name."

"That's alright, too. All that's necessary is your willingness to participate in a joint economic venture. If you can get something like that through parliament, later on, the company could really begin to cook for you," Doc says with enthusiasm.

"Talk about pooling resources through international trade is not new to discussions among heads of states in developing countries, Hampton. But, you know the pressures within the 'super powers' which work against that. There are those who are threatened by industrial development within the third world."

"True! Not only in the states and Russia, but all across Europe," Doc reiterates. "The Common Market doesn't reflect any major difference, either. But, present international events make a ripe situation for changing the market conditions, with a venture like that," he persists with the point.

"Well, right now, it's still a potential historical event," Adam remarks, philosophically. The governor was conservative, at times, and thought more of national development. After all, he depended, somewhat, on his ties with the same 'super powers' which he despised. His experience also gave him a sober hindsight which contributed to his view of the wiley and sometimes chaotic reactions of large scale political undertakings. "I'll have to think about your proposal further. Bring it up to me, soon . . ."

"You don't have to worry about that!" Doc was satisfied that he had gotten, even that far, with the governor. He was usually more tactful with the other old man, but the prospects before them caused the captain to be uncharacteristically forward. "Here, let me gather the ingredients together for you," he says, and begins searching for a pen and writing paper. "Just add a few pinches of jasmine and you'll feel like a new man!"

"You know, a governor of my age shouldn't be making little ones, Hampton. It wouldn't look right for my public image," jokes Adam.

Everett entered the galley in a light mood, just then, and caught the tail end of the conversation. "What's this I hear? Gossip about the first family . . . tsk,tsk!"

Adam wiped the perspiration from his brow, as he prudishly scrutinized the newcomer.

"Mr. Everett, how is the communications business," he says, dryly.

"I'm making headways, Mr. 'Governor', I'm making headways! And how is this summit conference progressing this evening," Doctor?"

"Well, at any rate, it's here tonight . . . talk to me after you've tasted some brew," he says, and points to an empty mug. "It should bring out the man in you, son."

"Then, I'll fill two pairs of pants, instead of the one that I now wear," Everett quips. "Is this what you seduce the leadership of our island with, Doc? I might've known that you'd conduct strategic meetings under the influence of brandy and water . . ."

"Is there always a noisesome tirade that follows you like a typhoon, Mr. Everett?"

"I'll tell you, 'Governor', I'm the baddest of the flock! Wherever I go, there's no rest for the tired and the weary," he shouts, and slaps Adam on the back. "You know, they wanted to bar me from the club for raising the tide in the morning," he laughs, and lifts his cup, quickly gulping the liquid. "But take you two old men. Now, you wouldn't know of the devilment a handsome young man like myself could get into . . . sitting here sipping tardies in the evening heat . . . tsk, tsk, tsk,"

"No, I guess it takes a very special breed to make for the life of a playboy," says Doc, ignoring the sailor's humor. "I'm afraid the governor and I are not that sophisticated."

Meanwhile, Adam's patience with Everett's bombastic remarks was wearing thin.

"Tell me, you wanton Rastafarian, just when is all that equipment due to arrive here," he says, testily. "We have deadlines to keep, you know!"

"Ah, monsieur 'Goveneur'," provokes Everett. "You do subdue the spirit of the hour. No telling what I'll have to account for, between you two patriarchs. Does the administration truly worry that I won't be able to fulfill my franchise," he continues to mock them, as he refills his cup with straight brandy.

"Right now, it frightens me the way you fill your cup," quips Adam.

The governor's sarcasm tickled Everett, but he choked in attempt to suppress his laughter while drinking the liquor.

"Now you remind me of Mr. Truman . . . have you ever been a young man, or did you come out of the box ready made with a walking stick, to spend your old age tending the government from a chair?"

"It's good to have something to cuff the young ones with," he responds, while rapping the cane threateningly on the table. "Now, about that equipment," Adam repeats, adamantly.

"Since I can't be diplomatic in the company of you two older gentlemen, I'll accede to your intimidation . . . the equipment should arrive via Jamaica by the end of this month, or the beginning of the next, at the latest . . . but, it'll take a month for installation and testing," he reports, more soberly.

"It can't be done any quicker than that, Mr. Everett?"

"You know, yourself, what type of transportation we have here, governor! Until adequate airlines are developed, there will always be a time delay in receiving commercial freight," Everett pleads.

"Well, we'll be ready to test the transmitter, once it's installed," Doc says, supportively, to smooth the friction between the two men.

"Thank you dearly, my good doctor," jests Everett.

The governor controlled his temper well, in the face of the younger man's impropriety. He knew the subtle class conscious resentment that still lingered with many of the islanders, which surfaced oftentimes in ugly ways during seemingly innocuous intercourse. Then, again, Everett was a particular kind of egoist, bordering on vaingloriousness.

"Just you have everything operational by the beginning of the fall," he orders, authoritatively.

"Cot-ton-peck, this man does not believe that I am the Messiah," jokes Everett. "So shall it be done, Mr. 'Governor'!"

Doc was unable to restrain his laughter at that point, and remarks, "doesn't that beat all!"

"Just so you get the job done, my son. Otherwise, there is a certain 'feathertail' from New York who I think would enjoy heading up that operation," Adam says, with cool provocation.

Everett's mood changed immediately from alacrity to depression. He reached for the bottle and dropped the affectation in his West Indian accent when he replied.

"No need for me to worry about that chap. They tell me his credentials are good enough to keep him on the mayor's staff," he curtly remarks.

Just then, the chauffer entered to remind the governor of his schedule.

"Are you ready, sir?"

"Ah, yes. . . well, gentlemen, your company and hospitality has been refreshing," Adam says, and cautiously raises his aching body from the chair. "But, before I go, Hampton, I want you to know that I'm going to need extensive details on those matters we discussed today. So, as soon as I can get a better idea of just what you have in mind, I'll be able to see whether it fits in with my presentation to parliament."

"Think about it in the meantime, alright," he replies.

"I will do just that! And, as for you, Mr. Everett, I do wish you'd pick up on your history lessons," Adam chastizes, then abruptly turns his back and ambles up the stairs, assisted by the chauffer.

There was an uneasy lull, after the governor left. Doc began cleaning the quarters, busily putting away empty cups. He left the half empty bottle of brandy in place on the table. Meanwhile, Everett thought perturbedly about the governor's statement. He scratched his head, somewhat befuddled, and asked Doc a question, uneasily, in an uncharacteristically subdued tone of voice.

"It was Truman, wasn't it," he says, while trying to figure out the enigma.

"No," replies Doc, laughingly. "I think you meant to say Alfred Smith. You see, Roosevelt wound up in the wheelchair, but I think the governor got your message. . . did you test the moorings?"

"As I came aboard. She's stable as can be. . . say, Doc, what the heck did the governor mean about Fred," Everett asks, still in a quandry from the old man's remarks.

"I don't know. You'll have to ask him. I can't read minds, Messiah!"

"Well, I hope he's not popping down here, anytime too soon. Things are just fine without that nuissance around," he comments, argumentatively.

"Ahh, you two are like a pair of sharks in the sea, trying to eat one another up," sighs Doc. "Why don't you talk to me about something else?"

"Why, don't you like my conversation, Doctor? It seems as if my company offends you," Everett teases him. He had gained his composure and resumed the boistrous affect. "Aren't I the aimiable sort," he says, while pouring himself another drink.

"Mr. Napolean will be company enough for you, if you keep on tasting. . . you shouldn't drink brandy like rum, you know!"

"Stop trying to be evasive. You haven't answered my question," Everett pressed Hampton.

"And I'm not going to, either! You're a good sailor, a class A engineer, and that's all I'm concerned with, understand! The other things you can file away in one of your cubby holes, and forget them! I'm interested in men, not a bunch of tempermental sissys," quips Doc.

"Alright, already! I won't ask you again," he says, apologetically. He saw that Hampton was truly irritated and figured he wouldn't get any further information from him in that state of mind. "And for that matter, I won't even walk upon the water for you," Everett adds, to clear the air with a note of humor.

The comic trist served to smooth the tension, and the two men shared a brief laugh as they relaxed once again.

"Say, monkey son, who you bringing to the Independence Day celebration," queried Doc, with a poor attempt at the native accent.

"Aie cabronia! You should see the lass I goin' ta bring to the regala. Make me feel ten pound lighta on my feet, man! A fetha in the air, my friend!"

Everett had become intoxicated with this thought. Not to mention the brandy. He got up and began dancing around the cabin, making a few sloppy calypso steps while holding the bottle of liquor up in the air.

"Goin' ta keep goin' all night long, till de sun come up!"

"Sounds like you got yourself into some more of that trouble, son. Watch out she don't grab you, in all your effusions, you know what I mean?"

"Shucks! Now, there ain't no woman alive going to catch up with an old seadog, like myself," Everett responds, confidently. "I'm very careful, lest I pluck the wrong flower and it goes to wilting on me. . . no, no, my mother, she didn't raise no stupid babies, you know!"

"Well, then, you're all squared away!"

"Right-o you are!"

"I sure hope Janice doesn't show up at the same location where you and your lady friend will be. . ." Doc just couldn't refrain from the antagonism. "That would be too much," he laughs, provocatively.

"Do you just sit around and think up situations, or is that a special short-coming of yours," Everett comments, dryly.

Hampton continued laughing. "You're the one that creates these situations, all

I do is enjoy them from the sidelines, buddy!''

"You, and your American sports-mindedness makes me sick! Everything was arranged perfectly in my mind. Now, here you come along and throw a damper in my plans. . . if she shows up, I know you would be responsible for the foul play, Doc.''

"Don't say that! It would be natural for her to come looking for you on an occassion like that, since she's supposed to be your girlfriend, isn't she,'' he remarks.

"Curses to you! You are an old meddling man!''

"I never claimed to be anything else,'' says Doc, as he lights his pipe.

Everett slammed the cup down on the table and got up to leave.

"Where is that stinking cologne of yours. . .''

"If it's so bad, why are you looking for it,'' he mumbles to himself. Then he hollers to Everett, who had disappeared into an adjoining cabin. "I think you used it all up!''

Everett returned, disgruntled, and says "you used to keep loads of that stuff around. What happened to all of it?''

"Well, as with everything, there comes a point of no return,'' Doc replies, nonchalantly.

"Then, I'm going to say goodbye and disappear into a night of debauchery.''

"Just be ready to pull out by five-bells. . . say the tuna's running about ten miles up the coast,'' Doc orders, as he settles down to enjoy his pipe.

Chapter Twenty Two

The Independence Day celebration was a gala event on the island of Martique. Each year, since the official decree, preparations were begun, as early as a month prior to the auspicious date. Thus, by the eve of the festivities, an infectious communal zeist geist pervaded the tiny nation which gave happy anticipation to both young and old. The islanders were proud of this new chapter in their national history and went about their last minute chores with a strong sense of cultural identity when the day arrived.

The governor delivered his traditional speech and signaled the beginning of the carnival-like celebration at sundown. When the affair officially began, the release of public excitement approached the level of frenzy. Mass singing and dancing occured spontaneously in the streets, accompanied by the lively sounds of calypso music. The governor made a hasty departure from the speaker's podium and rushed to beat the singing, dancing and parading crowds to the dock where he found his favorite vantage spot on board Doc's boat. The revelry continued throughout the evening and, as time progressed, the activities were gradually marshalled to conformity with the formal program. By then, the two old men were comfortable, and conversed intermittently as they watched the affair from a safe distance. There seemed to be no end to the individual and group dancers who performed a variety of cultural renditions, each having a unique interpretation. The steel bands were exciting also, and the people enjoyed the friendly competitiveness between the musicians who strove to enchant the audience with their special talents. The streets were the center stage for the performers, while nearby, little old ladies dressed in shawls wrapped about their shoulders, fed the teeming hordes on the sidewalks. The people had worked up powerful appetites during the celebration and lined up in droves to get their plates filled to the brim with a rich selection of delectable items. The combination of fish, fruit, vegetables, nuts and poultry seemed infinite, presenting inviting pleasure to the most discriminating palate.

Meanwhile, elaborately costumed performers paraded along the dock, as scores of noisy children ran excitedly among the congestion on the wharf. When the fireworks show was presented, the islanders took the opportunity to gather a 'second-wind'. The colorful display was even more impressive on the clear cool night of the affair. The governor enjoyed the fireworks most, and each year remarked how the show had improved. This time his enthusiasm stimulated Hampton to reminisce.

"Ah, 'Governor', this affair makes me homesick for the jazz festivals we used to play."

"Were they as enjoyable as this one, Hampton?"

"No, I imagine I'm just having a little reverie," he says, while leisurely puffing his pipe. "The sets we used to play were more restrained than this celebration. We never experienced anything quite like this, back home."

"Well, Hampton, here it's altogether different. We are accustomed to having all sorts of celebrations, as you know by now. One thing we have here in Martique is a sense of cohesion. Everything that affects the island finds its way into the lives of the population. It's like an extended family affair . . . of course, it is not without misgivings!"

As the two old men chuckle over the governor's sarcasm, a pretty young lady edges through the large crowd, down below, making her way toward the trawler. After beng jostled in the confusion awhile, Janice finally arrives at the craft's moorings. She calls to the two companions as they sit on deck, but her shouts are lost in the din of the multitude. Giving up that approach, she climbs aboard the gangplank.

"I can't even hear myself screaming, down there," Janice gasps, as she pauses to catch her breath.

The governor was surprised by the young lady's unexpected appearance and demeanor, but remained calm and cordial in his official capacity.

"Good evening, Miss . . . a happy Independence Day to you . . . "

"Janice," exclaims Doc. Her sudden visit caused noticeable alarm which he was unable to hide. "What are you doing down this way? I thought you were dancing with the other girls along St. John's Street . . . uh, how are you this evening" he says, while regaining his self control. "Can I fetch you some refreshment?"

"Oh, no, I'm not staying long. We don't go dancing until ten o'clock. I'm looking for Everett," she says, rushing the context of her reply together, as she struggles to gain her wind. "Have you seen him about?"

The governor was still being a charming official and thoughtlessly attempted to help the ingenuous lady, without a thorough understanding of the situation. "Isn't he over . . . "

Doc acted impulsively, interrupting the governor, before the cat got out of the bag. "No, we haven't seen hide nor hair of Mr. Everett about these parts, Janice . . . why don't you search over by the hotel. He might be puttering around the transmitter, working . . . I think you'll have time to get there and back, by ten."

"Thank you, Doc! If he should come this way, tell him where I'm headed, okay."

Janice didn't wait to regain her composure, but was off in a hurry. The two watched, as she was again jostled about in the throng, on her route toward the Hotel Anchorage.

"Oh, I see my friend, Mr. Carter, is putting the straw to the fire," says Adam. "He won't live long enough to get my transmitter working, I'm afraid."

"He won't live long enough to get 'your' transmitter working, you say. Shucks," grumbles Doc. "He won't live long enough to get the straw to the fire!"

"It makes me reflect on my younger days, Hampton."

"Were you a lady killer too, 'Governor'?"

"Oh, this island wasn't large enough to house all of the activity, my friend."

"I bet your memories are all pleasant!"

"It's like I was telling you, Hampton, the island is like a little family, you know?"

"You should tell that to Mr. Carter," Doc says, wryly. "It seems as if he doesn't realize how confining Martique could become, particularly when Janice gets wind of what's going on!"

"Fools like that always seem to lead a charmed life," Adam remarks, philosophically.

"Or have a charmed tongue," quips Doc.

The old timers shared a hearty laugh at the situation and passed it off, turning their conversation to other concerns.

"Did you bring in a good haul for the festivities, Hampton?"

"About two tons of the finest tuna you want to look at," says Doc, as he beams a self satisfied grin. "It seemed like bad weather, there, for awhile, but I'm glad it cleared up in time for us to get the catch in for the celebration."

"Yes," agrees Adam. "We were all concerned that the weather would break in time for the affair."

"Well, somehow things worked out just right!"

"Look there," Adam remarks, excitedly. "Isn't that Deputy Peterson over there?"

"Where," asks Doc, straining to see in the darkness. "Oh, yes . . . is that his wife with him?"

"Oh, my, I can't see that clearly. Don't tell me that this madness is becoming infectious!"

"Well, you know how festive feelings spread through a gathering like the plague! It doesn't take too much for it to catch up to the best of us. So, you'd do well by staying right here on this boat, 'Governor'. That way, you won't be getting into any trouble out there," Doc cautions, paternally.

"I started to tell you that I'm too old. But, I suppose you wouldn't believe me, seeing Peterson over there!"

"Hmm, maybe," says Doc. "But, especially after sipping that tardy I made for you. I know how that stuff makes a person feel!"

"Say, look here," Adam exclaims again. "How do you like that! There is Mr. Carter coming this way."

The two old sentinels strain their eyes to watch the caprice, as Everett approached the craft, arm in arm with his lady friend. He paused a moment, as he escorted the voluptuous female, and took a long drink from a liquor bottle. After wiping his mouth with the back of his hand, he kissed the apprehensive reveler and gave the near empty bottle to a passing stranger.

"Oh, no," sighs Doc. "Now I'm going to get caught in a lie, again. I wish he would keep his affairs away from my boat! He'll have the whole island coming down here, after too long!"

Everett was happily singing a folk-song as he came aboard, ostentatiously leading the shy lady. Doc and the governor gave him the silent treatment, pretending not to notice the commotion.

"Say there, fellow men," shouts Everett. "What are you doing aboard this tired vessel in the midst of the celebration! I should think you'd be dancing in the streets, or something."

Everett laughed at his own joke, a moment, but the two old cronies didn't comment. He paused to gain control of his intoxication, then became more bellicose.

"Say there, you two old men, I'm hailing my credentials to come aboard!"

"Well, come on aboard then, and stop raising such a rucus," grumbles Doc.

Everett responded to Doc's comment with boistrous laughter.

"You know darling, these two are among the island's oldest citizens," he whispers confidentially to the young lady. "But, not because of inhabiting Martique for such a long time, you see. Just in terms of their age," he concludes with a laugh. "Come on now, step lively!"

"I wonder if he believes what he's saying, or is too damned drunk to know better," murmurs Adam.

"Probably a combination of the two," replies Doc. The captain turned to the newcomers and hollered. "Be careful over there!"

"I thought the celebration was for the entire island," says Everett,, as he ushers his date along the deck. "What are you two gentlemen doing up here, when all the activity is down there? Have you gotten out already, and are too tired to continue through the night?"

"We can see everything from right here," replies Doc. "There's no need for us to venture out on a night like this, my friend."

"To hell not! With all the ladies out there looking for some lively accompaniment, you prestigious elders are doing the celebration a disservice by staying cooped up aboard this boat," Everett badgers, in a clumsly inebriated effusion.

"You are forgetting your manners, young man," Adam says, in a sober tone of voice.

"Oh, excuse me, 'Governor'. Gentlemen, meet Sonia. This, of course, is our illustrious governor. And this is the skipper of this fine craft, Doc . . . we all call him that because of the wisdom of his advanced age."

"So pleased to make your acquaintance, gentlemen," she remarks demurely, and beams a pleasant smile to the old timers.

"Now, isn't that something," laughs Everett. "She is pleased to make your acquaintance, and I am pleased to be acquainted with her!"

The governor ignored Everett's ostentation and began charming the attractive young lady. "It is a pleasant night for the gala, isn't it Sonia?"

"Indeed it is, sir."

"Are you tired from dancing, my child?"

"Oh, very much so. My feet ache as if I've walked twenty miles, barefoot," she sighs, subtly eliciting sympathy.

"Well, sit down child, and take a load off your feet," comforts Adam.

Everett became upset by the governor's paternal 'come-on' and fumbled awkwardly to regain his composure. He felt upstaged by the older man.

"Yes, Sonia, take a seat . . . here, I'll pull one up for you."

Doc found the situation humorous and joined in with the fun.

"Are you having a nice time, Sonia?"

"Oh, yes, we two are having a nice time, this evening," interrupts Everett. "Sonia wanted to visit the crew that brought in most of the tuna for the festivities . . . isn't that right, sweetheart?"

"Oh my, Doc, did you bring in all of that fine fish?"

"We hauled that load from about ten miles out," he replies, with a big grin animating his visiage.

"It must've been a fine catch for you," she says, excited with feminine curiosity. "My mother bought several pounds. She baked some and also made salad. It was delicious! Everett sat there and ate most of the bundle."

"I can imagine," mumbles Doc.

"You say?" Sonia hadn't heard Doc's sarcasm, and he quickly covered himself. "Well, I'm glad it didn't go to waste."

"In what section of the island do you live, Sonia," Adam asks, in a friendly tone of voice.

"The North sector, sir. I live with my parents and my aunt," she warmly replies.

"Ah, yes, that's a nice section," he remarks. "I haven't been there in quite some time now. Tell me, do you know Hilda Devoe?"

"Oh, quite well," Sonia answers. "She's a good friend of the family."

"Well, you tell Hilda, the next time you see her, that Adam sends his regards," he says, and winks.

Sonia quickly gathered the import of the message and beamed a broad smile. "I won't forget, sir."

Everett was again befuddled by the governor, who continued to be full of surprises. Unable to outfox the older man with bombastic humor, he groped about in a pathetically awkward manner. "Uh, why don't you let me show you the quarters, Sonia?"

"My, you are in a big hurry, Everett," she testily replies.

"I think we're disturbing these two gentlemen," he says, defensively.

"Not at all," comments Doc, while containing his mirth. "We have all the time in the world . . . "

"Wow, look at that man," interrupts Adam. "I haven't seen a costume like that, since my childhood days."

The foursome turned their attention to a wiry man on stilts, carrying an Independence Day banner as he paraded along the dock. They watched the excitement until the performer disappeared from view, into the darkness. Afterwards, the governor resumed his charming rouse.

"The evening air is quite refreshing, isn't Sonia?"

"Oh, yes, 'Governor'. I enjoy it immeasurably."

"That's good, my child. Now, tell me what you are planning to do with your life when you get older, my dear."

"I'm scheduled to teach school, next year. I'm almost twenty-two."

"Is that right? I hope you have prepared yourself properly!"

"Yes sir," she says coyly.

"Teachers are a premium, Sonia. As you know, many of our young girls have babies very early, before they have time to develop professionally," Adam lectures paternally.

"I understand what you are saying, 'Governor'," she replies, like an attentive student.

The conversation made Everett nervous and he interrupted, obtrusively.

"Uh, let's go below and see the rest of the boat, dear . . . it's really quite spacious inside."

"Oh, alright," she says, irritably, and reluctantly gets up and follows Everett into the hole.

Doc waited until the pair were out of hearing range, before conveying his thought.

"Say, 'Governor', you're doing quite a number on the lad. Do you have any reservations about mentioning Janice?"

"I don't think he will be staying that long. But, if you do say something, try to be discreet," Adam says, conspiringly. "She seems like a nice enough young lady."

"Alright," comments Doc. "But, it's against my better judgement, you know."

"Oh my, Hampton. I'm getting another migraine headache," complains Adam. "Do you have any more of that tardy you made? It's so good for ailments like this."

"Be right with you," comforts Doc " . . . just as soon as those two youngsters get out of the way."

"It isn't often that I get them. But nowadays, they just seem to go right through me, for some reason or the other. They started last year, about this time, and always seem to come upon me when I'm enjoying myself."

"Have you been to a physician about it," asks Doc, with friendly concern.

"I have to get a medical once every six months, but they can't find anything wrong," he replies. "I guess I'll have to do the best I can."

"Well, my old concoction might be of some help in the matter," Doc jokes. "You haven't been ordered not to drink, have you?"

"Indeed not, man! I'd have to find another doctor," quips Adam.

During the pause in the conversation, the activity on the wharf became their focus, once again. The two old men engrossed themselves in the spectacular sights and sounds of the celebration. They watched the affair quietly, and after a short while Sonia and Everett returned from the hole, engaged in a lively conversation. Everett was feeling a lot better, and somewhat more sober.

" . . . And so, I had to swim the rest of the way. And that water is colder than here along the island, you know . . . "

"Weren't you frightened, Everett?"

"Oh, I knew that I would have enough time to swim back to the boat, before the cold made me too stiff. And then, the crew always stands by when someone is in the water, you see."

"That is really scary," exclaims Sonia.

"What is scary, my dear," Adam asks, curiously, turning his attention to the youthful couple again.

"Oh, I was just telling Sonia how I got caught in the Gulf of Mexico when the rowboat capsized," Everett says, with an air of adventure.

"Oh, yeah, that was a funny one," adds Doc. "We almost steamed off and left the old 'blowfish' out there in the middle of the Gulf," he laughs.

"The crew was standing by, luckily," continues Everett, in a more relaxed tone. "Otherwise, this mother's child would have had a long visit with old father Neptune."

"That would have saved us a whole lot of aggravation in the long run, I'm sure," teases Doc.

"I find your humor misplaced, old man," Everett snaps.

"Everett said he might have frozen to death during that time of year," Sonia adds, with a feminine concern.

"I'm sorry he didn't get a chill and freeze up his lip, altogether," quips Doc.

The governor disdained the spar that was emerging between the two sailors, so he displaced the tension by tactfully flattering the young lady.

"Do you like to dance, Sonia?"

"Why indeed! My feet just got to aching so terribly this evening, that I can't seem to continue, any longer."

"Oh, that's a shame," he remarks. "I do so like to see the young ones move their limbs to the music . . . it reminds me of when I was young and chipper. Everyone thought I was the best dancer on the island."

"I bet you were, 'Governor'," she says, demurely.

"Well, that time is over now. It's all I can do to walk from one room to another, without falling down tired."

Doc was still anxious to put Everett straight. He had bitten his tongue while the governor played on the old jealous routine, but now he took the opportunity to introduce his own mischief.

"Say Everett, did you get over to the transmitter this evening?"

"Doc, you see how busy I've been today. I haven't had time to do that this evening, with all of the activity of the celebration."

"Well, if you were fixing to get over there, anytime this evening, you wouldn't be in shape . . . I guess everything will hold together over there."

"I'll go by sometime tomorrow afternoon, after I've had some sleep," Everett says, testily.

"It doesn't matter I guess, since I saw Jan going in that direction, any-how . . . Jan told me that, uh, he was going to check the transmitter anyway, you know what I mean? Seems as if he was, uh, looking for you," Doc emphasizes, with restrained humor.

The captain's rouse worked like a bombshell on Everett, who caught the drift of the innuendo immediately.

"Oh, is that so," he says, soberly. "Well, I guess everything is alright then. Uh, how long ago did you say you saw him?"

"About half an hour ago, I imagine," Doc replies, matter of factly.

"Uh, he didn't say he was coming back this way before ten, did he," Everett questions, calculatingly.

"Oh no, I don't think he'll have time to do that," Doc replies, mischievously.

"Yes, I see . . . well, uh, I think we'll move along then," he says, while getting up rather hurriedly. "Let's be going, Sonia. I think we better catch some more of the activities, before it gets too late. I'm going to have to turn in early this evening, it seems."

"Are we leaving, already," complains Sonia. "I haven't had time to rest my feet, yet!"

"I'm sorry, darling, but I'm on call early in the morning," pleads Everett.

"Alright, I'm coming," she sighs, and tiredly raises herself from the chair. "Good evening, 'Governor'. Good night, Doc. It was nice meeting you both."

"The pleasure was ours, dear," compliments Adam. "Do remember what I told you, and look after your health."

"You two take it easy now," adds Doc, restraining his laughter.

Everett led with a cautious pace, carefully looking about in the darkness, as the couple left the vessel and disappeared into the nights activity.

"Now doesn't that beat all," laughs Doc. "Here, the scoundrel has Janice walk all the way across the park to the transmitter, and she's got to dance, mind you, only to put sore feet on Sonia, running in the other direction."

"The trouble with you, skipper, is that you have no sense of imagination," laughs Adam.

"Aw, heck," says Doc, peevishly. "I can't imagine walking all over the island on a night like this, just because he's trying to play some jive-ass two-for-one. That's for sure!"

"Your life was probably just not that colorful, Hampton."

"I can't complain, 'Governor'. It's just that Janice is such a naive young lady, that I find myself feeling a little sorry for her.''

"What's more important to you, skipper, dancing or teaching?''

"I don't know if I find that so humorous,'' Doc replies.

"Well, I didn't know that you could have such feelings on the matter, my friend,'' consoles Adam. "I must say, Hampton, you're full of surprises . . . for a moment there, I didn't think you were going to remember to tell that poor boy anything.''

"Poor boy? Foolish brat!''

"My, you are frightful this evening,'' teases Adam.

"I'm not going to give it any more thought . . . say, what do you think Pelee is going to do, this season,'' he says, changing the subject.

"Bring in his usual million dollars. What else?''

"Man, I sure would like to see him play,'' says Doc excitedly.

"Shucks, I need a million dollars to take care of these legs of mine,'' complains Adam.

"Well, I have no particular need of a million dollars, other than the fact that I want it!''

"Don't we all, skipper, don't we all.''

"Well, hold on a minute, 'Governor'. I've got something that's worth about half that. Let me get some more of that concoction of mine.''

Chapter Twenty Three

The U.S. District Court was located in an austere building at 500 Indiana Avenue in downtown Northwest Washington, D.C. This was the site where Elaine would wage her battle against two formidable organizations of the establishment. She had guessed correctly that it would be a hectic day and had arrived early enough to secure nearby parking, allowing herself enough before time for last minute preparations. It was indeed, a characteristically busy Monday morning, with a full court calendar and numerous delays. It seemed as if everybody in the city had some legal matters to attend, on that day especially, as crowds of people entered the congested building, adding confusion to the already strained schedule of activities. The several clerks were kept busy, shuttling between courtrooms to transport documents, answering questions, giving directions and following the complex instructions of the irritable judges.

Elaine and the three plaintiffs had waited patiently throughout the ordeal, almost all morning. But, when the case was called, the defense counselors made a motion for an adjournment, claiming a need for more time to adequately prepare their case. Elaine was irritated by the motion and objected, because she felt the defense's strategy was unsupportable. Nevertheless, the judge over-ruled her and granted an adjournment. By now, she was seething, and asked her clients to wait outside while she had some words with the judge. The two men and young lady, all former employees of the notorious WKBC-TV, left Elaine alone to ventilate to the judge in private. Outside the courtroom the group talked shop-talk awhile, and Elaine soon emerged, somewhat more composed.

"They're really uptight about this case," she confided to the plaintiffs. "But, as long as defense has gotten the adjournment, I'm going to do some research at the Equal Employment Opportunity Commission. I'd like to explore some additional material. It must be a very tight case, before I interject the notion of spiritual assassination. So, I want you folks to go over the dates you were intimidated, very carefully. That way, there won't be any discrepencies. I'm going to have to pull the Federal Communications Commission down on improper regulation of programming, so I'll be spending a lot of time working on that."

She began to escort the threesome out of the building, in an unobtrusive rush to keep up with her busy schedule.

"By the time we start serving supeonas on those folks, we should have already established a pretty conclusive background of intent . . . now, let me say this up front. Attempts will be made to settle out of court, so be prepared to deal with that. Should any of you be contacted, note the particulars, but let the opposition do all of the talking.''

''So far nobody has said anything to me,'' remarks Jewel. She was an attractive light skinned lady who had worked as the station's token black news commentator. At twenty six, she was uncharacteristically naive about Black exploitation, although the management had manipulated her vanity about light complexion to the station's advantage in its relations with the community.

''But, don't you think it's pragmatic to talk to them. After all, if the situation can be resolved by keeping us on staff, inside leverage can be maintained to exert pressure on policy matters. Somebody's got to mediate the images being projected to the black community,'' she says.

''No! Let them do all of the talking, like I said,'' Elaine replies curtly. She wanted to school Jewel more thoroughly about the viciousness of the racism facing the young lady, but she just didn't have the time. She knew the importance of the T.V. career to the young lady, but apparently the broader issues that underlay both the communications dilemma and the Civil Rights Movement escaped Jewel's tunnel vision. True, it was a legal matter, but definitely comprehensible. ''Just note the particulars, right now!''

Edward was the oldest of the employees and had been around the station longest. He had worked himself up through the ranks to become a technician, and knew the score.

''You're right, this adjournment is just another stall tactic, but it does give me time to catalog abuses of the spectrum management guidelines, which you're going to need to deal with the F.C.C.

''Good. Then, the next sixty days shouldn't be wasted,'' concludes Elaine.

The group had reached the lobby and stood to the side of the entrance, away from the activity of the pedestrian traffic.

''Look, I've got to run. But, before I go, let's be in contact in about three weeks,'' she says. ''Call my office and have my secretary put a meeting on the calander, will you?''

Elaine hadn't intended to be rude to her clients by leaving so abruptly, but she was still smarting from the outcome of the court appearance. She rationalized that the time afforded by the situation was fortuitous for completing other business early, enabling her to continue research on the Neilson Report. She exited the building and walked the few blocks quickly to the parking lot where she picked up her car. She entered the Mercedes, got comfortable, and eased the auto into traffic, setting out to complete the day's activities.

It was almost four o'clock that afternoon when Elaine pulled the Mercedes in front of her house. Although the subsequent business engagements had been fruitful, she had developed a lingering headache, thinking about the court delay, and was too preoccupied to notice the dark blue rented Ford parked to the far end of the street. Wendell sat behind the steering wheel, attempting to remain inconspicuous, as he watched Elaine enter the house. Now, certain that he had the right location, he headed the sedan back to the hotel to work on his next stratergy.

Elaine didn't take too long unwinding her tensions. She gulped two aspirin, disrobed, showered and settled down with a heavy drink. Once relaxed, the astute lawyer phoned Lloyd in New York, to cool out and gain additional perspective. She needed moral support, as well.

" . . . No, I haven't heard anything yet . . . you mean you're willing to trust my judgement on the matter? Well, thank you, Lloyd . . . there's a sixty day interim period. It was adjourned! Okay, so there are some things that have to be handled that way in proceedings . . . look, if I had that material in front of me, I would be able to do something with it. That's your people's fault, my dear! This sister does work her cakes off. You don't question that fact, I hope . . . but, I'm talking about a weekend visit, at most. It's not as if I were taking a month off, or something . . . no, huh? Well, have you started moving that Zambian package yet? Great! Then, we're all going to make a killing. I'm going to purchase some additional holdings, I think. When that venture returns dividends, I'll be able to buy myself a vacation . . . how's the rest of the crew? . . . he is? . . . oh, don't tell me he's turning into a star salesman too! Why didn't you let Les handle that? . . . Alright, Lloyd, so it's about time Les begins to stretch his wings. That means mother will have to look after two birds, after a while . . . well, that's good . . . I follow you. Do what I can. Bye, now!

Elaine replaced the receiver onto the telephone and reached for her glass. It was empty. She raised herself from the chair and walked to the bar for a refill. After a sip of hennessy, she turned on the stereo to a contemporary music station. Elaine stretched her soft tender body which pressed delicately against the sheer voile negligee, revealing the full contours of her maturing form. Lingering awhile to get a feel of the cool romantic lyrics of Astrud Gilberto, she contemplated the day's accomplishments. The cogitation was brief and, after a few moments, she shook off the muse and went to work on the several documents and reports which lay, fastidiously spread on top of the table. She picked up the Neilson Report and settled down in a chair to study its contents. Elaine spent the rest of the evening researching and cross referencing information in the report and was quite surprised when she noticed the hour. A lot of ground had been covered, but many problems had to be resolved, she thought. Undoubtably, the adjournment was a blessing in disguise, she told herself, while putting aside her reading glasses and entering the kitchen. There was much work to do in the interim, and the time gained would be helpful.

Inside the kitchen, Elaine concentrated on her culinary artistry which was another talent she had mastered. She moved about like a woman familiar with domestic lifestyles, agilely handling the facilities with meticulous precision, and after a short duration, pulled a casserole from the oven and prepared a meal for one. It was at times, such as this, that Elaine felt especially reinforced about her decision to remain single. She was happy with her life and career, she thought, as she sat in the dining room eating, alone, contemplative, capable.

Chapter Twenty-Four

The young children made a flurry of activity playing in the yard outside the day care center. It was lunch time at the pre-school center. The teachers struggled desperately to maintain some semblance of order in the day's schedule while attempting to feed all the youngsters, with their different eating habits. The day care facility had been organized by a group of progressive black teachers who had received funding through the Chesapeake and Potomac Telephone Company, as part of a public relations gesture to address the problems of child care for poor working class mothers. The organization was characteristic of the social programming which was stimulated by the Civil Rights Movement, at that time. The first year of operation had been quite a success, Sylvia had told Elaine in their lunch-time conversation. The women had met professionally and developed an on-going friendship. Sylvia, a graduate of Howard University's school of Education, had coordinated the development of the day care concept and contacted Elaine to have the legal work completed on the proposal. The outcome of the professional collaboration resulted in an informal social relationship which was common to the manner networks emerged in the gemeinshaften community within the District of Columbia. The women had already discussed the more mundane topics about important local current events and subsequently turned attention to lighter conversation.

"When do you think you'll get started, Sylvia?"

"I have to find the right type of building for it to go over, really nicely. Everything else is set, from nurse to kitchen utensils."

"That's wonderful, honey. I'm really glad for you," Elaine comments, supportively.

"Well, starting a private school was always an important goal to me. I see it as a normal step from the various educational projects of today, so I just went ahead and did it! I'm kind of sorry about leaving the day care center though, it's been a rewarding experience," she remarks.

"There's nothing unfortunate in your leaving, sister. The experience provided background for a greater leap. The next step should be interesting to developing your educational ideas."

"Undoubtably. I've always been attentive to the philosophical concerns of my plans. That's one way I can contribute insight within an atmosphere of diverse educational practices. Educating black people is simply more than a 'custodial experiment'!"

"I know. I'm hoping to hear more about it, very soon . . . I suppose I should also keep my eyes and ears open for your housing needs."

"Definitely. That's the only thing that I'm really desperate about," comments Sylvia. "You can do the remaining paper work from the information I've assembled, I guess. But, I've got to get my hands on some decent property for the school."

"Watch out, friend! You don't want to get stuck when handling your property considerations. Real estate can be a little tricky, you know. Demographics, zoning, changing tax codes. . . get someone who's been around here awhile to help you," cautions Elaine, maternally. "Robert Mosses, or somebody like that should be helpful in selecting a nice location."

"Alright, I'll be careful. Do you think you can have the papers ready for me at the end of this week?"

"Within a week! Girl, you sure know how to knock a hole in a tight schedule!"

"Are you kidding me, or are you for real. Elaine, I know that nobody can catch up with your activities, these days, but I'm sure you're just simply busy socializing," jokes Sylvia. "I know how you rich lawyers get around, my dear."

"Pooh! Listen to that girl," laughs Elaine. "I should let you handle some of the engagements I have to keep. That way, maybe I can get your kind of paper work aside, for a change."

"Well, I'm glad you're not in such a bind for time today, that you can't have lunch with our problem eaters. Our menu is quite limited, I'm afraid, but I'm sure our nutritionist will balance your health requirements to normalize that liquor intake, girl," she jokes.

Elaine laughed at the dig. She was accustomed to the local folklore about alcohol consumption among the university alumni.

"That should be fun! Dining with the minor league will probably teach me something about social etiquette which I missed coming up," she remarks.

"Oh, there's bound to be some fun," says Sylvia. "They're quite fascinating. The little people will definitely fill you in on all of the relevant activities over lunch. We converse rather openly, you see."

"Gee, I don't know if I know how to act. Little societies are so demanding," she teases. "Do you think I'm versed enough to participate?"

"If you take your cues from me, I think you can get over," laughs Sylvia.

The two women continued their conversation while preparations were made to feed the few remaining problem eaters. Elaine took interest in the elaborate arrangement of play equipment inside the center, and Sylvia filled her in with a brief story about how she happened to find the material. During her tale, the staff rearranged the lunch tables. Finally, the teachers gathered together those children who had to be fed. Elaine was introduced to the youngsters as a luncheon guest. She made an impromptu greeting to get acquainted with the children and, after prayer, the group settled down to enjoy the meal.

"You haven't been out of the country yet, have you Sylvia?"

"Nothing to speak about. I've done my share of island hopping, but nothing heavy, like between continents. It's something I've always intended to do, specifically in terms of educational matters."

"Well, after a few years of private school, you can swing yourself a consultant's deal with one of the private foundations, or some government agency, and get an opportunity to do both."

"That thought has crossed my mind. But, tell me what other little tidbits you have tucked away under that skull cap of yours, Elaine.''

"Don't eat so fast darling," Elaine cautions an eager little boy sitting beside her. "Oh my, I see you have to have a hearty stomach to keep up at these affairs.''

"As I see it, the trick is to gear your pace with the children's. Their eager curiosity will keep your mature intuition active. So, when you communicate, the learning experience will always be a contemporary threshold. . . now, with that pedagogical advice, I think you should be able to come up with some real nice deals for this poor sister," laughs Sylvia.

"Girl, I'd have to restructure major systems, just for you to explore your educational ideas while visiting developing countries around the world!''

"Elaine, this is a new decade, you know, or has anybody on the hill informed you of the passing of time?''

"There's much to be gleaned from the administration's bag of tricky programs, undoubtably. Yet, there's still problems in the way of fostering exchange, Sylvia!''

"Okay, I'll agree with that. But, there's such a large educational appropriation, comparatively speaking, going untapped, because folks don't have inside information which some of us are more privy to. . .''

"Look girl, don't increase the amount of my homework. . . and what are you doing with yourself this summer, young lady," Elaine queries a shy little girl.

"There's got to be a way of writing around the 'legaleeze' to justify international exchange within grade school programs. People are getting our tax dollars for things that are far less important. . . and travel is such an enriching experience," remarks Sylvia.

"My goodness, Sylvia! You're more audacious than I imagined.''

"Let's not be too circumspect, for education's sake. If the possibility is there, I say let's explore it!''

"Somewhere along the line I missed the fact that the legal profession would keep me continually in school," laughs Elaine.

Elaine had decided to relax the rest of the afternoon, to cool out after her visit, and headed the Mercedes back to the Northwest. She had enjoyed the informal lunch with Sylvia and was in good spirits when she arrived home. Elaine parked the car, and was just about to unlock the front door, when she heard someone call her name. She turned in response to the call and was surprised to see the unexpected figure of Wendell, walking toward her from the opposite side of the street. He had switched cars at the rental agency, in the interim since his initial stake-out of her house, so as to maintain a veil of incognito. He hoped this precaution had prevented his detection. Now, as he crossed the distance to Elaine's door-step, a supercillious grin played upon Wendell's face while his mind reeled with hyped-up anxiety about the intent of the visit.

"My, my, Miss Peterson, you sure keep a busy schedule. I've been waiting all morning for you to show up . . . I called your office, but the secretary said you took the day off.''

"Oh, my gosh, it's you, Wendell," exclaims Elaine, somewhat perplexed. "What is God's name are you doing here in Washington," she says, as she regains her poise. Wendell's presence was unusual, as their relationship was casual and didn't involve a great deal of contact. She hesitated for a moment, as she felt the charm of his animus, and responded by giving him an affectionate kiss on the cheek.

Wendell sensed he had gotten over the first hurdle and relaxed somewhat. Nevertheless, he was sweating, and drops of perspiration gathered on his forehead, uncharacteristically, in the cold weather.

"Sister, you must really have the secret of success. Taking off in the middle of the week . . ."

"Are you alright, Wendell," asks Elaine. "You seem a little excited . . . look, you're perspiring."

"I, uh. . . yes, I'm okay," he replies, attempting to smother the incongruous situation by loosening his tie and buttoning the london fog raincoat. "Well, I guess I have been sort of rushing, sweetcakes. But, I thought I'd try to catch you while I was in town."

"I'm glad you thought of me . . . well, come on in, stranger, and let me make you comfortable," she says, with a warm smile.

Elaine unlocked the oak door to her pleasant tudor home, and they entered the living room. Wendell immediately began to scrutinize the household. His keen eyes darted feverishly around the living room while he made mental notes of the arrangement of the tastefully decorated furnishing, to coordinate plans with the empirical situation. After the brief, but thorough initial inspection, Wendell took off his raincoat and relaxed. He gave Elaine his outer garment, then struck a casual poise, straightening his worsted wool jacket with the meticulous care he was known to exercise. As he milled around looking at the art work and curios, he made thoughtful comments about her good taste to affect additional cover of a seemingly spontaneous visit. She responded appreciatively, in a demure manner, thanking him for his attentiveness to her personal lifestyle.

"Would you care for a drink, Wendell? I have scotch, bourbon, gin and hennessy." She took off her tweed coat and unbuttoned her white sweater, laying it on the couch while he decided.

"I'll have a scotch and water, sugar. You know, I really dig this crib! It's a cozy little nook, and you've made it quite comfortable," he remarks, while casually approaching her work table. Wendell glanced at the materials on the desk, quickly noting some of Elaine's legal folders. He would not have to search very far, he thought, and went to sit on the comfortable blue sofa. He was satisfied, thus far.

"Here you are, Wendell," says Elaine, as she brings him the mixed drink. "I'm going to freshen up a bit, sport. I'll be right back. Make yourself at home. The stereo is over there," she pointed to the expensive mahogany cabinet alongside the wall and disappeared.

Wendell nursed his drink and contemplated about his cover. Now that Elaine had left him alone, it might be good to review his strategy again. He got up and went over to the large selection of records. Thumbing through the albums, he was a little disappointed that she had no jazz. He settled for Roberta Flack, and meditated on his plan—an impromptu social call for some business advise. It seemed innocuous enough to catch her off guard, he thought. The music was soothing, and he tried to relax on the couch. The record hadn't finished by the time Elaine returned. Clothed in a plain yellow cotton dress, she appeared younger and less threatening to Wendell, who was still anxious about her probing his story.

"Wendell, I'm surprised by your visit, of course, but tell me what brings you to Washington? Are you becoming involved in our local political scene, here?

"Naw, you know that's not my gig. Petty hustling is nowhere! Truthfully, I've got other business that brought me to D.C., Elaine. That's actually why I had to see you, before I return to New York." Wendell lies, as he begins the deception.

"Don't tell me you've got one of those rags-to-riches routines. I'm not sure I want anything to do with some grand scheme which leaves me bankrupt,'' she mocks.

Wendell laughed boistrously and wiped perspiration from his head. ''Naw, naw, sweetcakes, you know I'm not the usual black con man. All my shit is up front,'' he remarks.

''I don't know that I can just buy that, friend! I'm well into my thirties and damn sure not interested in some charming pimp fleecing me out of my money. What's your story?''

''Patience, sugar, patience,'' he says. ''You know I've been working a long time to get my business into the mainstream. Well, it just happens I'm finally getting over, Elaine.''

''Tell me about it!''

''Sometimes you can be acid to a man, girl! But, I guess you're always a lawyer first, even though you wear skirts,'' Wendell smiled uncomfortably. He remembered that Elaine was a shrewd woman who couldn't be cajoled, easily.

''I think you're flattering my ego, Wendell, but, I'll listen to you. That's basic to good legal practices,'' she quips.

Wendell hesitated. He had her attention now, and didn't want to slip up with his details. ''I've been offered a big architectural contract by a private home builder, Maple Home Developers. My boat has finally come in. . . if everything pans out the way I see it, I'll be into some heavy duckets.''

''Good for you, darling,'' she remarks, with a serious tone of voice. His impression management was working on Elaine, who refrained from the platonic sexual competition, assuming the sober news of business success lay behind his visit. ''How were you able to come into such good fortune?''

''Well, it's actually not my own pull that got the deal moving,'' Wendell downplayed himself, as he stared into her eyes. ''You see, Yvonne's parents are the type of white folks who were willing to chance letting a token nigger into their private circles.''

''That's one way of getting something done, I'm sure!''

''Yeah, that's what I say,'' Wendell continues, with more assurance. ''You see, her old man is an investment banker and has privy to lots of inside dope. I don't know how many times we discussed minority business problems, but finally he pulled me into the private housing market through his connections with people at the National Association of Home Builders. From there, I made a solid contact.''

''My, that's a big conservative swing for you, I imagine.''

''That isn't the least of it. You see, the greenbelt communities that are springing up around the country now-a-days are linked into a whole economic plan in real estate development which is related to general business decentralization. That shit can mean a stable future for me, for a change,'' he says.

''Well, I hate to sound a sour note, but you may not realize your windfall if this current recession continues. The fact is, national unemployment and poverty might very well reverse the middle class flight to suburbia. That would mean a boondoggle.''

Wendell thought a moment. The deception was plausible, and Elaine had apparently accepted his story as gospel, thus far. He used a ploy, and fed her critical perception.

''I'm glad you mentioned that. It's one of the things which trouble me,'' he cajoled. ''But, at this point I can only rely on hearsay and party gossip.''

"What do you mean, Wendell? I don't quite understand you."

"Well, uh . . . I get a lot of political dope from Yvonne. You know, that's her thing. The Democrat Party and shit! She says there's talk circulating about the coming inflation. It seems like the president's economic advisor's even favor this kind of policy to get more money distributed. If that's true, people will continue to buy houses and indirectly keep me in business . . . what do you know about that rumor, Elaine? You're practically a neighbor to the White House."

"Well, first of all, I don't have direct contact with the inner circles of the administration to verify those rumors. But, if the democrat politicos are right, as Yvonne seems to think, then you have some economic security to look forward to," she replies.

"You think so, huh? . . . well, that's actually the first thing that I wanted to get advice about. You know, my politics are all about profit."

"That's understandable, Wendell. And, for your kind of business, it would be better to do more than public sector contracting. That just amounts to political parasitism. As you know, democrat programs in the inner cities are limited, anyhow. Your opportunity seems more viable, given an inflated economy, for a black businessman with vision to move beyond tax dollar dependency. That situation is the same old story of Pontius Pilate's silver coins . . . no salvation in that!"

"Your insight is like words of wisdom, sugar. for the life of me, I can't see what my black brothers see in all those phony games. It's a waste of time," Wendell criticizes.

"You've finished your drink. Would you care for a refill," asks Elaine.

"Yeah, sure . . . by the way, Yvonne asks about you often enough for me to send her regards."

"Oh,that's a nice way for you to cover-up her tacky manners. What the devil is that lady doing these days, anyhow? Still carrying her paranoic grudge against the establishment?"

Wendell laughed, uneasily, as Elaine poured his drink. He was sensitive to her intuitive remark and tried to avoid providing her imagination with anything she might eventually reflect upon which would reveal the sinister connection.

"She's still a hell-raiser, alright! But, she always thinks of you as a special friend . . . say, sugar, you mind puttng a little water in this scotch for me?"

Elaine responded to Wendell's request without any suspicion of malice and took his glass into the kitchen. Now, an opportunity was available, he thought, as she casually disappeared from the living room. Wendell moved quickly, removing a small capsule of seconal from his pocket. He opened the pill over Elaine's drink and poured the powder into the liquor while cautiously eyeing the kitchen door. Wendell was glad she drank hennessy and coke. The dark brown mixture would veil the drug as it dissolved. He stirred the alcohol quickly with his finger, then leaned back on the couch. He could relax. Seconal was extremely potent and would put Elaine to sleep shortly after fininshing her drink. Wendell continued the same personality affect and beamed a supercillious grin when Elaine returned with his drink.

"Thanks, sweetcakes. Say, listen, I want to impose upon you in another way. I need your services, sugar. do you think you can find time to check out the legal specs on this contract, before I sign my life away?"

"Here it comes again! . . . Wendell, I took the day off, just to enjoy a little quiet socializing and a lot of peaceful rest. I thought you got that message from my secretary," she scolds him.

"Aw, Elaine, don't be difficult," he says, with a low key come-on. He was stalling now, and figured his plan would be completed by employing a little circumlocution. "I'm supposed to be a personal chum, right! It's just a favor for old time's sake . . . look, I'm bound to be coming to you for more formal kinds of business, so it will pay dividends . . . who knows, maybe I can be helpful in connecting you with some of them white folks."

"I appreciate your concern for my welfare, darling, but I think I just have too many clients for me to haggle about finances, right now," she remarks, offhandely. Elaine assumed Wendell was being playful to coax her into work. She was totally unprepared for what followed and fell into the trap of his inducement.

"You mean you're content in your little black bourgeois bubble," he says, dryly.

"Don't play the devil's advocate with me." she quips. "I don't have to be defensive about my legal competence!"

"You're talking a whole lot of bullshit, sister. You know, as well as I do, you can't count on black folks for your future. Sometime or another you're going to have to drum up some white business to really get over," he continues, while nursing his scotch.

Elaine laughed and shook her head. "Wendell, you're a comedian. Here it is, the mid 1960's, and you're still hung up on that silly identity crisis that keeps black folks in the dark ages. We're supposed to be mature, you and I . . . "

"Forget that stupid crap, sister," he interrupts her, "I grew up in the school of hard knocks. What you're saying to me is not the way things happen in the real world." Wendell raised his animus and spoke with a sarcastic tone of voice which he felt would aggravate Elaine. Once she lost her temper, her body chemistry would quicken the effect of the seconal. "The folks just better take advantage of the times now, before it's too late," he provokes. "I haven't got any misconceptions, myself! For me, the important thing about the politics of integration is connecting with a profit. Otherwise, it's the same old shit!"

Elaine felt the surge from Wendell's energy probing her composure. At the same time she was relating to his statement. She reflected a moment, then reached fo her hennessy and took a long drink. She got up and changed the record. The music of Nancy Wilson filled the living room, and Elaine relaxed by the stereo awhile calming her temper. She had suddenly become very angry. There were a few things she wanted to tell Wendell, but thought better than aggravating herself further. Obviously, 'Skinner' was more fascinated with his own greed, but she wan't going to be induced into a confrontation. Elaine was sure of her own position. She had been exposed to the hypocrisy of the system and decided her interests were linked with the future of her people. Wendell could never be convinced that there were more important issues than monetary success. Elaine was frustrated by that situation and was also sorry he had come and attempted a cheap physical trick, for God knew, what reason. Perhaps his relationship with Yvonne was damaging, she thought. So many black men were being intrigued by the fascination of cultural contact, nowadays. Apparently, Yvonne's compensation for the rejection she experienced by her white fiance had a distorted influence upon the way Wendell viewed himself as a person. There was deceit involved, and she didn't want any part of it. Elained sighed and hummed along with the lyrics awhile. Finally, she felt she had more composure and strolled casually to the sofa.

"Well, Wendell, I've decided I'll do the favor, but forget about the other concerns. I think our interests differ. So, instead of making for hard feelings, I'll just see what I can do for myself, along with my black people."

"Damn, Elaine, you're being so contrary! You don't have to be offended! I'm not trying to sell you on my way of thinking," he says.

"Forget it, Wendell. It's not important," she remarks, dismissing the ploy. Elaine took another drink of hennessy and swayed in her seat to the rhythm of the music. "When can you have the contract in my office, Wendell."

"I've got it with me, right here . . . say, listen, sugar, I don't want any hard-feelings between us. Let's keep everything friendly, alright?"

"Wendell, I'm too old for personality conflicts. Let me see the papers," she curtly replies.

Skinner reached into his jacket pocket and pulled out some legal documents which had been drawn up for him to complete the plan. A wry smile emerged on his lips, but he held his anxiety in check. Elaine took the bogus contract and began perusing the details. She was a competent lawyer alright, and quickly found the flaws which Wendell had intentionally included in the preparation. She continued to sip the hennessy while reading. Meanwhile, Skinner kept a close eye on his watch to coordinate his strategy. Elaine didn't have time to complete the third page of the phony contract before the seconal took effect. She felt a sudden rise of nervous energy, but didn't think anything was unusual and continued reading. It was probably her temper calming down, she thought. But Wendell noticed the symptoms of the drug, as it quickly began to take effect upon Elaine; drops of perspiration gathered beadlike on her forehead, lethargy was making her dizzy and she struggled to maintain equilibrium. She rubbed her eyes repeatedly to keep clear visual focus while Wendell waited eagerly for Elaine to collapse. Finally, she succumed to the seconal, as a black veil suddenly descended upon her, shrouding her consciousness. She slumped in her seat, dropping the papers on the floor, as Wendell grabbed her to prevent an injury. He laid her limp body length wise across the couch, carefully placing her head toward the inside of the sofa. He figured he had about an hour to find what he was after and, if Elaine awakened unexpectedly, there would be momentary disorientation which would give him time to cover up.

Wendell went to the work desk, his keen mind alert for details, and began a very methodical search of Elaine's private papers. He looked through several documents, quickly putting aside material that was irrelevant for use by the party. Wendell spied the Neilson Report which gave him interim satisfaction in his quest to sabotage the organization. Apparently Yvonne had guessed correctly, he thought. Transcontinental Media Promotions was a very thorough company. Lloyd would undoubtably have this information in New York, also, Wendell figured. Thererfore, Yvonne's plan stood a good chance of success. He hoped TMP would swallow the bait, but he couldn't speculate. He would have to see where the company was vulnerable. Skinner continued to check the different contracts Elaine had prepared, to gain familiarity with her work for the organization, specifically. He found her legal briefs on the civil suit against WKBC-TV and paused to examine the notes. Wendell didn't have time to get a thorough understanding of the implications, beyond the obvious racial undertones of the case. He had no way of suspecting the critical link to the company's long range communication plans that this document represented. Skinner filed it away, since he could see no direct association with TMP. After thumbing through several other unimportant papers, Wendell saw something he felt was worthwhile. The portfolio labeled Swazi Bauxite had been prepared by the company.

Skinner was confused at first by the cultural identification. He refreshed his anthropological knowledge and recalled the Swazi were members of the Bantu tribe, part of the great Zulu nation. Wendell rubbed his chin, perplexed. The Swazi were a distinct people apart from the 73 tribes which comprised the Zambian nation. What was the connection, he wondered. The fact that Swazi was similar in dialect to Lozi, one of the seven major languages in Zambia, did not indicate the important relationship his critical mind was seeking. Wendell opened the prospectus and briefly scanned the information to get an impression of the subject. He moved to the economic statistics presented for investors. From a cursory reading, he thought this material was important, in and of itself. He looked further. When he turned to the section covering the company's long range projections he stopped. Wendell skimmed through the pages quickly and felt he had something. He took his time and re-read the details thoroughly.

Plans for future business expansion of Swazi Bauxite proposed a contractual agreement through a two stage developmental package. The first level dealt with capitalization, primarily, and was designed to present the investment prospectus to private investors, as well as specific national funding agencies with the Zambian Government. The second level was of particular interest to Skinner, because of its far reaching political impact upon international relations. The proposed structure of an international coterie among private businesses and African governments to resolve commerce and trade relations was critical. Wendell correctly perceived the hidden agenda immediately. Control of industrial development in third world countries would introduce major economic changes, pivotal to the balance of power. This document could be the reward for his elaborate scheme.

Skinner's mind was perculating. He would have to photograph the material. The party could always use the research to make counter proposals for its own purposes, thus gain influence with the Zambian Government, before Swazi Bauxite reached the second stage of its plans. It was an indirect tactic, but it might be effective to thwart the company's efforts. Then again, he surmised it would always be possible for the party to influence a political rejection of TMP's prospectus, altogether. Wendell thought that deception would be easy enough. Some sort of adverse propaganda. An ad hominem attack upon Fred came to mind, since he was already blacklisted in the states. If all that failed, he was sure the information provided good reference for the partry to use elsewhere. The important facts were known, it was up to the higher echelon to develop strategies to confront these new directions.

Wendell quickly exited the small house to get the Minox 16mm camera and electronic eavesdropping device from the car. He gathered the equipment and returned to complete his mission.

Elaine was still asleep when he re-entered the living-room. Skinner checked his watch to make sure he would have enough time to finish the activity. Approximately a half hour had elapsed. He turned attention to the documents, spreading the portfolio carefully to one side of the desk. Next, he set up the portable lights and camera stand. That task was quickly executed and he began to photograph the prospectus, page by page. Once completed, Wendell rearranged Elaine's work desk, as neatly as possible, leaving no trace of his espionage. He moved next to the telephone. This job was easier. Skinner unfastened the receiver and attached the small electronic wiretap in a short space of time. He stored the photographic equipment in the rented car and returned to relax on the sofa. His deed done, Wendell felt the calm satisfaction of success and finished the drink while his adrenalin slowly returned to normal balance.

Skinner turned to look at Elaine, whose sensual body lay in a drugged stupor on the couch, and experienced a provocative urge. Her well formed, partially exposed thighs, contributed to the exploitive fantasy which teased his mind, as he viewed her vulnerable condition. The muse appealed to his grosser senses, but he dismissed the thought from his consideration. Somehow, Elaine still threatened his ego. Even in her helpless state, Wendell had a great deal of respect for the woman. He rationalized that sex under those conditions would be less than enjoyable. Anyhow, he had good physical relations with Yvonne, he thought. That was one good thing about their partnership which compensated for the psychological decadence and avarice that motivated their behavior. He sighed, then meditated about the story he would give Elaine—'she had passed out from the alcohol, probably overtired, as she implied'. He decided it was an innocuous tactic. Anyhow, he couldn't feel sorry for her. She was merely a naive pawn to be used to get over in life, he told himself. Skinnner leaned back on the sofa and waited patiently for Elaine to awake.

Chapter Twenty Five

Rhythmic sounds of progressive jazz filled the studio, as the four musicians 'got down' in an early morning weekend jam session. The quartet was built around a portly middle-aged dark skinned saxaphonist from Chicago. His style was heavily influenced by Charlie Parker and John Coltrane. The distinct innovations he introduced to that Black-American tradition provided additional lyricism to his horn, which was superbly complimented by the melodeous exchanges with the trumpeter, pianist and drummer. The musicians were seasoned artists who had put in their dues around the jazz network for years. Through experiences with different groups along the way, their individual musical talents had matured, making for a successful collaboration. The artists had just begun their recording career and were at the threshold of a promising future. The group broke to check their scores. As they worked on the problem, Jomo and Sonny began a conversation, while sitting on the floor in a corner of the studio. Fred entered during the interim, glanced around to orient himself, and spotted his buddies. He went over and sat down beside them.

"What do you know, Baby?"

"I've been working hard, Sonny. This seemed like a nice way to spend some off hours . . . what's to it, Jomo?"

"I hear you, 'Governor' . . . say, uh . . . are all the ladies busy? I certainly didn't expect to see you here today!"

"You might say that I've been given the day off for good behavior. I don't have the typical middle class privileges of guaranteed weekends. But, as soon as I make a move toward Boston, I'll check out your friend, Jomo."

"There's no telling what you store in that gigantic recorder of yours, is there," he exclaims, in jest. He rubbed his head, emphatically, to further his point. "I had forgotten all about you, after that big performance you gave me about it."

"You know, Jomo, there's a menstrual affect that effects men's labor . . . sometimes, I find it better to make cutbacks, to keep things in some semblence of order, you understand."

"This must be the most analytical mother in the world, Sonny . . . I've never run into a dude with such a fierce battle going on in his mind with the ladies. I can't understand how the man's able to become prosperous, carrying around all that shit in his head . . . doesn't it stiffle your imagination, Baby?"

"Perhaps, that way he always feels the tension within himself, reminding him he's really alive," Sonny quips.

The conversation was momentarily interrupted, as the muscians tested the corrections on their composition. The drummer was dissatisfied, and the 'take' was scrapped. The group broke again, to continue working out the difficulty.

Jomo resumed his provocative spar to fuel the conversation.

"Composing themes to your lady is out of the question, right, Fred?

"It's alright, as long as it doesn't become a total lifestyle. My austerities clear my mind, Jomo. The more attention I give her, the more I clear my mind. That way I can continue moving, and we're both growing," he counters.

"That takes it out there to the limits of the galaxy," exclaims Sonny. He beamed his pearly white teeth, appreciatively, at Fred's clever trist. "What do you think about that, Jomo?"

"I'm going to make sure that I'm in close company with the ladies, so we can be on the same inter-galactic flight, Sonny. I'm not spacing nowhere without my compliment . . . It's not natural to do those kind of things."

"Well, let's just say. I want to be plotting the course," remarks Fred, dryly. "I don't have any problems, except for navigation . . . we can get along . . . she can even be the pilot, sometimes . . . but, I've got to be the one to set the direction! I want the ship to be going where I want it to be going, you understand?"

"I'm sure you'd have your purposes," Sonny chuckles. "But, just don't forget about the joys our brother here mentioned."

"Aw, that cat's just over-indulgent," Fred smugly comments.

"You might say that about some, but I don't think that's true of Jomo," Sonny remarks, protectively. "He's got a head on his solid shoulders, and he uses it, wisely."

"You know, I don't know how I can continue to like this guy," Jomo says, sarcastically. "Perhaps I should keep all my little things to myself . . . look, don't even ask me about that lady from Boston. After thinking about it, I don't think you'd appreciate my good intentions!"

"Where's all of your benevolence, Jomo? Doesn't one hand take care of the other," jokes Fred. "Since we all don't do the same things, I should think living would be that much more interesting, as we share resources . . . now, you do want to look out for my best interests, don't you?"

"I'm tired of looking after you wolves in sheepskins! Like I said, maybe I should keep all the trouble to myself."

"Hey, hey . . . then, nobody will come screaming in your face later on, about anything, will they," comments Sonny.

"People are so unappreciative . . . it's a cold world we live in," sighs Jomo.

"We're about changing all of that, aren't we," Fred cajoles, to edge the humor. "I mean, with all that space in the cosmos, I imagine there's room for your type of poetry."

The musicians were ready. Alan, the drummer, signaled Sonny, who got up to coordinate the take in the control booth. With the technical problem resolved, the musicians began to record the composition. Truly talented artists, they expended a tremendous amount of energy in their skillful performance. It was a very worthwhile recording session. Everyone listened attentively, enjoying the experience fully. Their progressive jazz was exhilarating musical harmony which left the critical tastes of Fred and Jomo throughly satisfied. After the set was completed, Sonny finished the job of marking and filing the master tape, then joined his friends who were talking casually with the musicians.

"That was a terrible jam! You really build some nice passages, man," Jomo commented to the portly saxaphonist.

"Thanks," Juno smiled. "We've been working on this piece, awhile now. I'm glad you enoyed it. Now to see what kind of reception it gets from the public."

"Well, I don't know what kind of distributing contract you worked out, but as I see it, the problem is just getting folks to hear your sounds. I'm sure you'll get a good response," remarks Fred. He was encouraged by the likelihood of their successful future and only regretted that he hadn't connected with them, himself. He had a keen interest in good music and was awaiting the opportunity to manage some talented artists.

"Yeah, with groups appearing everyday, out there, it really becomes hectic to record . . . like a listener's choice, without any tasteful discrimination," says Juno.

"Well, at least you won't have to stand around in your underwear, waiting for a gig," laughs Fred.

"Hmm," says Juno. "I've had my share of deprivation, man! It just takes too much time away from composition. I want to concentrate on creating some larger pieces now, and I need all the time I can get."

Sonny was busy pulling plugs and gathering the sound equipment, in an effort to close the studio for the day. He interjected a thought to the conversation, commenting as he passed by.

"Don't worry about it, buddy. We're going to start a top ten list in the jazz world and popularize the whole tradition."

"Is that right," says Jomo. He was still smarting from his spar with Fred, and took another stab at a pun. "You mean it won't be too long before 'ole' Fred here get's into the act and has a chance to beat on some skins to let off that anger?"

"Oh, you've sat on the stool before, huh," asks Alan.

"It's been awhile. My wrists have probably atrophied, by now," he feigns an uncharacteristic shyness.

"Aw, go on and sit down. You know you've been dying to meddle some sticks," badgers Jomo. "That's the only reason you came over here, turkey!"

Alan got up, and Fred reluctantly took a seat on the stool. He played a couple of bars, accompanied by Juno. The light passages were executed with competent precision, amazing the awe struck Jomo. Afterwards, there was general sense of levity among the companions.

"Aha," Alan comments. "You can do a little something on the skins, can't you?"

"Feels like I'm back in school again," he says, while examining his wrists. "That wasn't too bad, was it?"

"I think I'll take you under my wing for a little while," jokes Alan. "Twice a week, perhaps. Then I could probably make enough, teaching you, to buy some groceries, since the rent's going to be paid on time now."

Again, Jomo had put his foot in his mouth, but was too inspired by Fred's performance to be testy. "Man, you kept that skill all the way from high school . . . that's pretty darn good!"

"That's something else to remember, Jomo. A person's recall is very crucial. Something to be careful about," says Fred, relaxing with the thought of youthful experience. "There was a time, not so long ago, when I wouldn't have been able to do that. It seemed like everything was in chaos until I cleared my mind . . . It's somewhat like having charts on a boat.''

"Yeah," says Alan. "You have to exercise your mind all of the time, otherwise you recall suffers."

Sonny brought a duplicate tape from the control booth for Juno and joined the group while the men talked. Meanwhile the musicians began packing away their instruments.

"Keep this where you can lay your hands on it. The master stays here."

"I'll put it somewhere where it'll be safe . . . say, what was the time?"

"Four fifteen," he replies, and leaves them to attend his other chores.

"Trying to fill the album space, you know," Juno comments, as he returns to the conversation with Jomo and Fred. "Sometimes it can become very trickly. I don't like to tailor my work."

"I don't imagine any artist appreciates his hands tied . . . accomodations can sometimes be bad for aesthetics," Fred comments, supportively. "But, how do you feel about the session?"

"Pretty good, pretty good . . . although, I would like to hear these tapes, before leaving," he says, loud enough for Sonny to hear.

"The overhead is too steep, man," Sonny shouts from across the room. "You can't afford to hear those tapes today!"

"Old Sonny sure changes his tune when accounting for time. There's no love of labor involved in getting out of the studio when the hour is up," jokes Jomo.

"Well, at least he did squeeze you into a weekend session. That's a feat in and of itself, you know."

"Yeah, that's true. Tying up 'Olabisi' like this on Saturn's day is tantamount to sacrilege. I'm surprised he even came out of the house," laughs Jomo.

Meanwhile, Sonny continued his work unpreturbed by the 'dozens'.

"I had to seduce him with some lady all week long. He really made this an expensive venture."

"Chalk it off to communal sharing between the tribes, Juno. It takes away the avariciousness from the transaction," says Jomo, in a humorous attempt at philosophy. "We'll get over this monetary thing yet."

"In that case, we sure as hell better be clear about new ways of trading, whenever we liberate our brothers back home, because the way you cats sound is as if you're looking to get a firm footing in cocoa development in Africa. That could be worse than the South African monster . . . as much as I enjoy the lady, and all them big duckets, that would be a sad transaction," Fred interjects, soberly.

"Yeah, man, that's just another one of those political tricks that Blacks should avoid. Those mothers have already done a hell of a job messing up the social and cultural conditions in Africa, but we shouldn't fall for the quick money scam. When I think of how they've sucked all the vitality out of that continent, I just get sick with those niggers playing the 'man's confidence games'," Juno comments cynically.

The pianist interrupted the conversation to clear some details about the group's itinerary.

"Look, man, we're going straight uptown from here. We're not stopping to eat, before picking up the van. I guess we'll meet you in Long Island later this evening . . . what time did you say, about ten o'clock?"

"Right," Juno replies. "I should be there by nine thirty, or thereabouts."

Sonny returned to the conversation again, pausing in his frenetic activity to share in the small talk. He had completed the various closing down chores and released the engineers while the three musicians left the studio carrying their instruments.

"Phew! Now that that's over, what are you gentlemen doing for the stomach?''

"I hadn't thought about it, myself, Sonny. I guess we can stop down here, somewhere, for a light bite,'' says Fred.

"Oh, nonesense! With that beautiful houri at my place, you are all going to have to come and spoil your palates on some choice dishes . . . let me call and tell her how many she'll have to prepare for . . . ''

"Sounds like the man has a very interesting conjugal arrangement,'' laughs Juno.

"Wait until you see this sister,'' Jomo remarks, intoning a sotto voce and emphasizing each word. He rubbed his slick head, as he spoke, and gestured descriptively with his hands. "She is definitely made to order! Now you can get a chance to actually see what I've been talking about, Fred. My man is in perpetual bliss in his household.''

"Really,'' he replies, nonchalantly. "I'll be sure to note that. Then I'll be able to imagine what I can expect from my austerities.''

"Hey, listen . . . it's said that discipline inevitably leads to greater sensitivity of your surroundings,'' Jomo remarks, dismissing Fred's sarcasm. "Well, I appreciate home cooking, myself. I really can't indulge that pedestrian stuff, too often,'' he says, as an aside. "I'll tell you, man, there isn't anything more fascinating than to dine regale upon superb cuisine.''

"You mean with all the amenities . . . ''

"Say what you like, Fred, but it's mean to let the sisters wait upon you like those real old timers talk about.''

Fred smiled at the thought and began to share a moment's fantasy.

"The setting is probably reminiscent of a royal court, or someplace close, right?''

"That's it . . . plug into it!''

"She's one of the many mysterious attendants in the entourage who has come to wait upon you, out of all the members of the visiting officials,'' continues Fred. "She extends you the many allurements of the festive occassion while the grace and charm of her delicate being envelopes you in a sensual mood of relaxation.''

"The scene thusly set, I'm introduced to an infinite array of delectable cuisine, spicing my palate, while the natural elements contribute a soothing balm to my temperament . . . ''

"A constant smile plays about her face . . . ''

"Her eyes talk to me like gems of other heavens,'' Jomo sighs, as he gently rubs the smooth contours of his bald head.

"There's no chance for conversation and the evening is drawing to conclusion . . . ''

"We arrange to meet under the star filled sky, invoking our whims to meet the challenge . . . ''

"You play an interesting art form too, my man,'' says Juno, laughing at the exchange.

"The lady goes a long way to sustain my inspiration,'' confides Jomo. "I make a point of studying her . . . she takes you on many different trips. Each time it's a novelty, you know what I mean?''

"Yeah,'' he replies. "It's a pleasure, no matter how you look at it.''

"Watch what you consume, Jomo. With blissful ladies and all that eating, things could get confused," teases Fred.

"Oh buddy, here we go again with old glib Fred . . . wait until you've gotten through the meal first, then tell me if my imagination was really the case, or if it was really the case."

"Hey, man, I'm anticipating this event," cajoles Fred. "I've got to prepare for my audience with the princess, you know!"

Juno laughs, boistrously, displaying a set of smoke stained teeth, protruding awkwardly, from the constant pressure of the saxaphone's mouthpiece.

"I think my man has gotten away and done a slight solo on you, my friend."

"It's like him to be spoiled, anyway," says Jomo. "I guess I had been expecting that to show up in a different form."

"You see, Jomo, avijja has you so upset that you can't even spot a chameleon changing it's clothes on the kitchen table," Fred punned with him.

"You and your naked humor . . . anyhow, I really do hope you enjoy yourself, Baby. She's a real good cook and always has something special to tantalize your senses."

"Who doesn't have any sense," interrupts Sonny, as he rejoins the group. "What are you all talking about, anyway? Sounds kind of damaging to be making statements like that about people."

"I was just telling a disbelieving Fred about your queen," Jomo responds.

"Oh, yeah, everything is arranged. It should be about a half hour, so we'll have plenty of time to get down with some decent rap," he comments.

The men walked toward the exit, and Sonny turned off the lights to the studio. Each of them carried a part of the drum set downstairs. As the group emerged from the building, Sonny and Juno began the arduous task of hailing a taxi. Jomo continued the friendly spar with Fred, outside on the sidewalk where the exchange persisted.

"See the trouble with you is that you've been seeing nothing but demons for so long, you're beginning to imagine everybody's up to no good . . . now, I had that experience when I was running around with Margaret and that crew uptown. It all comes in periods, you know. Like leap year and shit! For a while things go along steadily, then all of a sudden, pow! Here I go through those gymnastics again. But, let me tell you, Baby, it's never a question of reneging the whole show. Hey, there are some pretty tough sisters out there who could really make a big difference in your attitude."

"I don't doubt that. It's merely that each one of them take a percentage of my time, I'm still telling you. And, that, is more of a concern to me at this juncture in my life, than at any other previous point in my growth," remarks Fred. "I'm not afraid of meeting demons or witches, or for that matter even goddesses, more positively considered. It's all a question of reframing my reference, in any case. But, I wonder how long it would be, before my considerations began to make me seem offensive, you dig?"

"Man, what do you think you are, anyway? Everybody has a restless soul, at times. That's not unique to yourself, you know."

Fred put the big bass drum into the trunk of the taxi, then moved back to straighten his clothing.

"I rather think it's a matter of clean spirit, Jomo. I don't want to become unnecessarily tired of moving in and out of pleasures. It would be debilitating to do so. Fun and games is a cheap pacification for the unproductive spirit. It's a choice you have to make, in just what you want to spend this lifetime working on. At any rate, I certainly don't entertain any wishes of coming back here. You see, I empathize with the Buddhist state of Arahant. Somehow it embodies much of the deeper meaning of Christ's passage, like overcoming the decadent world of spiritual poverty and darkness.''

The two friends concluded their philosophical exchange while entering the taxi from opposite sides. The doors slammed shut and the cab pulled away from the curbside, entering the light weekend traffic.

Chapter Twenty-Six

Latin music filled the air inside Fred's apartment with the sounds of Tito Puente flowing rhythmically from the radio. An opened book of yoga aphorisms lay on top of the work table, next to the stacks of documents, piled neatly to one side. The paintings had recently been hung, giving the small railroad flat additional interest, despite the congestion. An early edition of the New York Times, displaying a head-line of Ferguson's campaign, lay nearby a copy of the Neilson Report on the floor. A large cockroach strolled idly across the sunlit floor toward the newspaper. Fred's eyes followed the insect's movements while he sat comfortably in a lotus position. The lively music presented a comical accompaniment, stimulating the roach's prog-ress, as the first rays of sunshine glistened off its back. As the bug ambled on, Fred sat in quiet tranquility. His visiage appeared emotionless. Only his eyes moved, while his erect body remained motionless in a tense-free poise.

Fred began the exercise by focusing his mind in a disciplined concentration. Through regulated breathing, patiently, by stages of anapanasati, he was able to reach a state of samadhi without difficulty. An initial strain on his lungs from the smoking habit caused momentary distortion of his biochemistry, which contributed to a series of facial contortions, as his body adjusted to the rigorous breathing pattern. The tempo of the music increased, as the drummer made an intricate solo excursion, but Fred had become oblivious of the sounds, and movement of the roach. The music reached a climactic ending while Fred closed his eyes in the trancelike state of dhyana.

Fred's transcendental vision had transposed his mind's eye to the front of a Mexican restaurant. He found himself standing outside, looking around, in a languid dreamlike manner at the surroundings, as small groups of people clustered together, talking in an inaudible murmur. Fred looked at the activity in the restaurant through an opened door. The interior light of the cafe made the people inside appear shad-owlike, as they moved about speaking a peasant dialect. The atmosphere within the restaurant was reminiscent of Plato's allegory of the cave, he thought. Gradually, Fred's vision returned to the unpaved street where he found himself alone under the moonlit sky. No one sat at the exterior tables on the sidewalk under the portico, and he walked toward the chairs to sit down. As he drew near, his eyes focused upon a plethora of roaches of all sizes which congested the table tops like a living table-cloth. Their physical proximity created a virtual din of activity, as they milled and seeded all over each other. Fred stood there watching the insect infested table with objective aloofness, when, suddenly the deep metallic sounding voice of his spiritual guide interceded, giving ethereal directions.

"It becomes impossible to eat out of doors when the sun sets, my friend . . . it is alright, there is a place awaiting you on the inside."

Fred entered the cafe in a lethargic manner and observed himself seated at a small table. In his mind's eye, he was served a frugal portion of heavily seasoned chicken and rice which he consumed without the physical sensation of kaya.

Suddenly, it seemed that he had left the cafe and transported himself, dreamlike, along the Eastern coast of the country which was adjacent to the Golf of Mexico. Fred saw himself outside a parked Volkswagon, seeking directions with a flashlight, in the darkness of the rural countryside. A sign at the crossroads said—'Villa Hermosa'.

Again the voice came to him.

"This is a very ancient fishing village, my friend. As you can tell by the name, it is a beautiful little village. Accomodations await your arrival at the large guest house, just two streets East of the main road."

Fred returned, trancelike, to the car and started off down the road. His vision had interrupted the normal space-time continuum, so that events occured like a dream sequence. The guest house materialized before him. It was a large building of typical Spanish architectural design, with a spacious court and balconies enclosed by elaborate iron works. As the Volkswagon pulled up to the hotel, a wiry old man, clothed in a black sarape, stood watching the activity, in the shadows alongside the guest house.

Inside the hotel, Fred was shown to a typically spacious, high ceilinged, airy room with large bay windows. The quarters were very simply adorned. A finely crafted birchwood table sat next to the West wall, with a bottle of liquor, two glasses and a pitcher of water resting on top. Directly opposite stood a large metal framed bed. A chess board and one chair were arranged conspicuously in the middle of the room. Fred entered the room and turned on the overhead fan. He removed the key from the door and dropped it on the table. As he looked around, a large poster on the wall caught his attention and he moved closer to read the announcement.

"Annuncion! Corridor del Toros . . . did you enjoy the fascination of the bullfight, my friend? It is one of the more popular spectator events in Mexico City."

Fred was fatigued now, and strained in his attempt to reminisce. He looked at the poster awhile, then took a seat on the very large bed.

"Allow me."

Fred suddenly felt extremely small in the huge room, which seemed to expand and dwarf him, as the guide began to transpose his vision. His mind's eye saw himself from above, a tiny figure atop an enormous mattress. Continuing his concentration on the poster, he could hear the faint noise of the bull ring gradually becoming audible. The 'door' was opened, and Fred found himself in front of a similar announcement, posted on the wall outside of the stadium in Mexico City. He approached two waiting men, one Mexican and the other Black, and the three entered the arena. They hustled through the crowd to find their seats, as the activity neared its climax.

The men watched comfortably as the bull made several unsuccessful passes. Fred looked interestedly at the seven picks which were stuck in the animal's back, then glanced at the war-like procession of picadors who had tired the animal, beforehand. He turned his attention to the interesting faces amongst the spellbound throng.

"They really don't give the beast a chance at all, do they," he asks, offhandedly.

"It is a lingering folk pattern in our Spanish culture, but I am afraid, as your American writer Hemmingway has observed, the matadors, here also, no longer have the quality of refinement which characterized bullfighting in Spain, many years ago," Juan replies. Like Fred, he was very chauvanistic and projected ethnic pride as part of his keen personality.

Philip was busy indulging himself with peanuts, so engrossed with the activity as he anxiously stuffed his mouth, that his friend's conversation seemed indistinguishable from the background ambience. He was a young initiate to the journey and was just beginning to understand the Hindu concept of maya. Tall and well built, his lean body carried its 176 pounds with good proportion. Fred's companion also grew up in New York and decided early, to do something more with his life, rather than lag around the city. His youthful appearance was not an asset for him, he felt, because he sought the wisdom of age which removed his interests from that of his peers. Philip was not a handsome young man; his square face, broad nose and thick lips were rather ordinary. His reddish skin and closely cropped 'bad-hair' added a sense of self-consciousness, but his inner strength shined forth like a magnet which helped him develop good relations with people.

The bull made another pass, raising the clamour of the crowd, as the matador made a spectacular elusive move, deceiving the bovine again.

"Um, mm, mm," Philip moans, excitedly. "This is really too much!"

The animal was exhausted now, and stood listlessly in the middle of the arena. The matador began to make ready for the kill, measuring the distance and angle of entry of his sword which he held poised about eye level in front of his forehead.

"Now look here closely," says Juan. His dark narrow eyes seemed black, and were fixed steadfastly upon the ritual slaughter. The challenge of man against nature activated his animus, which indicated a great deal about his character to Fred. Sharp Caucasian features and straight black hair accentuated his light tan complexion, which further separated him from the peasant class. He was haughty, and viewed the sport of bull fighting in a calculating way, as part of his overall temperament about life.

"The matador shall attempt to do away with the brute in one stroke . . . let us see who will be the master of life and death."

As the matador closed the distance between the bull, the animal charged, raising a new outburst from the crowd. The bull approached. The matador plunged, while swirving his torso from the hips to avoid the hook of the animal's treacherous horns. Staggering, the bull listed, then fell to its forelegs, and finally rolled over on its side. The crowd was now wild with excitement, standing on their seats shouting praises.

"Wow, man," Philip exclaims. "That's some wicked shit!"

Fred said nothing. His eyes were intently set on the fallen bull. Meanwhile, the matador paraded around the arena with his arms raised high above his head, in a typical display of machismo, as flowers, hats and other paraphrenalia were tossed into the ring. Fred gazed reflectively at the slumped carcass, as the attendants fastened the animal's immobile legs to the team of horses which dragged the hulk out of the oval. He turned from the pathetic sight and looked around, observing the sublimated violence of the collective conscious, silently, as the images of the bull fight dissolved from his vision.

Rubbing his eyes to focus on the wall poster, once again, Fred looked around and found himself returned to the guest house. He was sitting in front of the chess set. After contemplating the sixty-four squares awhile, Fred moved the kings knight from the light court. He was still in the state of samadhi and saw himself get up and and pour a drink from the whiskey bottle. Once again, the liquor was consumed without the physical sensation of kaya. He studied the chess board awhile, then moved a pawn from the dark court. Again the 'door' opened, continuing the journey.

This time, Fred found himself at an outdoor cafe with Philip and an older white man. The threesome remained quiet, enjoying the solitude of their company, underneath the shaded veranda.

The voice of his guide came to him again.

''You intended to meet your friend in Oxaca, after returning from the South, to continue your search of wisdom. Now you must pay attention to the encounter with the spirits of the air, which the elders shall prepare for your understanding . . . there is a lesson to be learned from the old men of good will . . . ''

Background music of the local band became audible, as the distinct metallic sounds of the guide receded from the atmosphere, giving way to the sonorous tones of the brass instruments which gradually filled the air. The peasants played popular Mexican songs with their horns, as tourists converged to listen while sitting comfortably at their tables. A waiter approached the men to take their orders.

''May I serve you, senors?''

''Ah, si. Dos capacinos, por favor,'' Fred heard himself reply.

As the waiter began to move away from the table, the old man called his attention to place an order.

''Hombre! Uno momemto . . . damme un otro vaso de lo mismo,'' he says while holding up his near empty glass of whiskey. Then, he turned his attention to Fred. ''It's quite a long time that I've been coming down this way. The import business keeps me traveling, as far away as South America, at times. But, I find nothing as relaxing as sitting here in Oxaca around the village square, listening to the afternoon music . . . excuse me, I get carried away in my own little reveries, occasionally . . . you were speaking about San Mateo, if I remember correctly.''

The waiter returned with two cups of the coffee and cocoa mixture and a glass of whiskey on his tray.

''Excuse me, waiter, could you tell these two young men how to get to San Mateo?''

The middle aged waiter scrutinized the two Blacks, curiously.

''It is a very difficult journey to that retreat. Is there any particular reason that you go there?''

''We're making a pilgrimage to San Mateo to rid ourselves of some evils that we don't want in our lives,'' Fred tells the awe struck waiter. ''We hope to gain the teachings of the air spirits with the aid of mescalito and hongos.''

''Ah, por Dios,'' exclaims the frightened man. ''Of this I know very little. Only that it takes a strong constitution to speak with the forces on the mountain . . . I understand nothing else. Are you sure you want to go there alone, senors?''

''We're not afraid to speak to the forces on the 'misty mountain'. I understand that students make the trip quite often . . . can you tell us how we can get there?''

''If you desire to do this, you can take a train from here to Teochacan,'' the waiter instructs Fred. ''From there, a bus leaves to take you to the foot of San

Mateo. I understand that it is a day's climb up the mountain. The people there will give you directions along the way. It would be best to speak to the elders before seeking mescalito or hongos,'' cautions the Mexican. ''It can be very dangerous!''

''Can we use sleeping bags up there, or is that too dangerous,'' Philip teases the waiter.

''I don't think the banditos come near that part of the country. The superstitions about that retreat prevent them from disturbing its sacredness,'' says the old man, to allay the Mexican's anxiety. ''You will undoubtedly contact a source and have a good pilgrimage, once you get there. Do write me about your experience, I'm extremely interested . . . just a little too old to make an excursion in the underbrush, like that.''

''What are you planning to do, play armchair Anthropologist and fill your library with first hand accounts,'' quips Fred. ''That's no good for your own credibility . . . you should actually participate in the ceremony,'' he concludes.

The old man laughed at the bait. It was part of the luxury the younger generation could afford, poking fun at the stoicism of 'old folks'.

''I've been to far too many rituals. My door is already open to the journey, young man. I shall just offer one note of advice about good and evil for consideration, as you build your spiritual life, my friend.'' The old man shifted his position in the chair and transfixed his gaze upon Fred's eyes. As he spoke, his serious tone alerted Fred's keen mind to the sensitive temperament of the acquaintance who had hitherto been low key and casual. ''I can't tell you how I know, right now, but my intuition suggests you somehow would like to spread your spiritual growth, by helping black people find new foundations in the modern world. Don't answer whether this is true or not, just accept an old man's wisdom,'' he says. ''You must be attentive to the persistence of chaos from the 'lost souls' or evil spirits, which most orthodox religions mention in their various forms of dogma and ritual and the ancient kabbalists call tohu. People in all societies are continually fooled, you see, and tempted to court the forces of evil . . . especially when attempting to face objective problems of poverty. Just be careful of the limits of power in whatever work you're engaged.''

Fred had listened attentively to the old man's advice. He was no fool, and could tell that the empathic communication they shared was beneficial. His precaution against the illusions of maya was real. Fred, himself, had mentioned the traps of maya to the young initiate, Philip who was at that stage in his growth.

''I trust your concern for me, my friend. I'll take your advice to heart, because the problem of cultural lag and social revolution is a very real source for misperception,'' he replies.

''Well, perhaps my experience will be helpful to your understanding about what's to transpire. If you're interested, I'm available,'' the old man remarks, graciously.

He reached into his pocket and passed Fred a business card. it read, Timothy Rufus, Ltd., Imports/Exports, Philadelphia, Pa. (215) 756-6107. Fred heard the voice of his guide return.

''Reflection upon the seeds of this contact shall bear fruit in the future . . . ''

The three travelers sat in the village square of Oxaca, listening to the music and sipping their drinks in the late afternoon, while nearby, poor peasants peddled flowers to satisfy their basal needs, by hustling among the tourists sitting at the sidewalk cafes.

Fred was returned to the chess board again, where the game had progressed to an intricate climax. In his normal conscious state, he often challanged his mind by playing alone with himself. Thus, the exercise didn't seem awkward in his vision. He sat hovering over the chess board. The bottle of liquor sat half empty on the table nearby. Fred moved the white queen and took the black knight, then sat pensively awhile. Somewhere in his mind's eye, he knew he must penetrate the veil and get an understanding of the true nature of the transcendental journey. He tried to stretch his mind to the state of pativedha, but found himself laboring under the influence of alcohol in his trancelike condition. Somewhat confused by the sudden lack of control of kaya, he adjusted his breathing for another attempt. Physical sensation was not commensurate with the temporal displacement. Something was unusual. Just then, seemingly from nowhere, the apparition of a hand appeared directly opposite Fred's position in front of the chess board and moved the black castle to check the white king.

Fred watched the poldergeist with more concern than his prior experience in dhyana. Here was an explicit phenomenal occurance charged with meaning. Just then, the voice of the guide interrupted his momentary confusion about the symbolism. Although it was important to reach pativedhi, he would try again, later. But now to understand the message of the next lesson.

"You have learned to play with dharma very well . . . now, look at this!"

The guest house seemed to fade away before Fred's eyes, as if the surroundings were a wave of water. As his focus cleared, he saw three human forms hovering around a campfire in the dark of night. In his mind's eye, Fred saw himself sitting in the traditional lotus position while Philip was slumped over in deep sleep to his right. The third figure was an old Mexican Indian, dressed in a long black sarape which covered his body to the knees, revealing only the bottom of his thin cotton pants. He wore traditional sandals made of leather strips and old rubber tires which were common among the poor. His simple garments were accentuated by a large jade stone which hung as a necklace in front of his sternum.

The old Mexican was slender, yet his huge rough lands gave him the appearance of a craftsman. His wiry frame sat motionless also, directly opposite Fred, who gazed at the interesting contrast of the peasant's milk white hair and small dark eyes. The illumination of the fire played upon the dark tan wrinkled skin of his face, highlighting the stark aboriginal features, suggesting ages of weathered experience.

The old Indian had questioned the Blacks to great lengths, attempting to fathom their ethical convictions and spiritual strengths. After satifying the elder's rigid probes, the three men had discoursed in depth about the peasant's philosophy regarding the spirits of the air. Fred learned many interesting parallels about ritual purification which he understood in relation to Tipareth and the four breaths of life. The peasant had also warned him of the harm of hubris, as he comprehended the dialect, which could add confusion during the communion with the spirits.

Finally, the time had come for the ceremonial cleansing. The old man solemnly chanted his secret Indian prayers. He took the mescalito and hongos from a small cloth bag which was carried under his sarape. The mescal buttons were collected from certain cactus plants and the mushrooms were a peculiar variety of agaricaceae. But, when Fred inquired about the plants to increase his knowledge of their botanical properties, the peasant told him that this was a privileged secret. Although he knew about amanita, Fred listened to the caution against adventurism, lest he poison himself with similar lethal varieties. Then the Indian gave the plants to Fred and gestured for him to begin ingesting the hallucinogens. Fred ate the strange looking combination, as part of the ritual commensalism, this time, without the physical sensation of kaya.

It seemed as if hours had elapsed in his trance which allowed Fred a thorough communication with the spirits of the air. Fortunately, there was no encounter with the 'malevolent one' during his communion. Finally, he returned, and focused attention to the old man who looked on paternally. The peasant silently smiled and extended a hand crafted metal disk to Fred, who took the gift and put it in his pants pocket. The ritual was complete. The old Indian picked up the sturdy branch which he used as a walking stick and raised his thin body.

The etheral voice of Fred's guide resounded, as the old man chanted final prayers in the background, raising the level of the fire.

"Good bye, my child. May the good spirits which have been imparted to you protect you in your passage."

The peasant turned and disappeared into the night, walking with the aid of his sturdy branch, while Fred gently rested his companion onto the opened sleeping bag. A cool breeze flowed through the air, and he smiled at the gentle sound it made, rustling through the tree leaves. He returned to his position in front of the fire where he sat, meditatively tending the flames. After a few moments, he looked up at the dark sky where his communion seemed to have taken place and was enveloped dreamlike into the blackness.

Fred opened his eyes again, and saw Philip and himself standing nude under a downpour of water, cascading from the mountain waterfall. They were showering at a secluded spot, halfway down the mountain.

"Aggh! This water is freezing," Philip groans. "I feel like I'm in an ice bucket . . . let me out of here, at once. I gotta dry off."

"What's the matter," asks Fred, in a badgering tone. "Your blood can't take the extremes?"

Philip made a hasty departure, tip toeing on his bare feet, to prevent an injury from the rugged terrain.

"Phew? I didn't realize mountain streams could be all that cold. Especially during this season of the year," he mumbles, as he shiveringly towels off his head and body.

"Ah, that felt good," Fred says, as he emerges from the waterfalls. "Now, to walk down the mountain and find a cup of hot coffee at a friendly peasant's abode."

"Ahha . . . now you're talking," Philip replies and tosses him the towel. He pulled up his pants and began to struggle with his boots. "I must've slept through all of the good stuff, but I feel like a million dollars this morning. What about yourself?"

Fred finished drying himself and began to dress. "He didn't stay very long, after you fell asleep." He reached into his pants pocket and withdrew the metal disk. "Look at this talisman he gave me when he blessed our passage."

"Let me see." Fred handed the metal disk to Philip and continued to clothe himself. "Aha, this is very beautiful. Very intricate craftsmanship."

"He told me that events would begin to change for me in the near future, but the message that's inscribed on it will only become meaningful as I continue on my journey. It's supposed to help me understand the true nature of things encountered, as I reflect upon experiences in my way through life. It provides choice."

Fred turned to look at the waterfall, once again, while Philip examined the talisman. Somewhere in the background there was a faint ring of a telephone. As the noise from the telephone became louder, the surrealism of the journey to the past dissapated, and Fred's mind was transposed back to his apartment. He emerged from the bathtub, towel around his waist, to answer the phone.

"Hello." He dropped the telephone receiver and picked it up from the floor while trying to remain covered. "Hello, are you still there? Oh, how are you Elaine, I was taking one of my 'make-do' showers . . . good to hear your voice, too . . . no, I haven't come completely out of my meditation . . . I guess I am late for work. What time is it, anyway . . . really? Oh, you spoke to Lloyd already . . . hmm, okay I'm listening. The Neilson Report. Right." As Fred listened to Elaine's conversation, his visiage became pensive. He pulled the extension cord and went to sit on a chair. "You think that's where the money is coming from, do you? Well, I hadn't thought about that possibility, but it sounds logical . . . now, if you remember what I told you about languages, you can get a whole other perspective of the picture. Use the anagram on it when you're sure of a pattern . . . yeah, I see what you mean. It begins to resemble a black patriciate . . . sure, it makes sense. That's one way to handle the system's monster. So, that's the secret of the emerging black politician. Isn't that a tactful diplomacy of benignant virtue. Seems like giving up the notion of complete reign of sovereignty. I guess receding into the background is probably the only salvation for the 'man' . . . I agree with you, perhaps it would be better if we discussed this in private. When are you coming to New York . . . right. I'll mark that down on my calander . . . alright, I'll go over it again with that in mind . . . bye now."

Fred stood in the middle of the room, dripping wet, with his hand on his chin, thinking. As he struggled to organize all the questions about the rapidly unfolding events, the ethereal voice of his guide lingered faintly in the subconscious of his mind.

"It is important for you to pierce the veil."

Fred's eyes lit up with anticipation, and his body stiffened momentarily, as he suppressed the cogitation. He couldn't afford a residual lapse into meditative poise, right now. He consciously relaxed his miscles and began a regulated breathing pace, exhaling moreso, rather than inbreathing. He followed the muse, however, and went to the table to look at the Neilson Report for a clue. Thumbing through the pages he came across something of interest. The text read:

"In our examination of historical examples, through content analysis of key ancient civilizations such as China, Egypt and Rome, we have distinguished principle themes which are important to planning for future social and economic development. Within old world societies, cooptation of those dominent cultural configurations found especially significant, or useful in conquered groups, is one such pattern that was established in our historical presentation and is mentioned here, as a primary basis of control over indigenous peoples.

This fundamental control, residing with the emerging political institution(s) in old world societies, is experiencing structural changes at this juncture in world-wide developments. Conflicts often result in the interface between resurgent identity concerns of diverse cultural groups and immediate national priorities, in their mutual relationship to contemporary events within the international networks between countries.

Confrontation between ideological extremes and the emergence of marginal symbol systems within the overall charged political atmosphere, as these groups attempt to gain power, is a critical concern affecting institutional control which is a priority of social and economic development. National crisis ensuing from these kinds of conflicting interests lead us to the inference of a new role for the political tactician in the twentieth century who is a pivotal 'type' for organizing structures that are contributive to developing old world societies.

"As a public servant he represents the prevailing philosophy of the nation, whereas he remains a symbolic embodiment of kinship traditions, generally reflecting notions of 'grooming by the elders'. This description can be readily seen in the Chinese metaphysical system of casting hexagrams, particularly corresponding to lines five and two. The lines of the public official and the traditional ruler hold the delicate balance within societal organization. The social fibre is structured around these relationships.

Applying specific concepts based upon such principles to select the 'type' of political tactician capable of mediating the extreme factions presents one possible direction for effective governance during urbanization in old work societies; it offers a means of controlling the dynamics of traditionalism and modernity to continue social and economic development within national and international relations."

"That's a tremendous educational project, as far as I can see," Fred remarks to himself. "Damn, I can see why Ferguson is making such a headway into these kinds of considerations, right here in America . . . hmm, he's probably somewhat further along the line than I thought."

Fred searched for his clothes and dressed in a hurry, thinking pensively all the while. His activity was erratic and he experienced momentary forgetfullness. Finally, he shrugged his shoulders and heaved a sigh.

"Shit! What am I going through these changes for, anyhow. It's got to be that way. Old Doc was right about not wasting my time . . . try to do something while there's still an opportunity to shape the future. That Old timer really does see the design . . . building, internationally, through developments in city politics. Well, I'll be damned if I wasn't right. I wouldn't be surprised if he's in some kind of black patriciate . . . Fred, you ought to be ashamed of yourself for the oversight. Well, then, let's get it together . . . what time is it?" He looked at his watch. "It would happen on a day like today . . . Lawd Today!"

He scurried around the apartment like a chicken, gathering his personal belongings together. Quickly filling his attache case, he dashed toward the door as the telephone began ringing. Hesitating a moment, Fred thought it was probably Lloyd and disappeared through the door. He was already two hours late, and the boss just wouldn't understand the delay, regardless of the insight of his journey. The door slammed shut, leaving water marks of footprints all over the living room floor inside a vacant apartment. The phone continued to ring, but Fred was gone.

Chapter Twenty-Seven

The rush hour congestion inside the subway station reflected the large work force in the city at the mid-point of the 1960's. New York had a viable tax base, coinciding with the general popoulation density of a thriving metropolis and labor remained a major political influence at that time. Nevertheless, the transition in ethnic composition was the principle demographic variable which impacted upon the political process, as competing values of the new cultural awareness emerged during the election.

The multiracial masses exited from the succession of trains and thronged the Borough Hall station, bustling through the platform to their jobs. An express train pulled in, and Fred disembarked from one of the cars. He made his way slowly through the crowd toward the control booth at the end of the station while casually eyeing the urban renewal construction, designed to upgrade the subway system. He found Ferguson and Landers, who were just leaving the small quarters, as motormen and conductors checked in and completed their busy work. The councilmen had arranged the tour to inspect the system and view construction progress, as part of the council's response to the on-going labor issues.

"This is, by far, the worst of the express stations that we've seen," remarks Landers. He frowned with agitation, which was uncharacteristic for his normally composed demeanor. Ferguson noticed the expression immediately and his keen perception told him something else was on Landers' mind. "Almost one hundred people every three minutes, not counting the flow from the local side . . . I'm afraid we're going to have to consider another exit. Changing schedules isn't feasible. That would only tie up a greater number of people and result in larger traffic problems all around the city."

"Yes, I can see your point, Eugene. But, just imagine the type of static the union is going to give us on this matter while the hearings are going on. It would mean confrontation to try to schedule additional construction at the same time they're attempting a pay hike. The council's decision to hold the fare is going to be awfully hard for them to swallow, anyhow. And then, I can see the boys down there in fiscal when they see another allocation for capital improvements. Man, where do you think this problem is going to take us?"

"I'd be kind of careful of this issue, if I were you," Landers remarked caustically. "You've got enough on your hands as it is already. Let the Board of Estimate worry about bookkeeping. You don't want to add misery to hardship. Your educational proposal has already created a new front. You can't be serious about tackling organized labor on something that's an obvious pressure ploy to vitiate your influence in the campaign.''

Ferguson listened attentively and relfected on the irnport of Landers' remark. He knew the council president had direct contact with some of the powerful forces in the city and he wanted to know their future economic plans, which he understood were the real limits of municipal union demands. With this information, he could ultimately control the labor issue effectively in his campaign. Ferguson decided to use a little liberal diplomacy to induce what he could from his fellow councilman.

''You and I know unions are funny sorts of creatures, Eugene. But, from our work in office, I think we've reached a new understanding of how to approach essentially bureaucratic organizations, whatever they are . . . take the civil servants, for instance, who are a large segment of the voting population, I might add. Generally speaking, they have some vague awareness of the management games involved in running a city, based upon similar organizational problems in union structures. They're both political creatures. Nevertheless, no matter how tight a union structure, I think a frank, personal approach to the issues will make a significant difference to each individual within the membership. Look at it this way, our candid policy as councilmen had that kind of effect, by pointing out the abuses in the union pension fund. Some heads are going to roll, as a result of that . . . as I see it, my campaign has to continue promoting good accountability in government operation, at this point especially. By presenting efficient and effective management as a platform to the public, I can see how some union pressures can be nullified, through refocusing tax expenditure issues to public amenities. Simple operations research, used the right way. Because, I also think, as voters, union members appreciate being viewed as mature citizens,'' concludes Ferguson.

''That sounds like typical campaign propaganda, Charles. Gobble-dygook, right out of public administration textbooks. You know the usual response of the union worker is not that logical. They're politicized, by and large, because civil service is becoming an anachronism in the modern economy . . . well, anyway, I hope you're right, because we're going to have one hell of a problem on our hands, if the mayor gets called to Albany about state funds involved in this transit mess.''

''I know what you mean, a lot of trade-offs,'' remarks Ferguson, in a dejected mood. He had been unsuccessful with his probe. Speculation about the local economy based on innuendo wasn't helpful. At this point he would be in the dark, as far as support Landers might generate for his campaign. As he considered this problem of gaining 'inside' information, Fred casually approached in a light mood, which aggravated his tension further.

''Good afternoon, gentlemen. How's business going down here?''

''Hi, 'fellah','' Ferguson snaps, sarcastically in reply. ''Glad to see you could make it on time!''

''The way he comes on with that gentlemen approach is a sure way to smooth out a situation, I suppose,'' Landers says, laughing at the exchange.

''I'd say the man's concept of time relates with some other society, of which I am not familiar,'' quips Ferguson. He was still smarting from Landers' cold reception to his probe and ventilated his frustration on Fred.

''Hey, I hope I'm not getting too far out of sequence,'' Fred apologizes. ''I hate playing dissonant chords.''

''I'm not here to chastize your rhythm . . . just your concept of orchestration,'' he badgers Fred. "You know there are other people playing this set with you!"

Fred had had enough. His unusual lateness shouldn't warrant such hostility. "You know, I keep forgetting my raquet," he replies, with a blase tone, in an effort to check the councilman's attitude.
to check the councilman's attitude.

"It would be pretty difficult traveling with something like that on the subway during rush hour," Landers joked in response.

"Hmm, I know what you mean," he says. "Well, what do you think the recommendations will be? Are they going to get a pay raise," Fred asks Ferguson, attempting to avoid unnecessary tension.

"There seems to be a need for some improvement in services," the councilman comments in a restrained manner. He checked his deportment, for the moment. "I imagine that money would have to be spent there, before we can turn to wage negotiations."

"I see your priorities. Do some house cleaning first, then sit down and talk about justified compensation. It makes sense."

"Well, I'm glad you can still walk into a conversation. Landers says that I'd be presumptuous to make any statements directly linked to this transit issue . . . what do you think about that?"

"You have your own set of priorities with education at the forefront," Fred advises. "I don't imagine you'll reverse that platform at this stage of the campaign. We can always write a statement regarding your general views on the matter. There doesn't have to be a succinct focus on your specific position in this transit issue. Wait until later on . . . "

"Yes, I rather think that's appropriate for the present. There's no need for you to get strung out in the wilderness, so early in the game . . . take it easy, man. A whole lot of crises are going to pop up, in the interim, that'll attempt to draw off your energies. Stick with education. Let the transit committee appear in the public eye on this issue. We're less vulnerable than you. Don't go spreading yourself all over the city," says Landers.

"Both of you are just a little off base," Ferguson interjects. His political animus was already sensitized, so he used the situation to present a convenient view of the power confrontation with the union which, he thought, might help his long range strategy. He calculated like a fox. He would sound like the lion again, to make one lasting impression on Landers about his liberal commitments, and maybe later gain insight on economic directions within the establishment. "I have to keep abreast of issues from a realistic vote getting persepctive. As much as I can isolate essential elements of problems that plague the citizens, outside of their specific organizational or group interests, the more pragmatic my personal approach will be in presenting a platform."

"That sounds like an out of sight equation. You want us to hire some computer time to run that one through the machinery," quips Fred.

"That might keep you busy," Ferguson replies, dryly. "But, I'm sure you'd tell me that you had developed a program that was just a complicated restatement of my original idea, at any rate. Then, you'd tell me that it would be better accounting to let you tap your own resources to better inform me of the polls, right?"

"Hmm," sighs Fred. "I like the idea of contracting out, alright. But, sometimes I wonder who works for whom!"

"Sounds like you two have some complex relationship. Do you take care of any business, or are you still getting to know one another," jokes Landers.

"This guy does make me wonder what type of an outfit his people are running," Ferguson mocks Fred. "If it weren't for my implicit faith in his boss, I would swear I got a bad deal . . . Is that some kind of computer in an attaché case you're running around with, fellah?"

The three men had been slowly walking through the station during their conversation and finally emerged at the entrance of the cavelike facility. They entered the official limousine which was parked at the curb. The long black car meandered through downtown Brooklyn, across the Brooklyn Bridge and gradually entered Manhattan where it stopped at the reserved spot in front of City Hall. Landers was busy instructing the driver about the afternoon's itinerary while Fred and Ferguson alighted from the automobile and went to hail a cab at the curb.

" . . . And that's how I'd like you to write it up!"

"Alright. I'll put a press release together and have it on the wire service this evening," replies Fred. "It may be tomorrow when the news picks it up, though."

"That's okay . . . as long as it's coming from the work of the council."

The taxi had arrived and Fred entered the cab while Ferguson rejoined Landers in the City Hall lobby. With the immediate campaign tactic in motion, the candidate could return to his job with a relaxed temperament.

Chapter Twenty-Eight

New York was alive again with the arrival of the vernal equinox. The formerly vacant streets became crowded, seemingly overnight, as the city denizens fled their stuffy dwellings to indulge in the onset of warm spring weather. It was a welcomed change from the daily living patterns of the long cold winter, Fred thought, as he exited a taxi on Tenth Street. He paused at the newsstand to pick up an afternoon paper, as a young couple sped by on their bicycles. Lloyd had given him the time off to complete some writing and he decided to do some light shopping, before heading home to face the task. He strolled along First Avenue looking for bargains, casually browsing among the housewives and elderly at various open-air vegetable stands. Fred took his time and enjoyed the pleasant atmosphere of the ethnic and generational transitions in the neighborhood. He was in no rush to begin the work, as the job was a tough assignment. After finishing his shopping chores, he walked the short distance to Third Street.

Fred slowly climbed the three flights of stairs in the narrow hallway to apartment six. His springtime reverie was suddenly shaken, as he approached the door. It was slightly ajar, emitting lamplight from the interior into the dark hallway. Becoming upset at what he thought was an unusual oversight, he cursed at the situation, as he could not remember ever having left the apartment unlocked. Fred hurriedly entered the domicile, hoping nothing was taken in his absence. Fretful, but not suspecting malice, he pushed the door fully open with the weight of his shoulder, as his hands were filled with grocery packages, attache case and newspaper. He was shocked again at what he saw. A young black man stood awkwardly in the middle of the living room, nearby the work table where he had just finished searching documents. Fred's immediate thought was burglary, as he glanced at the rummaged condition of his apartment. His early return was unexpected and startled the intruder, who moved backward, cautiously, while still holding onto some papers. Dressed in an old dirty white polyester and cotton jacket, faded dungarees and sneakers, the thug could've passed for an adolescent, on the street. The momentary surprise was mutual, but Fred noticed the erratic body movements and unmistakable track marks on the junkie's bloated brown hands, before transfixing his gaze upon the burglar's eyes.

"What the hell . . . "

Suddenly, Fred felt a crushing pain in the occipital region of his skull. He dropped the packages from his hands, as he stumbled forward. He hadn't anticipated the accomplice behind the opened door. The blow wasn't incapacitating, but instead, stimulated his karate instincts. He sensed the position of the second thug and marshalled his resources for the onslaught. The accomplice attacked again. The large black man wore a full afro. Garbed in a tattered army field jacket, he was an awesome opponent, who weilded Fred's precious brass incense burner, menacingly. As he raised the implement to strike, Fred sprung. The action was lighting quick. He straightened from his bending position and spun his torso around, lifting his flexed left leg, and kicked. His reflexes were spontaneous, but his control was just a bit off from the disorientation of the attack. The defensive move would have been fatal with proper balance, but instead, sent the accomplice reeling into the wall. The incense burner crashed to the floor, as the man slid down the side of the wall and slumped over on his backside.

Fred's animus was kindled, giving him strength, as he struggled against both the killer instinct and the dizziness from the blow to his head. During the hesitation, the younger thug attacked, jumping upon his back. The momentum propelled the two men into the opened door. As he grappled with the junkie, Fred saw the steel blade of a knife and jerked his head sharply aside to avoid the weapon.. The burglar thrust the knife forward, slightly grazing Fred's temple, and slammed the weapon into the door. Making a backward sweep with his arm, Fred implanted a forceful blow with his elbow to the young man's rib cage. The thug bent over in pain, as Fred reeled around and struck the hoodlum across the larynx with the calloused side of his hand. The impact sent the junkie stumbling into the living room where he fell onto the floor, agonizingly gasping for air.

Fred felt wet blood and tightened his jaw muscle in anger. He went over to the moaning intruder and watched awhile.

"I should've killed you, you bastard . . . what's your name," he shouted at the junkie. He was irritated, but in control of his emotions. The young thug glared, in pain, and tried to spit in Fred's face.

"You son-of-a-bitch, I'll teach you never to rob again!"

Fred pulled the hoodlum to his feet and wheeled him around. He attempted to apply a 'full-nelson' on his neck, but the junkie ducked and bit Fred's hand. Applying tension to a pressure point on the young man's neck with his other hand, Fred caused the thug to cringe in pain and release his teeth. Just then, the accomplice grabbed Fred from behind, in a 'bear-hug.' His grip was like a vise, squeezing the breath from Fred's lungs. He was surprised by the resilience of the dope addicts. Apparently, the drugs had such a numbing effect on their nerves, that the junkies were able to continue fighting while sustaining major bodily injuries. He was sure he had broken a nose and a few ribs.

While the younger thug retrieved his knife, Fred thought fast. He wasn't about to give up to yama at this point. He would use his heel on the accomplice's shin bone, to loosen the grip, he quickly reflected. But, before he could maneuver, the knife-wielding junkie picked up some of Fred's papers and the two fled from the apartment, after pushing him onto the living room floor.

Alone now, Fred was disoriented from the ordeal and went to check on his injury. The cut was minor, so he covered it with a band-aid. He returned from the bathroom to assess the damage in his apartment. Fred looked around at the mess and shook his head in disgust. After painfully making the best out of an unbearable housing condition, because he liked the neighborhood and its proximity to work, he would now have to be in constant battle with drug addicts, he wrongly surmised. Fred didn't know where to begin the clean-up, so he went to replace the receiver onto the telephone. When he picked up the equipment, the cover fell open, revealing a very sensitive electronic eavesdrop. Fred disconnected the device and examined it closely. Although the job was sloppy, it definitely wasn't the usual modus operandi of junkies. He had never seen a wiretap, but knew immediately that something complicated was threatening his life. After thinking about the events in detail, Fred remembered that the thugs had taken some of his papers. He scrambled over to his materials, knocking the chair down, and searched laboriously through the disorganized documents. Something sinister was going on and he would have to get to the bottom of it.

It was important to reconstruct the general order of the various projects, to see what was missing. Fred tediously organized his papers again, and carefully thumbed through the material. He found the research notes on the Swazi Bauxite prospectus, as well as his preliminary plans for the Zambian communications project had been stolen. Fred was more perplexed than angry and sat down amidst the disarray wondering who could be behind the scheme. It looked like business espionage. He pondered the situation while looking around the apartment for other hidden complications. His bookcase was intact, the stereo and T.V. were secure, his clothes remained ordered. Finally satisfied, his gaze rested on the torn grocery bags, their contents strewn about the doorway. The newspaper was on the floor, slightly damaged from the conflict. The headlines announced the May 30, 1964 primary elections. Below the bold type, the characteristically polished smile of Charles Ferguson beamed, unmistakably, among the other candidates in the wrinkled photograph which accompanied the cover story.

Chapter Twenty-Nine

The entire staff of junior and senior public relations personnel were busy working on the final stages of the campaign at the offices of Transcontinental Media Promotions. A professional media blitz which the company formulated through extensive social science research was effective in opposing the traditional racist propaganda of the democrat machine, thus opening important doors within the conservative establishment. Ferguson looked good in the polls.

Lloyd was in his office, busy talking on the telephone with Dan Coleman, the excited campaign manager. It took all of his patience to allay the anxieties and nervousness of his associate, as the two men discussed lingering doubts. The door opened and Fred entered, holding a folder under his arm and a memo in his other hand. Lloyd completed the conversation with final assurances and placed the receiver onto the phone. Fred walked directly to Lloyd's desk and handed him the memo. The boss reclined in his chair while the worker leaned over the desk.

"Alright, what have you got working?"

"I'd like to sit down and play a game of chess with you, Lloyd."

"What the devil are you talking about, man? I don't have time, right now, to set up the board . . . besides, you can't play my game!"

Fred stepped back from the desk and pulled up a chair.

"Look, there's something I want you to explain to me."

"I will, if I can . . . what is it?"

"When was Ferguson selected to run as mayor of New York? I'm not talking about the formal mechanics of the Democrat Party organization." Fred transfixed his gaze on his boss's eyes, leaving no room for equivocation.

Lloyd interrupted the concentration and read his worker's inference, then laid the memo down on the table, reflectively.

"Oh, that goes back a long way. Look, you're not going to start asking me a whole lot of questions about who does the fingering, are you?"

"I'd be interested in that too, later on. But, right now, I'm concerned with the sources of his funds . . . you wouldn't be adversed to discussing that with me, would you?"

"Well, when you really get down to it, it really isn't all that confidential, anyway, is it? What are you and Les after, anyhow?" asks Lloyd, naively.

"Well, the brother did try to pry that information for me. What did you tell him?'' queries Fred. He had caught Lloyd off guard and conducted his own little Inquisition.

''Just what I shall tell you. Look it up in the campaign records,'' snaps Lloyd.

''But, you're not going to tell me that, right? I mean, I wouldn't have brought it up to you at all, myself, if I didn't think it was important.''

''I think I have an idea of where you're coming from, but go on, continue . . . ''

''What's happening along the twenty-fifth latitude that's so important for you to groom, me, and at this time? I'm talking about the trip to Zambia, true, but not solely in terms of our business relations. I'm concerned with other issues related to the philosophy of humanism . . . the framework for enlightened social and economic policy in that country is clear. What I want to know deals with political realities . . . like, how much influence does the embassy have on minorities in the urban affairs of this country, first of all? Next, where do I fit in?''

''Now, don't go off speculating! I don't think you'll find any contributions made through our relations with the embassy,'' Lloyd casually remarks. He regained control of the role reversal and became tactful, weighing the direction of Fred's intuition.

''It's just not part of the formal record . . . Here, read this and tell me if I see something important.'' He extended the company's copy of the Neilson Report to his superior and pointed to the elaborate statistical projections for implementing economic planning.

Lloyd perused the opened document while casually stroking his cheek. ''Well, I can see that you would be interested in the mathematics of the idea, but, ah, I really can't make out any heavy metaphysical connections. Perhaps, you can show me what you mean.''

''First, let me ask you one question. Do you plan to set me up for something that you haven't told me about?''

''Yes, I do, evidently.''

Fred reclined in the chair and smiled at Lloyd. He would try an indirect probe to pierce the older man's reserve.

''Well, then, you can't be planning to use the bishop, because you know where I stand on that matter.''

''Go on.''

''The knight is too limited a possibility . . . ''

''Feudal in essence. Non-applicable to the current times.''

''It . . . naw, it can't be the castle!''

''I see you must've been talking with Elaine,'' Lloyd digressed.

Fred wasn't entirely in the dark. He had assembled a fragmented picture from the insights of his exercises and made probable connections about the recent conflict within the logic of his memo.

''That sounds like bull, again . . . but, Lloyd, I'm not an official. Doesn't it frighten you that a liason through me is kind of tenuous?''

''If you really want to know, I'm planning on you and Helena reuniting and making the trip together. It's not so much you, by yourself, that will make the liason work, but rather what you represent about the folks back here at home.''

''But, Lloyd, I'm no symbol. I make my way through the hustle intuitively. I could never stand to be representative of anything, other than my own personal life values.''

''Stop playing my point down the drain!''

"Well, you be for real. You know I don't think that Helena and I have the same direction. What you need is somebody out of the civic domain, like Ferguson, to prop up as some sort of cultural image. I'm very selfish, you know."

"Since you bring this consideration up now, let me tell you a thing or two about your bombastic attitude," says Lloyd, in an irritated tone of voice. Fred's confrontation peeved him, and he lost his composure. "There's a responsibility that I see you meeting, by bringing together different forces that are necessary for the success of this operation in Africa. Now, the sacrifice is a personal one, and I think you'll agree that life just has larger issues than our personal worlds . . . Doc had to find that out the hard way. But, you were supposed to be picking something up while you were down there. Obviously, the lesson escaped you. Now that we have these types of international relations growing, there's no telling where the ball game might take us. What matters, is that we attempt to put forth the most wholistic and positive efforts to insure their maturity . . . who's to say who selected you to represent us over there, never mind the intrigue you suspect about Ferguson's political career. I'm your boss, only that . . . you'll have to get out there and find out the depth of the relationships we've worked out, before you can get any indication of the forces behind this network . . . I'm not going to tell you where Ferguson is getting a lot of his campaign money! The mystery is superfluous. Besides, I don't want you, or Les, for that matter, to be vulnerable. Perhaps, later on Les might be executing operations like this campaign, then he'll have that responsibility to consider, himself. Anyhow, you're going on a completely different route, altogether."

"Wait a minute, Lloyd, I resent that! I'm not a blind man and I don't see myself fumbling haphazardly in the dark, unnecessarily . . . you know me too well, to arbitrarily force me into something that I have reservations about, because I don't usually resist directives!"

"All I can tell you is that you will be amply taken care of, as long as you do the right type of job. The task is very heavy, and you'll just have to get a first hand picture, which I'm unable to give you at this point."

"Look, I'm willing to work on communications packages, as long as the idea relates to viable socio-economics. But, at this point, it all sounds pretty macabre . . . "

"Well, you'll just have to change your frame of reference and look at things from a larger scale than you're accustomed, Fred."

"And resume a lifestyle which, from all indications, can't work," he quips. He wasn't completely satisfied and provoked his boss further, to get clarity.

"That's a minor problem you should be able to work out. I'm concerned with the Murphy family representing TMP over there. Not just Fred!"

"Now, there's no way in the world you can formulate a profile for me, as an expatriate . . . I don't rank! I keep telling you, I'm not an official."

"I can see you have the wrong picture in mind, already, Fred. It's not the politician that's ultimately important for our work . . . what we have in mind is the successful businessman. Zambia's socialist government is solvent. What's needed in that country deals with economic relations, with connections extending beyond, the mere, political arena . . . what do you think something like a television satellite operation would amount to, if it were solely a state operation? It's a major consideration of your project, you know?"

"Lloyd, I see the direction of your point, as far as my work in communications. But, I keep telling you that family life is over with me . . . that wouldn't be a forward moving step to consider, as part of the package."

"We'll have to talk about it a little more."

"This is as good a time as any, Lloyd!"

"I have some telephone work to do," he curtly replies.

"Bull," says Fred, gesturing a karate advance. "Messing that directly with the economics of a foreign country is too subject to political quagmire, and one must be able to protect himself . . . I just don't think I want my family to be vulnerable to those pressures."

"You always sound as if you're speaking in the first person!"

"Getting away from my mother taught me that! Man, I realize that it won't be done in isolation. That others would be involved is all part of my cognizance. But, I still have to make some personal discriminations in my role, as a change agent in the world," Fred persists. He wanted his position clearly understood, as a defensive precaution of his hindsight from being black-listed.

"Well, you've been selected for this assignment by some very powerful people. I won't say anymore to you about it at this time. Just get your shit together and be ready to travel in the next couple of months," Lloyd concludes.

"Hold on, man! This report covers a lot of information about international trade and commerce, based on complicated patterns of economic development. Translating just that source, to develop communications packages is a lot of homework for me, don't you think? I mean, with your contacts, you could at least get me briefed on the undercurrents involved, before I make a tragic mistake."

"You're already linked with Elaine. I expect she'll be helpful. You're going to be meeting some heavier international financiers through the embassy, now. She'll be your contact, so you might as well prepare yourself, thoroughly, with her help. All of our efforts must be geared to make our timing pay off . . . managing cities is the first important step toward realizing stable world governments. It's all a matter of finances, at this point. You can agree with that, can't you? It's a critical event now, but has always been part of world history. Well, realize your responsibility in creating a viable communications industry along those lines," Lloyd counsels him.

"Alright, so I leave out political intrigue and mystery, for the moment . . . still, I want to find out what type of designs there are for me to become a patrician, once I've had an opportunity to get into the problem at hand."

"It wouldn't make sense, right now," Lloyd remarked, closing the inquiry.

"Well, that's one hell of a way to conspire," quips Fred.

"Call it what you like, but don't refuse the key when it's extended to you!"

"That's about the same thing you told me when I got into this business. Now, I don't have any family life for the two years we've worked together. Based upon those prospects, I wonder what's going to transpire in the future . . . I keep telling myself, I'm only thirty-five, I can be recycled. But I wonder!"

"I understand your feelings, Fred, but don't start shaking up the campaign accounting at this point. It could only lead to trouble, if somebody gets wind of what your thoughts have brought to light . . . And, lay off Lester! He doesn't need to be concerned with that type of information to do his job effectively."

"Lloyd, this is incredible! I've never known you to hold back on me, once I've told you what I was after . . . why so secretive?"

"It's not peculiar, Fred. See me through to the completion of the project. It will all become clear to you in the near future."

"Sounds like we're operating out of the State Department, or something . . . "

Fred got up from the chair. He knew his efforts would go nowhere, now. But, at least he had satisfied his premonition. "I guess I'll get my passport renewed. Maybe that will push the matter out into the open that much sooner."

Lloyd got up and ushered Fred out of the door. For the moment he was successful, but he knew Fred's personality. The matter would have to be resolved while he continued nurturing the talented young man. He was important to the organization, even though a bit idealistic. "I'm glad I have your confidence!"

"Trust in me saith the man!"

Fred closed the door as he left the office. Lloyd stood alone, momentarily reflecting upon the conversation. Finally, he returned to his desk and picked up the telephone.

" . . . It's me, Lloyd . . . yes, alright, I guess. Look, this thing has got to move more swiftly. Fred's come across something . . . oh, scrutinizing the Neilson Report. He uses languages very well, you know. Sometimes it inspires his mathematics. I, ah, imagine Elaine fired him up somewhat . . . no, it didn't come entirely as a surprise. I had to play dumb though . . . I think I stalled him, temporarily . . . uh, huh . . . getting them back together is going to be the really difficult thing . . . alright, I'll wait for you to come up with something . . . "

Lloyd removed a very large reference book and began searching the details of the index. After finding the subject of interest, he reclined in the armchair with his filled pipe lit, reading the text.

Chapter Thirty

Work by the Civil Rights Movement was progressing steadily in the Federal Courts, at that time, through the charismatic leadership of Dr. King, who had gained national prominence in the media. The impact of the social revolution awakened a new sense of solidarity among the Blacks, particularly, as the policies of integration swept across the country. The local reaction to accomodate the increasing numbers of minority voters led to a series of convenient political realignments, behind the scenes in New York. Ferguson emerged within the party struggles and capitalized on that power to ultimately succeed in his primary bid for mayor in the city. His election victory was front page news around the metropolis and was also reported extensively by the major radio and television networks, following immediately after the formal tally.

After the event, the elation over a prospective change in administrative patterns lingered for several days among the civil servants who gossiped continually about the primary while performing their diverse functions. Ferguson's scheduled meeting with the Black Teacher's Caucus at offices in the municipal building contributed additional excitement to the otherwise typically bureaucratic atmosphere of the worker's activities. He sat inside the conference room entertaining the representatives who arranged themselves, semicircular around his chair. Jomo was busy taping the group with his nagra sound recorder.

" . . . So, that's about the extent of it, my friends. The governor will not endorse the entire platform. His reservation stems from the position that I take on school decentralization," Ferguson remarks.

"Well, we can't really be concerned with his view of the Constitution, because he'll never be able to run for national office, anyway. But, our concerns are being soft peddled, because they do raise basic fiscal issues about accountability . . . regardless of the city's tax structure, we've got to make a real attempt at community control, just as you put forth in the proposal," says Rupert Andrews. He was the principal representative of the Black Teacher's Caucus who had consulted with Ferguson on the draft proposals. Like his political counterpart, he was an old-timer to the system, and felt happy that his tireless battle to effect educational changes for the young black and other minority students had finally paid off.

"That's my feeling on the matter, as well. In the end, he can't get away from the problem by paraphrasing Mayor Bailey's talk about a tight budget . . . judging by the election. nobody around town wants to hear that kind of crap. Eventually, he's going to have to change his position to maintain his political constituency in New York.''

"Perhaps, if more serious attention had been paid to white liberal propaganda, then community control within the Board of Education could've been anticipated. The voters can see the import behind the issue," says Omira Bay. She was an attractive, dark skinned, middle aged woman whose flair for African attire had caused personality conflict with her colleagues on the job. The resentment carried over into her professional work where she found administrative closure in her attempt to introduce black history into the curriculum.

"Probably! Because, we're only telling them what is inevitable in their current short-sighted programs," remarks Callander.

"Well, we're continuing to map out our plan and disseminating it nationally. Our efforts coincide with the general thrust in other cities around the country. I just hope our projects are considered in future city planning. Whatever is on the drawing board for the year two thousand, we have to face it as educators. So, our suggestions should be recorded in the public record for consideration by the citizens," says Andrews.

"Right," adds Fred. "There shouldn't be any difficulty in presenting alternatives to the situation . . . what's relevant is right there in the package for general understanding!"

"This will be the first real meaningful change in public education in decades."

"Well, I'm glad to hear you speak so positively about the outcome of the proposal, Omira. How do you feel about taking a part in the machinery, once this change occurs," asks Callander.

"It's another way of making room for the others coming behind me!"

"Yes, it has a great deal of potential in all of the key motive parameters," Fred comments. "As you see, it's flexible enough to provide that important challenge to the people to build their communities, and get over poverty."

"Teachers eventually become administrators, if they're progressive minded. So, what's more natural than to make that a principal concern in community control of the educational process," observes Andrews. "Educators have a responsibility for policy formulation, also. They tie in at the board level along with the community interests. Therefore, an approach like that would create a different kind of balance in the dialogue. I think it would be more meaningful."

"You don't have to convince me, dear," Callander glibly interjects. "That complex out there on Livingston Street is a pitifully archaic structure, to say the least."

"Well, I hate to introduce a note of political realism, but at this point, it really depends upon the type of reception the proposal will have on the people," remarks Ferguson. "That's the ultimate test. And that has a lot to do with presentation and dissemination . . . you'd be surprised at what never reaches the public attention. I can remember my field days in Mississippi, visiting a health care center which had to get support from UNICEF, because it couldn't get a dime out of the state, after it had exhausted its federal funds . . . now, just think about that for a moment, as far as the direct awareness needed by the voting public about issues that affect the body."

"Even though that's going on down South at this time, I still feel the city dweller has more overall pressures that keep him in economic flux and thereby in a worse state of tension," Omira comments, reflectively. "Take school, for instance. Workers know how much money is taken out of their pockets, but there is no social accountability when they look at the educational situation. That's why I think this proposal has its own justification written into it.''

"You're perfectly right, it does," remarks Ferguson. "But, to make sure that there will be no problem for the ideas to be assimilated, I suggest that you utilize the communications expertise that Fred represents. You all know that he's working with my campaign . . . I want you to feel free to discuss any other problems with him. He's ultimately charged with keeping these areas of my platform alive in people's minds.''

"It's his nice way of easing on to other parts of his schedule," Callander jokes. She was accustomed to Ferguson's gentlemanly style and made fun of his overly tactful way of relating to black folks.

"Oh, have we kept you too long?''

"I've got about ten more minutes, Rupert. Then, I'm really going to have to leave.''

"Since it might be a problem getting the governor's endorsement, where do you think you'll go from there?" asks Omira.

"I think we discussed this strategy, didn't we Fred?''

"Yes, I mentioned to the campaign staff that an endorsement by white mayors and other Blacks in official capacities on the national scene, might be an alternative approach. That way, we'll keep Ferguson close to the headlines and people will continue to follow the details of the proposal, to keep up conversationally.''

"Well, it's a hot issue with city workers, so I understand," says Omira. "And, of course, the community is keeping up with it.''

"Some of the college groups are doing strategic work on it, as part of their civil rights activities," Fred comments.

"That's good! It increases the amount of dialogue in the home, in a lot of cases," observes Omira. "They're also a sizable vote in their own right.''

"Yes, students can be very perceptive. Often it's just a matter of organizing a communications channel for that audience. In the end, a greater population is reached," says Fred.

"Students often realize issues more poignantly, in terms of their own transition into adulthood," remarks Callander. "Once they get a gist of the ideas, they can follow a precept pretty steadfastly. It's all a part of coming of age.''

"Thus, they become a different kind of lobby to be galvanized by the astute politician," adds Fred.

"Well, somebody ought to recognize those young people," says Callander, emphatically. "They're trying to get home the same way we are, you know.''

"Well, I can see further implications of this proposal, myself," says Omira. "It could lead to setting up an extensive private school system. All it would take is some imagination and the right type of forceful contacts that your company represents, Murphy.''

"I wish it were that easy, sister Bay!''

"Don't act as if you're sitting on a diamond mine," quips Callander. "You know you'll have to give that to somebody else while the campaign is in process, Fred.''

"What are you prepared to do for us?''

"I can function as your consultant, Rupert. At the same time, I would attempt to further some of my own ideas, on behalf of the caucus.''

"What did you have in mind, Murphy?''

"A suggestion to include a comprehensive exposure to the arts. Basically traditional, in the direction of character development. Then, I can see the virture of increasing the dialogue betwen various classes of students to foster a spirit of cooperative endeavour. Things that could enrich the relationship between students, as they begin to move from probelm solving to creative enterprise. I guess, right now, the only concrete focus is to use municipal facilities and services, more thoroughly, for these kinds of activities," Fred summarizes, briefly.

"You mean sponsoring cultural events during the school year," asks Omira.

"That's a limited example, perhaps," says Fred. "Ultimately, the notion is to engender individual respect and appreciation of human life. It's a normal outcome of the battle for full citizenship rights which is part of the responsibilities of community control."

"That sounds very interesting, Murphy. I'd like to bring that back to the body, if you don't mind."

"Hey, wait a minute! It seems as if you're getting ready to disgress with all that 'body' talk, Omira." Callander was having her usual fun, poking little digs at black leadership. Although cynical, at times, it was part of her down-to-earth informal personality.

"Do I detect a note of jealousy, Rita? You didn't think that I had anything in mind, did you?"

"You've ceased surprising me, Baby. But, I just wanted to let you know that I was listening closely to your conversation."

"You'll have to excuse me, Omira, I always seemed to get seduced away from serious concerns through personal flattery by our black politicians," says Fred.

Ferguson checked his watch. He would have to cut the meeting short to continue his official duties. "Well, I can see a lighter tone has developed, so I'll make my exit about now. I imagine you people will let me know when we'll be getting together, again . . ."

The group got up, and Ferguson shook hands with the representatives.

"Don't worry," says Andrews. "We'll keep you boys down at City Hall busy on this matter. There's a lot of work in store for you people, now that the ball is rolling so well."

"Just remember to make sure and give all of the work to the right person over there," Ferguson jokes, as he points a finger at Fred. "His group represents a vital organ to this campaign."

"Oh, we can see that they're on top of the situation," says Omira. "As long as that type of publicity is forthcoming, neither of us should have too much to worry about . . . But, then, it's always good to have reservations. That way, one hand will cover the other and very little will be overlooked."

"You're quite right about that! It's a good thing to remain conscientious until the end," observes Callander. "That way, no matter what occurs, you've provided a learning experience of some value."

Ferguson left the conference room while the meeting broke into an informal conversation. Andrews moved casually to the table at the rear and perused campaign literature left by the caucus.

"That was a pretty decent suggestion, 'Baby'. Where did you conjure up that idea? It had to be in some pretty far-out quarters, I'm sure," teases Callander. She was in the mood for the dozens and began her provocative behavior, again.

"Rita, stop trying to project difficulty in keeping up. Those little political ploys that you're so adept at using are beginning to tire me.''

"Well, you're kind of cute when you're on the spot. Fred!''

"Is that how the spiders nurtures its web, by playing upon gross vanity? Or is it a genuine pleasure you have in poking fun at the layman?''

"That's the best one I've heard, yet! Imagine, you, being figured as a political neophyte," Callander laughs. She became theatric and affected a deep voice. "Oh, uh, Fred? He's just a down-to-earth city boy, you know . . .''

"Well, that's an easy enough mode for me to fall into.''

"Sounds like we have another potential candidate here," laughs Omira . . . "Excuse me, but I do want to take that idea back to the caucus. Do you have any objections?''

"No, not offhand," replies Fred. "But, why don't you wait until I can map it out a little further? First, I'd like to talk to you some more about it, if that's possible. Then, perhaps we can come up with a more thorough package.''

"That sounds fine. Just contact me and let me know when.''

"Say, Ferguson is really on the ball, isn't he," Andrews comments. "You know, I haven't known anyone to move up through the ranks, as quickly as he's done it. It certainly will be an interesting administration with him in office.''

"I suppose you see a tremendous amount of work that went into his preparation," Callander remarks, matter of factly.

Jomo had packed his recording equipment and was headed back to the office. "Excuse me, I'm wrapping up. You don't need me to do anything else today, do you?''

"No," replies Fred. "Just be sure to edit around the personal stuff. That's scheduled for a radio talk show later this evening.''

"Got you!" Jomo exited the conference room with his smooth cat-like movements.

"Say, Fred. Do you think you can get a short informational film together for us to use in other cities?" inquires Andrews.

"Yes, there's no problem in getting that done. There's almost enough material for something like that already.''

"Well, it would be helpful for the caucus to communicate, as we branch out across the country, if you know what I mean.''

"Indeed! You could start by sending a copy to the principal civil rights organizations. That's an important sphere of influence that you people can exploit. There are probably some other organizations that will come to mind, once I sit down and talk to sister Bay, here," says Fred.

"Good! We can start this ball rolling right away. You know, I'm really impressed by Ferguson's agility and swiftness . . . and, I see there's a carryover in the associates around him," Andrews remarks, complimentingly.

"There's no grass growing under Mr. Murphy's feet, darling. He knows all the options of speed and specializes in weathering the storm. Don't you, Mr. Navigator," teases Callander.

"I try to know where I'm going, Rita . . . thank you!''

"In that case, we can look forward to our work coinciding with the election," says Omira. "There's undoubtably a great many things that will be developed by the fall, once nature begins her pruning. . . then, we'll be able to see the birds in the bush.''

"Yes," Fred agrees. "Then, our timing should be right for scheduling communications activity, since autumn is a good time to discriminate complicated fiscal matters. It's quite a creative art of planning the transition between final and first act, during that season. It's precisely why we should coordinate around the campaign. Programs should be ready to begin, by the time Ferguson's in office . . . and, we all know, there are a million things to get done.''

''Well, if you feel anything like I do, you're a very anxious man,'' says Andrews.

''I hope I can contain myself long enough to get some of these ideas under way,'' Fred comments, as he smiles, charmingly to the group.

''Isn't that the biggest understatement you've ever heard,'' sneers Callander.

''It sounds like the man has a good direction, to me,'' Omira remarks, thoughtfully. ''I'm sure there's a great deal of credit he deserves.''

''You'll find the collaboration with him to be decidedly one-sided, I'm afraid, my dear,'' Callander pestily criticizes him.

''Well let's not get too carried away, Rita. I know how to work with other people . . .''

''My, that's incredible! How long have you been aware of orchestration, may I ask?''

''That's one of the more immediate goals, since we're operating in an urban context at this time,'' quips Fred.

''There's no doubt about it. It just happens that education is wrapped up in urban policy, but it's certainly a national concern,'' Andrwes reflects.

''Yes, and as usual, it takes us folks to perceive ways of handling the mess that's been organized over the years,'' says Fred, sarcastically. ''We're just going to have to start directing events through our perception of the greater goals. There's really no other way!''

''I'll buy that,'' says Andrews, enthusiatically.

''What are you two doing? Planning to run for office, the next time around, perhaps,'' badgers Callander.

''From my understanding, Rita, one never knows when one's hat is tossed into the ring. It's always wise to have an ongoing platform.''

''Well, you go right ahead and keep working at your constituency, Baby.''

Fred paused in his conversation to drink some water. ''All of the time, Rita . . . all of the time!''

''Then, you and Omira Bay will be able to start working on the communications project right away?'' asks Andrews.

''Let me check with the office, before I make a final statement, alright.''

''You wouldn't want to get caught chasing birds in the bush, prematurely. Would you, now,'' cajoles Callander.

''You know, Rita, there are other things indicated by the square, besides opposition . . . but, let's just say, I'm writing in a little rest among the other little notes to provide musical interest. It gives the composition the ability to continue building,'' Fred says, to downplay her dig.

''Tell her, brother,'' Andrews edges the spar.

''Hmmm, it seems that I'm entirely out of place in this company. It must be time for my exit . . . see you children, later.'' Rita had caused enough trouble for Fred, she thought. So, she departed, in her characteristic nonchalant manner, and left the little group of eager bourgeois civi servants to their task of solving the problems of black society, she joked to herself.

"Gee, that woman's got a lot of fire in her," Andrews reflects, with an affectionate smile.

"Is it my imagination, or does she take you under her wing?" asks Omira.

Fred was used to Rita's teasing. He had accepted it as part of the mutual respect they had for each other. He smiled at the womanly insight of the representative.

"Since you noticed it, I don't think there's any more to say about it, do you?"

"I can dig it, Fred. After all, I'm not as old as she is, but I can respect that type of relationship," Omira remarks, demurely.

Chapter Thirty-One

The large bay windows of the spacious three room apartment were opened, allowing the fresh air and Northern light of the early morning sunshine to pour in and enliven the atmosphere of the dwelling. The intermittent chatter of sparrows, linnets and gosbeaks presented natural harmony, as the birds played amongst the trees in the backyard. The Golden Gate Bridge could be seen picturesquely in the distance, reaching upward toward the overhanging cumulus clouds. Several large paintings hung on the walls inside the sparsely furnished domicile, complimenting the African statues, Oriental metalwork and a small British rug, placed in the center of the living room floor. A colorful antique globe stood in its frame, next to the small bookcase. An opened book rested, face down, on the simple couch, next to a pretty stuffed rag doll. While the television emitted an inaudible series of pictures to an empty living room, a woman's voice could be heard talking on the telephone in the kitchen. Helena was seated upon a stool, conversing in a hilarious mood. She was a petite, yet sensual woman, whose light brown eyes accentuated the large bush of black silken hair which she wore in an Afro style. Her casual demeanor complimented a keen, alert mind. Still youthful looking at thirty-two, she sat, dressed in dungarees and opened blouse, entertaining herself during one of the many daily telephone conversations with local girlfriends.

"You know, that's really a very funny coincidence," she says, while smothering her laughter. "All of the people we know are in that same position . . . trying to keep a balance between some situation, or other, and their old men. What's Ann doing . . . " she laughs, rioutously, at the reply. " . . . Is that right? You know, Dorothy, those reggins that they made during the thirties are really something else. They must have all come out of the same mold. I'm telling you, Dot, all of the sisters are having the same kind of trouble with their men . . . Anita tells me that Cliff has finally decided to sit down and do some serious writing. Nothing else seems to matter to him, these days, except writing. So, he's pushing the keys, now. Before that, you remember, he was going to take over the movement and set Blacks right in the world . . . Pan has got Amy looking at the world through rose-colored glasses, even though they might get thrown out of that new development which they've just recently moved into, you know. He's still peddling the revolutionary magazine business and pimping like some pseudo-intellectual storefront priest. And

Wendy's husband, Van! That sucker is still trying to make all of the money in the world by conjuring up those ridiculous deals with those jive-ass associations. She never sees the reggin!'' She laughs a moment at the comical situation. ''I'm telling you, I can stand this relaxation . . . right! I know you do, dear . . . isn't it unbelievable what you can get into when they're not around? . . . I didn't know that! How's she doing? Well, I'm just over an operation that I had and it's been more than a month, now . . . yes, well, I'm glad I went for a check-up. I would have never thought that my appendix had to be removed . . . you're kidding me, Dot . . . well, a body has to take care of itself when it starts getting old. Although, I'll be the first to let you know how young I am,'' she says with flattering laughter. ''The trick is to think young and let your experience work for you . . . aren't you too much! What did Hal say about that? Well, that's wonderful! Let's see if he keeps his word. You know how those reggins promise you everything to try to console you . . . okay, I don't want to run away with the time on the hot line. Call me back later, if you get a chance to use the phone. Bye now.''

As she put the receiver down, the bedroom door slammed shut, suddenly, which changed her whole demeanor. Helena reflected a moment, then lifted herself agilely to investigate the situation. She stood contemplating the closed door, then opened it and looked around curiously. Not finding anything unusual, she returned to the living room, shaking her head.

''Damn! What kind of spirits are working around here today? Take it easy, fellows!''

She went over to the couch and picked up her book again. Helena had just settled down comfortably when the doorbell rang. She got up, reluctantly, and glided across the room. When she opened the portal, Fred's unexpected presence startled her, causing an awkward facial expression during the silent interplay of emotions.

''Oh, my God! This is unbelievable,'' exclaims Helena, as she recoils from the doorway. ''What are you doing here?''

''What am I doing here? I thought you were supposed to be in the hospital!'' Fred entered the apartment during her momentary confusion. ''What is this, your idea of a joke of something?''

''What do you mean? This isn't even oddly entertaining,'' she replies, adamantly slamming the door to display her irritation.

Fred pulled a telegram out of his pocket and held it before her face. ''Didn't you send me this?''

''What is this foolishness?'' Helena shrieks, as she grabs the telegram from his hand and walks to an open window.

Fred controlled himself, taking time to scrutinze the apartment, first, while she read the message. ''Why did you have me come across the country, if you're not in the hospital?''

''I was in the hospital, for your information,'' she quips. ''About a month ago.''

''So, what made you wait until now to get me out here?''

''I didn't send that message. I don't even want to see you, Fred!''

''Well, thanks to someone's pranks, I made a trip for nothing,'' he glibly remarks. ''Where's Amber?''

''She's in school. She's been doing that for a year now, or don't you remember how old she is?''

''Oh,'' says Fred, somewhat disconcerted. ''Who took care of her while you were in the hospital?''

"I took her to Los Angeles. Why? Were you coming out here to babysit?"

"Don't chastise me, Helena! You know you've never let me know where you were living during all this time. Even though your friends seem to think I'd have some possessive interest in knowing your whereabouts, I wasn't the least bit interested in chasing you around the country. I pay my dues through the court. It's your business with them, after that!"

"I didn't expect that you came all the way out here to San Francisco, just to see how your money was being spent," she quips.

Fred sensed Helena's belligerent attitude and tried to circumvent an unnecessary argument. He avoided the issue tactfully, by taking interest with her parenting of their child. "It's a nice apartment. Did you have any difficulty finding it?"

"We seem to be getting along alright?"

"Who's that," queries Fred, uneasily. She had a way of plying his chauvinism through petty ego deceits.

"Amber and myself! Are you coming from the airport, Mr. detective?"

"A little hurried, but I imagine I can find someplace to stay until I can catch a return flight."

"Oh, now that you've put in your appearance, you're ready to leave, just like that, without seeing your daughter! What kind of a man are you, anyway? . . . you're her father! Or, have you disavowed that fact. It seems to me that you would at least be responsive in some way to your role, since you're out here! She knows that you exist. Don't pretend she doesn't! While you're here, you might as well see how she's grown, in the past two years," Helena remarks, furiously. She still lacked emotional control, and the seemingly surreptitious visit ignited a resurgence of feelings from the past. She was overwhelmed by his appearance and found it a convenient issue to ventilate her temper. Fred was upset, but he checked his anger.

"I imagine that some changes have taken place . . . "

"Your cruel sense of reality doesn't disturb me, Fred! I'm talking about your child, not some vague abstraction! You certainly had better find some time to see your daughter, now that you're out here!"

"After all, her mother made that statement and the whole world will judge me according to your sentiments, isn't that right?" quips Fred, with biting irony. "You really mean I could have put aside my personal responsibilities, trying to survive, and gone searching for your whereabouts. That would be a better description of the situation, wouldn't it?"

"Probably about as easily as you went to Martique . . . you know, I call that being very blatant, the way you made my brother get all uptight," she shouted at him, with tension straining her voice. Frustration blocked her reason, and she lambasted him, verbally, in a temperamental rush of random associations. "I really don't think you ever take time to consider human feelings, do you?"

"I have a right to my personal tastes," Fred retorts, defensively. "Your brother is merely related to me through marriage. As far as those kinship bonds extend in our relationship, we're legally separated. There's no need for him to feel a loss of faith. Sometimes, two people don't make it, right? It's not the fault of the marital institution, in and of itself. But, he doesn't understand that and I'm not really interested in making my frame of reference adhere to his personal prejudices . . . I don't like him for getting into my affairs. He think's it's because of other reasons. That's his problem."

"He was only doing what he thought was his responsibility," exclaims Helena, quickly rationalizing her outburst. "Obviously, you don't have any concept of what that is! Anyway, you could have been more civil. Isn't that part of male camaraderie," she says, to provoke his ire. Helena knew how independent Fred was, but attacked his personality out of frustration, adding more confusion to the situation.

"What the hell do you think you know about that, Helena!"

"Enough to see that you don't even have that anymore! What do you represent, Mr. Murphy? Do you see anything in the mirror at all?"

"I'm getting old! I don't have to look at myself to understand that," he sighs, with exasperation. "Besides, there are far too many things to be done!"

"That is, besides being a father!"

Fred saw himself being dragged into the web of antagonism. Somehow, he had hoped that time would've taken the bitterness out of their relationship. "I'm not going to get into that sophism with you, Helena. You already have the floor. Before long, I'd be here attempting to present a case to you. I've told you many times just where I stand on that matter."

"That's right, I can't understand you, no matter how hard you try to explain yourself," she badgers. "After all, as you always say, you're the mother, Helena, you should understand your daughter's problems . . . meanwhile, you don't have to stop living, because that's not the way you see yourself as a father."

"She'll always know where to come, if she needs me."

"That sounds so deplete of any kind of compassion, man. When are you going to get wise to your child's needs? Even if she is a little girl!"

Helena was crucifying her husband for all of the emotional tension she remembered in their marriage. She worked the confrontation up further, from a closed mind, although her rational thinking was cognizant of the cold economic facts and social influences which fundamentally plagued their family. She marched into the kitchen with a fretful display of disdain and began cleansing the dirty pots, angrily banging them on the sink.

Fred followed her, trying to maintain control. He hated these scenes. Black people should be more mature and leave pettiness behind, he thought. If only he could make Helena understand! "You've always told me that little girls grow exceedingly swift. Much quicker than little boys, so it's said. But, that doesn't make me feel that her life is any-the-less handicapped without a balanced home. That's something that I've continually brought to your attention, if you remember correctly!"

"Oh, I'm glad to see that you realize the need to come around, once in a while."

"If I take a different position, you'll argue with me about that. What am I to say to you, Helena. I've told you a thousand times to use a tape recorder when you speak, so you would avoid sounding so redundant. Obviously, you didn't believe me."

"I'd like to cut your tongue out . . . if I were a witch, I'd poison your speech. That would probably be worse than castrating you!"

"I'm tired of these adolescent conflicts. I'm not trying to hurt you. It's the only thing that you've been able to see in all that I've attempted to encourage. Some antagonist trying to outscore you. I've just been too busy trying to do the many things that have to be done in other areas of life, than to concern myself with keeping up the constant infighting. Who's got time for the irrelevant competition?"

"I know. That's energy wasted," she analyzes his thought with cold sarcasm.

"Oh, how brutal it all sounds to a mind fascinated with imagination. What else could you put into a little child's mind?"

"That the only way through this miasma of life events is to build for personal salvation. It's no different for Amber because she's a little girl. She'll grow up to be a little lady. But, the same situation confronts her, as a black person. She's going to have to make some decisions in life, and I'm more concerned with her ability to exercise her own values in her judgement. If I were to stop what I'm doing now, I don't think I could be any more of a father to her, than in continuing what I had set about, in the first place," he replies, incisively, attempting to awaken her intellectual sensibilities.

"Your self-importance is so ingratiatingly supercilious," she snaps, with dry callousness, downplaying Fred's point.

"Well, from that description, I have enough opposition in my life, as it is, than to become schizophrenic," Fred remarks, caustically. "It's been a long time and a lot of hard work in getting to where I am now. If, for a moment, I thought it wasn't worth it, I wouldn't spend any more time with these kinds of activities." He paused a second to calm the atmosphere, before making his next point. It was important that he, at least, contribute sober clarity to engender maturity in their parental communication. "The fact of the matter is that Amber Ujima will grow up wholesomely, precisely because I refuse to stop trying to change the oppressive conditions of the black family. You keep thinking that a person takes some time out, somewhere within the work. That's just not so, I'm afraid."

"Hell, you don't ever reverse your opinion," Helena remarks. She had been moved by Fred's sincerity and tried to be less of a bitch. "When was the last time you related to Amber like a child, instead of a little adult?"

"Now, that doesn't sound at all like you. You know we touch one another in our own ways. I only make her aware of the fact that she is the center of her growth experience. It's one of the more beautiful mysteries of life, but it is a responsibility," Fred comments.

Helena was embarrassed, but she didn't want Fred to be comfortable. Although she knew their separation was not entirely his fault, there was no other concrete focus for her to ventilate the agony of her love-hate tension for the man. She fled the complication and went into the living room while continuing her tirade.

"Oh, you are so overbearing! I don't see how you're able to work your field with an attitude like that. How did they ever select you to work on an election campaign centered around education?"

"Perhaps, they couldn't argue my philosophies," Fred casually replies, while standing near the bookcase watching her every gesture, as she sat on the couch.

"Everything is so real, it's crystal clear, isn't it, Fred Murphy?"

He shook his head in dismay. "I hope other people don't pick up that idea of politics. Otherwise, we'd be counting on a lot of misinformed voters . . . "

"I might've asked you about the campaign, if you had shown real interest toward my illness. But, apparently, I didn't present a classical picture of recuperation . . . In case you want to know, I had my appendix removed."

"I'm not here to hold an Inquisition, Helena . . . it's good that there wasn't anything else more serious wrong with you. You might've contacted me, though."

"You really move me with your concern," she says, with indifferent laughter. "How's the party making out? We've been getting reports out this way. You people are just about ready to go to the polls, in a few months, isn't that right?"

Fred relaxed somewhat. He sensed that Helena had spent her emotional energy, and was psyched-down. He was glad of the opportunity to turn to other comfortable matters. "One of the most decisive contests across the country. It all has to mean something, you know."

"You look tired, man . . . are they working you hard?"

The unmistakable change in Helena's tone of voice sensitized Fred. Beyond the tension of their estrangement, he was still captivated by his alluring wife. He felt an upsurge of physical longing and looked away so as to avoid her eyes. "I could use about an hour or two of sleep . . . maybe a cup of coffee."

"Nonsense! You'll have to stay and eat dinner. Amber will be in about three fifteen . . . I can whip up something nice for the occasion," she says, decisively. Helena told herself she was responding to Amber's paternal needs, but behind the rationale was more than the physical agony of their estrangement.

Fred dismissed the sexual hunger and searched Helena's eyes.

"You don't know anything about that message?"

"You can be sure that I didn't send it to you," she curtly replies, as she got up to evade his stare.

"What are you doing for yourself, Helena?"

"Keeping busy!"

"I mean . . . "

"Really now, Fred. What with taking care of Amber . . . plus, I've started painting, again. I'm over at the Art Institute a lot. I just don't have time for all of that."

Fred was sorry he had expressed his jealousy. The situation tempted lust, but he was certain of his deeper emotions. "Maybe I am, just your little boy!"

"Huh, listen to this one. I have enough on my mind than to be thinking about taking care of your crazy self. Go on in there and get some rest, before I change my mind," she says, in a charming manner.

Fred hesitated a moment, unfastening his tie, then went into the bedroom, leaving Helena alone in the living room. She gathered her composure and put the earplug into the television, turning the volume up, comfortable. Although calmer now, the character of surreptitiousness within the tense awkward events played on her mind, as she sat on the couch idly watching the daytime soap operas.

Chapter Thirty-Two

The silent television glared at the empty living room, contrasting with the chatter of birds which presented pleasant background sounds to the otherwise serene atmosphere of the apartment. Long shadows crawled along the floor from the rays of the afternoon sunshine which had just departed from its zenith. The Chinese characters on the unique wall clock read three twenty-five. The front door opened, and Helena entered with Amber, who peeked inquisitively around the apartment. She carried her school books in a knapsack which dwarfed her tiny six-year-old body. She was a gorgeous golden brown miniature of her mother.

"Is it in here, mommy?"

"No, I think the surprise is in my bedroom. You can go and open my door." Helena helped Amber with her knapsack, then went to turn on the television set. She had a change of mind and opted for the stereo, instead. Helena listened to her daughter's surprised voice in the background, as she selected music appropriate to her mood.

"Daddy! Daddy! Mommy didn't tell me you were coming to see me!"

Fred awakened when Amber shook his head. He was elated to see his beautiful daughter. "Come here, darling and give me some sugar. My, you've grown so. You're going to be as tall as I am, before too long."

The deep melodious voice of Nina Simone drowned the conversation with the subtle nuance of her poetic lyricism, while Helena stood smiling. Unable to control the growing warmth which filled her womaness, once again, she left the living room and began preparing an early dinner, attempting to displace her emotions. After awhile, Amber entered the kitchen, full of childish excitement.

"Mommy! Mommy! Daddy says he wants to take me fishin' on a great big boat. Can I go mommy? Can I go, please, mommy?"

"Wait a minute. Excuse yourself, little lady . . . now, what's all this commotion about a boat?"

Fred entered the doorway in his undershirt and socks, looking on affectionately while straightening his wrinkled summer slacks. "I was telling her about the trawler down in the islands. Perhaps I can take her with me when I get another chance to get down there. Is that alright with you?"

"Fred, what are you talking about? You know she's in school now! She's missed enough time, as it is already, without running around the world with you on some fishing boat.''

"Well, from her report, she's doing alright in school. A little time off won't hurt, I'm sure,'' Fred pleads.

"That's easy enough for you to say. You don't have to face her teacher, do you? Look, it was hard enough finding a decent school for her to enroll in this year,'' Helena went on like a typical mother hen, as she moved around the kitchen busily fixing dinner.

"Well, it probably won't be until after the election, anyway. I'll have to wait until my next vacation comes around . . . she'll probably get a lot out of the experience.''

"From one extreme to the next,'' mumbles Helena, as she shook her head. "What type of salad dressing do you want?''

"Oil and vinegar is fine. What are you making?''

"Abalone steak and mushrooms, with a lot of spaghetti. I know you don't like heavy meals in the summer, but you do look like you could use a couple of pounds . . . what's the matter, don't you have anyone to cook for you?'' she began the war again.

Amber interrupted with her childish innocence. "I don't like mushrooms, mommy!''

"I know, dear. I won't put any on your plate,'' Helena says, distractedly. She didn't know why, but she was trying to get at Fred's goat, again.

"Thanks to Amber, I'll skip what I started to say. But, what do you mean you don't like mushrooms, little lady. Don't you realize how good they make your food taste?''

"She's a little young to understand the esoteric import of mushrooms, Fred. I think she'll have to grow a great deal more, before you can converse with her about their hidden meaning. Besides, these are the ordinary garden variety. There's no psilocybin in them for us to go tripping around the apartment in some 'misty melancholy','' she downplays his overture to their daughter.

"Nevertheless, they're a good food item,'' he replies. "There's a lot of fairy tales based upon the mushroom, Amber.''

"I don't like them,'' she childishly persisted.

"Alright, darling, you don't have to eat any,'' Helena babied her daughter. "Your father and I are just talking about the mushrooms among ourselves.''

"Are you going to stay with us daddy?''

Amber's naive comment brought the awkwardness of the family's affairs out in the open, causing her parents momentary discomfort. "Your father is very busy, Amber. He's doing a lot of things that take him far away from us, so let's not worry him about staying in one place,'' Helena tactfully covered the issue.

"I'm glad daddy came to visit us. I haven't seen him in such a long time.''

"Will you two stop chattering so much . . . get out of the kitchen, so I can finish cooking . . . go and wash your hands!''

Fred took Amber by the hand and led her into the living room. "Come on, sugar. Tell me about you friends in the neighborhood.''

"I should fix up a bitches brew, sure enough,'' Helena mumles on, in sotto voce, as they left the kitchen. "Hmm,'' she reflects. "Now, stop that, Helena, don't be unnecessarily troublesome!''

Fred relaxed in a way he had not known for two years. Although, he couldn't forget the pain and agony, the circumstance allowed him to share precious time with his family. Amber's exuberance reinforced his comfortable feeling as she responded to his paternal warmth.

" . . . And Ritchie and Bobby are in my class. They don't play nice. When we go outside to play, they always take the rope from us and the teacher has to scold them . . . but, little girls don't play that way, do they, daddy?"

"Well, I hope you don't play that way! Little girls are so much prettier when they play nicely, don't you think?"

"Yes, I think so . . . my teacher is very pretty too. She's always fixing her hair to stay neat."

"Really now? Well, what about your dancing lessons? Do you like going to dance class?"

"Oh, yes. Look, let me show you what we learned to do." Amber located a comfortable spot on the rug and began performing her ballet skills. Her tiny body moved like a manequin, pirouetting and extending delicately for her father's enjoyment.

"Well, how about that," Fred compliments, as he beams a proud smile. "I think that's just gorgeous, dear. Do you like dancing . . . ?"

"Come on now, crew," Helena interrupted. "The food is still hot. Let's get something to eat now . . . did you wash your hands, Amber?"

Her daughter ran happily off to the bathroom to take care of herself while Fred casually strolled into the kitchen.

"Are you raising a new dancer?"

"She's crazy about it. I'd never be able to forget the dance classes. She keeps right up with the calandar. I had to show her which day to mark, once, and she never forgot . . . I guess she's like you with that punctuality phobia," she makes a smug dig.

"It's been running me ragged these last couple of months," sighs Fred. "I can hardly keep up with my exercises."

"I bet you find time to fit in your personal habits, though," quips Helena. Her jealous tease was less deceit, than for pun.

"Why are you trying to crucify me?"

"Oh, excuse me! Did I say something out of place," she smirked.

Fred sat down at the table somewhat deflated. "I try to watch my habits, as best as I can, Helena."

"Really," she drawls. "How was your Washington visit?"

"You must spend a great deal of money in long distance phone calls," Fred remarks, sarcastically.

"I pay my bills, dear."

Amber returned, just then, hiding her hands behind her back with an air of secrecy. "Guess what I have . . . ?"

"Gee," says Fred. "I can't imagine what it could be!"

"Here!" She gave him a handmade card, with an unsophisticated picture crowded by uneven crayoned letters scrawled on the front.

"Ah ha," Fred says, upon deciphering the message. "It's a father's day card! Did you save it for me?"

"We made them in school last year, but I didn't know where to send it to you."

Fred was hurt. He searched for Helena's eyes, but she avoided his glare and continued dishing out the food. "Oh, did you forget my address, by any chance?"

he says, dryly.

"Your food is going to get cold, Amber. Put that card over there on the counter and come eat your dinner."

"It's lucky I didn't leave the country," Fred continues, in a perturbed manner. "I probably wouldn't hear from you people, at all."

"You did the right thing to come and see Amber," she curtly replies.

"Never mind, It wouldn't be wise to continue the discussion, since I see you're changing the subject . . . considering my situation, now that I'm here, I'll make the best of it." He tasted the food. "This is pretty good! I see you still have a good hand in the kitchen," he remarks, smothering his feeling, in the presence of his young daughter.

"Yes, a mother is supposed to be proficient at all of the household responsibilities," quips Helena. She was pushing the tease again, but controlled herself. "Oh, shucks, what am I getting into this mood for. Go on and enjoy your meal, man!"

"Thanks! My mind is awfully tired, you know. I couldn't keep up at this point, even if I wanted to . . . "

"What I meant to say, was that I spoke to Elaine, and she told me that you were in Washington for awhile."

"She told you. You didn't ask?"

"See, there you go now," pleads Helena. Fred tried to get out of the intimidation by stuffing his mouth. "No, no, I didn't question. She called me to find out something about private schools, which I was able to help her with, and somewhere in the conversation she mentioned you two were working on something. That's all."

"You're sure that's it," teases Fred.

"Yes. She wouldn't go for my probes. I guess I did try, though . . . "

"Look, Helena, if you wanted to reach me for anything, all you had to do was contact the office. I can always be reached there!"

"Ah, Fred, you can function so well in an official capacity," she says, disdainfully. "Does your whole world revolve around such civility?"

"I really didn't want to discuss this," he says, defensively.

"Do I detect a note of disapproval? You know, I really should have been more drastic. But, you didn't even allow me to do that . . . I could curse your coldness!"

"I was merely being pragmatic . . . eat your spaghetti, baby," he disciplines his daughter.

Helena suddenly realized her impropriety in Amber's presence, and felt perturbed. "Hmm, I better get up now, before I spoil your meal." She put her fork down, got up, emptied her plate and left the kitchen. Meanwhile, Fred's keen eyes caught the bewilderment of his daughter's inquisitive stare.

By nightfall the tension of Fred's serendipitous visit had subsided in the apartment, making for a convivial atmosphere. He was stretched out on the floor with Amber, who relaxed in her dainty pajamas. Books were open, allowing father and daughter to explore the fantasy world of fairy tales, as they shared a precious moment of growth together. Helena lounged comfortably on the couch reading a novel.

"Okay, now that we've finished all of those stories, don't you think it's time to go to bed?"

"I'm not sleepy, daddy. Can you read me another one?"

"Nope! It's almost nine-thirty, sugar plum."

"Just one more, daddy, please."

"You heard your father," says Helena, looking up from her paperback. "Put your books away and he'll tuck you into bed. Don't forget your prayers."

"Alright, mommy." She picked the books up and put them neatly away, then headed dejectedly toward the bedroom.

"Don't you say good night, young lady?"

"Good night, mommy," she mumbles, demurely. Amber regressed, momentarily, and went to her mother with pre-school affection, giving Helena a big hug and kiss, then dashed into the bedroom.

"Wait for me, sugar," says Fred, as he followed her spontaneous flight from the living room. "I want some of those kisses, too."

Helena resumed her reading and, after a short period, Fred emerged from the bedroom. He milled around the living room, like a bull in a china shop, not knowing exactly what to do. Finally, he picked up a magazine and anxiously thumbed through the periodical. Helena peered over the book and eyed his awkward nervousness with humor, smiling mischievously.

"Are you bored?"

Fred dropped the magazine onto the end table. "Maybe I'd better make reservations for the return flight," he says, uncharacteristically lost for words.

"Oh." Helena's mood changed, noticeably.

"I don't think I've been good company."

"You can't make up for a couple of years in a matter of hours, you know."

Fred was pensive now, and her conversation made him edgy. He changed the subject. "Let me see if I can reach Lloyd. What time is it?" He looked at the Chinese characters on the wall clock.

"Say, that's clever."

"I don't know what was on my mind when I bought it, but it reminds me of you. Can you read the characters?"

"Yes. You know, I read something in ancient history about their sophistication in clock making . . . let me try to reach him," he says, briefly foreclosing her conversational lead. He went into the kitchen to call, but the line was busy. Somewhat out of his usual, he returned to the living room where he found Helena eagerly awaiting the outcome of his call. "Well, it seems like somebody's there. I'll have to try again in a few minutes . . . so, tell me, what have you been doing with yourself, old lady."

"You mean, you're genuinely interested? Well, that's a scream," Helena remarks, as she casually accepted his affection. She raised herself on the couch for a friendly conversation.

"I'm serious. You look well . . . you must be doing something right," Fred flatters her.

"Well, I'm glad you noticed," she smiles. "I've been keeping up, but I stay pretty much to myself. That way, I can stay out of situations."

"That's a marked improvement. You do have a way of being in the middle of whatever's going on around you, lady."

"Oh, I just think you're jealous of seeing other people, besides yourself, with social graces," she teases. "Anyway, your selfishness could never allow me to blossom in my own right."

"Is that how you read the situation, Helena? Well, I'm sorry to let you down so hard, but I never saw all of that socializing as being productive. For instance, if you had spent more time with your painting, then perhaps you'd have had a showing by now . . . what happened to all of your work?"

"Ah, it's in storage in Los Angeles," she lied. It was important to keep her little secret to herself, she thought. In the meantime, she would lead him on and, eventually, score a big rouse. "But, what makes you think a showing is all that important? I still have my articles to write, and there's also the possibility of teaching at a small school. There's ample time for me to have a show, you see. Anyhow, I feel that I'm still growing. What's important is that I'm working more now, than was ever possible before . . . that's undoubtedly due to less aggravation."

"It surprises me how you interpret events. I imagine it just hasn't been long enough for you to exercise a degree of objectivity," Fred criticizes her point. He felt that she was shortsighted about the subtle pervasiveness of societal pressures upon the marital institution. "Why don't you face it, you became lazy when you and all of those other women got mixed up in that 'Mumbo-Jumbo'."

"The wives in that group were only trying to keep marriage from digressing into the ordinary. After all, we were attempting to broaden ourselves, as parents, to meet our responsibilities to the children's growth . . . you always claim to look at things in depth, I wonder why you could never make that connection," she chastises him.

"Perhaps it was never clear to me that the goals and means coincided."

"No, that's not it, Fred. You looked at that group as a bunch of 'flighty' ladies, gathered together to sustain each other from the onset of old age . . . that's why you never offered your assistance to any of the projects we tried."

"I didn't feel any of the things you were doing were important enought to warrant my time. You know what a struggle it was trying to make a comeback, after being black-listed. It was virtually impossible for me to do anything, but get myself off the ground," Fred exclaims. He became angry remembering the experience. The estrangement was just another outcome of the system, he thought.

"You know, there's one thing I don't understand. Maybe you can make it clear to me," she comments, offhandedly. Her concern was tainted with lingering personality issues and she spoke without fully weighing the import of her husband's statement. "What is it that's so important about your life, that's any different from a million other black cats out there?"

Fred was deflated by Helena's perennial insistence on, what he termed, 'the no-man' oversight in her view of his personality. That closure, on her part, restricted the communication of their mana in his work to raise them to higher spiritual levels.

"All I can say is, that it's what I'm doing with my life that has importance. I'm concerned about the quality of my life. Therefore, what I do can only be compared, with the million other dudes that you speak about, as far as what is genuinely beneficial to the living experience."

"Isn't it all a state of mind? That quest to be what you are, by choice?"

"Helena, that's childish! You know that choice is consciously acting upon available opportunities. Most people in the world are locked up, in some or another closet, with a limited field of experience, just because they've never made the right choices. Why," he emphasizes, pausing for her to consider his point. "It's not solely due to the forces which stiffle imagination . . . I think the real problem is the failure of people to exercise judgement in their lives, despite increasing opportunities."

"You use such an analytic temperament to view life. Aren't you afraid of becoming over precise and unemotional?"

"No, but it would be worse if I weren't blase! An individual has to plan his life in the midst of many forces, so it's important to exercise discrimitive choice," Fred concludes.

"Blase, huh? I think it fits you. But, not for those reasons. You have a good head, but you're very pretentious! It makes a woman feel somehow subservient."

Fred smiled demonically. "You know, that's the crux of our misunderstanding . . . Its precisely at that point where we diverge in our life views. You think the whole show is basically a matter of natural emotions, but I think there are other forces to explore."

"That's just because you're a stubborn male chauvinist! How does that song go . . . 'I wish that you could be in my shoes for just a moment!'"

"Oh, no," exclaims Fred. "I know too many aspects of myself which I don't like, as it is. So, it would be best for me to wear my own shoes. Because, in the end, each of us has to judge in order to account for one's self."

"You must have caused your mother some hell of a maternity pain when you were coming here, fellow," she laughs at her own pun.

"I was a big baby, if that means anything," Fred replies to her humor with a wry grin on his lips.

"It's a good thing you weren't blessed with a son, like you hoped, Fred . . . if you didn't make the kid a genius, he sure would've been a pure replica of your ego."

"Is that what you see, Helena?"

"Partly . . . but, I did get a premonition you were coming. You know, I can read your spirits through my natural emotions . . . don't laugh, it's true," she replies.

"It's funny that I wound up in your bedroom."

"That doesn't surprise me a bit. It just goes to show you how interwoven you are with that which you try so hard to play down!"

"We all have the beasts and demons to deal with, I suppose."

"You really think you got out of my thing, huh? That my natural view of life couldn't take it . . . is that why you think I left you?" Helena emphasized her glib remark to pierce his 'stubborn intellectualism'. She wished she could hurt his pride enough for him to truly feel, for once, rather than rationalize her position.

"I think we saw different goals! You decided to do what was best according to what you saw. I'm trying to do likewise with myself."

"Well, then, you can lift your cover," she changes the focus. "What did you really come here for?"

"You know, Helena, I've been running that through the back of my mind for awhile now. It appears that there is quite a determined effort to get me to participate in a model for a business project that's about to occur."

"Well, don't involve me, because I don't want to be a part of your schemes, anymore," she remarks indifferently.

"That's the only reason that I can think of for my awkward presence here."

"What!"

" . . . To somehow convince you to go to Africa with me, in an amiable familial arrangement."

"Are you crazy, Fred! I'm just getting settled here. I'm not about to be continent hopping with you around the world!"

"You asked me. So, I told you what kind of pretext brings me here. Essentially, I don't argee with the plan, either."

Helena lost all composure. Her brown skin flushed red. She raised herself abruptly from the couch while her light-colored eyes darted anxiously around the room for a cigarette. "If this doesn't beat all! I knew you were involved in some madness, but I didn't really think you were mad, until this point," she screamed. "You mean to tell me that after two years you've come back here with a proposal to try and repatriate a land you lost hundreds of years ago? Come on Mister, tell me something else!"

"I've long since grown accustomed to these awkward positions, but I haven't contrived an international game, just to return to a marriage which I feel has failed . . . the setting is part of the ground rules," Fred calmly explains.

"Well, you can tell Lloyd and the rest of those pompous idiots that I'm not interested in being a model, anything," she says, slowly emphasizing the words with calculated sarcasm. "The charisma of that type of life has left me . . . can't you see how busy I am raising my child and getting back into some serious work? What is he thinking about, anyway . . . sending the worst kinds of representatives of that institution to a growing nation? What could they learn from us?"

"Perhaps, what to look out for. Maybe they're anticipating a higher divorce rate, or something, and want to scrutinize us like guinea pigs . . . I'm not sure! But, everything changes significance from a future perspective . . ."

"They've got a hell of a nerve," she interrupts, exhaling smoke through her nostrils. "And, you mean to tell me that you go for that kind of nonsense!"

Fred was uneasy with both Helena's temper and his own doubts, but figured he would make a genuine effort. After all, he had just about committed himself. "I vaguely recollect you speaking to me about team work, somewhere in the past. I am speaking to the same person, I think! Who knows, maybe there's a way of working around a societal situation to eventually getting it out of our personal relations. Anyhow, I can point to some virtues, as far as expanding Amber's world view."

"She can always visit that part of the world later, if she chooses."

"Needless to say, you know how I feel about taking the opportunity when it knocks," Fred consoled her. He was careful not to overweigh the issues with career concerns. True, it was important, but he didn't want Helena to focus on his being selfish, as she was bound to do.

"Right. There should be no looking backwards. Only forward movement!"

"Okay, so I'm not saying that now . . . but, a person should go as far as he can, before turning back. That way, he has more to offer upon his return."

"What could I look forward to . . . a life centered around the embassy, perhaps?"

"You have your painting. You could probably teach," he coaxes her. "Look, let's talk this thing through, seriously, calmly, okay? I want to go because of the opportunities it affords me to do something really important . . . I can't do it alone, so I'm asking you to consider it as a step toward making amends."

"That's some hell of a consideration you're asking me to make, Mister!"

"Can you do it without being limited by past circumstances? By looking positively toward the future?"

"I've been doing that all my life, it seems . . . are you asking me to try something else now?"

"Helena, you sound as though you think a man can't apply himself to change objective situations by merely facing life's realities. You hesitate, at the point where man separates from avidya and ascends to the bliss of atman. I try to communicate that principle of trancendance from my overview, because I want you to understand how important it is to coordinate our life forces. Yes, sometimes chances have to be taken in order to do things. But, it's important not to let events control our lives. Think about it in that sense.''

''Oh, you're serious . . . do you want me to set up a date for my reply, or must I give it to you now?'' Helena understood, but she was angry about past events and perplexed by the sudden possibliity of their reunion.

''Look, I'm not going to stop now. Not when I've begun to feel my own impetus,'' he says, intensely. ''I'm trying to design my life in concert with the new pulse in the world which I don't think is solely custom or habit. Sometimes, I let myself be intrigued by imagining beyond historical limitations. In that way, I can see many nuances of my own intuition. Somehow, I feel my actions make a difference in it all. I'm so close now, Helena . . . I know the trip will be an important catalyst for our future.''

''You're really presenting a case, aren't you? I don't know whether to laugh, or to be glad this nut is not in my house, any more.'' Helena remarks. She had been weighing his words more carefully, watching as Fred's excitement transformed his visiage.

''Why, because I can't stop long enough to catch my breath, sometimes . . . I don't think I'll die of stagnation though. More likely a heart attack!''

''What are you griping at now?''

''Oh, I don't know Helena. What are we doing here together that's really important? Why not think about this proposal as something entirely different, at this time. It's an opportunity . . . make the trip with me . . . make your experience work for you all of the time, to change our lives for the better! I'm not a person to lose sight of reality,'' he remarks, changing his pace to remind her of important aspects of his character. ''You know that! And, I don't think it's too big of me to come to you with such a request . . . nothing could stand in the way of our joint forces, Helena. We have a basic structure to work with. Think of how much this means for Amber's life.''

While Fred emphasized his points, his gleaming eyes transfixed upon hers with a piercing stare. The uncanny effect was disconcerting, as she looked, quite mesmerized, at the metamorphosis of his body. An aura of light emanated from him, surrounding his entire being which slowly transformed into an image of an old man. He seemed to be alive with primordal energy as he began to rub his loins in a delicate sensual manner, directing the force with precision toward her. Helena attempted to thwart his onslaught, impulsively, as the light enveloped her. She felt vulnerable, but was unable to contain her emotions. Finally, she was overwhelmed, and emitted a loud catlike shriek from her larynx. Her body trembled from the inducement of his mana, and she struggled to regain her composure. The empathic communion was cathartic, and Helena felt renewed.

''You still are into some weird shit, aren't you,'' she sighs relieved. ''I knew today was going to bring something startling. Something ethereal was about. You know what I mean . . . I got to feeling that all of my growth would be necessary to see me through the developing situation . . . now, I'm really taking the time to think about what you said, and I'll have to say, it makes sense. I was fortunate that I paid attention to you when we were together, Fred. I'm glad now, that I never got hung up in the dirty thirties . . . although I felt that I had to get away from you, it has really been a lesson for me. I was thinking today, about how much experience has shown me, already. But, now I know that's not exactly true. I've just been fortunate in my experience, thanks to you . . . there's a whole lot of agony in life.''

"Yes, but out of that agony beatitude can come to fruition. As long as there's judgement, a person can realize proper goals. Right direction can be discoverd through good discipline of one's intuition . . . we've been here a long time, Helena, don't you think we should live blissfully?''

"Don't take me to your church now, Fred. I think I'm ready to bear witness to your testimony without all that,'' she laughs. Helena was purged now, and allowed her true feelings to emerge. "I just want to know if you can find someplace to buy material for me, so I can make our own clothes.''

"You mean you will come with me?''

"So, I've got to wind up being a sucker . . . alright, I'll go for it,'' she joked. "It may come as a shock to you, but I'll do it. Don't ask me why, Fred. I'll just pick up my bag and leave my roots, and we'll do it . . . when is all of this going to take place?''

"I don't know. The details haven't been worked out yet,'' he replies, momentarily surpised by her sudden change of attitude. "I think within the next couple of months.''

"What do the configurations say?''

"The second and fifth line . . . I would imagine it has something to do with traditional leadership patterns. There's still more homework to do, but I'm sure we can figure it out!''

"From sarapes to galees,'' she laughs, as she lights another cigarette.

"What do you think about living on a farm and raising baby goats?''

"I think I could really dig being a part of a growing black nation . . . don't think that it hadn't ever occured to me before.''

Fred was elated. He got up from the couch and did a soft shoe dance on the rug, clapping his hands. "That tension between capricorn and cancer is just too much to overcome. I know how our past travels captivated your imagination. We can't stop now. There are other places for our life forces!''

"Okay, okay. You're my reggin! But, you still haven't told me what is really involved in this African sojourn.''

"It hasn't all been divulged to me either, yet,'' says Fred, soberly. He remembered his own reservations, but felt he would have Helena's strength now, to help weather the storm. "I'm entering it as a consultant in urban affairs, specializing in communications. That way, there's an avoidance of any direct politics . . . more, or less, a private citizen doing business in a different culture. That's the important thing in us being a part of that society. Once again, you see, who I am is important to what I'm doing. What I'm about is where my family fits in. The rest develops from the personal ties that bond us together.''

"You really get a kick out of doing adventurous things!''

"I certainly do! But, I hope that enthusiasm gets me through the other mundane shit . . . you know, just because the cycle of wars returns to prosperous times doesn't mean that we should cease working to prevent wars, altogether. What it does mean to me, is that Black people should be controlling that continent. Even though the game is up, as far as violence, there's still work to be done on very realistic levels. Like building the kind of civilizations that our intuitions tell us is possible . . . I'd reather be doing that, rather than something else in this life.''

"Oh, my," exclaims Helena. "I forgot about all of those shots we have to take . . . you know how I hate needles!"

"Yes, I guess I have been carrying on, haven't I."

"I've kind of missed that fire in my life."

"I told you, you could never walk away from me," Fred jests. "I wore your nine for a long time. A thousand times over. You know I had to do something to contribute direction to your growth."

"Yes, strange people beget strange company," observes Helena. "And, what has Elaine been putting into your fire?"

"She's been trying to get these kind of forces to work along the same principles in the Capitol. You know, the judicial process is something to be recokened with, in terms of the law."

"Ah, I see. The lawyer has been counseling you on the proper moves, huh?"

"I would say she's one of my team mates," he teases her.

"How exciting." Helena drawls, affectedly. She wasn't really jealous of Elaine, but had always felt a womanly competitiveness with his professional associate.

"Good! That means you'll do it with me. Let me call Lloyd and tell him that it's going to work out alright, after all."

"I never could understand you on matters like this, man," she snaps. "You should curse him out for making a fool of you."

"I know I should, but it can wait until after I've gotten there. I'll play along with, he who laughs last, in this case."

Fred went to telephone New York while Helena put a recording of Leontyne Price on the stereo and reclined on the sofa.

"Hello, Lloyd. Well, I'm glad I caught you. That was a pretty risky thing you did. Having me come all the way out here, like that, takes a lot of gaul . . . what do you mean, where am I! I'm in San Francisco, as if you didn't know . . . well, I though you did. I got a telegram that stated Helena was in the hospital. It proved to be dated information though . . . early this morning. . . well, who would have sent it, in that case? Alright, it doesn't matter. I'll play along with the script. Eventually, it will come out in the open. The important thing is that I worked it out with her, so you can put that into your pipe and smoke it . . . of course I know how to get back to work. I figured that since I was out here, I'd do some preliminary ground work for the Black Teacher's Caucus. Yeah, I can be back by Thursday . . . Les can handle anything that comes up, until I return . . . alright, will do . . . uh hun . . . see you later."

He returned from the kitchen, reflecting on the conversation and sat next to Helena on the couch.

"What's the matter now, Baby?"

"Oh, nothing." he says, dismissing the mystery. "Everything is alright. I'm just going to have to get some straight answers, I suppose." He turned to look at her and pinched her nose, in a light mood. "It's alright, you don't have anything to worry about."

"I'm putting us completely in your hands, once again. I hope it doesn't hurt as much, the second time around." she says, cautiously seeking his assurances.

"Amber looks a lot like you now."

"It's funny that you bring that up. I was just remembering how awkward you were at first . . . do you remember when she got into the hair grease that time and spread it all over herself . . . you two were a mess trying to wipe it up." she laughs.

"You made such a big project out of it, that I had to spend the whole morning cleaning up behind you and your daughter. What a riot!"

"I was somewhat clumsy. I couldn't entirely appreciate having a little daughter, way back then."

"Yes, I know. You were too hung up with that male chauvinism to notice it," she reflects, consoling him as a consort, once again.

"Naw, I still think the first child should be a male, but I'm not entirely rigid about that any longer," he remarks, reflectively.

"Well, that's a big adjustment!"

"I'm going to have to be back in New York by Thursday . . ."

"Hmm, I think I can put you up until then," she teases. "Since we are partners, once again, that's permissible."

The sensual smile on Helena's alluring face caused Fred's eyes to light up in response to the subtle invitation. He moved closer, as she moistened her lips with a delicate motion of her tongue.

"You can't conceive of all the trouble I'm going to give you."

"I already know two years of turmoil. I'm ready for something else to happen, Baby." He kissed her lightly upon the lips. "You can't make another one like that, you know," she responds, softly.

Fred felt his passion rising and kissed her lingeringly, as they fell back upon the couch, while the melodious voice of Leontyne Price filled the air with the rich tonal resonance of a classical aria—'O Patria Mia.'

Chapter Thirty-Three

The late summmer evening was pleasant in the city. Following the long day of sweltering heat, the typically cool nocturnal weather of San Francisco made comfortable socializing ideal. Fred and Helena were concluding the day's activity, casually strolling the dimly lit paths of a municipal park. They had dined earlier at Fisherman's Wharf and were now meandering leisurely toward the local museum to see an exhibition of her paintings. She mentioned the art show, conversationally during dinner, and he made spontaneous arrangements for the two to attend the affair. As they walked through the overhanging trees, soft zephyrs flowed through the air, causing Helena's blue chiffon evening gown to caress her petite body, delicately accentuating her femininity. They paused a moment while crossing a small foot bridge which spanned a clear brook and embraced warmly.

"You're full of surprises, lady! I've got to feel like some kind of fool, the way I came out here talking so badly about you," he says, reflectively.

"So, I'm a pixie! I've got to work my stuff, you know . . . I thought about sending you an announcement, but then, I said to myself, that's verboten! It wouldn't seem right to let you know about the showing, after all the changes . . . I'd trump you, by letting you find out through the grape vine. I was hoping to make you stop, for a moment, and be jealous," she chuckles.

"Did you really think that would happen?"

"Well, I kind of felt that way. You know, like I could be just as independent as you!"

"I guess you played a good enough game of it. And, if I hadn't shown up, it might've worked," he laughs.

"Nothing like a good try, sport," she quips, as she adjusts her dress.

"Hmm, I thought you had droppped out of it all!"

"I have a few resources myself, you see." They looked affectionately at each other, momentarily. "How did it go today?"

"How did it go today . . . oh, just wonderful! The caucus was very receptive to the idea . . . you know, this city is more quaint than Los Angeles. I think I like it better," he says, changing to relaxing matters. Talk of the job took his mind away from the peace he had not known for so long.

"I'm going to be sorry to leave, myself. I've gotten to like it, for several reasons. It's comfortable here," she remarks, as she watches the reflections of the evening starlight upon the clear stream, quietly flowing under the bridge. She thought, like the water ultimately reaches its level, her own life had finally arrived at proper balance.

They finally arrived at the museum. It was a low modern building, spaciously designed to compliment the landscape. After stopping a moment to chat with the hostess, they entered the gallery and began browsing.

Fred was impressed. He took his time to appreciate his wife's talents, which he looked at through new eyes. "Hmm, this one is nice. I haven't seen it before."

"It took me about a month," she responds, informatively. "Quite a few of these are new. I left the older ones in storage at the school. I wanted to show something more indicative of my growth, so I did a whole new series . . . look at this, for instance." She led him to a mural size painting where they stood viewing her rich stylistic variation.

"Hey, you're really stretching out on that large canvas, aren't you?"

"My work seems to get better as Amber grows older," she says, with a warm smile of womanly fullness.

"I can understand her being an inspiration to your talents. Children can make you look differently at the world due to their search for self identity, I imagine. It's all a matter of work," he comments, as they continue through the gallery.

"She wanted to paint a couple of pictures for the show."

"I'm sure she would have gotten some immediate sales," he remarks, with a happy smile on his face. Her comment brought forth memories of paternity. "What's this about?"

"Oh, I painted this after a very bad experience . . . I really don't feel like talking about it. It's kind of a reminder for me."

Fred decided not to pursue the issue. She would have to overcome whatever personal conflict she had, he thought. "Well, I'm glad to see you moving out on your own . . . no more women's groups, huh?"

"Not exactly," she murmurs, coyly. "I try to keep things limited to the telephone though."

"That's some improvement . . . how do you feel about being some kind of laboratory experiment for the posterity of social science?"

'That sounds more relevant for a woman's coterie. I can think of a million projects that I'd like to try, you know."

"Is that right," he laughs. "Well, I'd rather see you busy at work, as Mr. businessman's wife, myself." He pinched her behind.

"Ouch! Don't do that with all these people in here," she exclaims. "That's bad decorum. You'd better not do anything Italian, like that, in Haille Salasie's court . . . we'd really cause a hell of a cultural shock!"

"Then you'd better wear different clothing, so you won't be tempting me all the time," he teases her.

She smiled sensually, then whirled her petite body in front of him, clutching her delicate garment like a fashion model exhibiting her wares. "I'm never going to stop doing things to upset your composure, Mr. businessman! I'll just find some other style to accentuate myself . . . "

"I don't know how that's going to work out," he laughs. "I believe we're supposed to be a bit more stoic."

"Hmmm. I'm just waiting to disprove your philosophy that women are less universal than men, Baby. You'll see! I'll be quite sufficient and able to do my part,'' she says coquetly.

''I just hope I'm right in making this move,'' he replies, shaking his head in mock dismay. ''I don't mind being an expatriate, if it comes to that. But, I'm more than a little concerned about us being representative examples of the future of black people . . . too many folks have noticed my individual proclivities whenever there's impedence to working in concert.''

''But, you're forgetting the reason I'm here with you, honey! To give added dimension to your character and balance your temperament for you to get over high hurdles,'' she remarks, soothingly.

''My, how charming you are now! You can sure turn a hundred and eighty degrees in the course of twenty four hours, Helena. I guess that's half the journey.''

''Well, anyhow, how do you like the showing?''

Fred cleared his throat and became glib. ''I think it's fantastic!''

''My, we haven't had one of those in quite some time.'' She mimicked his statement, affecting a deep tone of voice. ''I think it's fantastic! . . . After this show, I'm hoping to be included in a permanent collection. But, the prospects are vague now,'' she remarks, with satisfaction.

He smiled at her accomplishment and casually glanced at his watch. ''Shucks, I wanted to see Amber, before the baby-sitter put her to sleep. Now, it's too late. Come on, let's pick up a bottle of wine on our way back.''

''Ah, monsieur, in a moment I will arrange our transportation,'' she replies, and disappears in a flurry of activity to speak with the hostess.

''Cheez! I must've cut my throat with a straight edge, without knowing it,'' he jokingly mumbles to himself, as he feels the tightness of his collar.

Fred took a seat and watched, as other guests gradually filled the gallery to visit the exhibition. After awhile he lost interest and became meditative. As he reflected, his face became tense with the strain of an emerging muse. His mind's eye opened again, and he saw the dream-like figure of the Mexican Indian walking away into the ethereal darkness. Fred watched himself lower Philip onto the sleeping bag, in a re-enactment of his prior vision. Just then, he heard a distant voice in background.

''We're ready!''

Fred was jolted back into consciousness by Helena's statement.

''Are you alright . . . we're ready to go now.''

He looked up at his wife, somewhat perplexed. A sober mood characterized his thoughts of the premonition. ''Yes . . . I must be getting tired.'' He smiled at her, to cover his cogitation. ''Are we off?''

They joined arms and walked toward the exit while the spectators busied themselves critiquing the art work.

Chapter Thirty-Four

The few days spent together passed, altogether too quickly, Helena thought, as she sat in the terminal at San Francisco International Airport. Traffic in the waiting area was sparse. The few idle travelers relaxed comfortably awaiting Wednesday evening departures. Fred returned from the reservations counter waving the ticket and sat next to her.

"Well, here I go again." He turned to watch a black red cap moving luggage through the terminal. "Boy, I'm sure glad I don't have to push that cart for a living!"

"That wouldn't be too relevant for your talents. Anyhow, you could leave those tasks for younger brothers to come to grips with . . . maybe, when they truly understand labor and career, there will be clarity about job propaganda which the would-be executives pass on to folks who should be working."

"These days, they'll tell you anything to keep you from thinking. The situation is conducive to self defeat," he sighs. "I can't stop to feel sorry though . . . it's too important to maintain a future tense in my work."

"You just have a clear idea of purpose which guides your direction to what has to be done," she remarks, supportively. "That's not hard to fathom . . . you're just not the prophetic type, that's all."

Fred internalized Helena's insight quietly. He felt she was beginning to understand his values, at last. Hopefully, his plans for their family would be successful, he thought. "Hey, I'm glad you invested yourself in this project. It could mean the answer to some of the questions we've been asking about our lives."

The flight announcement interrupted their conversation. They got up to kiss, but stood looking reflectively into each others eyes for a few speechless moments. Finally, they parted company and left the airport terminal, walking in opposite directions.

Chapter Thirty-Five

Autumn progressed toward winter, bringing the end of the campaign closer to election time. Political cacophony charged the atmosphere in New York City, making a kinesthetic impact upon the anxious population in October 1964. The candidates made last minute bids for marginal votes during the excitment of the concluding month in the decisive contest. Fred and Lloyd were lunching at an inexpensive Spanish restaurant on Fourteenth Street. They had taken time off to relax from the hectic schedule and share comfortable conversation at a more 'civilized' pace. Lloyd's manner, typically reserved and officious, was uncharacteristically informal. He was glad to put aside anticipations of the election, and listened patiently while Fred talked exuberantly about his transcendental insights.

"It seems like I've just returned from a celestial excursion, Lloyd. But, I think . . . yes, I do know how to convey it to you. Maybe it won't sound so strange, after all. I was working on another communications plan for Zambia's satellite package. You know, establishing normal T.V. and radio patterns. Then I had an idea . . . you remember how Einstein's theory described gravity, right?"

"Vaguely. What's so important about gravity, Fred?"

"Immediately, energy! Look, the spinoff of satellite communications into navigation, telephone and telecommunications is already part of today's technology. But, hypothetically, the commercial use for agricultural and industrial development remains an open field," he says, as a brief prelude. "Anyhow, the way Einstein described gravity, as a warping effect on bodies in space, may be a key to employing the satellite project for agricultural and industrial development in Zambia."

"I don't see the connection . . . "

"Well, it probably wouldn't be impractical for a geophysicist to develop spectometer technology. Then, the satellite could also be used for locating basic raw materials, arable lands, underground water and even vital energy sources. All of those needs are important in planning future urbanization, even down to site location," Fred continues, enthusiastically.

"How do you imagine it will work?"

"It's a matter of using the earth's physical electromagnetic fields and the satellite's warping effect in a geometric relationship to the sunlight, which is deflected normally by gravity, like a vector force . . . the idea is to analyze the refracted light of vapors emitted from the earth in that country, to pinpoint its natural resources," he concludes.

"Hmm," Lloyd reflects. "Well, apparently insights are unfolding for you, man. So, a note of caution! Around about now, you'd better take care of yourself. You know what I mean? See, sometimes abstractions take on a different meaning. But, you don't want to lose yourself in the multitude of it all," he remarks, with a cryptic innuendo. " . . . I suggest you continue to concentrate on those possibilities until you can develop a good investment package. Just be sure your specific direction has adequate enough scientific substantiation to draw capital."

"I keep my meditations under close observation all of the time, Lloyd. Doc taught me that, long ago . . . that's why I'm intrigued about Einstein. You know, his work theoretically implies the notion of longevity, beyond the gravitational field. That's close enough to my discipline to look, forward, through the 'space-time' continuum. Hey, if the universe is open to us, once understood, it's possible to control events to make meaningful changes," he interjects.

"Your exercises surely have paid off in the end, haven't they, Fred? But, the question of exercising those powers is a matter of discretion. Are you in tune with that?"

"I have a sense of purpose! Besides, I don't want to come back here, anymore. I've had it with all the petty constraints on life. I'd rather prepare for whatever comes next, do you understand what I mean," Fred remarks, philosophically. He lit a cigarette and inhaled deeply, then leaned back in his chair to weigh his next point. "I don't think about dreams. I live intuitively. That's what makes dreams come true . . . All that to say, going to Zambia should take my disciplines even further . . . it's about change, as I see it, Lloyd. In this case, changing my center of gravity to open doors . . . What can I tell you! It's like removing veils, but in a different sense. And, since Africa is the most logical place with enough space to step off into the universe, I'm getting my directions together to coincide with this project. I don't want anything to intervene."

"I understand. You're exercising good thinking to apply your skills, and opening up new ideas for our organization, as well. That's moving doors, I'd say . . . but now, what's the question you're subtly trying to bring up?"

"Ah . . . how many business ideas should I explore?"

"You know the point in your going, Fred. I'm not limiting you in the manner that you get there. Whatever your forces are, bring them into play for our work . . . yes, I'm aware that you're ready to make the trip. It also seems that you're capable. Just remember, we're as anxious to make it happen, as you are . . . for as many reasons, I might add. All these events are part of a major change to a forward outlook in policy matters regarding black people. It's time to create new directions, and leave history alone to an extent. After all, when all of the evils and social injustices are removed, where are the personal dimensions of living going to take us?" Lloyd used the convenient interlude in work to continue tutoring Fred in their mutual growth with the developing company. Thus far, his worker's ideas were inspiring, but he was cautiously mindful of his elocutions about the insight. " . . . As long as you know what you're doing, see what your journey reveals. It may be teachable! Having a family should prevent anyone from being afraid of what you're exploring, so you could study pretty openly. I suppose Helena could do all of the immediate editing . . . just so you write something," he smiles in an uncharacteristic manner.

Fred chuckled at his boss's comment. It was Lloyd's typical officiousness in directing the black company. "Esta bueno, no," he changes the tone of conversation, as he fills his mouth with yellow rice and pork. "That's what the folks here are accustomed to saying." Lloyd's point was understood, but Fred wanted more definitive outline of his specific business responsibilities. "Say, Lloyd, I appreciate your taking me to lunch, but I don't understand the gesture . . . "

"I like to get outside from time to time, to see just how manu operates," he says, offhandedly, to avoid the probe. "That way, I can keep in shape too . . . put some of those exercises of yours to work. I already have some respiratory control, but that took me a while."

"Stay with it, man. It shouldn't be long before you shake off that dead weight and began to experience intuitive thoughts. Then, it's just a matter of recognizing events in time to do something productive."

"It sounds like having a mind sensitive to problem solving," Lloyd remarks. "You know, we're always looking for solutions. So, perhaps what you're doing can be applied elsewhere."

"You sound like you're running a foundation . . . I think I can take myself far enough to make it worthwhile for strategic planning. National defense is still a reality . . . "

"Well, everyone is using one or the other technique, these days," Lloyd reflects. "I don't think it will be too difficult to get a green light on your practices . . . hell, if there's some sort of whole in the universe, all the better for the forces in that part of the world, I guess."

Fred smiled at Lloyd's pun and continued more soberly.

"You know, people like Dubois understood the mythic within history that helps working with leadership principles. My concern, however, is to go beyond the symbolism of the thirties, which has shaped the thinking of many Blacks in this country."

"Yes, the great race for discovery and knowledge has been going on for a long time, but we just seem to be overcoming the debilitating impact of the depression," he remarks, with vague understatement. He was curious of Fred's thoughts, and left the point open to glean the younger man's perception as the conversation continued.

"As a change agent, I want to be where the next great leaps in Black development occur . . . man, when I put this stuff down on the chart, I should definitely know something. What to do becomes easy, then."

"First of all, you're going to have to develop more of a business attitude in setting up this communications network. It has to be, first of all, an economic consideration . . . I know you see other things, but the company's profit and the country's developmment needs are the immediate realities. Progression within those constraints will pose less complications for you . . . and dig, watch those vipers out there. Obviously, there are many negative forces about, and if they get wind of what you're exploring, you could be wiped out in a moment. I wasn't kidding when I said I want to keep in shape, myself. Especially after that incident at your apartment," Lloyd counsels him with a severe tone of voice.

"I'm not nervous about that anymore," Fred replies, as he puts his cigarette out. "I don't think I'll overlook any direct threat in the future. And, as for manu, being close to city politics during this campaign has taught me a lot, in a short space of time . . . I'll just have to view the project more so in relation to international events, as you say, and be personally on guard now."

"Well, I'm emphasizing these cautions, because I don't want you to wind up a modern day Oppenheimer!"

"What are you talking about, Lloyd? I think he's got the kind of economic and political attitudes that Blacks can profit from in their social planning."

"I don't mean the businessman . . . I'm clear on his position about Africa. Especially the pragmatics of attracting foreign capital. That's important for our success, as well . . . I meant the physicist who got censored by the government on security matters, here in the states, back in '54. You remember?"

"Oh, yeah, now that you mention it."

"Good, because your esoteric way of work on such a sensitive project could encounter trouble through power ploys, due to its military significance."

"Lloyd, look at it this way. A person has a responsibility as a citizen, in this country, or in Africa. Somehow, through this project in Zambia, if we can convey to people in Africa that an enlightened electorate is the best defense for future growth, perhaps on an immediate level, a reduction in tribal conflict will result. People all over must understand salvation in terms of their own self development, because public organs are only worthwhile, if there's personal value . . . one develops within the other to ultimately transcend . . . my child gave particular meaning to that perception."

"Well, I just want to caution you . . . oh, another thing, you'll have to be clearer . . . a lot of people haven't done as much homework as you have, so anticipate shortsightedness as another obstacle. What you encounter must be translate able, so that some sense of the ideas can be conveyed . . . it's a big step you're taking, man. Don't let me down!"

"I'll try my best, Lloyd," he replies, with a polite smile. "I'm usually more abrupt, but I guess I'm getting inspired." Fred paused to flag a waiter. "More tea, please." He turned to the conversation again. "I got an important lesson about clarification from Ferguson. He's not afraid to use his image. That makes a difference, even with all our directions considered."

"Yeah, standing out against the background is undoubtedly a virtue of the man. Probably the reason he was selected," Lloyd casually comments. " . . . Never had to step on anybody's toes, is another good thing. Just constantly at work toward making a way, and it paid off. By the way, he has a great deal of respect for your mind. But, he doesn't understand your motives. Anyhow, it seems that you two would get on very well together."

"The opportunity hasn't come up yet. He's always very busy."

"An astute political scientist. He could tell you some things about Africa. His views are based upon 'social darwinism', though."

"Just goes to show you that you can't always be too hasty," says Fred. He was intrigued that a black man would hold such an ambivalent theoretical view. "I would never have thought of him as being a conservative."

Skinner passed along the sidewalk outside the restaurant, just then, while Fred relaxed, sipping his tea. Wendell stopped and reflected a moment, then returned to peer through the large front window. He watched the two men relaxing at the table while attempting to make himself inconspicuous. Fred felt a sudden discomfort in his subconscious and turned anxiously in his seat. Impulsively, Skinner withdrew from view, to avoid detection of his surveillance. When he looked, Fred saw nothing unusual, as he gazed at the street activity, and resumed the conversation, somewhat perplexed. Lloyd was still talking about Ferguson's background, unpreturbed by the erratic behavior.

" . . . he learned the importance of screening himself very early in his career, therefore he has no trouble being clear and precise on matters. But, only a few know what he explores behind closed doors. It's only recently that he's become a visible public figure."

"It seems like he's been out there for so long," Fred says, offhandedly, while dismissing the premonition. "You know, once he advised me to become a professor. I told him that was a task public officials should pursue . . . I guess the shoe's on the other foot now!"

"I would really pay attention to his views. He's got some very heavy credentials you're not aware of."

"Oh, really . . . " Lloyd responded to Fred's inquisitive glare with a cold stare. "Alright, never mind!"

"Sometimes you seem as if you're contemplating your navel, or something."

"When it opens, I want to know about it." quips Fred. "Lloyd, why do you continually thwart my resolve to explore issues in depth?"

"I want you to get there, first of all. Events will fall into place soon enough . . . why don't you let the business plans develop, first?"

"What's the matter with you, man? I can't help being impetuous, with everything there is to know about this venture."

"So, what else is new, Baby? Look, you're going to spoil my lunch, with all your inquiries. Let things rest, for awhile!"

"Alright, Lloyd! But, I'm not going to stop putting ideas together for my own edification. I don't want to get caught relying on implicit faith and what have you promises."

"What can I tell you? Talk to Elaine. Maybe she can satisfy your imagination better than I can, anyway! She has to promote you to her contacts . . . why don't you make a phone call when we get to the office . . . I'm trying to enjoy my lunch."

Chapter Thirty-Six

The fall transition culminated, turning the splendid array of foliage brown. Dead leaves fell gradually from the trees, clustering haphazardly underneath into little piles, as the weather changed throughout the state. The pastoral view of Northern New York slowly receded in the dusk, on the Southern journey down the Hudson. With the onset of evening, illumination from early stars replaced the last rays of daylight, which disappeared, imperceptibly with the lingering reflections it cast upon the water underneath the Tappanzee Bridge. The distinctive architectural contrast of Grants Tomb and Riverside Church that bordered the Harlem community, was still visible from the West-Side highway as darkness set in. Further downtown, from the West Nineties to the Seventies, large expensive apartment dwellings loomed pompously atop the granite parapet overlooking Riverside Drive, on the route to lower Manhattan.

The campaign celebration began shortly after the polls closed, and was in full swing at the Plaza Hotel in East midtown. A large assemblage of campaign staff, party hacks, city officials, socialites and select party members crowded into the reception hall, anticipating the outcome of the epochal event in New York City politics. The anxious gathering waited, as the hour approached for the unofficial tally, while talking nervously over drinks. When the count finally came in, Ferguson had won. Jubilation erupted among his excited supporters. Although elected by a narrow margin, the candidate's victory was thought to epitome a new direction that would ultimately unify the disparate factions within the Democrat Party. Ferguson moved around the reception, animated by the news of success, stopping occasionally to speak briefly with different people, as the typical fawning process began to engulf the incumbent mayor into the throngs of his constituency. Fred watched curiously, as the pecking order ensued, while his mind pondered the next assignment. He had worked laboriously on the campaign and was satisfied with his contribution to Ferguson's success. His next task was much more difficult. As he dwelt upon the important connection of these events to the future of black people, he reflected about his own growth and the many obstacles he personally had overcome. The time had finally come for positive change, he thought. Fred turned away from the spectacle and focused attention to Lloyd and Rita. The old duo made a curious spectacle, unto themselves. They sat, reservedly, in adjoining chairs, formerly attired in conservative evening garments, each wearing eyeglasses. They projected an image of professorial precocity. He smiled at the sight while listening to their conversation.

"I wonder if these people now realize the scope of this unfolding performance. It's been an interesting prelude, don't you think?"

"Yes, quite, Rita! But, I haven't missed the rumors circulating around town about where all this is going to wind up. It's being down-played as passé . . . you and I know better!" Lloyd paused to take a draw on his pipe. "The skeptics are speculating failure. I guess the prospects have really shaken folks up."

"I kept telling you all along that we had the keys. Although, it does make me reflect a little about Moses and the promised land, since I'm not as young as I'd like to be . . . there's definitely a lot to think about in it all."

"Those are my feelings, precisely! We've got a longer way to go, than we've come."

"Well, that's good, Lloyd. You know I hate to be tired of anything! This race has just shown me how anxious I've been," sighs Rita. "But, I guess you'll say that's normal for a woman my age, isn't that right?"

"Your anxiety is understandable, once a person gets a sense of your direction," interjects Fred. "It doesn't take long to see your sense of purpose."

Callander smiled graciously while delicately adjusting her hair-do. "You still flatter me, even at my age, darling. Can you see why I'm so uptight about not being young?"

"Ah, but what your experience is doing for you makes all the difference, Rita."

"I couldn't imagine too many other sisters filling your role," remarks Lloyd, with unusual charm. "You're still much ahead of the game."

"Really, Lloyd? Does that mean I'm putting pillars in the way of those who come behind me?"

"Ostensibly, dear heart. There has to be some return from what you put in along the way," Fred comments, supportively. "I'm just glad that you chose to do what you're doing in this life . . . it does make a difference!"

"I'm happy that you show your concern, Baby. It makes me feel less barren as a woman."

Lloyd finished his drink and sat the glass down. "Well, it's good to hear that Fred didn't go into some complicated discourse about the propitiousness of the opportunity according to your astrological configurations," he laughs.

Fred chuckled at the humor and took their glasses. "Let me get you folks a refill . . . excuse me."

He bustled through the crowd, slowly, pausing to chat with the new mayor, momentarily, then continued toward the bar. As he departed, Ferguson turned to look for Lloyd and Rita. Lloyd's eyes caught sight of the mayor's searching gaze and he raised his pipe in a victory gesture while Callander nodded her head. Ferguson returned a warm smile, then continued socializing.

"Now there's a man who's realizing a purpose!"

"I know he's glad to get over a lot of anxiety. He looks better, doesn't he," remarks Lloyd, as he casually puffed at his pipe.

"Once he gets some rest from the race, we'll really be able to see how ready he is. He did a good job in keeping the lid on his anxiety, I want you to know . . . heck, I would have never made as good an image in his position!"

"I doubt if too many others would have either. You know, this is turning out to be quite an interesting experiment."

"Hmmm, I see Fred has some influence on your choice of words, too," Rita puns. Then she continues soberly. "Lloyd, I just want to tell you now, you better straighten that young man out, before sending him on this international venture . . . you don't want to lose him. Especially at this point."

Lloyd reflected a moment, removing his glasses to wipe his face with a handkerchief. "I guess he has made a point of staying on my mind, these days . . . he's not put off too easily. But, I can't tell him too much, because he's already got more than enough work on the project, as it is."

"I'd like to know more about that, if you don't mind!"

"What can I say? Fred is a different kind of man. The way he approaches life is so different than what I see others doing, that sometimes I find myself taking lessons from him." He leaned back in the chair and crossed his legs, casually conveying his observation like a school teacher. "Essentially, the way he's organized himself makes it hard for me to deal with him on a consistent basis. He's not to be programmed."

"Hmm. Well, you say it surprised you that he pulled his family together, after all that time, huh? Not me! He couldn't stop along the journey, any more than either of us can, for that matter. But, he has a sense of ensemble, or structure, if you like . . . I see him as the kind of person who would take time to make sure his offspring would follow in his momentum."

"I'll have to say, he's much easier to communicate with these days!"

"Well, at any rate, that's this woman's view of the situation. You can tell me anything. I'm an open person, I think . . . but, I want you to hear me now! First of all, I would have prescribed that course of action a long time ago, you understand. Then, secondly, you had better be careful not to make his family vulnerable in future circumstances," she admonishes him.

Lloyd laughed in an uncharacteristic manner. "Well, perhaps your concerns are clearer for you, in the accusative sense, but I didn't sanction that tactic at all. It was out of my hands. You realize that!"

"I'm not going to argue that point. Despite the terrible lack of tact, it's brought him a tremendous amount of sustainment, since then."

"Well, then, you can say we have a lot to be thankful for."

"Keeping that in mind, Lloyd, don't you think he ought to be getting some answers to the questions he's posing?"

"Crowding him with those responsibilities may be detrimental," Lloyd snaps. He became curt. "I can't do it, I'm afraid ! He'll have to rely on his intuition, as far as that's concerned."

"Oh, my God, you're about to make me tired again," she sighs. "Alright, I'll come clean. I haven't divulged anything to the suspect. Will you subpeona me for testimony, or is my word holding any weight with you?"

"These days, judging by the election, I'm willing to hear anybody's epic . . . I might not commment about it, though!"

"You know, the only spirit you raise is that reactionary old philosophy of Booker T. Washington at Tuskegee!"

"Come on, it's not that bad! Anyhow, nobody has a monopoly on black talent any longer," Lloyd reflects. "I'm just being cautious."

"I don't think you're reading me correctly," says Rita, as she leans forward to emphasize her point. "That young man has talents, yes. But, it's really a question of how he's using his intelligence that's making him a threat to power circles. You should do all you can not to stifle him with a lot of charade and 'double-think'."

"I'm going to make every effort not to do that. It wouldn't help in the least! He's smart enough to assimilate the ideas he'll come in contact with, but I just don't want things to be premature."

"You know, you're going to have to get off the clutch, sometime, and put the show into gear, because you're never really sure when the baby is going to decide to come," she quips. "It's a matter of being ready for the arrival!"

"That's what I'm saying, isn't it." Lloyd gropes momentarily, and straightens his jacket. "Now, how would you know about things of that nature, anyway, Rita?"

"You'd never understand, counselor!"

Fred returned to the conversation, just then, interrupting the diplomatic spar. "What's the point, crew?"

"Rita's starting a campaign of her own to have a baby."

"Is that right," Fred says, while passing their drinks. "Why did you wait so long before deciding to do that?"

"I developed slowly," she remarks, smugly. "Oh, there's Mrs. Ferguson! Doesn't she look like she'd make a fine first lady?"

The threesome watched as the new mayor's wife spread her charm, as she mixed with the friends and supporters of her husband's successful campaign.

"Our man says he's ready for the television cameras, downstairs," says Fred. "I guess our work on the campaign is finally coming to a close."

"Well, I'll take the time now, to congratulate you for a job well done. I might not find the time, once I get back in the office. There's a lot of finalizing to do."

"While you're doing all of that accounting work, Llloyd, do you want me to assist Elaine, or work further on the Neilson Report?"

"You can keep the lines open with her, but I don't think you should go any further with the case, yourself. It may come up later to inconvenience you. So, start building on your research. Maybe you'll glimpse some answers to your questions in the report."

"Nope! I'm not going to let you antagonize me," jokes Fred, as he shakes his head in playful jest. "I refuse to bring up the issue!"

"Don't tell me you've exhausted your inquisitiveness?"

"Don't goad me, Lloyd. I'm not about to sound ridiculous tonight, predicting the possible change of the earth's axis to melt the polar caps . . . I don't think that would solve the drought problems in blighted regions of the world . . ."

Lloyd gave forth a blank stare and took a drink. "Hmm, how long did it take you to be toilet trained?"

"I was a nasty brat. I held my bowels long after the toddler stage. My mother couldn't do anything with me."

"Oh, you cats turn my stomach . . . let me go over there and speak with the next first lady," says Callander. "I might pick up some pointers for selecting the child's father." She breezed away theatrically with her typical aloof demeanor.

"I guess she didn't enjoy our conversation," Lloyd says, smugly. "Well, it looks like we should move a considerable margin on the boards. For a relatively new outfit, that's not bad at all."

"You mean I have a piece of something that's serious, eh? Well, I'm glad I took your offer," says Fred. "It saved me from going completely under, if you want to know about it."

"There are different ways of getting at a person's potential. But, the important thing is that it's there, to begin with . . . in your case, you left no room for doubt."

"So, you think I'll be able to pull this operation together?"

"Yes, the satellites can be developed for the variety of informational needs in Zambia. There's no need to get into spectacular commercialism, Fred. That can be left to other interests. Our major concern is toward developing formidable business relations with Africa through stable communications operations. Then, we're in at the ground floor."

"I see, I see."

"As long as the people over here can see progress unfolding, I think we can safely say we've accomplished something worthwhile."

"Keeping progressive propaganda on the screen could eclipse the negative effect of television, altogether," Fred remarks. "It would be, most decidedly, a very revolutionary step."

"Especially since the folks in Detroit have opened that television station . . . now, that's something you can work on. Give me a market survey for setting up a black network. You might use that Neilson Report in your research. Extrapolate important demographic patterns that correlate international to domestic trends and estimate a time factor for such an endeavour."

"Alright," replies Fred. "I've already progressed some charts which I can use for that, so I'll take a look at the substantive materials for statistical details. That shouldn't tie me up too much.

"Good. I don't want you too busy while waiting for definite dates of your departure . . . I hear you got your shots."

"Yeah, they did the same out there on the coast. We're all set to go."

Ferguson approached the two men, followed by a cadre of enthusiastic supporters.

"Well, let me congratulate you people for such a professional job . . . I'm going down to face the cameras now, can I get a little bit of your feelings?"

He embraced each of the two respectively, giving power signs to them.

"Congratulations, Mr. Mayor," says Lloyd, with typical officiousness.

Ferguson beamed a smile to the twosome, who did likewise. He wheeled around to lead his entourage toward the exit. As the crowd began to filter out of the room, Rita chatted with Mrs. Ferguson, on their way to the news conference. Fred and Lloyd remained upstairs. Their job was done. They looked for comfortable seats in the vacant reception hall and found a spot near the bar.

"Phew! I thought that would never come," Lloyd sighs, as he slumped into a chair. "I guess I'm partial to an armchair, when you get right down to it."

Fred laughed, as he eased into the adjoining seat. "You sit in that damned chair all day! No wonder it's hard for you to stretch out!"

"The fact that I'm there is the important thing. I can only make this kind of formal engagement. I don't have the time to stretch out, in between contracts, and practice austerities, like you. All of my time has to be spent next to that phone . . . you know, with all of the business the company gives to ITT, we ought to have more of that action too."

"Now, that's one way of getting around the bill," quips Fred. "Well, now everybody is aware of the ancient sleeping giants. So, the big fear of facing the bastardized history is just about over. Now it seems like the whole future in the 'melting pot' will be wrapped up in a dialogue with, the so called, lost civilizations. I suppose there must be a million adages about the mythic return of the native . . .the way events are headed now, there should be no doubt that we're the catalyst of change in this society."

"No place to run, no place to hide, huh?"

"That's the way things were planned, I'm sure. But, now folks can see how to change important events within the recurring cycles."

"Yeah, it really gets hairy when you begin to analyze the international consequences of social control." Lloyd reflects. "look at that rice lobby, for example. Isn't it unfortunate that they can cause all that devastation in Indochina through political manipulation of the economic market. That type of foreign policy doesn't have to be part of Africa's development also."

"I think we're too far ahead now, to passively accept events like that hoax. You know, when you consider the political folklore of, war, to stimulate economic expansion, the question stops being a matter of political theory and becomes a real danger for business in future planning, as it turns out. There are just too many other beneficial alternatives of the profit motive that can prevent the inevitable attrition in human resources," remarks Fred, sarcastically. "Anyway, I don't think this country can afford a foreign policy based upon reparations, succeeding each armed conflict, forever. That's a false premise for social planning . . . of course, the possibility of war in social interaction is real. It's just not feasible for the future of human life."

"Yeah, that's why this communications plan is so importnat. Propaganada based upon scare tactics, just to make cyclic repetition seem palpitable, are mere counter productive excuses for change . . . Well, since this business is coming together, we don't have to fear being black-listed, anymore. Pretty soon, nobody will have to go underground."

Fred leaned back in the chair and comfortably stretched his legs. "Yeah, I was thinking about a travel agency, with all that transportation taking place. You know, Lloyd, I could retire with something like that set up."

"I don't know who ever accused you of not having an imagination. Shit! You've already talked up a bunch of amenities, haven't you?"

"Well, I imagine this excursion should amount to something! After all, I did pull my family back together, like you all wanted, so now I'm going to have to take care of them, somehow."

"You might as well talk to Bill about that," Lloyd replies, as he refills his pipe. "He's into all of those kinds of ventures."

"Hmmm. It seems like this plan should work out very well, indeed, in answer to Langston's Deferred Dream."

"I'm glad you feel the time spent there will be important. But, ah, use the World Bank for Zambia's benefit. I just want you to have a business relationship, my man. Whatever investments we can generate, our contract shall be with INDECO. Anyhow, if you're successful in developing this communications project, you'll always be financially mobile, no matter what route you take."

Fred smiled mischievously. "The total commercial potential is seducing, but I'll heed your advice on the matter, Lloyd."

"If you don't mind, please try to work through the company, as much as possible . . . we have a good pension plan too, if you remember."

"The thought never left me, Lloyd."

"Well, let Elaine handle anything that you should stumble upon, okay? This operation has a lot of expansion potential."

"Alright, buddy. But, what happened to Elaine, anyhow? I expected to see the Washington lawyer tonight. Did something come up?"

"I don't know what happened to her."

"It would be a good time to speak with her, now that we've found the comforts of a 'barber-shop'," Fred comments, whimsically, as he leaned his head back and casually looked up at the ceiling.

"Has she told you about the Mister Dawson you're supposed to meet?"

"She mentioned he's very sharp, spends very little time with affects, and has a pair of piercing eyes which scrutinize all your movements . . . I don't really know what I got from that description."

"You know, of course, that he's been very active in Latin America during the last decade," says Lloyd, as he casually puffs his pipe.

"So she said. I understand he comes from a wealthy family and made his killing in commodities when he was still a young man."

"I think he's fifty six now, but he's not afraid to make this type of venture . . . "

"That's interesting. He's still active, even at that age. Now, if it were me, there would be no time wasted in easing out of the back door," jokes Fred. I think it's good to slow down by fifty. Then, a body can appreciate the armchair."

"Thinking, organizing ideas, and writing . . . all that, and golf too. That's really mellowing into old age, gracefully," Lloyd reflects.

"Yeah, it's a pleasant archetype for a man's mature experience, if it works out quite that way. But, I think you overlooked teaching . . . speading the Gospel, as you see it!"

"Oh, how could I forget that. That's implicit to each stage of life."

Chapter Thirty-Seven

Activity around the office had normalized after the successful election campaign, as once again, the daily routine pervaded life in the city. Fred had subsequently turned his attention to work on the Zambian project, restructuring the Swazi Bauxite prospectus for funding through INDECO, as well as private investment sources. He thought Abiola's business ideas would work well through coordination with the Zambia International and Mining Corporation to help that government prevent an uncontrolled depletion of its raw materials. Fred was also able to complete another draft of the extensive communications package in the interim and stood leaning over his desk, busily proofreading the report. He paused, momentarily, to glimpse the wall clock and adjusted his watch. Although everything seemed appropriate, he wanted to be correct when Lloyd's deadline arrived. While he scrutinzed the document, the secretary approached in her characteristic display of sensuality and stood next to him. She shifted her weight at the hips to make her presence felt. Fred looked up with mock surprise.

"Ah, Wanda. What can I do for you this morning, Chica?"

"You've been proofreading that report for the last hour. Wouldn't you be more comfortable sitting down?"

"Oh, I didn't notice that I was standing," he says, as he straightens his body. "Do I look awkward?"

Wanda shook her head with amusement. "Now, we both read this report several times. Are there going to be more corrections today? I'd really like to go to lunch, you know."

"I think you do a wonderful job, Wanda," he says, as he motioned with his hand for her patience, while thumbing through the remaining pages. "I just want to make sure that I said what I wanted to say. They've been after me for clarity."

"That doesn't surprise me. It usually takes me twice as long to type your drafts."

Fred casually took her hand as he closed the report. "Wanda, that's because you're so new to the complexities of this operation."

"It's just that my inquiring mind demands that I know what I'm dealing with," she says, and moves her hand to the folder.

"That extra effort will get you going places, lady," he remarks with a smile, while nonchalantly scratching his face. "I think this is ready for the inner circles."

Wanda eyed him teasingly. "Well, I'll have to say, it's about time!"

Wanda left Fred's desk, walking with a typical undulation of her physique. As he watched the voluptuous movements of her body, his gaze was interrupted by his co-worker.

"I see you finished your report. Are there going to be any shocking revelations?"

"I don't know, Les! I took it through the next decade. It seems like there will be some decisive elections in the seventies. From what I can see, it looks as if the impact will extend into the next century."

"Cheez! That sounds pretty tenuous. Over that space of time, the technological changes, alone, could be catastrophic, aside from their application."

"Well, I just dealt with the last part of what you said. Because, technological innovation must have utility, otherwise it's not important. Organizational strategies battered around by labor and management for reducing the work week and staggering the work force would do more in the long run, than setting up poorly planned mass transit systems . . . just like I was telling you about the jingoism in Washington and it's closure for mature activity."

"But after all, Fred, it is the Nation's Capitol."

"Of course, but that fact just furthers the point I made to you and Jomo, that new directions should emerge in that city, more than anywhere else."

"Well, it sounds good, at any rate."

"Hopefully, my ideas will be picked up in the district, because there are a lot of front operations that tie into other networks across the country," Fred replies.

"Do I hear you correctly? It sounds like you're proposing to change the traditional order of ye ole hen house. That could be potentially dangerous for business," Les observes.

Lloyd emerged from his office and handed the secretary a memo, then returned to his quarters with Fred's report.

"I thought you might have slowed down somewhat, after the moratorium on the campaign information. I guess that's not the case."

"Indeed not . . . you'll get a look at it during the meeting. As a matter of fact, your talents are important for implementing positive propaganda, here in the states. I specifically mention that you should be charged with that responsibility," says Fred.

"That sounds good, but I hope you're not just giving me all these beautiful palliatives for you to escape the sweat and agony of it all. You know, Fred, I could wake up one morning out of a job."

"Or perhaps be appointed special envoy to an emerging African nation. Now you would dig that, wouldn't you?"

"I can't fathom your smile, friend . . . anyhow, I did come across something, by chance, which might interest you. It might come as a surprise to you that a lot of the current social and economic strategy for Africa dates to World War I. It was even part of plans developed by The League of Nations. Ideas put forth by prominent social thinkers and statesmen, at that time, contributed to the ultimate break with colonial organization. Many of the social concepts didn't die with the League, but are prevalent in debates regarding African nationalism at the U.N. today."

"Is that right?"

"UNESCO is one such outcome. Abiola belongs to one of the member associations, by the way. It appears there are hosts of fascinating international experiments being conducted about future life in cities. That's where you might find the connections you were looking for," Les continues briefing Fred.

"That sounds feasible. What are the details, Les?"

"Well, concern among the private organizations about detremental forms of social organization has led to a clandestine venture of economic control by these powerful groups, outside the official policies, of course . . . various investments made in key institutions to apply the principles of societal order and stable growth. One way that's occuring is through city politics. Their influence is downplayed, for apparent reasons, due to its extreme sensitivity to national governments. Coincidentally, their rationale relates to the symbolism of your philosophy regarding the importance of the city in the progress of civilization."

"Ah, ha," Fred comments, reflectively. "I understand. The millenium concept . . . that correlates with premonitions Elaine developed while researching Swazi Bauxite. What I gleaned from her insight points to a black patriciate, somewhere in the background. Did you come across anything like that?"

"Well if you remember, the idea of the black official almost failed during Reconstruciton."

"Right."

"It seems the momentum got bogged down in international intrigue, as well as the backlash of Southern white democrats."

"How so, Les?"

"At that time, political and economic inroads that Negroes had in American government furthered spiritual ties to Africa, especially through the inspiration of Liberia's establishment."

"Yes, yes, I remember the history. Go on, Les."

"Subsequent events, regarding international commerce, introduced other political considerations about favorable balance of trade for the economies of the developed nations. Gold became an important form of payment which contributed to the persistance of African colonialism . . . South African apartheid, is perhaps, a more apparent outcome in Africa. But, the subtle impact upon Blacks in the United States relates to the succession of World Wars and the periodic migrations to the inner cities. Subsequent events are clear. The political-economic changes distorted the link of interdependence, further loosening the bond between cultures in the two continents."

"Of course! You're right about the impact of the constant change from the gold standard . . . that is a chauvinistic deceit to thwart capitalist expansion in America and also throughout the world . . . "

"Precisely, Fred. Unemployment and racial issues facing Blacks, which subsequented the turn to big business concerns resulted from deceptive profiteering by political pimps who tricked the unwary into programs of accomodation to populate the cities. Thus, the big sellout of Reconstruction politics became apparent after McKinley's administration, when the cooptation of labor concerns, and the rise of criminal elements controlling jobs programs just put additional stumbling blocks in the way of developing viable Black economic institutions," Les concludes.

Fred reflected about the information. The answers clarified his mind, somewhat. He would meditate further, to help organize his directions, he thought. "What's on the agenda of this organization for the immediate future?"

"The organization has worked out an overall timetable to implement different projects according to an international strategy for social planning in the twentieth century. The specific policy is capital investment in cities with stable administrative organization. Of course, they have their parameters for assessing the political climate conducive to social and economic growth. Ferguson's election is the first major success of civil rights tactics, which has been monitored awhile in the states, for instance. So, now I imagine there'll be financial and programmatic support commensurate with old Northeastern patterns. You know, the usual investments in municipal bonds and specific authorities. A matter of leveraging control, just in case," says Les, with a cryptic air. "That kind of fiscal influence shall underscore much of the degenerative outcomes, resultant from collusive arrangements between those unorthodox proselytizers, public interest groups and traditional political organization, which tend to overshadow productive business and contribute to diseconomies. It's obvious that communications is critical . . . that's where you figure into the picture. Your public relations career has been noticed. You, and others, are being sought to translate their concepts into specific communications packages, for acceptance within emerging countries, to promulgate the idea of better ways of living. It's an attempt to offset criminal effects of the more politically volatile, and economically exploitative ventures, similar to their activity in the states. That's why Abiola opened the door for TMP in Africa."

"It sounds pretty cogent. Lloyd told me about Abiola, but where did you get all of that other information, Les?"

"It's a long story, Fred. But, here's a brief synopsis . . . I met a former professor, by chance, who's currently with the World Bank. He's an economist, but was very interested in the election and invited me to a soiree for a retiring staff member. I went, and met a lot of agency types from different departments, several embassies, as well as some people from the organization. Later in the evening, he gathered the group's representatives together for a rap. They expressed a great deal of interest in the successful campaign, but, you know me, I was all ears. Despite long delays, it seems the organization is back on schedule. They're maintaining a low profile, to keep the greed out of their financial dealings. I was told that certain forces wouldn't hesitate to jeopardize the project, since stable cities threaten the political and economic profiteering of chaotic systems," he concludes.

"It seems like their work is toward realizing New Jerusalem," remarks Fred.

"Perhaps. Just be aware of the malady of power in all of that international intrigue, my man! You know, a lot of people in society get conned by the money game programs, but the end of power is poverty."

"True . . . although I'll have enough on my hands, I don't quite know how a confrontation can be avoided. I'll probably make a couple of mistakes, before I get a sense of all the various innuendos. You know Les, there are a lot of sensitive cultural issues involved in satellite communications. One could easily build a case against me in the beginning . . . "

"That's how the organization stands to be wrecked. Misrepresentation of their ideas, to stimulate cultural conflict . . . somehow, opposition has already gotten wind of the idea," Les interjects. "That's why parasites are trying to muscle in on the ground floor like that Dawson character, whose name came up in the discussion . . . oh, by the way, my economics professor told me that the Neilson Report is a fraud."

"What! . . . . are you sure?"

"After finding inconsistencies in the report, he checked with the agencies at the U.N. that were cited in the research . . . "

Just then, Lloyd emerged from his office and interrupted the conversation. His demeanor was very serious.

"Listen gentlemen, something critical has come up. I want to see you both in my office, right away!"

The three men headed into the office and made themselves comfortable; Les stood over Fred, who reclined in the armchair, while Lloyd sat stoically upon the desk. The workers waited expectantly, during the long silent pause, before Lloyd finally began.

"Unfortunately, I must be the bearer of bad news," he murmured. "I just got word that Doc passed away."

Fred was shocked. He got up from his chair, and almost fell, as he stumbled forward toward the desk. "What! Oh, no!"

"I'm afraid he suffered a heart attack early this morning," Lloyd sighs.

"That just can't be . . . I," Fred choked on his words.

"I understand how you feel, Fred . . . It was a big shock to all of us." Lloyd lowered his head, momentarily, as Fred sat down again. Les consoled his co-worker's grief by rubbing his friend's shoulders.

"What were the details?" asks Les.

"Everett found him on the trawler, unconscious on the floor of his cabin. He summoned the hospital, but by the time they arrived it was too late," he replies. "The authorities are trying to contact his relatives, here in the states."

"Florida, I believe. Do you think that . . . "

"Once we get word of when the funeral is to take place, I'm sending you down there, Fred . . . I, uh, hate to sound officious, right now, but there are some serious matters that his death brings to the forefront," Lloyd says, as he gains his composure. "You both realize what an integral part he played in the overall operation of TMP. Now, we'll have to let serendipity dictate just how to fill that spot. I'll have to choose between the two of you, based upon considerations of both seniority and competence. Doc established quite a coterie and had a great deal of influence. I doubt if either of you could adequately replace him, right away. Nevertheless, it's vital that that link be maintained, immediately!"

"What about Everett? Was there any thought about using him?" asks Les, off-handedly, to displace the moribund overtone from the conversation.

"Not really," he replies. "He still has more to learn, before being considered for something like that . . . although, he'll be next in line, since Doc had been training him for that responsibility."

"I wonder if he got any indication that death was about to visit him. It seems that I was getting a premonition of yama, recently, but his passing just seems so odd. A heart attack, huh? Well, I'll have to look at his papers . . . let's hope that he's surrounded by good karma in his passage," Fred remarks. He had become sober again, and reflected about the wise old man from an eschatological perspective.

"More than likely," interjects Lloyd. "Now, the effect of his work will have to be continued, and I'll tell you quite frankly, I think it's going to be you, Fred . . . "

"I wonder if that's the proper choice. I might think your assessment of the situation would point to a younger person, who'd be able to prevent negative forces from causing havoc, more readily than myself . . . "

"You were closest to him, Fred . . . therefore, I don't think it would be such a shock for you to go up on his behalf."

"But, what about the Zambian project? I've been preparing myself for that, quite awhile now," pleads Fred. "Do you want me to leave than undertaking altogether?"

"In either case, Les is going to have to exercise a little more autonomy. There would just have to be a temporary setback in those designs, as far as I can see it."

"I don't know, Lloyd. That's a completely new project," Les remarks. "It's not the same as stepping into an ongoing program, which I'm more capable of doing . . ."

"Plus, he doesn't have that family structure which you advised me is critical to the social dimensions of the plan," adds Fred.

Lloyd weighed their arguments, then slowly put forth his point. "For you, under those circumstances, Fred. But, the same considerations don't obtain for Les, in this new situation of crisis," he says. "We might have to write in another type of profile, but that can be done without too many extraneous considerations. The important concern, even if we have to introduce that kind of change, is to keep Doc's spirit from being annihilated. You are both capable of doing that, to varying degrees . . ."

"Look, I don't want to sound in any way negative," says Les. He was considering his friend's leadership ability and the impact he saw Fred having upon such a complicated endeavour in the future of black people, rather than his own career. "I feel that I can meet either of the proposed challenges. But, ethically, I think that Fred's the better choice, at this point . . . it's not only the question of time put in, you understand . . . He's taken his studies further. I was just about to tell him, when you brought this unfortunate message, of anticipations in high quarters about the kind of work he'll be able to accomplish in Africa . . ."

"I can't be so concerned with who's in what position, or where! I have a task to accomplish. I've got to make an assessment based on other considerations, not opinion polls . . . even if they're conducted within high circles," Lloyd shouts, and slams his fist on the desk. "Just remember how Doc got the shaft, in the beginning, by the same kinds of cliques . . . now that we've reached this point in history, there's all types of reversals and new interests, eager to have a say in the directions of this operation . . . I'm sick and tired of the bull!"

"Take it easy, Lloyd, I know you really don't mean that," Fred consoles him. "It's just as much of a shock to you, as it is to me, I imagine. But, don't let yourself get all unstung! There's a way around this situation, as you were saying, and it has to do with realizing the impact of all Doc passed on to us. I'm sure you will use the best discretion in making the decision."

Lloyd began to pace around the small office, in an effort to regain his composure. "I just didn't think it would happen so suddenly . . . look, I'm going to have to think this thing through, thoroughly. I want you two to help me, by meditating on Doc's passage, if you don't mind. Maybe we can come up with a solution by the time of the funeral."

"Are you going to handle any other business, in the meantime?"

"We'll move the staff meeting forward, Fred. I don't think we should let our progress slow down, too much."

"Right! Plus, it seems that Fred is making some startling revelations again," Les remarks, encouragingly.

"Well, that'll be all, for now . . . see how far you can get by then."

The two men got up and began leaving the office. Fred paused a moment, then turned to add. "I'll recite some vedas tonight."

"That would be in keeping with his soul and dharma," says Lloyd. They looked at one another for a few silent moments, then Fred exited. Lloyd remained standing awkwardly in the middle of the office. He raised his glasses to his forehead and wiped his face with his palm, as he overcame the lingering emotions.

Chapter Thirty-Eight

Early morning sunlight shined through the rear window of Fred's apartment, partially illuminating the small railroad flat. He sat, stoically, in a yoga position on the floor, quietly chanting in a shadowy corner of the living room. A single tear rolled slowly from his eyelid down the side of his cheek while he reflectively fingered the metal talisman from Mexico.

" . . . Fourth from his navel came mid-air; the sky was fashioned from his head; earth from his feet, and from his ear the regions.
Thus they formed the worlds.
Seven fencing-logs had he, thrice seven layers of fuel were prepared, when the gods, offering sacrifice, bound, as their victim, Purusha."

Fred finished the verses and raised himself, wiping the tear from his face, and walked toward the bathroom to relieve his body. Someone knocked on the door, interrupting his activity. He responded, and found Skinner standing in the doorway.

"Hey man, you sick or something? I just called the office, and they said you were out for the day," Wendell says, affecting concern.

"Nah, nah, come on in, Skinner . . . what's to it?" Fred stood aside as Wendell passed his large frame through the door and into the apartment.

"I've been working my cakes off, to be sure! Anyhow, I finally got that architectural package together for your people and I want to talk about it . . . got some time?"

"To tell you the truth, no," Fred remarks, curtly. "I had some bad news recently."

"Oh," says Wendell, with mock surprise. "Well look, I'll be brief, man. It'll only take a couple of minutes . . . you got a brew, or something?"

Fred looked at Skinner, whose steel gray eyes returned a cold stare, shrouding the malice behind his friendly smile. "Yeah, just a minute. Make yourself comfortable." He went to the refrigerator while Wendell strolled idly around the room, looking at the decor and casually perusing Fred's work materials. He finally stood before the poster of Krishna, with his back to the living room, and surreptitiously pulled a pistol from inside his jacket, then patiently waited. It wasn't long before Fred returned with the beer and, as he approached, Wendell turned slowly around and pointed the weapon at him.

Fred grimaced at the sight of the gun. "What's to it, Skinner?" he says, dryly, as his jaw muscles tightened. "You couldn't wait to get the blood off your conscious, huh?"

Wendell knew Fred's temper and weighed the situation carefully. "I'm fully aware of your mastery of martial arts, Baby, so don't attempt anything foolish . . . have a seat and enjoy your last refreshment!"

Fred smiled demonically, carefully controlling the killer impulse, as he methodically calculated his position. "So, you're finally showing your hand . . . how do you feel, selling your brother into slavery, again?"

"This is no time to be cute, Fred. I'm doing what I have to do to survive. You understand how it goes, Baby. It's just too long a story for me to tell."

"Oh, I know that, Skinner," he says, as he casually sits in a chair. "Besides, you're probably too ashamed to go into details. But, apparently this is my last conversation, so please make it interesting!"

"Okay, Fred. I guess you've got that coming," replies Skinner, as he cautiously sits down. "It's not so different, man. It happened some time ago when I was trying to get my company going. You know how hard it was during those years. You suffered some consequences, yourself," he remarks, defensively.

"Yeah, I suffered, buddy! But, I don't see the sympathetic connection you're making . . . all of the dues I paid, never led me to sacrifice my principles, Skinner," quips Fred. "But, anyway, you're trying to tell me that your operation is a front, is that right?"

"I guess I wasn't too wary. The money looked good and the prospects didn't seem too complicated. That's the real reason I could never take you folks up on the offers the organization made to me . . . "

"Well, it's not too late, Skinner," Fred interjects, in a final attempt to help his adversary.

"Out of the question," he replies, with a sudden change of attitude. "I'm in it too heavily now!"

"What the hell did you do, man? Sell your soul?"

"I was actually supposed to get you involved, somehow. But, you never gave me an opportunity to seduce you . . . one thing I can say about you, man, you never let pleasures ruin your disciplines."

"Ah, ha, I'm beginning to see the picture. It's back to the ancient war of the knights," Fred remarks. He was drawing as much information from Wendell as possible, before confronting the battle against death.

"Precisely!"

"But, what do you do with me, afterwards? How do you explain an outright killing? Doesn't that pose some problems?"

"It's a high powered air pistol, Fred. The darts have been soaked in nembutal which stimulates an overproduciton of adrenalin in the blood, leading to anarythmia. The traces disappear long before an autopsy, giving the appearance of a heart attack."

"Did you do the same thing to Doc?"

"Not me! But, essentially the same process was used," says Skinner.

"What's to be gained by all of the intrigue?"

"Come on now Baby, you're pulling my leg! Stalling isn't going to get you out of it."

"No kidding, I'm really ignorant," he lied.

"I suppose you don't know about plans for you to become a member of the Society of Nine?"

"Never heard of it," replies Fred. "How does it figure in?"

"An international society, working through the U.N. and other kinds of organizations, promoting law and order. It represents the biggest threat to our survival. If we can't profit through human conflict, then we're out of business. You know, it's the classical extortion game . . . now, in your case, you've opened too many doors that pose a threat to our existence. Realizing that you'd never make a one hundred and eighty degree turnaround, you simply have to go, Fred!"

"That's really macabre, man! I mean, after all that shit we faced in Korea, together, and the effects of McCarthyism we experienced, you're just going to ice me like that! No compunction, whatsoever, huh?"

"Sorry, Baby, but that's it. I've grown accustomed to life in the party!"

"Wait a minute, Skinner. What comes after this?" asks Fred. He was pushing to get at more strategic information.

"Whatever this group has planned, we'll find out," Wendell remarks, confidently. Skinner wasn't being tactful, since he felt he had the upper hand in the situation, and overlooked the way his own hubris was subtlely used against him by Fred.

"How? I mean, who's your source . . . is Elaine mixed up in this conspiracy some way?"

"Naw, I've just used her, without her knowledge, to poinpoint the key people in your outfit. With you out of the way, Les will probably take over your activities. So, all we have to do is get to him."

"Through Dawson?"

Wendell was taken by surprise with Fred's knowledge of that key person and became irritated at what he thought was his own oversight. He felt the leak was due to a slip-up in his work, somewhere.

"What do you know, Baby? Come on, speak up!"

"Nothing really," Fred replies, nonchalantly. He figured he had activated Skinner's animus and would play his cards prudently, allowing Wendell to trip himself with his own hyper-activity.

"Only, that we know what Dawson represents," he edges the tension. "I suppose it was you who arranged his contact with Elaine?"

"I just follow orders, buddy. The Communist pay me well. That's all I'm concerned with," he snaps.

"Oh," remarks Fred, with a blasé air. "I thought greed might've led you to play both sides of the fence, Skinner, since there must be a lot of money this Society of Nine is spreading around," he says provocatively.

"Ferguson and I get ours!"

Fred felt disgust grip the pit of his stomach, but he maintained his composure. Although he was successful in teasing the information from his opposition, it was a pyrrhic victory. Well, it was finally true. The nightmare was real and his people were about to be duped by political machination, he thought.

"You're practicing emphatic degeneracy, you bastard . . . " He reached for the beer to quench his thirst.

Wendell anticipated conflict and reacted impulsively to Fred's movement while watching him diligently. "Don't do it, Fred! You can't win," he says, nervously. "There's no sense in becoming violent at this stage of the game!"

"You know what, Skinner, you've been heading for hell, right along. So far you've got one foot in the coffin. Do you think you can get out of retribution by worshipping mammon?" Fred's eyes lit up as he talked. He began to activate his psyche, animating the natural forces around his apartment. "Once you've sacrificed yourself, there's nothing they won't have you do," he says, while reaching deep within his cultural heritage to evoke his mana. "You're a programmed zombie without salvation!"

"I can't worry about it, Baby! The monster is already in motion. You see, the trouble with you and all of those black apostles and vanguard organizations is basic hypocrisy," Wendell shouts. "The man has got you so spooked about communism, that he continues to keep your pockets empty while you lead black people on some useless 'tail-chasing' about the devil." The sounds of drums and shrill voices became slightly audible, as Fred filled the air with African chants from his distant background. Wendell paid no attention to the distraction, and continued his tirade. " . . . Meanwhile, he's organized a nation of servile idiots through the indoctrination of democracy who are locked in a fierce competition among themselves . . . for what? The meager tid-bits of society's welfare state . . . "

"You and Ferguson appear to have adopted a Machiavellian perspective. But, do you think you two will fare any better in Russian society, as black people?" While Fred spoke, his visiage began to metamorphose, as he ordered his forces for the encounter.

"What does it matter," quips Skinner. He looked at the strange transfiguration occuring before him, and paused to wipe his eyes, then continued in the heat of his self-deception. "The United States is going to wind up with a cancerous service economy, in the near future, and a frustrated population, and the party will do everything to help America change hands, one day. Look, the Central Committee has already transmitted their operational directives, I understand. In this country, for instance, work through such front organizations as the Progressive Labor Party has led to infiltration of young radical groups which are appearing in the background of the present Civil Rights Movement. A cadre of dedicated workers will be recruited and screened from groups like the Students for Democratic Society, the Weathermen, SNCC, CORE, the Panthers and others, who will eventually leave their demonstration activities behind for the masses, you dig."

Fred watched Wendell with a wry smile, as he listened to the strategies of destruction planned for America. He gleaned everything which he could use to warn his people while simultaneously projecting his psychic energy to engage Skinner's soul.

" . . . These cats will don a conservative image. Some will enter business organizatons and labor groups while others, like Ferguson, will become the political apostles of liberalism. You know, only fifty percent of eligible voters turn out for national campaigns. It only takes twenty-six percent of the Electoral College to control the Executive Office. You can see how that will work. Local politics is easier, as you now realize."

"So, I suppose the party will pursue its policies of cooptation in Africa the same way, through direct political and economic exploitation of cultural patterns within developing cities . . . but, of course, you realize it will be difficult to fool the black patriarchs," Fred remarks, dryly. His light brown eyes glittered with an amber light, as he pierced the veil into Wendell's aura.

"Oh, you're talking nonsense, man. I figured out the nomothetics of that part of the Society of Nine, through anthropology. Abiola's problem is that he's too damn smug in advertising his connection to Swazi culture. It just took some research to identify the principles of democracy in Shaka's Zulu empire, which he's promoting. Yes, I'm aware of the protective oath, for whatever it's worth," Wendell glibly comments.

"Well, it's not going to work this time, because we know there's been sabotage and have been waiting for the source to appear. The Neilson fraud has been uncovered, also. Now, if I go, it won't be too hard for the others to piece this little mystery together . . . I understand you now, Skinner. You are the legacy of Cain furthering the city of Babylon," Fred intones, provocatively, as he induces the evil power which controlled Wendell to manifestation, by the force of his mana.

Wendell shook violently, as the awesome power released its energy within his body to thwart Fred's attack. Skinner stood up awkwardly, with his arms flailing wildly about the air and his widely dialated eyes darting feverishly around the room, shouting hysterically in the deep droning voice of the spirit which possessed him. "I will make wholesale violence in the inner cities through racism and tribalism throughout the world. Financial upheavals will follow . . . scandals of all sorts will rock this nation and abroad. Families and churches will be filled with chaos and war will plunder the globe into the darkness of poverty and disease . . . I will take your life, as an example to those who would confront my sovereignty over the living."

Fred's eyes were still transfixed upon Wendell as his light skin became imbued with the black aura. He steadied himself for the battle, raising the tempo of the chant to feverish pitch. Skinner raised his arm and pointed the pistol at Fred, who directed a vector force at his enemy, hurling the large man backwards over the chair. The impact seemed to have no effect upon Wendell, in his possessed state, and he quickly got up from the floor, assembling himself for the attack. Fred was in control of himself, but he knew the demon was both powerful and cunning. He didn't have time to pursue the offensive further, as he planned. Suddenly, he felt a numbness in his chest, spreading rapidly through his lungs and heart. Excruciating pain shot through his nervous system and he began to lose his equilibrium. The intense shock almost broke his will, but Fred's intuition sensed the voltaic reaction in the biochemistry of his vital organs, and he responded. Fighting desperately to maintain his defenses, Fred struggled against the pain and attempted to regulate his breathing. Although he had stopped smoking, his lungs labored with the severe pressure which the evil spirit directed at him. He invoked his ruach to restore himself, momentarily warding off the attack. It was important that he keep his forces coordinated, as a shield around him. He knew the major danger he faced was the devil's control of the air. Fred continued to fill the apartment with African chants, thinking to disorient the malevolent creature. He was soon surprised, as the evil spirit began a sound attack of its own, imploding the atmosphere with a cacophony of high pitched discordance which grated upon his eardrums with a deafening din. He grabbed his head in painful distress from the confusion of the piercing drone, as the capillaries in his ears and nose began to burst. The room became blackened with a vile shroud, blocking the rays of sunlight from the rear window.

Fred thought it was all over for himself, as he doubled up and fell off the chair. As the unrelenting eerie sounds continued, he began to smell the unmistakable stench of death surrounding him, smothering his breath, as he lay helpless on the floor. Fred thought feverously about how to stay alive, as the whole extent of his epistemological knowledge rushed confusedly through his mind, and somewhere within his dulled senses his intuition responded. Death was an abnormal operation of physical forces—an entropic state. Maybe he would be able to survive the drain of vitality. Fred began the slow process of inbreathing, drawing his mana gradually within himself, again. There wasn't much time. His shield was faltering. Everything had to be accomplished at the right psychological moment. When he had gathered his life force into his sushumna, he directed all his remaining energy toward reaching the state of pativehda and concentrated on Jude–9, thus opening the door to the fourth dimension.

Fred's journey through the ethereal world occured with a flash of light. The interruption in the space time continuum had caused a momentary transmigration of his vital forces. Death's stasis, which impeded the circulation of air, was propelled away from his body with a tremendous electrical effect similar to joining like polarities in magnetic fields. Fred slowly regained consciousness and laid still on the floor awhile, as his vital forces returned, gradually enlivening his bodily sensations. After what seemed an interminable duration, he struggled to his feet. He leaned against the wall, still dizzy from the ordeal, and assessed the physical damage to his head. He was a bloody mess.

Finally, Fred examined his ravaged apartment. The stench was gone and the railroad flat remained quiet. He looked away with disgust of the havoc, focusing on the light pouring into the rear window. The sounds of sparrows playing in the backyard seemed normal to his ears, so he figured they hadn't been ruptured. He turned toward the front door and saw Wendell's large body laying face up on the floor. Fred surmised he was dead, but went to examine him to be sure. He looked at the pale hue of Skinner's light brown skin, without remorse, and closed the lids over Wendell's dialated gray eyes. Fred searched among the overturned furniture and disarray for the phone, pulling the extension to the rear window. After he reported the apparent heart attack to the police emergency unit, Fred stood looking reflectively through the window at the graveyard in the rear. He had battled the prince of the air and overcame death.

Chapter Thirty-Nine

Hampton's funeral was arranged within the week and Fred took his family down to pay their respects to the old man. The early morning ceremony was conducted at an Episcopal Church which stood atop a hillside, stoically overlooking the seaport. The procession left the building and moved slowly through the gray mist. The dawn light contributed to the somber atmosphere, diffusing demure rays upon the bereaved relatives and friends. The bishop read the last rites and made a special aside to psalm 107, as Doc's coffin was interred.

" . . . They that go down to the sea in ships, that do business in great waters; These see the works of the Lord, and his wonders in the deep. For he commandeth, and raiseth the stormy wind, which lifteth up the waves thereof. They mount up to the heaven, they go down again to the depths: their soul is melted because of trouble . . . "

EPILOGUE

Fred was down below on the trawler looking through Doc's logs and papers. He had set aside Hampton's personal effects for his relatives and continued organizing the voluminous materials. He opened a file folder and perused some documents, briefly. They contained the old man's charts. Putting them aside, he took a break and entered the galley for a drink. Fred poured a liberal shot of cognac and sat down, taking time to listen to the natural sounds of the harbour. He would have a lot of work to do on Doc's charts, he thought while he relaxed to the background harmony of the ocean, as its waves rushed rhythmically against the shoreline. Occassionally a seagull flew by, breaking the lull with the shrill staccato of its cry. Fred finished his drink and returned to the task of sorting files. He opened another little box and a small metal disk dropped onto the floor. He turned around and stooped to retrieve the object and was surprised by the sight of Everett and Helena standing in the doorway.

"Oh, I didn't hear you folks coming."

"We thought you might want some company," says Everett. "What's that?"

"Doc's talisman. Perhaps I can find out a few things, between this and his papers. He kept very intricate reports."

"Yes, man! All the time writing. If not in the ship's log, then in his other notebooks. I couldn't imagine what all he could find to write about, as much as he did . . . and that talisman is connected with his writings," asks Everett.

Fred scrutinized the talisman, fingering it delicately. He reached into his pocket for his own and examined their similarity.

"Hmm, in a way, Everett. It describes his spiritual potential. I suppose, when I look at this writings, I can get an idea of whether or not he's finished his work. What I can see right away, is that he's finished samsara."

"Does that relate at all to what Les is doing with his project?" Everett probes, cautiously.

"Quite a bit! Doc has compiled an extensive knowledge of the forces governing events in our people's lives . . . once I code this information, Les should have very little problem developing his strategy for the project. Then, we can look forward to working in concert with other people of good will to realize a better world."

"That's important, Fred. Does the work of the Society of Nine reflect that same view? Especially your thought about Africa being more conducive to change, at this juncture in time,'' Helena inquires. She was still assimilating the import of so many epochal events and sought clarity in her attempt to be a supportive wife and mother.

"Yes," says Fred. "The impetus is world wide. It's directed from patriarchs working in the background of society. The elders, if you like. Doc's guidance and, people like him, have provided folks, like myself, important insights in developing their wisdom.''

"Then, it's important that you teach,'' Helena interjects, intuitively.

"Yes, it is.''

"I think you'll make a good headmaster, 'feathertail','' jokes Everett.

"Oh, by the way, I found out that it was Doc's charade which brought us back together . . . I came across some notes in his writings,'' remarks Fred, as an afterthought.

"Well, I'll be! It took all of that time to find out who was really behind that plot,'' Helena chuckles. "Bless him, the old patriarch.''

"Fred, when do you think you'll have all of your material down here? I'm anxious to get started, you know!''

"In about a month, Everett. Lloyd is having it shipped down by air freight . . . I guess it will be awhile, before we can skipper the boat the way Doc used to do it . . . ''

"We'll manage, somehow. Now that the broadcast operation is moving along, I'll have more time to spend with you at sea.'' He stretched and yawned. "You know, with all the forces in the universe, it still takes good men to channel them properly.''

"Well, I've got to buy that. Because, I'm going to be forcing you, to make us, a son . . . feathertail,'' Helena chimes, teasingly to Fred.

They smiled happily at each other and Fred thought he had finally reached inner peace. Some day he would realize his communion with Jehovah.

About the Author

MICHAEL JOHN MURRAY, M.A. is an independent Writer/Producer who has developed professional talents in communications during a period of seventeen years. Educated in Urban Sociology and Motion Picture Film Production, the author has worked in television—WRC/NBC-TV, practiced independent photojournalism, trained as a newspaper writer, managed a multi-media project and studied theatre production. The artist has created several manuscripts that are planned for future publication and/or film production. A native New Yorker, Mr. Murray is married and a father of two children of Negro ancestry.